Three Women and Alfred Nobel

A Novel

Erika Rummel

First published in 2018 by Endeavour Media Ltd.

Table of Contents

In memory of Jim Ryder

Vienna

Late nineteenth century

Ida

The dream begins with a bright flash, an explosion that tightens my heart and triggers a panic. I know nothing about explosions. I have never seen severed limbs or mangled bodies. Yet they intrude on my dreams: lacerated flesh and shattered bones. The moan of a dying man fills my ears. I see him stretched out on the cratered earth, his mouth blackened as if he had swallowed soot. I see a woman standing by a stove, stirring a dish with a wooden spoon. The force of the explosion throws her against the wall and crushes her head. Her body slackens as she slides down to the floor. Her eye sockets are filled with blood. Bloods runs from the cavity that was her nose and from her gaping mouth. A voice comes through the shattered window, indistinct at first – something about a tragedy that could have been avoided. Then the words become clearer. It was an accident caused by an apprentice who didn't watch the temperature gauge. The sad Nordic voice of the announcer grows louder and turns into a roar. He is screaming at me, no, *I* am screaming.

I wake up with a jolt, sink back onto my pillow and stare up at the ceiling until the bloody images in my head dissolve and fade to the color of plaster, until my breathing returns to normal and I realize where I am: safe in my bedroom, in St Veit, a quiet suburb of Vienna where life's drama plays out in trivial scenes – petty theft, misdemeanor, spats between neighbors. There are no explosions, no violent deaths, no shredded bodies in the street. People here die in their beds, peacefully. The mourners weep decorously and stifle their sobs, pressing handkerchiefs to their mouths. This isn't the Balkans, where people beat their breasts and hire wailing women. The people in St Veit suffer quietly, but I don't fit the mold. It's years since Georg's death, and the nightmares keep exploding in my head. Even now that I'm awake and the bloody images have dissolved, I can't stop the chain of memories. I'm back with Georg. It's the day of his departure for Heleneborg, a factory town in Sweden.

We are on our way to the railway station, walking on a path between overhanging trees. The gravel crunches under our feet. It's early morning, the sun has barely burned off the fog. Georg is carrying a suitcase secured with a leather strap. The weather is unseasonably warm for September. I feel hot in my wool jacket. Georg sets down the suitcase and puts his arms around me. He is so tall he has to lean down to kiss me. He slips his tongue between my lips.

It started that summer. At first, he kissed only my hands, then my lips chastely, but the night before his departure, we went beyond what was allowed. At the back door, we kissed like lovers for the first time. His hand wandered from my waist to my thigh. I let him ruck up my skirt and slip his fingers between my legs. I leaned back against the wall into the trellis, feeling weak with pleasure. The branches dug into my back, the leaves brushed against my neck. I barely felt them, I no longer knew myself. Georg pushed against me, and with a sudden ferocity, with a wild desire, I bit his lips. Something gave. It was a sweet release, but sweet only for a moment before I came to my senses and pushed him away, heart pounding. What if my mother came to the door and caught us like this? For a moment, we looked at each other with apprehension then I pulled him close again, all fear suspended. I no longer cared who saw us. Georg was going away.

The next morning, on our way to the railway station, we embraced like that again, and I kissed him fiercely, with insatiable desire. Something had happened to me, unfolded with a cry and couldn't be silenced. How could I live without Georg? I looked into his eyes, our faces so close that I could feel his breath. I pressed my body against his, I wanted to remember every curve, every tendon and muscle. I passed my hands over his neck and face to memorize their contours, the texture of his skin.

Even now, I tremble with the memory of his body, that last embrace before we went on to the railway station. The words come back to me.

"When you turn sixteen in a few months—" he says.

"—Four months and three days," I say.

"—I'll ask for your hand. It may be a long engagement, though. It will take me two or three years to get enough money together to support a family. Will you wait for me, Ida?"

"I'll wait. But you'll come home for Christmas, Georg, won't you?"

"If I can manage it."

We kiss one last time. At the station, where we are no longer unobserved, we stand apart. We shake hands before he gets on the train. I wave my handkerchief as the rods and pistons of the locomotive start their shuffle and the train leaves the station in a cloud of steam. I stand there until the last carriage has passed out of sight.

Georg's farewell gift to me was a dictionary and a primer, *An Introduction to the Swedish Language*. He intended for us to settle in Heleneborg. He had been hired to work in Nobel's factory there. They turned out dynamite, a word that meant nothing to me then. It was just a mouthful of letters. I didn't know what dynamite was, only that it had something to do with detonations. Georg wanted to become a chemist, and Alfred Nobel & Co had offered him a position as a trainee. It included room and board. He was hoping to save up most of his salary so we could marry sooner. We wrote to each other twice a week, not what was important to us, not what I wanted to hear, only what could be shared with my mother, who would have been suspicious if I had not shown her Georg's letters.

He wrote about his work, about the town of Heleneborg. He always included one sentence in Swedish to show what progress he had made in learning the language and to encourage me in my lonely studies back in St Veit.

I've made friends with the brother of the owner, he wrote. *His German is better than my Swedish, but he puts up with my stammering and corrects me. Emil is nineteen, and we get along very well.*

All the trite things we put into our letters, all the things we omitted! I said nothing about the heat between my legs, the longing when I lay in bed at night. I wrote about other people instead and about trivial things. My mother had a cold. The woman down the road had given birth to a child, her fifth. In church, they lit the first advent candles. They looked pretty. That's the sort of thing I wrote to Georg.

I was doing one lesson a day in my primer, and it wasn't difficult to learn the words. Swedish was close to German, I wrote, *When you come home at Christmas, we'll do practice dialogues.*

But that time never came. Georg died before Christmas. Nobel's lawyer informed his parents of the fatal accident. The letter arrived together with Georg's possessions, neatly packed in a crate, and a money order for the pay owing to Georg, plus something to compensate the parents for the loss of their son. The lawyer's message was full of clauses that started with *notwithstanding*, to protect Alfred Nobel & Co from any claims, from any responsibility for Georg's death: *This is not to be construed as an admission of fault on the part of Nobel & Co. Indeed, it was the young man's negligence that caused the catastrophe, which resulted in the loss of property and lives and caused considerable financial loss to the company. The payment is a goodwill gesture and meant as a mark of compassion and sympathy with your bereavement.*

There was no consolation in the lawyer's letter, so I read the newspaper article he had enclosed, a description of the accident which appeared in the *Post-och Inrikes Tidningar*. I read it over and over, with the dictionary by my side, going through it line for line. I don't know what I expected – Georg's last words or the comforting words of someone holding his hand as he was dying. But the article only added to my distress. It turned into fodder for nightmares. *The tragedy could have been avoided*, I read. *It was caused by negligence or inexperience on the part of a recently hired trainee who failed to keep a check on the temperature gauge.*

Then came the story of the woman in the house next to the factory whose skull was crushed and a description of the scene of carnage, the huge yellow flame, the enormous pillar of smoke, windows blown out and shattered, workers ripped to pieces, unidentified body parts on the ground, bloody limbs, formless masses of flesh, tattered pieces of clothes. *That's all that was left of the victims, a few charred fragments*, the paper said. And wasn't Georg one of the victims? He was a trainee. Who was supervising him when the accident happened? Why wasn't there a relief valve on that gauge, or a warning light, or a bell that alerted him that something was wrong?

Alfred Nobel, the owner of the factory, was unhurt. He was not on the premises at the time of the accident. Georg died at nineteen. Nobel lived to old age and made millions from his lethal invention. Yes, I tried to suffer Georg's death quietly, like his parents who lowered their heads and mumbled, "God in his wisdom." They sold up and moved away because they could not bear to live in a place where everything reminded them of their son. That was St Veit's way – yield to God's will. But when I passed their house – their former house – I gave no thought to God. I cursed Nobel. My mind was filled with thoughts of revenge, of hunting down the man responsible for Georg's death. There should have been a safety procedure in place, there should have been someone to supervise Georg, but a supervisor had to be paid, and installing a safety valve would have cost money, and factory owners thought only of their profit. A man's life was cheap. I wanted to see Nobel punished for his shoddy practices, for his profiteering. I wanted him to atone for Georg's death. The longing, the desire I had felt for Georg turned into thoughts of revenge. And the desire for avenging my lover turned into an obsession.

That's how I am. My mind gets into a groove and keeps going like a painted pony on a merry-go-round. When I was four years old, an aunt gave me one of those spools on which you can weave strands of yarn into a multi-colored cord. It was a toy popular with little girls. I fell in love with it immediately. I was fascinated by the fingerwork required, by the pattern of the yarn laid around the tacks, by the cord appearing at the bottom of the spool and growing with every gentle tug. I wove yards of cord. The coil accumulated at my feet. I didn't want to stop for dinner. I refused to go to bed. In the end, my mother had to take the spool away from me, and I cried furiously for hours. It was the first indication of that inconvenient trait, my ability to concentrate fiercely. When I got older, I read books with the same deep concentration I had brought to the weaving spool. And I went about collecting and categorizing leaves, mosses, and stones with the same devotion that I gave to memorizing poems and practicing scales on the piano. I could not stop myself. By the time I fell into the scale-playing rut, I was old enough to realize that I must somehow check my compulsion or risk alienating everyone around me. In fact, I confessed my strange desire to continue whatever I was doing to our parish priest, and he agreed that my behavior was sinful, if only because it distressed my mother, and thus contravened the fourth commandment: Honor thy father and mother.

By the time I turned sixteen, I had learned to control the repetitive behavior which irritated people, but I could not overcome the intensity of the feelings that drove my compulsions. It was in my blood. After Georg had kissed me like a lover, I wanted his touch every night. The desire for him swamped my brain and left me helpless. When Georg died, the desire for revenge took over. I could not dampen it. I railed against fate, and because fate was too vague and shapeless to satisfy my obsessive mind, I seized on Alfred Nobel, the owner of the factory in Heleneborg. He had neglected to ensure the safety of his workers, had been too cheap to install safeguards because he wanted to maximize his profits. It was Nobel who was responsible for Georg's death – that was my line of reasoning at any rate, although obsession does not need a rationale.

My grief was passionate, desperate, vehement. I could not quell my desire for revenge. I could only hide my feelings behind a mask, a frozen look. Inside me, all was turmoil. Outside, I was calm and presented a blank face to my neighbors, to our charwoman, to the greengrocer, to the parish priest. During the day, I was like a creature in a cocoon, tightly wrapped up in silent wrath. At night, I dreamed my catastrophic dreams. They came like riptides, invisible to the eye but perilous to the swimmer caught in them. I was pulled under and trapped in the same subterranean cave night after night, rocked by the same explosion over and over again. I heard the blasts and the screams of the wounded and the dying. My own agonized cries rarely broke out into sound. They stuck in my throat and remained soundless or issued forth in mewls and whimpers. At the time, I shared a bedroom with my mother. She was the only witness to my agony. She heard my stifled cries or woke up because I flung out an arm or trembled violently or writhed as if I was trying to escape a stranglehold. Then she took hold of my arms and shook me awake. My face was wet with tears, but when she asked me about my dreams, I pretended to remember nothing. I had no wish to put my hellish visions into words and experience them a second time in the retelling.

Sophie

The cab turns into Morzinplatz and draws up in front of the Hotel Metropole.

It may not be as classy as The Ambassador, Sophie thinks, but it has *tone*. It tells the world that she is no longer an outsider, no longer living in the shadows. In a few weeks, she will be a married woman. And on the guest list of respectable hostesses, she hopes.

The hotel has the solid look of tradition – a classical portico over the entrance, caryatids flanking the windows on the second floor, a balustrade running along the roofline. And the location is good, close to the center of the city. True, the Metropole no longer attracts the crème de la crème, but that's the fault of the management. They haven't kept up with the times. Why don't they install electrical lights and ensuite bathrooms in every apartment? That's what the better sort of people expect nowadays. Then again, if the Metropole had all the modern conveniences, she couldn't afford to rent an apartment there. Alfred isn't as generous as he used to be.

The driver hands her down from the carriage, and the doorman bows to her, not quite as attentively as he ought to – that's the problem when you don't tip them extravagantly. Sophie swishes by him into the foyer, and yes, she has to admit the atmosphere is a bit lackluster, in spite of the gleaming marble floors. The maroon sofas and chairs have a dull look about them, but the reading and reception rooms beyond offer a vision of elegance. The doors are flanked with bronze torches. The rooms have gold-coffered ceilings and paneled walls, marquetry tables and slender French chairs. No doubt it's the stylishness of the reception rooms that has kept the permanent residents loyal to the hotel. They are impoverished aristocrats for the most part, but they can keep up appearances and receive their visitors in worthy surroundings.

Sophie checks the clock above the reception desk. Alfred will be here in half an hour. A lot depends on that meeting because Nikki won't marry her – can't afford to marry her, he says – unless Alfred agrees to continue her allowance. She must look her best when he comes. She *will* look her best, that's not the problem. It's the conversation, what to say to Alfred now that it's over between them. He can be so severe. Maybe she shouldn't have written that letter.

What you have done is a sin, she wrote. *I wasted my youth on you and have to be grateful that Nikolaus Kapy has agreed to marry me. No one wants a wife who has been another man's mistress for so many years.*

No, she was right to speak out. Every word in that letter was true. And Alfred hadn't even bothered to answer her. Just forwarded the letter to his lawyer. Why didn't he do the right thing years ago and make an honest woman of her?

I won't marry a young woman whose philosophy of life has little or nothing in common with mine, he said when she begged him to take care of her. *We aren't suited to each other.*

That's not what he said when they first met. She remembers the passionate letters he wrote when they were apart even for a day. *A thousand ardent kisses! How is my sweet little child?* And when she gave him the tiniest hint that she was unhappy, he was full of sympathy. *Don't admit any sad thoughts, my love. Go for a drive in the country, find entertaining company. Don't brood, my little froggie. I worry about you so much.*

But then he changed his tune. When she was unhappy and complained of boredom while he was away on business trips, he lectured her in that pompous style of his: *You feel anxious? That's just female foolishness. You are bored because you have nothing to do. Get yourself a couple of entertaining novels, and you will transfer your anxiety to the heroine. Keep yourself occupied and everything will be fine. Prolonged idleness is unhealthy for anyone. You don't work, you don't write, you don't read. You don't even think.* But he was wrong. She was thinking all the time. She couldn't stop thinking about her precarious situation. Her reputation was ruined, and she had no means of supporting herself. What if he deserted her? He was no longer in love with her. He barely wrote to her when he was away, and if he did, he sent her only a few rushed lines.

I can't tell you how busy I am. Meetings from eight in the morning till dinner time, and even dinner tonight was a business affair. And now it's midnight. I have time only to write you a few lines. I'm sorry I can't join you in Carlsbad, although I need a vacation more than you do. In any case, it isn't the right time of the month. Meaning, not the right time to have sex the way he liked it. She was willing to pleasure him in any way, but he wanted the same old thing. Lights out, groping under the covers, brushing his hands over her breasts, fingering her between the legs, as if sex was taboo, their dirty little secret, when everyone in the hotel knew what was going on, from the bellhop to the hotel manager, and the bathers at the mineral spring and the couples in the carriages on the promenade smiled knowingly when they saw them together. Alfred wouldn't come out with it, but she knew what he was thinking when he had his finger in her thing or rubbed himself against her until he came. He told her a story once, about a father having an incestuous affair with his daughter, and she could tell the idea turned him on, even though he pretended he was talking about a historical drama by some medieval Italian. So that's what he wanted her to do: play at being his good little girl. It wasn't her idea of fun. Alfred was no good in bed. She wanted something livelier, something more adventurous. And over the years he turned from a sweet old man into a grouch, forever criticizing and lecturing her. All the nasty things he said when he was in a bad mood! That she was a greedy little Jew. *True to type. Just like the whole tribe of Hebrews.* Of course, when he was in a good mood, he made up for those tirades, took her out to the fashionable shops and bought her anything she wanted, dresses, shoes, jewelry. Life with Alfred was hard at times, but being separated from him was even harder.

I will never forget the way people treated me when I got pregnant, she thinks. But that's how it is in Vienna. If you don't display your marriage certificate on your back, they think you are a common whore. Married women sell themselves to the first-comer for a hat or a dress and cheat on their husbands, but that's all right because they stood up in front of a clergyman and signed the parish register. She sighs. What's the use of rehashing all that? It's over between them, and she has to take what Alfred is willing to give her and the child. Yes, the letter she wrote him was mean, but it was the truth. He was cruel. *What am I to do now?* she wrote. *I am desperate, and there's no one to give me advice.* Or money. She had made it clear in her letter: Nikki was willing to marry her, but he had no money, or not enough to support her and the child.

The worst part was finding a place to live, she told Alfred. *There is nothing to be had in Vienna under two thousand florins a year, and those apartments are all on the third floor, which is too high up for me because I'm sick and can't climb stairs, but the worst thing about those places are the cockroaches. Every place is crawling with them!*

So, finally, he agreed to pay for an apartment at the Metropole, not the best solution, but a decent place at any rate.

I don't know what I would do without my sweet little Gretel, she thinks. Alfred refuses to see the child. Perhaps he is afraid she'll win him over. She is such a cute little darling. *You can't imagine what Gretel means to me*, she wrote to Alfred. A *little girl like her holds my mind together (even if it is a small mind, as you say). She keeps me from any bad thoughts. I should have had my little piggy-wiggy much earlier. Then she would be real company for me now.*

Even Bella was sad when she and Alfred broke up. Poor little dog. She, too, felt neglected. *When I stroke her,* she wrote, *she growls and ducks out of my way. She misses her master. I am depressed when I think of the wonderful times we used to have when I lived with you in Paris or in the villa in Merano, away from those dreary winters here. To spend the cold months with a small child in a hotel in Vienna – it's cruel, Alfred! I am sick of life. I am wretched now that I am apart from you. I am lonely. They all shun me. Nobody calls on me. Nobody invites me. I am so desperate, I sometimes think it would be best to take my life.*

But Alfred no longer answers her letters.

Bertie

Lady Suttner provided me with a letter of reference, but it lacked warmth. She acknowledged that I was competent and had fulfilled my duties as a companion to her daughters, but she pointedly omitted any good wishes for my future. Anyone reading the letter understood at once – the countess did not regret my departure.

When I left the Suttner household, I had been with them less than a year. The family lived on a grand scale. From the marble hall, you entered a suite of three drawing rooms with silk tapestries that cast a weather spell. The first room was green like the stormy sea, the second a sunny yellow, the third a wintery blue. The library, which also served as the gentlemen's smoking room, had wainscoting polished to a soft glow and a fireplace so large you could roast a pig in the hearth. There was an army of servants below stairs: a valet, a lady's maid, two housemaids, a cook, a scullery girl, serving men, a gardener and his boy, a coachman, a porter, and me.

The Suttner girls, who ranged in age from fifteen to nineteen, were curiously alike in temperament as if they had been tuned by the same fork. All three were meek and had a tendency to whisper and lower their eyes. The oldest was engaged to be married to a Prussian count she dreaded. His bristly moustache was hateful to her, she said, and his voice terrifying. It was my task to shape the younger daughters into debutantes who might find more genial suitors. The girls and I were soon on the best of terms. I did not parade the dignity of my thirty years and wasn't too strict in my supervision.

There was also a son, Arthur. He was twenty-three, handsome, with a cheerful disposition and very charming. Of course, I fell in love with him. He was irresistible, a magnetic force. When he entered the drawing room, the atmosphere grew bright and warm. Smiles appeared on everyone's face, and conversations became animated. We all loved Arthur. He had returned to the family home without completing his studies and was hanging around the library, reading Descartes and Hume. He had no interest in the legal profession for which his family had destined him and no desire to take the civil service exam – until I offered to study with him.

We went through the questions in his textbook, and he answered me readily enough, but his zeal diminished when I was called away to look after the girls. In my absence, he fell to daydreaming. His father called him a lazy dog. His mother suspected that he was an idealist and feared for his career.

Soon, my study sessions with Arthur turned into trysts. One thing led to another, and he asked me to marry him. I knew his parents wouldn't welcome me into the family and wasn't surprised when his mother took me aside and with great delicacy but icy coldness gave me to understand that my position in the house was untenable, and I must leave. I had expected nothing else. I came from an excellent family but was absolutely penniless and seven years older than Arthur. Women were crazy about him. He had every chance of making a brilliant match. How could I stand in the way of his future?

I resigned from my position and looked for other employment. Scanning the newspapers, I came across a notice: *An elderly gentleman, living in Paris, desires to find a lady, also of mature years, with a knowledge of German and French, as secretary and manager of his household affairs.* Secretarial positions were usually reserved for gentlemen, and the wording of the notice was odd. It read almost like a matrimonial advertisement. I hesitated, but I had no other prospects. So far, my applications had not been successful. I was in dire need of employment and confident that I could do the work of a secretary. I knew I could handle the German correspondence. After my father's death six years ago, I had taken on the task of looking after our finances, dealt with the lawyers and answered business correspondence. My mother was useless when it came to money matters and gladly left them in my hands. I was fluent in French, thanks to a nanny who was a native speaker. No doubt I could pick up the phrases needed to write proper business letters in French. And so I applied for the position. The gentleman, Mr Alfred Nobel, invited me to come to Paris for a trial period. The tone of his letter was stern rather than romantic as I had feared from the style of his advertisement. He seemed to be an unhappy man, not to say a misanthrope, and I wondered what I was getting into. But it was the only offer I received, and poverty forced me to accept it.

I braced myself for a sour old gentleman and was pleasantly surprised when I arrived in Paris and met Mr Nobel in person. He was gray-haired and walked with a stoop, but his face retained a certain youthfulness. His moustache and beard were neatly trimmed, and his blue eyes radiated intelligence, although he had a way of fixing them on me that was unnerving.

Nobel lived in a newly built mansion on the Avenue Malakoff, not far from the Arc de Triomphe and the Trocadero gardens, in the very center of Paris. The house looked austere, but I suppose the plain and rational style of modern architecture suited a man like Nobel, who was a scientist. The house was a four-storey building with a flat roof and a façade, unadorned except for a wrought-iron balcony running the length of the third floor and a garlanded arch over the main entrance. The outside held no attraction for me, but the interior had a certain charm. Nobel's study overlooked a fine private garden and was furnished with bookcases from floor to ceiling. A massive oak desk stood before the great window and offered a view of neat flower beds and a water fountain in the Moorish style. My desk, in the adjoining room, shared that pleasant view. There was also a winter garden that offered respite on cold and rainy days and seemed to have been designed by a more playful spirit than the rest of the house, with a checkered marble floor, domed glass roof, potted palms and comfortable sofas and chairs.

Compared to the Suttners' household, Nobel's style of living was simple. There was no army of servants. He relied on the services of a middle-aged couple, the Perrins, who acted as housekeeper and driver and were aided by a maid of all work. An old valet looked after Nobel's wardrobe and personal needs, and a chemist assisted with the experiments he conducted in a laboratory attached to the house. The rest of the staff were day laborers who went home after their work was done. There was no sense of community among the live-in servants. In the evening, each retreated to his quarters, and I went to my room, where I felt alone and unprotected. At the Suttners I had often shared the family dinner. In Nobel's house, the maid brought a dinner tray to my room and left me to my own devices. Arthur's letters were my only comfort. A cousin of his had agreed to be our go-between, but I could not write as often as I wished because my letters had already attracted the attention of the cousin's older brother who teased her about her mysterious Paris correspondent and threatened to tell her parents of her "admirer". She, therefore, asked me to curb my letter-writing fever. I had no friends in Paris and passed my free time walking the boulevards and parks and browsing the department stores but my thoughts were with Arthur. I read and reread his letters and kissed the lines in which he professed his love for me until the ink dyed my lips and the words became smudged.

When Nobel was away on one of his frequent business trips, I wandered through the rooms on the first floor, admired the art he had collected, the walls of rich red damask, which was very much in vogue then, and ventured into the winter garden to savor the tropical air. The house was silent as a grave, even when Nobel was home. There were no musical evenings, no balls and no formal dinners except on rare occasions. Nobel preferred to entertain his friends and associates in the private dining room of the Grand Hotel, but when he did have guests, I glimpsed famous faces – the Goncourt brothers, Emile Zola and the white-haired, white-bearded Victor Hugo, who had returned from his self-imposed exile on the Channel Islands and was the hero of the liberal thinkers. From my infrequent conversations with Nobel, I did not think he was an admirer of liberal thinkers, but my impression of him changed from week to week.

I usually began my day sorting through the mail he received and entering them into a log with a brief summary. I set aside the ones that needed answering and brought them to him in the course of the morning. He returned them to me, with notes indicating the replies I was to send. Sometimes he dictated a few phrases to me, but more often he left the wording to me. I set to work and presented the letters for his signature in the afternoon. During the first few weeks, he barely looked up from his desk when I came into his study. He said not a word more than needed to be said. But over the weeks, his reserve began to melt. He put his work aside when I entered and remarked on the weather or the politics of the day or a play he had seen but always in a gruff voice. At last, he relaxed his manner, asked me to take a seat when he was at leisure and began to talk to me at greater length, about life and art, about problems of the moment and eternal problems, but in spite of his efforts to treat me kindly and with courtesy, he never succeeded in making me entirely comfortable. I think it was the way he trained his eyes on me as if he wanted to give me a secret message.

I confided my unease to Arthur. *I find Mr Nobel puzzling*, I wrote. *There seems to be a hidden meaning behind his words and gestures which I cannot fathom. And sometimes, he turns sarcastic.*

One day, he received a pathetic letter from a man who claimed he was reduced to starvation and beseeched him to send money.

"Well, Miss Kinsky," he said to me. "What do you think of the merits of this letter, or rather the rhetorical skills of the writer? I've never read a more touching description of poverty. There ought to be a literary competition for begging letters, don't you think?"

"I wish there was no need for literary skills to arouse pity," I said. "Poverty is moving enough in itself, and the poor have a claim on us if we want to call ourselves Christians."

"Quite so," he said. "I only wish I had a bag of tricks like Christ and could multiply my money the way he multiplied fish. But even if I'm too clumsy to work that sleight of hand, I'll follow your admonition and do the Christian thing. Send the man what he asks for, with my best wishes."

I could not make out his motives. Did he truly pity the poor and cover his feelings with sarcasm? Was he ashamed of his feelings, perhaps, and feared to look like a dupe? He said no more and only gave me one of his penetrating looks which made me so uneasy. I did not know what to say in answer to his quip about Christ's sleight of hand. I fear he was an agnostic or worse, an atheist.

I told Arthur about our conversation. *Nobel can be caustic*, I wrote, *but in his defense I must say that he is generous. After he has vented his spleen, he doles out his money without bitterness.*

Another time, when Nobel gave me instructions to send money to a supplicant, he stopped me as I was leaving his study.

"Turn around, Miss Kinsky," he said and made a great show of eyeing the back of my dress. "Bustles seem to be all the rage among fashionable women nowadays. I see they have found favor with you as well."

I was deeply embarrassed by his close scrutiny of my dress. When he saw the color rising in my cheeks, he laughed. "No need to blush," he said, without taking his eyes off me. "I'm not referring to your sense of fashion or your fine proportions about which a man of literary gifts might wax poetical. I am talking of the waste material in your dress, the over-drape, the gathered puffs, the ruffled skirt – now if we could cut out that fullness, we might supply some poor mother with enough material to sew dresses for half a dozen children."

His words left me speechless. I lowered my eyes, but he continued his harangue.

"Not to mention hats for which they charge a fortune at Virat's, whereas they can be bought for a quarter of the money down the road. Now, if those customers at Virat's were to donate the difference in price to the poor, each hat would feed a family for a week and keep them in fine fettle. Am I right, Miss Kinsky?"

I quoted his rambling speech to Arthur in my next letter. *Nobel has no social graces*, I wrote, *but I forgive him because his actions are good. He is a charitable man.*

He'd better be, Arthur wrote back, *because he is in the uncharitable business of war.*

I knew that Nobel was famous for developing the chemical formula for dynamite. I also knew that he had factories all over Europe, but until Arthur enlightened me about its military uses, I thought of dynamite only as a means of blasting rock used in mining and construction. The thought of its murderous use in battle added to my unease. Nobel's business interests and their deadly purpose seemed at odds with his philosophy of life. *But then he is a strange man*, I wrote to Arthur, *and I am still puzzled as to why he wanted a female secretary, why he advertised in a Viennese paper and why he hired me. Of course, I cannot ask him such personal questions.*

No, don't encourage personal conversation, Arthur wrote back. *You mustn't let your guard down. From what you write, it is difficult to tell what he is up to. In any case, I hope you will not have to work for him much longer.*

We had talked of eloping before I left Vienna, and I sensed that Arthur's plans were coming to fruition, even if he did not mention them explicitly, for fear of our letters falling into the wrong hands.

I never asked Nobel about the circumstances that led him to place that advertisement in the newspaper. The housekeeper hinted that there had been an unsatisfactory arrangement with another woman from Vienna whom he sent away. "We all wondered that he did not send her packing sooner," she said. She was willing to tell me more, but I did not think it was right to inquire into other people's affairs.

One day, Nobel offered me an explanation himself.

"How do you get along with Mrs Perrin?" he asked me.

"Very well," I said, since I was keeping on friendly terms with the housekeeper.

"That's good," he said. "I find her awkward to deal with. When I give her instructions, she stands there slack-jawed, winding her apron around her hands and giving me breathless replies. 'Yes, sir, no, sir.' I can't get an intelligent word out of her. You may have wondered why I advertised for a female secretary, Miss Kinsky. I was hoping she would take that chore off my hands and combine secretarial duties with supervising the household staff. I did not think a gentleman was suited to that double duty."

According to Mrs Perrin, my predecessor had not been up to the task either, and I doubted my ability to give Nobel satisfaction on that point.

"I have no experience running a household," I said.

"But it will be your duty once you are married, and you might as well try to gain experience now," he said and gave me one of those stares that penetrate the soul.

To overcome my discomfort, I asked him: "And you believed the paragon who could combine those tasks was to be found in Vienna?"

"I placed my notice in a Viennese newspaper because I have a liking for the people there. I find them pleasant. They have a willingness to oblige. And I did receive a large number of applications." He paused and drew back his lips into a sarcastic smile. "Some applicants included photographs and added descriptions of their feminine charms as if I had advertised for a wife. Yours was the only intelligent letter I received, which contained no shallow words, no falsity and no frivolity. I knew at once that I had found the ideal candidate and a woman to my liking."

He got up and advanced on me as if to take my hand.

I don't know what his intentions were, but I backed away at once and thought it timely to tell him I was pledged to Arthur.

"Ah," he said and retreated behind his desk. "Then your heart is not free?"

"Mr Suttner has asked me to marry him," I said, "but his parents do not approve of our union."

I thought of the last time I was with Arthur before I departed for Paris. He came to my mother's house. She protested and said she could not permit us to meet without the knowledge of his parents, but she relented when she saw how wretched I was. "I shall allow you ten minutes by my watch," she said, leaving us alone in the drawing room. We clung to each other, wept, and exchanged salty kisses and trembling words of endearment. When our time was up, Arthur knelt and kissed the hem of my gown. "I adore you," he said. "You will always be my goddess." I stood at the window of our drawing room and watched him get into the waiting carriage. As he drove away, I knew I could never let him go.

Nobel had turned his back to me and looked out into the garden. Silence descended on us.

"I understand," he said at last.

When he faced me again, there was a softness in his eyes I had not seen before. "I was in love once, a long time ago when I was young," he said, "but I encountered an obstacle which cannot be overcome. Death carried away my love and deprived me of all hope. You have hope at least, and I wish you happiness, with all my heart."

Ida

The nightmares did not let up even after I threw out the Swedish dictionary and the language primer and everything else that reminded me of Georg except one photograph and a locket with a braid of his hair. I could not bear to part with them. My grief kept me in a state of suspension, where everything seemed to be at a great distance and the air that entered my lungs was different from that which everyone else was breathing, an air filled with the fine ash of a volcanic eruption, of a catastrophe remembered.

I came to my senses only when the past collided with the needs of the present, when my brother announced his decision to emigrate to America. He had been offered a position at Kuhn & Loeb's investment bank in New York. He wanted me to join him, to come away from the toxic atmosphere in St Veit, poisoned by sad memories. He wanted me to snap out of my funk, as he put it, but the enormity of my pain and the memory of Georg held me fast. I had unfinished business here. I wanted revenge. Besides, there was the practical question: Who would look after our mother? She trembled at the thought of Fritz going so far away. She was a widow and afraid of being left alone in her old age. She wrapped her arms around me and begged me not to go. She wept at the thought of losing both of her children at once. She pleaded with Fritz.

"Don't take Ida away from me. She is all I have, now that you are deserting me. No, I shouldn't have said 'deserting'. I don't mean that you shouldn't try and better yourself, Fritz. I don't want to hold you back, but—"

In the privacy of our little parlor, she allowed herself to sob loudly. I sympathized with my mother. I knew what it meant to lose a loved one. Fritz brushed her off with an impatient gesture, the kind that stopped all argument. He was only twenty-four, but he already had that aura of authority which makes for success in life. He was tall and square-built, had a firm jaw, steady gray eyes and a commanding voice. He was a dutiful son and willing to provide material support for my mother if need be, but he did not believe in making personal sacrifices for the sake of an old woman. She belonged to the past. He was a man of the future.

"I've made my decision," he said. "I can't stay. If you are unwilling to let Ida go, very well, I won't say any more about it, but at least make sure she gets out of the house. Get her into society. She's eighteen. Don't let her mope around like that. You don't want her to turn into an old maid, do you?"

"Oh, she won't be like this forever," my mother said. "Time heals wounds. Wounds turn into wisdom." She was full of pious platitudes, and for all I know believed in them. She wanted to see me happy again and happily married.

Neither of them said out loud what was surely on their minds: that I was no beauty. An extra effort was required of me if I wanted to catch the eye of a suitor. I had no charms other than the charms of youth. True, I had no obvious faults. The problem was that I had no obvious attractions either. I was no heiress and did not come from a distinguished family. I would inherit only a small annuity. The proportions of my body, the features of my face and the color of my hair were all so ordinary that men's eyes passed over them unseeing. Brown hair, brown eyes, a pleasant face and nicely curved lips, a compact figure – not bad in themselves, but nothing to arrest the eye. In any case, I had no desire to attract a suitor.

"I'll never forget Georg," I said defiantly. "And I don't mind remaining unmarried. I have no love left for any man."

"Well, then, what will you do with your life?" Fritz asked.

I shrugged.

"You can't expect me to support you both," he said. "Besides, I don't know how it will work out for me in America." He ended up doing very well and could afford to leave the house to me when our mother died. But when he set out for America and gave me that warning, there was no guarantee that he would be successful.

"You'll have to make your own way," he said to me. "You'll have to earn your living as a governess or as a companion to an old lady. And I'm not sure you have the right qualifications. You will have to improve your skills, Ida."

I saw his point. What skills did I have? I played the piano and had a pleasant singing voice. I had a smattering of knowledge in history and literature. But was that good enough?

"You'll be up against a lot of competition," Fritz said.

"I could teach French."

"Yes, you have an ability for languages," he said, and my heart contracted at the thought of Georg's Swedish lexicon and the useless progress I had made in that language.

"Why don't you take English lessons?" Fritz said. "That's in demand now and might give you an edge over other applicants when you look for a position."

Mother agreed that it was a good plan. "Who knows," she said, "when I'm dead, you might want to join your brother in America and then a knowledge of English will come in handy."

The thought of my uncertain future made the past recede for a time and cleared my head sufficiently to stop brooding and start planning. The gritty scenes still played regularly on my dream stage, but during the day, I rallied. I worked hard to untangle my mind and make it go through the motions of forming thoughts and acting on them, although it felt as if another person within me was giving the command and choreographing my steps. Still, I did it and imposed order on my thoughts and set myself two goals: supporting myself and avenging Georg's death. Revenge, I thought, was the only way to end the crippling nightmares, although I had no idea what form that revenge would take, and indeed how to go about tracking down Nobel and putting my plans into action. Improving my qualifications to obtain work was an easier task.

Twice a week, I took the train from our house in St Veit to the main railway station in Vienna, then the tram to the fourth district. From there, I made my way on foot to the farmers' market. The tenement where Miss Schmidt gave private English lessons was on the far side of the market, which was bustling with customers inspecting the produce laid out on wooden trestles. I crossed to the other side, along a dusty aisle, littered with lettuce leaves and squashed fruit. Farm women ladled milk from wooden buckets and housewives haggled with vendors for chicken, so cramped in their cages that they looked like brown and white feather balls. I stood for a while at the edge of the street, waiting for a break in the row of drays rattling by, then dashed across and passed into the tenement through a wooden gateway. It was pock-marked as if someone had demanded entry with an axe. Miss Schmidt's apartment was on the third floor, up a dark staircase.

My English teacher was a meek little woman in her thirties with a voice so soft you had to lean in to hear her. The drab color of her dress barely stood out against the equally drab walls, which had not seen a coat of whitening in many years. To take advantage of the daylight, we sat across from each other at a table pushed up against the window. It overlooked a courtyard, where lace curtains were tacked to drying boards. The braying laugh of washerwomen floated up to us as we practiced English conversation. I was always struck by the contrast between the laughing women below and the stillness of Miss Schmidt's apartment where we carried on a stilted dialogue, the genteel patter I would have to master as a lady's companion.

"How do you do, Miss Schmidt?" I intoned.

"I am well, thank you, and how are you this morning, Miss Lassick? Did you go for a carriage ride?"

"No, I chose to walk because the weather was mild."

"How is your aunt, Miss Lassick? Is she feeling better?"

"Much better. It is very kind of you to inquire after her."

We went on through the questions a traveler might ask in foreign cities.

"Where is the museum? How much does this postcard cost? When does the train leave?"

I answered Miss Schmidt's questions impatiently. What good were those words to me? I would have preferred to learn a different vocabulary. What are the safety regulations in your factory, Mr Nobel? Do the deaths you have caused haunt your dreams? Do you think that money can redeem the lives you have ruined? But then I would probably speak German with Nobel, or French. The papers reported that he lived in Hamburg. Paris was mentioned as well. He had bought a mansion there. But all I had to go on were incidental reports. I had no method to pinpoint his whereabouts, no means of arranging an encounter with Nobel or exacting revenge once I had him cornered. All I could do was keep my eyes and ears open for something that might shape the disorderly heap of ideas in my head into a cogent plan. In the meantime, I played imaginary scenes in my head, encounters in German, French, and English, watching Nobel go pale under the bombardment of my words. I did not know what he looked like. I pictured him as a hulking man with a proud and arrogant face. Yet when I screamed my accusations, his face contorted with shame. He cringed. He begged me not to make a scene. *Keep your voice down, miss*, he pleaded.

In my daydreams, I reduced Nobel to a pitiful creature. In my nightmares, he was a ghoul rising up from the gutted factory in Heleneborg and attacking me bodily. I fought back, got my hands around his neck and pressed my thumbs into his flesh, trying to strangle him, but I could not vanquish him, even in my dreams and woke up drenched in sweat, with my heart pounding and my throat raw from silent screams.

The night terrors left me limp, but I rallied during the day and continued with my English lessons. My knowledge advanced under Miss Schmidt's guidance. She was a good teacher, even if the words she taught me were useless for my purposes, even if I disliked her because she was old, or seemed old to me, and yet cherished romantic thoughts. She had a predilection for Elizabeth Browning, whose sonnets she recited to me in a trembling voice and with her eyes closed. I watched her performance with distaste.

My youth made me impatient with Miss Schmidt. I was hard on older women when I was eighteen. I thought their age did not entitle them to thoughts of love. Now I am Miss Schmidt's age and – like her – still cherish romantic notions. Or let us say, I feel a twinge of longing for affection now and then, for someone to put his arms around me, for a sympathetic ear to share my thoughts and worries. And yes, I admit, sometimes I feel pricks of a more lascivious kind when I see a good-looking man. I was disgusted with Miss Schmidt for having romantic thoughts. My thoughts are worse. My voice does not tremble, and I do not close my eyes the way she did when she recited poetry, but my mouth softens, and I feel the blood pulsing in my neck when I imagine a man's embrace. Not all the scenes playing in my head are stories of revenge. Some are stories of love and desire. For years, I modelled those scenes after my farewell from Georg, our last walk together to the train station. The man I kissed in my daydreams was him. The body I felt was his. My arms were around his neck. He pressed against me, or rather I pressed my own hands against my breasts as I was lying on my bed dreaming of him. I let my hands slide down to my stomach, to the mound between my legs and stroked it, softly at first, then harder. Oddly, my imaginary love scenes were not much different from the revenge scenes playing in my head. They both had a climactic ending, a spasm that brought the scene to a stop. The two scenarios – love and revenge – shared other features as well. There was the same closeness of bodies, the same wrangling and beating of the heart, the same breaking sound at the back of my throat. But when I came to the end of my love scene, the part where I rubbed and fingered myself until I felt the spasm of relief, my conscience took over and lambasted me for what I had done. It was a sin to pleasure myself. And even if it had not been a sin, I was a fool cherishing fantastic notions. How could any man fall in love with a plain-looking woman like me? And did I want a man to fall in love with me? I wanted to be true to Georg, but there were days when I wavered, when I wanted to attract a man's attention. I did have assets – good hair, clear skin, trim figure. Why not make the best of them? I pulled myself together and made an earnest effort to look decent, but, my God, it was a Sisyphean task. Like pushing a rock up a hill. I brushed my hair until it was glossy and pinned it up carefully. By noon, it had slipped, and strands of hair were straying down my neck. Or I had a bad night, full of clouded dreams and nightmares and woke up drained and with dark circles under my eyes. Nothing I could do about that or the fine lines that began to form at the edges of my eyes and the corners of my mouth. Still, there were mornings when I looked into the mirror above my washstand and was pleased with what I saw – the healthy glow of my cheeks, the brightness in my eyes. Those were the days when I was willing to take on all odds and find a man to love.

Miss Schmidt taught me serviceable English, and I quickly became competent in the language. I went about the task with my usual determination, obsessively reading the English dictionary and memorizing the textbook. I carried it with me wherever I went, even to Sunday mass. I sat in the pew, clasping my hands together with special devotion to keep myself from taking the book out of my purse, but the words I murmured under my breath weren't prayers. They were English dialogues. It was a great wrangle to free myself from that particular obsession, by convincing myself that I had completely mastered the content of the textbook and could, therefore, discard it.

In the end, I did not have to apply for the position of a governess or compete with other candidates for the post of a lady's companion. Instead, I was offered employment by a friend of my late father who wanted me to translate newspaper articles for him. Mr Olmuth, a man who had inherited money and knew how to increase his wealth, subscribed to half a dozen international papers, British, French, and American. He wanted to keep up with what was going on in the world to protect his investments. Every afternoon, I went to his house and cut out the most important world news, pasted them into a ledger and added my translation. I read about battles and peace treaties, parliamentary debates, steam engines, motor cars and dynastic marriages. Mr Olmuth had already cut out the business news that interested him. The Suez Canal in which he had bought shares, to his great satisfaction. The Panama Canal, which had cost him money, although there was a chance that the construction might start up again and his shares might recover their value. The rubber plantations in the Amazon, a sure money maker. The oil fields in Baku. He wished he had invested in them earlier! I pasted the business news into a separate ledger with my translations alongside.

The routine motion of cutting and pasting was very pleasing to me. In fact, it was like my childhood pastime of collecting and labelling leaves and seemed to have a healing effect on my mind. The slow word-for-word consideration of the text aided my recovery. In my grief over Georg's death, I had shut myself off from the world and kept to my own thoughts. Now I allowed the words and ideas of others to penetrate my mind, or at least to cross my mind on the way from one language to another. It was like opening up a channel to irrigate a fallow field or a window to expose a vista. My surroundings came back into view, piece by piece, and resumed their place in my mind. For a long time, I made no room for thoughts, except thoughts of revenge, as if the explosion in Heleneborg had shredded all other ideas. Reading the papers in Mr Olmuth's study and discussing world events with him, I began slowly to refurnish my mind with less distressing sights and sounds. My mother noted it with approval, and I myself thought I had succeeded in taking the edge off my grief, but my nightmares continued and my thoughts of revenge did not go away. On the contrary – for a long time they had been rather vague. Now they began to firm up and take shape and crystallize. Nobel had become a demon haunting my nights. I was convinced that I must exorcise him if I wanted to regain my peace of mind and rid myself of the nightmares. The first step, I thought, was to scour the newspapers in Mr Olmuth's library and find sufficient information on Nobel to track him down.

Nobel had taken out a patent on dynamite, I read. There had been many accidents involving his invention. The paper quoted Nobel as saying: "*Even if the explosions continue, it is my hope to be able to convince competent and scientific authorities that dynamite is, at any rate, less dangerous than gunpowder to handle and store.*" The accidents did continue. A container with dynamite, left behind in a hotel lobby in Bremerhaven, exploded minutes after being carried out into the street. Hundreds of people were killed when dynamite exploded on a steamship in the Panama Canal (and were there any survivors I could contact?). In Sydney, a warehouse was levelled by a blast. A dynamite factory on the outskirts of Hamburg blew up. Fourteen people were killed in an explosion at a warehouse in San Francisco.

The information immediately turned into fodder for my nightmares. The carnage shifted from Heleneborg to a hotel lobby with shattered chandeliers and bloodied carpets, then to the deck of a listing ship with steam hissing from a burst boiler and screaming passengers, their skin flayed. Splintered wood and corpses floated in the ocean, and I too was drowning, waking up, gasping for breath. The nightmares made me more determined than ever to carry on with my plan of revenge. It was the only way to overcome my terror, I thought.

I bought a special notebook to write down information on Nobel. It wasn't one of those pretty silk-covered aide-memoires women use to jot down epigrams or their own genteel thoughts. It was a black leather-covered book with a clasp and lock and marbled end pages. I weighed it in my hand. It was hefty, suited to the weighty matter I would entrust to its pages, accidents and deaths. I copied out all the quotes attributed to Nobel. Apparently, he had nothing to say about the Heleneborg incident beyond one succinct statement. The catastrophe had been caused by negligence, he said, and could not have happened in the normal course of things. *An accident of this nature should not occur again during nitroglycerine manufacture.* Should not occur *again*? Isn't once enough? Can you kill a man twice?

Reading the papers served my own purpose as much as it served my employer's commercial interests, but newspapers weren't the only source I consulted as I gathered material on Nobel. Mr Olmuth introduced me to an old lady who had met Nobel at Aix-les-Bains some years ago. She was willing to talk to me, and I was excited by the possibility of hearing from another person who knew him personally.

Mrs Bottig, the widow of a general who had sacrificed his life for his country, lived on the belle étage of an apartment building overlooking the grounds of Belvedere Castle.

She threw open the doors to the balcony to let me admire the view of the sprawling lawns and topiaries, the cascading fountains and graceful statuary lining the gravel paths of the Belvedere.

"Magnificent, isn't it?" she said with a proprietary air. "I have been to Versailles, Miss Lassick, but I must say, Prince Eugene had better taste than the Sun King. The Belvedere has more agreeable proportions than that pretentious French palace, don't you think?"

"I'm afraid I've never been to Versailles," I said.

"Then take it from me, Miss Lassick. The Belvedere is superior to King Louis' palace."

She turned back to the room.

"Ah, there you are, Menzel," she said to the servant who was setting down a tray with coffee things on a small Japanese table. "Thank you, Menzel."

She closed the balcony door, led me to the sofa and poured coffee for us. The black silk of her dress rustled when she moved. She was a doughty matron who had settled into permanent mourning.

"You wanted to know about Alfred Nobel," she said. "Mr Olmuth tells me that you are doing research and are interested in the business affairs of the Nobels, but I'm afraid I know nothing about that, except what my cousin Marie tells me about the Nobel brothers in St Petersburg. She married a Russian count, you know, who turned out to be—" She drew a deep breath as if to say more then changed her mind and let out a sigh instead. "—but you want to know about Mr Nobel in Paris, isn't that what you said?"

"Yes," I said, "I would be very much obliged if you gave me your impression of him. What was he like?"

"Like?" My question confused her apparently. She hadn't thought of Nobel as being *like* anyone other than himself. She had no concept of the difference between seeming and being, between a man and his reputation. "He is an inventor, a genius, they told me."

I waited politely for more.

"He has a splendid winter garden in his palais in Paris, and he is interested in orchids," she said after racking her brains for additional bits of information.

"You talked with him about his house in Paris?"

She gave me a startled look. "My dear!" she said. "You don't ask people about their houses. It's not done."

"I'm collecting material for a biography, Mrs Bottig," I said. "I meant: is what you are telling me hearsay, or did Mr Nobel mention the winter garden and the orchids to you himself? And did he say anything else to you about his life in Paris?"

"Well, now that you ask me, he did say something about collecting art and about the pictures he has in his drawing room. He mentioned Courbet.

Yes, now I remember – he said Courbet's *Waterfall in the Mountains* was his favorite painting."

"You talked about his taste in art?"

"We talked about many things. An estate he bought outside Paris and a laboratory he built there. A laboratory! I was so surprised. I thought he was going to say, a villa. But he was a strange man and said some very odd things."

"Odd?"

"Well, they sounded odd to me. He said that Paris was truly civilized. Even the mongrels smelled of civilization. Don't you think that's a strange way of putting it? And then, oh, I don't know whether I should tell you. It's rather rude, I'm afraid, and he didn't say it to me personally, but it made the rounds, you know."

She hesitated.

"Don't worry about offending me, Mrs Bottig. As a biographer, I need to know what Nobel was like."

"He thought that the conversation of French women was insipid and preferred conversing with Russian women. Unfortunately, they had an antipathy to soap, he said, but one cannot ask for everything. Isn't that the most ridiculous thing you have ever heard?"

That was all I could get out of Mrs Bottig. I added it to the other witticisms and apocryphal anecdotes I had gathered. I had one more question, however: Could she put me in touch with Mr Nobel?

"Oh dear, no," she said, raising her eyebrows. "I wasn't on close terms with him. No one in my circle was. As I said, he was a most peculiar man, not at all *comme il faut.*"

The Olmuths also introduced me to a gentleman who collected quotations. I sat next to him at one of their dinners. He had a long face and close-set eyes, which gave him a dreary look, but he turned out to be quite entertaining and a veritable storehouse of anecdotes. He came up with two quips about Nobel. The illustrious writer, Victor Hugo noted that Nobel travelled constantly. "Trains are his rolling prisons," he said, and, "Nobel is the wealthiest vagabond in Europe."

After these interludes with Mrs Bottig and the collector of anecdotes, I went back to scanning newspapers and extracting more snippets of information about Nobel. One article said that Nobel had *borrowed his plumes* from Sobrero (Who was Sobrero? I looked him up. He was the discoverer of nitroglycerine). Nobel denied the accusation and pointed out that it was he who had made nitroglycerine workable (workable! And the accidents?). Later Nobel – the hypocrite– contributed money to a bust of Sobrero, which was unveiled in 1879 at Nobel's Italian factory.

I also found earnest testimonies to Nobel's indefatigable spirit, his salesmanship, his business acumen. But the whole didn't add up to a clear picture of the man. I still hadn't found a means of getting in touch with him and still didn't have an answer to the question which interested me particularly: What drove him to engage in the lethal business of selling dynamite? Did he have any conscience at all?

My renewed efforts to find information on Nobel fed straight into my dreams, the same old nightmares and other dreams, less terrifying perhaps, but disturbing nevertheless. In one of them, I was in a storeroom filled with boxes and crates packed with papers. I rifled through them but could not make out what they were. They bore no labels and were tied with twine which I wrenched off with difficulty as I had no scissors and no knife. Sometimes, I glimpsed Nobel's name on a page, but the lines were always smudged or the page torn so that the crucial information was missing. Sometimes, the boxes were stored in what looked like an old stable in an interior courtyard. I sat at a wooden table, wrapped in a coat to protect myself against the cold rising from the stone floor and the thick walls. The broken cobbles were covered with puddles the color of spilled blood. The room had a heavy oaken door, the upper half of which was hinged and could be opened like a window, but the courtyard also housed the shop of a tinsmith and rang with the fall of his hammer so that I could not concentrate on what I was doing. At other times, the courtyard suddenly filled with people who stopped at my door and leered at me or made threatening gestures. I was therefore forced to shut it and work by the light of a smoking taper. Again, I spotted Nobel's name, but the smoke got into my eyes so that I could not go on reading. I woke up rubbing my eyes and was chilled to the bone, because my featherbed had slipped to the floor, and my arms and legs were exposed.

The Olmuths were very kind to me and treated me almost like family. They shared their box at the opera with me, they took me for carriage rides in the Prater park and invited me to join them for dinner if they needed to make up an even number. In that way, I was taken into society, as my brother wished, and was introduced to plenty of gentlemen, mostly old but also a few eligible ones, only my heart wasn't in it. Mrs Olmuth was the motherly type, round-faced with soft old eyes and a gentle voice, full of goodwill and anxious to find me a husband. My brother had encouraged me to marry because he saw it as a guarantee that I would be taken care of. Mrs Olmuth and my mother saw marriage as a validation of womanhood. It meant that someone found me lovable and was prepared to sign his name to it. In their eyes, marriage was an indication of a woman's worth. Remaining a spinster somehow marked me a failure, and in a way, implicated my mother and Mrs Olmuth as well, making them failures in the matchmaking department. I was in my thirties and still a spinster when my mother died quietly in her sleep. She had resigned herself to my unmarried status, but Mrs Olmuth was not a woman to give up easily and redoubled her efforts after my mother's death. She discreetly reminded me of my precarious financial situation. I continued to live in my mother's house. What if my brother demanded his share of the inheritance? I had no money to buy him out. If the house had to be sold to satisfy his demands, I would be left without a home. I knew my brother was a hard-nosed businessman. I expected no charity from him, but I could not bear the idea of selling myself to a man, for that is what matchmaking amounted to – my body and my services for the financial security provided by a husband. I repressed the anxiety I felt about my future. I will deal with it when my brother demands his inheritance, I thought. So far, he had kept silent about the matter, and I saw no reason to raise the question myself. Mrs Olmuth was right to remind me about my uncertain future, but I stubbornly refused to enter into her matchmaking schemes. I made no effort to ingratiate myself with the gentlemen she presented to me. They were eligible, yes, but lacking in looks or brains or charm, in the characteristics that might have made me forget Georg and my plans of revenge and replace them with an obsession to get married. Some of the acquaintances I made at the Olmuths' house proved useful at any rate, a matron who needed a chaperone for her daughter travelling to London, another who wanted a companion on her travels in France and Carl Volker, who encouraged me to take up writing, who kept promising to publish a collection of my essays and would have published them sooner if I had been more receptive to his advances.

I suppose I should be grateful to Carl for starting me on my writing career. Mrs Olmuth seated him next to me at dinner one night. She was desperate because the woman she had meant to be his dinner companion had sent regrets at the last moment. There was no good match for the publisher among the remaining guests. I was the stand-in, as usual. As we assembled in the drawing room, I noticed Carl fixing me with a multi-layered look, of observation, appraisal, and discreet admiration. No, more than admiration. He looked smitten, but I didn't take his attentions seriously because Mrs Olmuth had told me that he was a confirmed bachelor. Even if she had said nothing, I would not have taken a sentimental interest in Carl. His body was well padded. He had a look of plenitude about him that promised comfort to a woman, but he did not inspire romantic feelings and certainly was no candidate for playing a role in my imaginary love scenes. His wit and knowledge did not make up for what he lacked in physical attraction. Yet I found his talk engaging enough to ease my restless mind for a time, give me respite from my thoughts of revenge and guide them into a broader channel.

The dinner conversation that night turned on women writers. I said that they had become popular in other countries – Austen, Gaskell and Eliot in England, George Sand and Delphine de Girardin in France. Why was there no woman writer with comparable success in Austria?

"What about Ebner-Eschenbach?" Carl said.

"One swallow doesn't make a summer," I said. "In Vienna, writing is still considered an unusual, not to say, questionable aspiration for a woman."

"You think so?" he said.

"*I* don't think so myself, but when the subject is mentioned, people draw back, as if there was a whiff of something unbecoming about a woman author."

"And rightly so," an elderly cousin of Mr Olmuth put in. "You must admit that writing is an act of public exhibition."

No lady could wish to expose her thoughts in that indiscriminate manner, he went on. It was like going on stage, and everyone knew the life actresses led. They lost all sense of decency. That was the result of exposing themselves to the public eye, to an audience whose qualities they had no way of vetting or limiting.

"A writer can vet her audience," I said, a little heated perhaps. I saw Mr Olmuth raise his eyebrows and scaled back my voice. "By publishing in a reputable magazine, I mean – a magazine that will be read by discerning readers."

Mr Olmuth's cousin sniffed. "Academic journals may guarantee such a readership, perhaps, but you will find no women writers in academic journals."

"Besides, the women you mentioned, Miss Lassick, are novelists," his wife added. "And the audience for novels is certainly very broad. A novelist has no way of telling who will read her words or, worse, what anyone will read *into* her words."

A published book, she said, revealed the author in the private act of thinking or rather fantasizing. It was indecent, to say the least.

After that, Mr Olmuth put in a few calming words, and the subject was allowed to lapse, but Carl turned to me and said softly:

"You were right defending women authors, Miss Lassick. I read one of your essays – on London playwrights."

He almost won me over with his quiet voice and his steady eyes. For a moment, I thought of the comfort such a man might bring me – balm to a mind chafed by obsessions. Then my eyes wandered to his pudgy hands, and the moment passed.

"So you've read my essay?" I said.

I had tried my hand at writing and had the satisfaction of seeing a few of my pieces accepted for publication in a literary magazine, but they were no more than safety valves to blow off steam before I returned to my all-consuming passion, chasing down Nobel.

"Written with great perception," Carl said about my essay on playwrights. "I was impressed with your judgment, and I hope to see more of your work. If you don't mind me asking, are you planning to take up writing in a professional way?"

I blushed a little under his compliments and at the idea of becoming a professional writer. At the same time, I realized that this was exactly what I ought to do, take my revenge on Nobel by writing up the story of Georg's death and raising the issue of accidents in dynamite factories. It was a eureka moment. I must take up writing in a professional manner.

Answering Carl's question, I said boldly, "I have given it some thought." Carl smiled amiably.

"Have you decided on a genre?"

"Biography," I said, thinking of the exposé I might write, which would trace Nobel's rise as a merchant of arms and reveal him as the monster he was, a man who traded in death.

"Ah," he said. "Then I have a proposal for you, if you are interested in taking on a commission, that is."

I was interested, of course, and he told me of a lady who wished to hire the services of a writer to help her with a piece of work she had in hand: a history of her illustrious forefathers.

And so I embarked on my writing career, discreetly, almost secretly, with short histories of prominent Viennese families. They were all commissioned pieces. Carl provided me with the necessary introductions at first, taking me along to soires. Mrs Olmuth thought she was nearing the goal of her match-making labors and began shifting her attention to my trousseau, but I regarded Carl as no more than a business partner and was soon able to do without his introductions. The booklets became popular, and my services were in demand. I no longer needed to solicit orders. People contacted *me* rather than the other way round. They asked for a genealogical study, as they called it, although what they really wanted was a past to brag about. They liked the idea of a family history, stitched together from anecdotes featuring their witty, noble and wealthy ancestors. These biographical studies were for private use, printed by Carl in a suitable quantity to be sent to relatives and friends. One copy was kept on display in the drawing room beside an album or two of landscape photos. The "genealogy" was invariably on top of the pile, opened to a desirable page, as if someone had just consulted it, and the visitor was invited to consult it as well.

The writing process was always the same. I interviewed the ladies of the house. They showed me the portraits of their ancestors and pointed out their names on the family tree, drawn on the last page of the family bible. They told me about reputed ghosts and crazy aunts, cautioning me at the same time not to mention them. Then I was given the run of the house library, for additional research, and put together a flattering story. It contained nothing that was untrue but omitted much that was unbecoming, questionable or simply boring. Once the text was approved by the head of the family, I took it to Carl Volker, who produced a limited edition, paid for in advance. Needless to say, my name did not appear on any of those publications. I was a ghostwriter. Only Carl knew that I had put them together. The pretense was that one of the ladies of the house had written a family history and that Carl had found it so captivating that he asked for permission to print it and make it available to a larger audience.

Sophie

Sophie stops in front of the mirror and looks at her reflection with a critical eye. She is wearing her new dress, close-fitting to show off her figure. It's the perfect cut. That dressmaker can work miracles. Her prices are outrageous, but she is worth every penny.

She is no longer as slim as she was before her pregnancy but her complexion is still faultless. Like alabaster, Alfred used to say. For a moment, she plays with the idea of putting a knot of ribbons around her neck and fasten them with the diamond pin Alfred had given her on her twenty-fifth birthday. He was so loving in the early days of their courtship. But when she needed him most, he deserted her. It was a miserable time. She had to borrow money. She pawned the jewelry he had given her, everything except the diamond pin. She couldn't bear to let it go, even when she had to beg and borrow to scrape together a meal. *It's your own fault*, Alfred said. *You squander the money I give you, gallivanting around Europe from one fashionable spa to another: Carlsbad, Ischl, Trouville. You make extravagant presents to your family, those leeches, and give lavish parties for your so-called friends.* Yes, she thinks, he is right. I spent his money recklessly. I gave no thought to the future. I was a fool, and now I'm paying the price for my stupidity.

Of all the jewelry Alfred had bought for her over the years, only the diamond pin is left, but it is too early in the day for wearing diamonds, and she doesn't want to give Alfred the impression that she is well-off when she needs to press him for money. Instead, she puts on a black velvet neckband with a little rosebud to set off the whiteness of her neck and bosom, showing as much skin as she dares to expose in the afternoon without looking like a coquette. And she has rinsed her hair with a lotion that turns it honey blonde, the way he likes it. *My little angel*, he used to say, burying his nose in her ringlets and ruining her hairdo with his caresses.

And, of course, she is wearing his favorite perfume.

She has set the stage carefully, sent away the maid and told Nanny to take the child for a walk in the park. Her future depends on the meeting with Alfred, their last meeting perhaps, and there must be no distractions.

When he rings the bell, she opens the door herself and takes his coat, well-padded even though it is a mild day. He is always cold, she thinks. When he takes off his silk hat, his gray hair is a bird's nest, but everything else about him is neat. He is very particular about order and cleanliness. The maid looked sour this morning because she made a fuss about tidying up the drawing room, making sure that everything was perfectly aligned, the mirrors polished, the table tops shiny, no speck of dust anywhere.

She presses Alfred's hand and looks into his eyes, but he doesn't kiss her. He merely brushes his lips against her cheeks and pulls back his hand. It's not a good beginning.

He looks around the drawing room and nods at the pictures and the furniture she has chosen with such care. For once, he can't accuse her of wasting her money. Everything is of the best quality and in the best of taste.

"Nice place you've got here," he says, sitting down stiffly. She expected more praise, or more warmth at any rate. His eyes linger for a moment on the photo of Gretel prominently displayed on the piano. The child is wearing a frilly, lacy dress with a white sash and has a string of corals around her neck. Her pudgy little fingers are holding onto a bamboo chair. Alfred's heart would melt if he could see her, she thinks. No one can resist my little charmer. Her eyes are the softest blue, and she has the sweetest and most trusting smile! But he refuses to see the child.

He looks at the photo.

"Isn't she beautiful?" Sophie says.

He merely nods.

"And I was so afraid for her when I was pregnant. I thought my suffering would make her ugly," she says. "I cried for hours, I couldn't sleep at night because of all the brooding thoughts crowding into my mind. I thought she'd be born with a yellow complexion. They say that children often turn out thin and ugly if the mother is troubled."

"You have caused your own troubles, my dear," he says.

"I don't know why you'd say that, Alfred."

When she sits down across from him, she makes sure to arrange the folds of her dress to give him a good view of her tiny feet which he loved – so much so that he used to kiss her toes, the silly old man. And now, he was so hard on her and blaming her for her troubles. "After all, it's natural for a woman to want children," she says, "especially when you were away so much, and I was always alone."

"Hardly alone."

"Well, not alone but with people who didn't care, who were around for a few weeks and gone again."

"Yes, a merry-go-round of worthless people, hangers-on, ne'er-do-wells. And your family. Bloodsuckers all of them, expecting me to feed the whole Jewish tribe."

Her mouth goes into a pout, but this isn't the time to argue with Alfred. "I know you don't read my letters," she says, "but didn't the lawyer tell you? I converted. I'm a Christian now."

"Don't say you did it for my sake, Sophie. You know perfectly well I don't care about religion. It's all hypocrisy to me. You did it for Nikolaus Kapy. He wouldn't marry you otherwise. And, by the way, wasn't he supposed to be here today – or has he changed his mind?"

"Not at all. He will be here shortly. I just wanted us to have a little time to ourselves, Alfred." She smiles and gives him a meaningful look, but he doesn't return her smile. He sits there like a wooden statue.

He has aged a great deal since I've seen him last, she thinks. He has lost weight. His voice is thinner, and when he came in, she noticed a slight stoop in his walk. He always fussed a lot about his health when they were together – to get her attention, she thought. He wanted to be mollycoddled. But perhaps it was for real this time, and he was seriously ill.

"Of course Nikki is willing to marry me," she says, "and I am willing to go ahead, for Gretel's sake. I am determined to sacrifice myself to give the child a name, but it's your opinion that counts with me, Alfred. Just tell me what arrangements you want me to make."

"What financial arrangements I'll make, you mean."

"Well, yes, that too. I am taking this step for the child's sake. I don't want her to suffer later on. People would point a finger at her. An illegitimate child! If the mother erred, why should the poor creature suffer for it? No, you can't be so cruel, Alfred, and not make the necessary financial arrangements. You owe it to me."

"That's what your father seems to think. Your virginity is worth so many shekels to him. But I have no legal obligation toward you, my dear. You lied to me, you know. You told me you were eighteen when you were twenty-four. You swore you were a virgin. You had a whole lot of tricks up your sleeve, didn't you? You knew how to play the innocent little girl. But never mind that now. I will do the decent thing, not because I owe you anything but out of pity for you. I won't deny that I enjoyed your company. We had good times together, and I don't want to see you suffer."

"I have suffered enough for whatever I did wrong, believe me, Alfred. The birth was so painful I thought I'd die. And I have never recovered my health. I keep thinking what will happen if I die? You promised to take care of me and the child and bear me no grudge. In any case, I know what you pay your lawyers, a huge sum of money! So why would you begrudge money to the woman who has lived with you for all these years? And you used to remember Gretel's birthday and send her a present. She turned five last month, you know, but not a word from you. And the lawyer treats me like a criminal. I am no criminal just because I got pregnant. If you could see my sweet little Gretel you'd fall in love with her. She's such a beautiful, charming child and so clever." She sees the impatience in his eyes. If only he would allow her to kiss him or go on her knees before him and play the penitent. He used to love that, to press her cheek against his groin. "I know," she says. "The child hasn't inherited her cleverness from me. I am just a silly goose. You've told me often enough."

But he waves her off. "I haven't come here to talk about the past. I've come to talk business with your husband-to-be and make the necessary arrangements for the marriage to go ahead and for me to put paid to the whole affair." He shuts his mouth in a decisive manner that leaves her helpless.

For a moment, they look at each other silently, in mutual dissatisfaction. Then there is a knock and Nikki comes into the room. He looks smart, even without his uniform. You can't take the military training out of a man, the upright bearing, the firm step, the spare, disciplined movement.He kisses her hand and gives Alfred a deferent smile.

The two men shake hands.

"How are you, Captain?" Alfred says.

"No longer Captain," Nikki says, "but otherwise well. And how was the train journey?"

"Becoming more tiresome with every year. I used to think nothing of taking the overnight train from Paris to Vienna, but now I feel every bone in my body. I can't sleep in those narrow berths. Not to speak of the food they serve in the dining car. My stomach revolts – but never mind the ailments of an old man. How do you like your new position, Mr Kapy? It's a comedown, I suppose."

"It's honest work," Nikki says, "and I am grateful for your recommendation. They would not have hired me without your intervention."

"And your family? Are they reconciled to your new life?"

"I am afraid not. But that can't be helped."

Sophie listens to them with relief. Nikki always says the right thing. The tension in the room dissolves.

"And how are the preparations for the wedding coming along?" Alfred asks.

"It's all arranged," Nikki says. "My cousin Josef will be the best man."

Josef is the only family member who has stood by Nikki. The others have cut their ties with him. They are scandalized. Well, let them be.

"I thought it best to keep the wedding a private affair," Nikki says, and Alfred nods approvingly.

"Very well," he says, "then I wish you all the best for the future." He bows in her direction and gives her a distant smile. "All the best to both of you."

He hands Nikki a draft to cover the wedding expenses and gives him a copy of the instructions he sent to the lawyer. Sophie will be paid a monthly retainer.

The two men stand and shake hands as if they had just completed a satisfactory business deal, and that's all it is to Alfred, she thinks. He has bought his freedom.

He kisses her hand politely and takes his leave.

"I don't see why the wedding has to be so low key," she says to Nikki when they are alone. "You have nothing to hide. Everything is in order. The lawsuit has been settled."

"We've talked about all that earlier," he says. "There is nothing more to say, Sophie." But she won't let him off.

"I don't know why your family can't accept the settlement. You went through all that trouble and all those procedures."

"I couldn't have done it without Alfred's financial support."

"So what if he paid for it? That's no reason to grovel. He almost had you on your knees."

"It was proper to thank him for his help. I don't call that groveling."

"Thank him for what? He owes it to me. He agreed to set us up. He has the money to pay for it. And he hasn't been very gracious about it."

"Let it go, Sophie," he says. "It's done. No use going on about it. In any case, I have to be off. I have an appointment with a client."

He gives her a peck on the cheek and makes his escape.

But she can't let go of the past. *You are selfish*, Alfred said to her. *Like all Jews.* He liked to put it that way because she has no comeback for it. Her father is a Jew – she can't help it. Baptism makes no difference. I may be Christian now, she thinks, but I remain a Jew in Alfred's eyes and in everyone else's.

I wish Nanny and Gretel were back, she thinks. Now that she is alone, the black thoughts are coming back. *Sometimes I feel like ending my life,* she wrote to Alfred. She presses her hands against her ears to stop the echo of those words. All those pleading letters she wrote him. *Don't desert me. I can't go on without you.*

She gets up and paces the room. The words in her head won't stop. A tidal wave of blackness breaks over her head.

Then she hears the key turn in the lock and Czerny's iron voice: "No running in the corridor, Gretel."

"Why can't I run, Nanny? I like to run."

Gretel comes bouncing into the room, and Sophie feels a new will to live. The malaise fogging up her brain clears. The weight lifts.

"Come here, poppet, give your mama a kiss," she says, sitting down on the settee and pulling the child into her lap. She strokes her hair fondly, and Gretel nestles close to her.

"Take off your shoes, child," Czerny says. "You'll scuff up the sofa."

"Never mind the sofa! How was your afternoon, sweetie?" Sophie says. She takes the child's face between her hands and looks into her eyes. "You look tired, sweetie."

"She is," Czerny says. "It's time for her nap. I'll take her to her room, madam."

"No!" Sophie and the child exclaim in unison, and Czerny looks very cross.

"Just rest your little head in my lap, sweetie. You can take your nap right here." She pats the sofa.

Czerny shakes her head. "Your mama is pampering you," she says to Gretel. "At least let's take off your dress." She helps Gretel undress. Sophie fetches her mohair shawl and wraps it around the child.

"There now. Are you comfortable, sweetie?"

The child nods sleepily.

"I'll put away her things," Czerny says and retreats.

Good. Sophie wants to be alone with Gretel and look at her face, so beautiful in repose. Her eyes are shut except for the lashes fluttering a little with dreams, of Bella, perhaps.

Gretel shifts a little under the touch of her hand. Her lips move. She finds a more comfortable position and falls asleep again.

Ida

Writing family histories on commission was good practice. I was finding my way with words, edging toward my real goal which was never far from my mind: an exposé of Alfred Nobel's unscrupulous business practices. I did the commissioned work, but I always circled back to my obsession: revenge on the man whom I held responsible for the death of my fiancé.

I kept scouring the papers for information about Nobel: his whereabouts, his habits, the company he kept, the circles in which he moved, but he was hard to track down. He had homes in three cities and stayed in none of them for long. He kept on the move, travelled from one factory to another, from one lab to another, *the nomad millionaire*, the papers called him. He attended business meetings in London, Paris, Hamburg and Vienna but seemed to have no personal friends, attended no public functions, did not allow his picture to appear in the papers, almost as if he feared an attempt on his life. Perhaps I was not the only one who was after him.

I made my first attempt to contact Alfred Nobel directly, writing to him in care of his branch office here in Vienna, explaining who I was, demanding a justification for carrying on his lethal business, threatening to expose his unscrupulous practices to the public. I am not sure what I expected – a confession of guilt, an apology, atonement? If he had answered me in a suitably contrite form, would it have been the end of my desire for revenge, or would I have only used it as material for another imaginary scene in which we screamed at each other and fought bodily? I assume my letter was forwarded to Nobel in Paris or wherever he was living at the time, but I received no reply. Then I wrote again, this time addressing my letter to Max Philipp, the head of the Viennese branch of Nobel & Co. I was careful not to spell out my first name when I wrote to him. I signed my inquiry "I. Lassick" and described myself as a journalist, allowing him to believe that I was a gentleman. I told a few necessary lies: that I had been commissioned to write an article, tentative title, *Alfred Nobel: The Man and His Work*. I was hoping for some insights into the mind and habits of the famous inventor.

Mr Philipp replied promptly. He was a business associate of Mr Nobel, he wrote, and had no knowledge of his life beyond the transactions in which they were involved and the meetings they had attended jointly during Nobel's visits in Vienna. I shuddered with excitement at the thought that my enemy had been here, in this very city, where I might have run into him, where my imaginary shouting match might have turned into a real scene.

"It is Mr Nobel's habit to keep to himself," Max Philipp wrote. "He is not inclined to speak of personal matters." Mr Philipp had a suggestion, however. I might be more successful with my inquiries if I applied to a certain Bertha Kinsky who had been Nobel's secretary in Paris and was now back in Vienna. I took up his suggestion at once.

When I wrote, asking about her acquaintance with Alfred Nobel, Miss Kinsky – Bertie, as I came to call her – replied and invited me to come and talk to her. We met at her mother's apartment, an elegant suite which spoke of past wealth and noble ancestors.

The wallpaper and the drapes had a rich darkness about them, and the gold frames around the oil paintings added a glow to the room. A large pastoral scene hung above the fireplace – a landscape of ancient ruins. The other walls held portraits – ladies in Biedermeier finery and gentlemen in hunting gear or in uniform. The dainty tables and chairs, the display of figurines and flower arrangements all seemed to have more symbolic value than function, a little like the owners themselves. The Kinskys were connected to the premier families of the empire, but they had suffered the common lot of households deprived of their father and protector. The source of their income had died with him, or their funds were curtailed at any rate. When I made the Kinskys' acquaintance, mother and daughter had sunk into genteel poverty. In some ways, Bertie's lot was not so different from mine, although her financial decline proceeded along a gentle slope, and her prospects were certainly brighter than mine. She and her mother still wintered in fashionable places in the south and were received in the great houses. Yet, when I got to know Bertie better, I realized how straitened her circumstances were at the time, and how carefully the two women had to manage their resources to keep up appearances. In any case, Bertie, like myself, had to make her own way and took a position as governess in the household of Count Suttner.

Bertha is a dowdy name, at least to my ears. It made me think of a stout elderly woman, but the woman who received me was slim and tall, with striking eyes and a mouth that seemed forever poised between a smile and a pout. Her hair was arranged in coils at the back of her head, with a waved fringe over her high forehead. She was wearing a dress in the Parisian fashion – a skirt with diagonal stripes and a blouse with a lacy inset – and moved with a grace that was bound to attract admiring glances from the gentlemen. She was, moreover, irrepressibly cheerful. All her talk was exuberant and accompanied by lively gestures. Poverty must be the reason, I thought, why she remained unmarried.

I asked about her employ as Alfred Nobel's secretary, and she told me of the odd circumstances in which she made his acquaintance. She was a governess in the Suttners' household, fell in love with Arthur Suttner and was dismissed when their affair was discovered. She spotted an advertisement Nobel had placed in a Viennese paper. He was looking for a secretary of mature age and hired Bertie, sight unseen, on the strength of her letter of application.

It was an odd relationship, she said. Her tasks were conventional enough – dealing with Nobel's correspondence – but the way he treated her was not conventional at all. After he had overcome his initial stiffness, he was more like a kind relative than an employer and seemed to take a genuine interest in her welfare.

"One day, he asked me if I was happy. I said no and poured out my story: I had exchanged promises with a young man of good family, but his parents were dead-set against our marriage. I wasn't good enough for him." She stopped and wrinkled her brow as if she was surprised at herself. "I don't know why I said all that to Mr Nobel. Surely, it was inappropriate to have a conversation of that nature with my employer, a man I had known only for a short time. He might have taken advantage of my distress, but he was every inch the gentleman and acted like a fatherly friend."

Nobel expressed his sympathy for her plight. He, too, had been young and in love once, he said. He, too, had been deprived of happiness, not by the parents of his bride, but by the inexorable hand of death.

"And do you know how he overcame his grief?" Bertie said, pausing for effect. "He poured it all out in a long poem! Written in English, he said, because the extra effort that was needed to write in a foreign language made him think more deeply about his condition."

"Did he show you the poem?"

"He did, and I was so taken with it that I asked if I might copy out the beginning. Would you like to read the verses, Miss Lassick? They might help you form a picture of the man."

Of course I wanted to read them. I felt as if I had learned English for that very purpose. For a moment I was tempted to say, "God in his wisdom," as Georg's mother used to say, but I immediately chastised myself for that facile thought. Indeed, my religion was in crisis, and every Sunday, when I attended the obligatory mass, instead of praying, I railed at God. Where was his justice? Where was his mercy? Why did he let Georg die and Nobel live?

Bertie had taken a sheet from her bureau and began reciting the first lines of Nobel's poem:

The solemn silence of the midnight hour
Unchains the fettered spirit, and the power
Of reasoning takes a visionary flight
Beyond the limits of defective sight
Which may deceive us, yet attracts the soul
Even with its wild and daring uncontrol.

"Beautiful – don't you think?" she said when she came to the last line. Her voice was reverent.

But I had heard only the words that echoed in my own heart – *unchained, visionary flight, wild and daring uncontrol*. Was Nobel describing a nightmare?

"Powerful at any rate," I said in confusion. "May I read the verses for myself?"

She handed the page to me. I ran my eyes over the lines and realized my mistake. The verses did not speak of violent dreams or emotions. Nobel was describing reason stirring at the midnight hour.

"He counselled me to take a rational approach," Bertie said.

"Love is not subject to reason," I burst out. "If Nobel counselled you to be reasonable, he cannot possibly have been in love himself or truly have mourned his loss – unless men are very different in that respect from women."

"I quite agree with you," she said. "I refused to listen to reason. Mr Nobel advised me to wait and let time be the judge of my feelings, but I was too impatient. I couldn't stand being apart from the man I loved. A thousand miles between us! I cried when I thought of it."

"And so you quit your position?"

"Worse than that. When Mr Nobel went away on a business trip, I bolted. I can't put it another way. I pawned a diamond cross to pay for my trip back to Vienna, and here I am, looking for employment again and with very little chance of anyone taking me on. I can hardly expect Mr Nobel to give me a reference."

"And your young man?" I said, talking like a friend of long standing because there was a feeling of instant rapport between us, a mutual understanding even at that first get-together. When she told me her story, I saw that we were equally helpless in the face of our passions and had the same compulsive need to pursue a course to its end, however troublesome. I began to think of Bertie as a soulmate. At least I think it was me who initiated our friendship, but it may have been Bertie who brought about that feeling of mutual sympathy. It was in her nature to befriend others without a second thought, without consideration for a person's wealth or standing. She was made for friendship.

"I saw Arthur as soon as I got back to Vienna," she said. Her face lit up with a smile. "Nothing has changed between us. We are as much in love as ever. But we'll have to be discreet. We can't be seen together. Not in public."

"There is no chance of the family approving your marriage?"

"None," she said. She offered no explanation, but I understood. Her pedigree was quite good enough. She was related to the Liechtensteins on her mother's side. It was her lack of money that made a marriage impossible.

"But you can't go on forever 'being discreet' as you put it."

She sighed. "We'll find a way."

When I got up to go, she squeezed my hand. "Come back next week, Miss Lassick. I'm so glad I told you about Arthur – I needed someone to talk to, and my mother is the last person to lend a friendly ear to my 'folly' as she calls it."

It was a successful interview. My talk with Bertie had yielded quite a bit of personal information about Nobel. The picture she painted of him was rather flattering – a cultured gentleman who gives discreet fatherly advice to his secretary, but I suspected that she had been taken in by him. That "fatherly" gesture sounded like a clever way of decoying a woman. Nobel's interests were probably more salacious than he let on. In any case, I wasn't looking for praise when I asked Bertie for an interview. I needed material to shore up my exposé and was determined to elicit information about the darker side of her employer and about his profiteering. She had read his daily correspondence. She must know about his business practices.

When I visited her on the following Wednesday, as arranged, it was her mother who received me. Bertie had found a way to get around the Suttner veto. She had eloped with Arthur! The two lovers had gone to live in exile in Mingrelia, her mother told me.

Mrs Kinsky was as tall as her daughter. Her face retained traces of delicate beauty, but she had run to fat. Her large bosom heaved and her chin wobbled as she wiped her eyes with a tear-moistened handkerchief.

"Mingrelia?" I asked. I had never heard of the place.

"A godforsaken tract of land in the Caucasus," she said, and I remembered a newspaper clipping I had filed away for Olmuth. The article reported about Nobel's company building oil refineries in the Caucasus and shipping oil from the port of Baku. I had made a note of it because one of their tankers exploded while loading kerosene. A spill had leaked into the engine room and caused a fire there. Half the ship's crew was killed in the explosion.

Was there a connection between Bertie's choice of exile and her ex-employer's investment there? Did Nobel have a hand in the pair's move to Mingrelia? No, Mrs Kinsky offered another explanation.

"I rue the day on which I decided to spend a few weeks at a German spa ," she was saying. "That is where we were introduced to the Princess of Mingrelia. She was charmed by Bertie and invited her to visit. Bertie showed a keen interest, but, of course, I thought it was only common courtesy. I never—!" She shook her head. "But here I am, forgetting my manners and keeping you standing. Why don't you have a seat, Miss Lassick, and I'll ring for coffee."

So I had coffee with the mother instead of the daughter. I was the only visitor that day, although it was the Kinskys' afternoon "at home". I heard the doorbell ring several times but Mrs Kinsky had given orders for all visitors to be turned away. She couldn't face the questions, she said. No doubt, rumors were flying already. She had made an exception for me because in the farewell letter Bertie had left behind, she mentioned that I knew about her affair with Arthur. She was sure of my discretion, she wrote.

"I hope you will honor my daughter's trust," Mrs Kinsky said, plucking nervously at the braid edging her dress. It was billowy in front, but the loose cut did not succeed in hiding her ample figure.

She gave me a pleading look, and I understood why I had been admitted to her drawing room while everyone else was turned away. She was anxious to ensure my silence about the affair.

I could see she was hurt by Bertie confiding in me. She couldn't understand why Bertie would speak to me, a stranger, rather than making a confidante of her mother. At the same time, she was probably glad to talk about the affair with someone who was at arm's length, instead of facing curious friends who might spread the news of the calamity. Yet we both knew: there was no way of keeping the thing a secret for very long.

"Oh, the foolish girl!" Mrs Kinsky said. It was all so embarrassing and so disappointing too. "She could have had her pick of men."

She didn't say much more at the time, but later, when I had earned her trust and was accepted as a friend of the family, she told me about all the suitors Bertie had fascinated and rejected. Men of quality, she said, pursing her lips. A prince once, then a famous opera singer, and at another time, a sinfully rich manufacturer, whom she agreed to marry but jilted after the first kiss.

"At least that's how she explained it to me," Mrs Kinsky said. "The kiss disgusted her. She felt a passionate protest arising in her breast. And that was the end of that. Such a willful girl! She sent back his presents and broke the engagement."

I must say I was on Bertie's side. A man whose kiss is disgusting isn't acceptable as a husband, sinfully rich or not.

There was no dearth of men to take his place, Mrs Kinsky said with deep regret in her voice. "Bertie was always in a social whirl and carried everyone along with her. She had so many admirers—" She paused and left me to supply the rest: Bertie could have done better than eloping with Arthur, even if he was a count.

I said nothing because I didn't agree with Mrs Kinsky. What can be better than marrying the man you love?

Bertie and I had met only once before she eloped with Arthur Suttner to Mingrelia, but it was clear that we were in sympathy with each other. We were in tune, equally driven by our passions. Bertie sent me greetings from the Caucasus through her mother, and we ended up corresponding. My God, the nerve she had to go to that wild country! Reading her letters was like reading a novel in instalments, and she wrote the way she talked, breathless, with laughter stuck in her throat. Every sentence could have been punctuated with an exclamation mark. I had a thousand questions, and she answered them eagerly as if she wanted to spread the gospel of Caucasia. Of course, I asked Bertie about Alfred Nobel's investments in the area, but she knew nothing about them. After a few months, she and Arthur settled in a place called Kutaisi – if living in a little wooden cottage can be called settling. She was excited about her new home at any rate and suggested I visit them and report on the conditions there. You are a writer, she said. You have published articles in magazines. Yes, and I was desperate to get away from the commissioned genealogies, the sedate style required by the dowagers, the gravity of other people's history. I was keen on something more visceral, something that mattered to me. I wanted to insert myself into the narrative and speak in my own voice. The story I wanted to write was about Nobel and how he had blighted my life. If I accepted Bertie's proposal and travelled to Kutaisi, it was as much to vary my writing as it was to be close to my only source of personal information about Nobel. Might I not find out more about him if I was Bertie's guest in Kutaisi and spent my days in her company? And what about Nobel's commercial activities in the area? I had read up on the economy of the Caucasus and discovered that Alfred Nobel had two brothers in St Petersburg, who were the principal suppliers of military equipment to the tsar. Their factories produced artillery shells, gun carriages, mortars and cannons. All three brothers owned shares in an oil company in the Caucasus. How many people had lost their lives there on account of those merchants of death?

I wanted to know and therefore was willing to go to Kutaisi. Mrs Kinsky was willing to pay my travel expenses. She did not entirely trust the buoyant mood of Bertie's letters. She wanted an eyewitness report on her daughter's life in that unimaginable place, the Caucasus.

"Bertie is an optimist," she said to me. "I don't mean to say that she does not tell me the truth in her letters, but I fear it is a truth tinted rosy by her enthusiasm. I would like a report from someone who is more down to earth, and you strike me as a realistic woman, Miss Lassick, someone whose account I can trust."

I thanked Mrs Kinsky for her confidence and her belief in my veracity, although I had already made up my mind to lie to her if necessary. If I found Bertie in dire straits, I wasn't going to betray my friend or alarm her mother. Parents are altogether uncomprehending when it comes to love and adventure unless there is a demonstrable advantage to be gained from an affair and a favorable outcome in the offing. I didn't tell *my* mother about my ambitions to become a writer until I had a measure of success and could show her the evidence, the printed booklets for which I had been paid good money. And I never mentioned the subject of men to her at all. Nor did *she* after I turned twenty-five. By that time, she had come to the conclusion that I had no reasonable prospect of finding a husband. I was too old and too single-minded. So what was the use of talking about men? She would have been deeply shocked to find that I, a spinster, took secret pleasure in looking at handsome young men or harbored a clandestine desire to be touched and held close by them. I had no reason to think that Mrs Kinsky was more liberal in her thoughts than my late mother.

"I would visit Bertie myself if I was up to it," she said to me, but I could tell that it was not a question of health or strength. There was wonder in her voice that I was willing to accept her offer, that a *woman* would volunteer to visit Caucasia and expose herself to the hazards of travel to faraway lands. Bertie had done it for love, which was a mad enough thing, but what motive did I have to accept her offer and go there? It could only be for the sake of adventure or from idle curiosity, motives entirely out of her range.

I could not look at Mrs Kinsky without remembering my mother's kind face and the innocent, vaguely helpless eyes which seemed to beseech me and the whole world to take pity on her and spare her all distress. She had passed away in her sleep two years earlier, and I missed her. But after I had decently grieved her death, I felt an indecent sense of relief. I could make my own decisions now, without having to explain or to argue my case. I no longer had to put on an act and play the virtuous woman to satisfy my mother's sense of what did or did not become a lady. Even during her lifetime, I had developed a certain facility of putting on that chaste persona and taking it off again at night, together with my clothes, but the delicacy which the role of the model woman required wore me down. The patience, the cheerful smile and friendly concern I had to show in my mother's company took a toll on me – and I was in her company during much of the day. I haven't entirely freed myself of the virtuous carapace I wore for the sake of my mother, but now I only put on my armor in the company of old ladies interested in my services as a writer. The rest of the time I am myself, in my thoughts at any rate, and it is a great relief to go on thinking my bold thoughts without blushing under my mother's gaze. Those mild eyes of hers always made me feel guilty. She was an innocent soul and somehow managed to remain innocent and keep her mind pure and unsullied by reality. Or is my brother right when he says I'm putting her on a pedestal? "You are making a saint of her," he said to me. "Our mother grew up in an age of innocence. She was no saint. She was just a woman of her time, that's all."

I took up Mrs Kinsky's unstated question: Why was I willing to travel to the Caucasus? I could not tell her my true motive, my obsession with Nobel which drove me with the force of a cattle prod. My career as a travel writer was still in the future when I talked to her, but the idea was on my mind now that Bertie had suggested it, and I said boldly:

"I am thinking of giving an account of my travels in a series of essays. Writing has turned into a profession for me. I came to it by chance when I was helping an acquaintance put together a family history, but I believe I have a vocation to write."

Mrs Kinsky gave me a strange look. "Oh dear," she said. "You and Bertie, both. I suppose that's why you have taken such a liking to each other. She wants to be a writer, too. And her husband approves!" She paused as if to say: at least you don't have to worry about the approval of your family. "Perhaps it's just as well that he does," she continued, "but what about the rest of his family? It's my hope that he will be reconciled with his parents, and I fear Bertie's ambition will be a roadblock on the way to a happy reunion. The Suttners will hardly approve of their daughter-in-law becoming a writer."

Bertie

We are to meet Ida at the border of Mingrelia. Princess Dadiani has been gracious enough to invite our friend to her summer palace in Gordi and provide Arthur and me with an escort. The men have put up a canvas shelter for us by the river, laid down a carpet over the bare ground and arranged a table and two chairs under the canopy. The roar of the rushing stream makes conversation all but impossible. We sip tea, keep our sights trained on the road and wait.

And here she is at last! The bridge is too narrow for a coach to pass. The carriage halts on the far side of the river and the driver helps Ida down. She catches sight of me waving wildly and mouthing, "Welcome," and starts walking across the bridge. I gather my skirts and rush to meet her halfway. We embrace fondly.

"How was the journey?" I say after introducing my beloved Arthur to her.

She eyes our now-faded European garb and sighs. "You said I would find everything terribly exotic. I'm afraid I found it all terribly inconvenient, especially the flea-infested hotels, the smothering heat, the reek of sundried buffalo dung and the boring diet of mutton, mutton, mutton."

Ida is like that, a little too candid, but I forgive her. She is sincere at any rate, and she struggles to come up with something more heartening.

"You are an intrepid woman, Bertie. I admire you for that."

"I don't know about intrepid," I say. "I never thought about danger when I set out with Arthur. I felt the intoxication of hope."

Arthur corrects me. "The intoxication of adventure. You love adventure, my dear. Admit it."

Ida gives me another hug. "In any case," she says. "Adventure becomes you, Bertie. You look very well. And very happy."

"I am, and I hope mother will be reassured when you tell her. She finds it difficult to believe that anyone can be happy so far away from Vienna."

"It was kind of her to pay my travel expenses."

"And kind of you to come."

"Oh, I jumped at the chance of seeing you again." Ida laughs a self-conscious laugh. "*And* to embark on my new career."

"Your new career?"

"As a travel writer. I intend to return to Vienna with the first draft of a travelogue."

She is tired of genealogies, she tells me, and wants to try her hand at something new. I wonder what happened to her other plan, the book about Nobel.

The porters transfer Ida's luggage to their donkeys and strap down the bags with leather belts. Ida mounts the gelding we have brought for her use. There is no more talking because we are obliged to ride single file along a narrow path looking down on canyons and forested valleys. At last, the castle comes into view, and I hear Ida exclaim with wonder. Gordi is awe-inspiring – a town built on a plateau, buttressed by a sheer wall of rock, and a palace that is a fairy-tale castle, flanked with towers and adorned with balconies and terraces.

A triumphal arch of flowers awaits us at the entrance to the palace. Ekaterina Dadiani has come to greet us in person. Her upright bearing belies her age. Her figure is concealed under a long flowing gown and her face, veiled according to the custom of the country, shows only her lively dark eyes. She is surrounded by her ladies and a fierce-looking bodyguard with bands of cartridge shells across their chests and daggers stuck in their belts. To honor us, she is in full regalia, wearing the royal crown, a slim band of gold from which a jeweled pendant hangs down, dangling between her brows.

We dismount and bow to her. Taking my arm, she asks me to introduce Ida: "Présentez-moi votre chère amie, Contessina." Like all members of the aristocracy and the upper classes, the princess speaks impeccable French. The ease with which her courtiers speak foreign languages amazed me when we first came to Mingrelia. Conversations at lunch and dinner were carried on in French and sometimes in German for our benefit.

The princess has always treated me with the greatest kindness, and on this occasion, too, she gives us and our guest a magnificent welcome. A troupe of dancers perform the *Lesginka*, a wave of forward and backward moves with endlessly repeating motifs which always put me into a trance. The next piece is livelier, with the young men leaping like ballet dancers and the women gliding along in heavy silken garments that conceal their feet so that they look as if they were rolling on invisible casters.

After the performance, we are conducted to the princess' private dining room. The company includes her son and heir, Prince Alexey, the younger members of her family and several gentlemen of the court.

As we cross the hall, Ida takes my arm. "What a marvelous place! This will make a great opening scene to my travelogue. I can't wait to write it all down."

"And the biography of Nobel?" I say. "Have you given up on it?"

"Oh no, it's still very much on my mind," she says. "We must talk about that when we have an opportunity."

As it happens, the subject comes up during dinner. Prince Alexey mentions Nobel's name. He is in the area, recruiting men for his factories in Baku, he says.

Ida leans forward eagerly. "Mr Nobel, here?"

I am as surprised as Ida. It takes only a moment to sort out the confusion. The prince doesn't mean Alfred Nobel. He is talking about Emanuel Nobel of St Petersburg.

"It's a family enterprise, of course," he says. "Alfred Nobel handles the dynamite production. The clan in St Petersburg manages the factories producing military equipment, and they are all involved in the oil business. Emanuel Nobel is their man in the field. He's here recruiting workers for the new factories in Baku and Kazan."

"Workers?" Arthur says. "Let's call them what they are: slave labor."

"That's what the laws of emancipation have done for the peasants, Count Suttner," one of the gentlemen puts in. "They flock to the cities, hire on as factory workers and are happy because they have a few kopeks jingling in their pockets, but they are nothing but slaves and too stupid to think of the future. In fact, they are worse off than before when they were serfs and the landowner took care of them for life. The factory owner will kick them out when they are too old or too sick to work. Then what will they do? Starve to death, that's what."

"I am sorry for the poor wretches," Arthur says, "but the solution isn't undoing the laws of emancipation or going back to the old system. We must go forward and provide better working conditions for the men."

My own dear Arthur! He can't help speaking up for his ideals, even if there is no hope of convincing anyone here. He has a philosophical bent, or perhaps I should say, a Utopian bent, dreaming of an ideal society without class distinctions. Of course, he gets black looks from the gentlemen around the table. No doubt they have suffered financial losses in consequence of the new laws and do not share in the revolutionary ideas of liberty, equality and fraternity.

The prince takes up Arthur's challenge:

"Then, my dear Count, you will be happy to hear that the Nobels are building houses and schools and hospitals for their workers – at least that's what I've been told."

"Very commendable," one of the guests says with a sneer. "In that case, they'll go bankrupt soon, and that will be the end of that fool's paradise. If you ask me, the peasants are children and should be treated as such. Feed them but don't put money into their hands, or they'll drink themselves stupid. And whip them if they are idle, or you won't get an honest day's work out of them."

Arthur opens his mouth and shuts it again. He can see that his ideas are too radical for the company assembled around the table. There is no use preaching social reform to them, and he doesn't want to give offense to the princess. She has listened politely but hasn't said a word, and that means she disapproves.

"Well," the prince says. "The Nobels are all a bit crazy. Do you know that one of them dressed up as a peasant and went on a walking tour around Baku?"

"To find out about the living conditions of the poor?" Arthur says hopefully.

"No, my dear Count, he was looking for walnut trees," another guest says. "Wood for gun barrels, you know. If the word had gotten out that the Nobels are buying wood, the merchants in Baku would have raised their prices. So he went directly to the suppliers. Those Nobelskis as sly foxes!"

"I'm not sure how much of what we hear about them is true," the prince says. "Don't put too much trust in those stories, my dear Count. They are hearsay. The same man who told me about the workers' houses also said that the Nobels were putting in telephones. Either he was lying or the Nobels have truly gone mad."

A nephew of the princess is seated between Ida and me. The young man is well into his drink by now and breathing alcoholic fumes into my face every time he turns to me. He addresses the prince: "Perhaps you should invite Emanuel Nobel, so we can get at the truth."

When the prince ignores his drunken mumble, he turns to Ida and says in a leering voice:

"You should ask the prince for an introduction to Emanuel Nobel. He is very generous to the ladies. He is a mongrel, of course, born on the wrong side of the blanket, but I am told he once folded a diamond necklace into his escort's dinner napkin."

Ida puts up her hand to stave off his noxious breath and says coldly: "I am afraid my knowledge of French is not good enough to follow your remarks."

Good for her!

"Perhaps you can translate for us, Countess," the young man says to me. His whole body is listing to one side. I am afraid he will topple into my lap, but the princess has risen to signal the end of the dinner. The young man rights himself at the last moment and is helped from the table by one of the footmen.

The company moves to the music room, where we are entertained by a chamber quartet. After their performance, we linger and talk a little longer. Arthur takes his seat beside the prince and, to my regret, returns to the subject of the Nobels and their workers. Alexey frowns.

"I'm inclined to think that those stories are a pack of lies," he says. "The newest rumor is that the Nobels are building a pipeline to take oil from their refineries to the port of Baku. What nonsense! For hundreds of years, drivers have transported everything on their *arba* carts, and they will go on doing it because the ground is too treacherous for any other kind of transportation. A pipeline! Next, they will be telling me that the Nobels are building a ladder to the moon. Come, let's talk about something else, dear Count."

"Very well," Arthur says. He is willing to let it go, but now Ida who has been listening to them takes up the subject.

"The Nobels in Baku seem to be very enterprising, Your Highness," she says. "And Alfred Nobel is involved as well?"

"Yes, he is the financial genius behind it," the prince says. "Now there's a man I'd like to meet, but I've been in Paris twice now and couldn't get anyone to introduce me to him. He lives a retired life, they say, and doesn't go into society. But enough about the Nobels." He gets up, making it clear that this is the end of the conversation. "If you will excuse me," he says. "I believe my mother wants me."

He makes his escape, and Ida fastens on Arthur, trying to persuade him to take the initiative and get in touch with Emanuel Nobel to find out how the family is running the factories. I see she is back on the old track, thinking about her biography of Alfred Nobel. Unless, of course, she believes the St Petersburg branch of the family would make a good topic for a travel essay.

"I suspect the Nobels are taking advantage of the situation," she says to Arthur. "They are looking for slave labor as you so rightly put it."

I am afraid she will fire him up again. This really isn't the place to talk about slave labor. I give Arthur a warning glance. He acknowledges it with a nod.

"I wouldn't want to tar all the Nobels with the same brush," he says. "I don't know anything about the Russian branch of the family. Bertie thinks highly of Alfred Nobel at any rate. She tells me that he is a generous man, and for all I know, those reports about the housing project for workers are true."

Ida doesn't give up. "If that's the case, it would be good to meet with Emanuel Nobel in person and hear what he has to say about the emancipation of serfs," she says. "He comes at the subject from a different angle. You can't expect the present company to be pleased with emancipation. They are landowners and have lost their serfs. They will hardly sympathize with your liberal views. If the account of the housing project is correct, the Nobels may be more amenable to your ideas."

"Perhaps I should make inquiries of my own," Arthur says to me later as we are getting ready to go to bed.

"I wish you'd leave it alone, Arthur. The prince behaved very well, but I could see he was annoyed by your questions."

"Oh, I won't bother the prince again. I thought I might question the house servants about Emanuel Nobel's whereabouts."

The next morning, he asks around and reports back to us. One of the stable hands, a young man by the name of Luka, knows where Emanuel Nobel is staying – at a manor house some ten or fifteen miles away. He is willing to take Arthur there. Of course, Ida begs him to take her along.

"I want to write about local conditions," she says, "and a talk with Nobel will make a splendid addition to my travelogue. Won't you come as well, Bertie?"

"I have promised to spend the day with the princess," I say. "I can't very well absent myself now, although I must say I am curious about this whole business and wouldn't mind joining you. Why don't you put it off until tomorrow, Arthur?"

"Very well, my dear," he says, although I think he would have rather gone on his own, for a man-to-man talk with Emanuel Nobel.

The three of us depart after breakfast the following day. To avoid giving offence to the princess and her son, who does not seem to approve of our interest, we announce that we are off on a leisurely ride in the countryside. We set out with Luka in the lead, riding along a road that quickly deteriorates into a stony path. Soon, we are making our way through dense brush and fighting off gnats and horseflies. My itching skin makes me irritable. Arthur is impatient as well. He asks our guide how much further we have to go, but Luka pretends not to hear his question and forges ahead.

"I suspect the fellow has lost his way," Arthur says.

Ida gives me an uneasy look.

"I hope he isn't leading us into an ambush," she says.

"Oh come now!" I say. "You are letting your imagination run away with you."

"I don't know, Bertie. That man's face doesn't inspire trust. There is something sinister about him – his sharp eyes, his thin lips and beaked nose."

I haven't paid much attention to Luka's face, and he is far ahead of us now. He has rolled up his shirt sleeves, exposing his brawny arms with muscles like cords. If he is leading us into a trap, we have little chance of defending ourselves. But that's nonsense!

Arthur calls out again, asking Luka if he knows where he is going and demanding an answer.

The man turns, showing us a face dripping with sweat. "I know the way all right," he says and moves ahead briskly.

"What did he say?" Ida asks.

"He assured Arthur that he knows the way," I tell her, but Luka's insolent answer grates on me and no doubt on Arthur as well. We ride on in silence. The horses' hooves strike a low echo on the hard ground. The only other sound comes from the buzzing of horseflies and the swishing of branches against our sides.

"I really don't trust the fellow," Ida says. "Perhaps we'd better turn around."

"We've come too far for that," Arthur says. He tries to calm her. "Don't worry. We are safe."

Finally, after a steep upward climb, we come to a clearing and a shelter made of weathered boards. It is a tumbledown building with three walls.

The fourth side is open to the elements. As we come nearer, we see a dozen sheep milling around in a pen and an old man milking the bleating animals. A boy is chopping wood nearby. He puts his hatchet down when he sees us approach and is about to slink off, but our guide is faster. He jumps off his horse, catches the boy by the arm and talks to him in the local dialect. The boy twists under his hold but nods assent.

Luka lets him go. "He will look after the horses, Count," he says to us. "We'll take a rest here."

"How much further is it to Nobel's house?" Arthur asks.

"Not much further, sir," Luka says. "But the horses need rubbing down." His voice is polite, though not particularly obliging.

We dismount. The boy takes hold of the reins and leads the horses away while we follow our guide into the shelter. The reek of animal dung is unbearable. Luka is speaking to the old man, who looks back at him with sullen obstinacy and keeps on milking his sheep. He is sitting on a low stool in front of a stile that allows the animals to come out of the pen one by one. He pays no attention to us as we stand, watching him lock one sheep after another between his knees, squeeze their teats and direct a few squirts of milk into a wooden pail before releasing them again. Luka, who is standing by his side, pours out a steady stream of words, presumably explaining our predicament. I am certain now that we are lost The lines on the old man's wrinkled face harden into disapproval, but he never takes his eyes off his sheep and says nothing in reply to Luka's harangue. When he has finished milking, he gets up and doffs his cap to us, but the expression on his face remains fierce. He says a few words to our guide and points toward the back of the shed.

Luka takes us around the back to a creek, which has been channeled into a trough. A metal cup is attached to it by a wire, and we use it to slake our thirst. The boy has taken the saddles off our horses and rubbed them down. They are peacefully grazing. Ida and I wash the dust off our faces and necks and tidy up, smoothing down our skirts, picking leaves and twigs out of our hair and re-pinning it as well as we can.

Our guide suggests sending the boy ahead to Nobel's house to announce our visit. Is there any particular message we want him to relay? Arthur gives the boy his card and instructs him to say that we hope Mr Nobel will give us a brief interview. We are the guests of Princess Ekaterina Dadiani. To give us a better claim on his time, he adds that Mrs Suttner knew Alfred Nobel and had been his secretary in Paris. Luka repeats Arthur's words in the local dialect. I am not sure how much enters the boy's brain, but he nods and takes Arthur's card, marches off along a path leading back into the forest and is soon out of sight.

When we get back to the shed, the old man is standing at a trestle table. He has set out three cups of milk and a loaf of coarse dark bread. It is only now that I realize we are standing in the middle of his living quarters, which he shares with his sheep. Apart from the trestle table, there are two rough-hewn chairs and in the corner, a bedstead covered with a ragged blanket. A coat made of sheepskin is hanging from a peg on the wall behind it.

Arthur gives the man a few coins to pay for his hospitality, and his face brightens. He pulls out from under his straw pallet an earthen pot filled with cheese curds and places a knife at our disposal after wiping it off on the hem of his shirt. Ida and I sit down on the two chairs provided. The men eat and drink standing up. Our guide shows a healthy appetite. Arthur spears two or three pieces of curd with the knife and politely chews on the bread, but Ida declines to eat anything at all, and I manage only a few sips of tepid milk. It has a beastly smell. My stomach churns at the thought of the matted fleece of the ewes and the shepherd milking them with his dirty hands and black-rimmed fingernails.

Arthur thanks our rustic host. We get back on our horses and move on, following the path the boy has taken. After half an hour's ride, the path widens. We come to a stone wall, skirt it and reach a wrought-iron gate. Luka jumps off his horse, opens the gate and leads us along a gently rising gravel drive. When we reach the top of the hill, we see, nestled in a grove below, a manor house.

"This is where Nobel is staying, Count," Luka says.

The house looks rather picturesque in its solitary setting. A well-tended lawn runs down from a stone-flagged terrace to a little stream and a copse of birch trees. A servant appears on the terrace and calls off the dogs guarding the steps and barking at us fiercely. He greets us with deference. The master is expecting us, he says, and gives directions to a stable hand to take away our horses.

We cross the terrace and enter a high-ceilinged hall, furnished in the French style. After our ride through the pathless forest and the encounter with the shepherd in his tumbledown shed, I expected a primitive hunting lodge, but the furnishings are those of an elegant townhouse.

A liveried servant leads us into a study, lined with glass-fronted bookcases, each topped by a bronze bust. I catch a fleeting sight of my flushed face and wind-blown hair in the mirror above the fireplace before Emanuel Nobel steps forward to greet us with a gesture of easy friendliness.

He is a handsome, rather soft-faced man in his thirties, wearing a frock coat and cravat. His elegance makes me uncomfortably aware of our disheveled appearance. There is something intent and searching in his eyes as he makes an obeisance to me and Ida and takes Arthur's proffered hand. I think I see a shadow of disappointment pass over his face as if he had expected better company.

"I am greatly honored by your visit," he says in fluent French as he leads us to a settee. "My servant announced a lady who knew my uncle in Paris," he says, addressing his words to me. "I visited him there some time ago and was introduced to his secretary, Miss Hess." There is a barely noticeable hesitation as he pronounces the word "secretary". "You must be her successor, madam."

"I was only briefly in Mr Nobel's employ – last spring," I say.

"Ah," he says, "that explains it."

I'm not sure it does.

Nobel rings a bell, and two servants enter, carrying trays of zakuski – venison patties, caviar, pirogies, mushroom pies and other delicacies.

Our host takes his seat across from us. "You are from Vienna," he says. "You must speak to me in your native tongue. I find the Viennese intonation charming."

He turns to Arthur: "I can still picture Miss Hess, who didn't like to be hurried, raising her finger to my uncle and saying in her droll way: 'Just a little moment, please – *ein Momenterl, bitte.*'"

His perfect rendition of the Viennese phrase makes us laugh.

"One of these days I will travel to your celebrated city and listen to the music of those charming voices," he says. "Alas, business forever gets in the way of my private plans."

The servants have set small tables in front of us and serve us the canapés, arranged on exquisite gold-rimmed plates, complemented with iced vodka and Tokay in crystal glasses.

The conversation turns to the subject we have come to investigate.

"You have heard of my father's project then," Nobel said. "We believe in looking after our workers' health, in developing their skills and training them in good work habits. It will be to our as well as their benefit."

His speech sounds practiced. Perhaps it is his recruiting talk.

Arthur relates the story we have been told about telephones being installed in the workers' quarters. Is that true as well, he asks.

Nobel laughs heartily.

"I haven't heard that particular story, but people are fond of making up fancy tales about us. I dare say we have a reputation for doing things in an odd way. That is to say, people consider any deviation from long-standing traditions odd and are inclined to think of any liberal approach as crazy."

"And does Alfred Nobel share your liberal approach?" Ida asks. She is trying to bring the talk around to the subject that interests her.

"I couldn't tell you," Nobel says with an ambiguous smile. "We never talked about such matters when I was in Paris. But I assure you, my uncle is liberal to his employees. Or was to Miss Hess, at any rate."

There is a puzzled silence as we digest this piece of information and guess at its meaning. Then Arthur asks about Nobel's hiring practices, but he is no more successful than Ida in eliciting a conclusive answer.

"I'm afraid you've caught me at a bad time," Nobel says. "I was on my way out when your message was brought to me. I mustn't miss my appointment, but I wanted to welcome you and hope you will stay and join me for dinner tonight."

We demur, telling him of our little adventure.

"We are late already," Arthur says, "and expected back at the palace for dinner."

"Most regrettable," Nobel says. "Then you must give my compliments to the Princess Ekaterina. As to your questions about our hiring practices and the working conditions in our factories, I hope you will have an opportunity to come to Baku, my dear Count, and see for yourself how we operate. If you give me sufficient notice, I will show you around myself."

We leave, impressed with his urbanity but dissatisfied with his evasive replies.

As we mount our horses, Arthur repeats the Viennese phrase Nobel quoted.

"*Ein Momenterl, bitte!*" He shakes his head. "I can't imagine any secretary saying that to her employer."

"I must find out more about the droll Miss Hess," Ida says, and I wonder whether this is the woman Nobel's housekeeper mentioned to me – the secretary he let go and "should have sent packing" sooner rather than later.

"I wish we had made Mr Nobel's acquaintance earlier and arranged for a visit to his factories," Arthur says, as we pass through the wrought-iron gate and turn back in the direction of the palace, this time, by a smoother road and with a second guide supplied by Nobel.

Ida

It seems that all my inquiries end in question marks, but at least I know now that there is another witness to Nobel's life, a woman who knew him, perhaps intimately, if I interpret Emanuel Nobel's enigmatic smile correctly. When I am back home, I will search for Miss Hess – but where? In Paris or in Vienna?

Before I retire to my palatial bed, which looks like an altar strewn with cushions, I take out my notebook and jot down my impressions of the day. I must have cut a ridiculous figure in Bertie's eyes, the way I carried on during our ride in the forest, in a senseless panic over nothing. There was no danger. The threat was as imaginary as my nightmares.

I'm not a good traveler. I don't take new situations in stride. I don't like surprises, although I enjoy writing about them afterwards. Putting my life into words is putting it in order. It wasn't a lie when I told Mrs Kinsky that I wanted to write a travelogue. I was tired of genealogies and wanted to switch to a new genre. Since then, the idea of putting together an account of my travels has grown on me. I have come to observe my surroundings more closely and am writing down my impressions conscientiously. I mean, these aren't diary entries, written on the spur of the moment to give expression to overflowing sentiments. They are the kind of notes I imagine journalists take, precise and to the purpose. There is certainly no shortage of material for a travel essay or indeed a whole series of essays. I have filled a respectable number of pages in my notebook: a description of the first leg of my journey traveling in the company of a missionary and his family who were on their way to Tiflis, then the lonely coach ride to the border of Mingrelia and my meeting with Bertie and Arthur. I have jotted down my first impression of him. *He is a slight and rather delicate-looking man in his twenties. Although his receding hairline and his serious eyes give him a mature appearance, it is obvious that Bertie is older than he.* Then comes the account of the splendid reception we were given in Gordi. I describe the women's dress, their gowns and the gauzy headscarves with one side drawn down to conceal their faces, the men's jackets reaching to the waist and open at the breast to show brightly colored kaftans, their wide trousers gathered with silken waistbands, their pointed shoes, embroidered in red and gold.

It is a detailed account, and with every word I put down, I am moving further away from my own past and from my original purpose – to talk to Bertie about Alfred Nobel.

I am lying on my bed, looking up to the dark ceiling, waiting for a nightmare that doesn't come. I feel – what? Relief? The new impressions seem to have lightened my mood and taken a weight off my shoulders. I need not have warned my travel companions that I was suffering from nightmares. I always woke up in time to suppress alarming shrieks. I am wondering now: was I able to control those fits because I made a special effort, or did the new experiences deaden the effect of the old ones? The night panics seemed to ease with the new sights and sounds invading my mind. The Heleneborg of my dreams no longer resounds with explosions or resembles a battlefield strewn with bodies. It has turned into a black and pathless forest through which I wander, lost and in confusion. I still suffer a nameless fear, but I no longer feel the terror that gripped me before.

The desire for revenge, which has been upmost in my thoughts for so long, is losing its overpowering urgency. I don't mean that I have let go of my obsession entirely, but something has shifted. Do I feel relief then? No, the waning of my compulsion has not given me peace of mind. On the contrary, it is making me uneasy. I feel like a deserter. I am no longer true to myself or to Georg's memory. I try to tell myself that this is only an interlude. I will get back to Nobel and my purpose once we reach Kutaisi and I have a chance to talk to Bertie in a more private atmosphere.

The next day, we take our leave from the court and by nightfall reach Bertie's new home. Kutaisi is a dusty town, but its central street is planted with a row of mimosas that fills the place with a drowsy fragrance. The house is a modest cottage. Bertie has dressed up the walls of their low-ceilinged "drawing room" with red fabric and furnished it with a table and a few chairs. There is also a wooden divan, covered with a rug and lined with long bolsters. A large veranda with carved wooden pillars overlooks the courtyard. It quickly becomes my favorite place to talk with Bertie over cups of scented tea. As soon as we are alone, I bring the talk around to Alfred Nobel, but I can see that the subject no longer holds Bertie's attention. Kutaisi is the focus of her interest now.

"I thought you came here to write about your travels," she says.

"I came because your mother was worried about you."

"Well, now you can put her at ease. You see how comfortably we live here."

"And I came to see *you.*"

"I'm so glad you did. It's wonderful to have your company."

I hear the flatness of her response. I know Bertie expects more from me than companionship – an interest in reporting on the exigencies and peculiarities of life in Kutaisi. She is no longer the light-headed woman in love I met in Vienna. She is married to a man who has the spirit of a reformer. Under his influence, she has developed a social conscience. She wants me to write about the Caucasus and provide a universal lesson: We are all brothers and sisters under the skin, united by the same thoughts and emotions. Or: One can be happy without living in the lap of luxury.

"I know you want me to write about Kutaisi," I say, "and I will. In fact, I have started putting my notes in order, but once I've polished my account and readied it for publication, I intend to go back to writing my biography of Nobel."

That's the word I have settled on with Bertie, a nice neutral word that gives nothing away – my "biography" of Nobel.

"You must bear with me if I keep asking questions about Nobel while I'm here and have a chance to talk to you," I say.

"But that world seems so far away now," she says. "Paris, my secretarial tasks, the painful time of separation from Arthur. Thank God that's all in the past! Still, if I can be of help to you—" She sighs. "What would you like to know, Ida?"

"About Nobel's business practices, for example."

"I know nothing about them."

"But you handled Nobel's correspondence when you were his secretary. You must know something about his business affairs, his travels. Just tell me whatever you remember, whatever you consider significant."

She gives me a martyred look. "What can I tell you, Ida? He travelled a great deal, mostly to Ardeer in Scotland and Krümmels near Hamburg, where he had factories and laboratories, and he also talked about going to America. A certain Shattner was giving him trouble there and had involved him in a lawsuit."

"A lawsuit about the accidents in his factories?"

She wrinkles her brow. "Accidents? No, I believe it concerned patent law."

"And what became of the lawsuit?"

"I can't tell you. I left Paris before it was settled."

"You handled only business correspondence, I suppose."

"I handled Mr Nobel's official correspondence. It did not always concern business. He received many honors."

I know about the honors conferred on Nobel. The French enlisted him in the Légion d'Honneur. The Bolivians gave him their highest distinction, the Order of the Condor. He received the Brazilian Rose. He was made a Knight of the Order of the North Star and was awarded the Swedish Letterstedt Prize.

"A much-honored man," I say, barely keeping a sneer out of my voice.

Bertie raises her eyebrows. "Well, yes," she says. "And he deserved it."

We look at each other silently. It is clear that we disagree about Nobel, but it won't do for a hostess to argue with her house guest. Bertie's raised eyebrows merely give me warning. What she means to say is: I have personal knowledge of Nobel. You don't. So why do you question my judgment? And if you do, why do you persist in asking me about Nobel? There is nothing I can say in reply to her unspoken words without betraying my real purpose, revenge for Georg's death.

So I give up on the past for the time being and live in the present. I listen to Bertie speaking enthusiastically about *her* town. She and Arthur are making a modest living in Kutaisi. Bertie gives music lessons. He teaches languages and designs wallpaper. In spite of their reduced circumstances, they are content, she says.

"People treat us very well, not at all like a pair of runaways but rather like exiled aristocrats," she says. "We didn't know the first thing about setting up or running a household in Kutaisi. We felt helpless, always depending on the favor of the princess and her friends and relatives – until she sent us Totia."

Totia, whose full name I never learn, speaks a few words of French and acts as a kind of steward in the Suttner household.

"He can get his hands on anything we need, knows every workman in Kutaisi and has a way of keeping the servants in line," Bertie says. "The princess has kindly provided us with domestic help. We ourselves couldn't afford them, but she cannot imagine anyone living with fewer than three servants."

If you listen to Bertie, Totia is a miracle worker, the biblical savior who *will make the crooked road straight and the rough ground smooth*. Since the cottage has no guest room, he had a hut built for me at the end of the garden. I sleep in this glorified shed on a divan filled with horsehair and banked with pillows. There is also a low table on which I fold up my clothes at night and a washstand with a basin and pitcher, which is filled with fresh water by a servant every morning and evening. The floor is packed earth but covered with a woolen carpet, woven in a fine pattern of indigo and purple. The roof of my shed is supported by four slender columns, slightly taller than the walls, leaving a narrow gap to allow for the air to circulate. A heavy curtain on a brass rod serves as a door. I pull it aside when I want to let in the light of the day and close it at bedtime, sleeping in the black night of my windowless bedroom.

When I thank Totia for the arrangement, he modestly lowers his eyes – I wear a headscarf in deference to the custom of the country but no veil. I regard that piece of gauze a conceit. It is so flimsy that the slightest breeze or a rapid turn of the head will make it flutter, revealing the face of the bearer.

Totia turns from my naked face politely, but for a moment, I feel the heat of his black eyes on me. He is not a native of Kutaisi. His features have a far-eastern delicacy. The faces of the local population are dusky. Totia's skin is a darker shade and has a marble smoothness. The light gray kaftan he wears brings out his brown complexion. He is tall and slender, unlike the majority of men in Kutaisi, who are of a sturdier build. But what I find most attractive about him are his full lips, as red as a painted woman's or rather as red as a lush fruit. He is the descendant of a magus, the head of a sect of fire-worshippers in Baku, Bertie tells me. He showed her a picture of the temple of Artech-Gah with perpetual flames rising from its four corners. It is near Baku. The only other temple like this was in Bombay, he said. I would have liked to ask Totia questions about Baku, the site of the Nobel family enterprise, but he does not have enough French to fully understand or answer my questions. Our communication is mostly through looks and gestures, but what fiery looks!

"Totia has taken a liking to you," Bertie says to me one day. "He makes sure your towel is changed every day. That is a mark of great favor, you know." She thinks Totia's attentions to me are amusing. I do not tell her that he also brings me flowers every day, that my heart has been singed by his hot glances, that his hand touched mine once as if by chance, and his touch was like ice and fire.

I watch Totia, captivated by the way he moves with the erotic languor of a tiger. He is discreet and never addresses me directly. Our eyes meet only furtively, but I have seen his desire, and it gives me a sense of power such as I have never felt before. I believe it is the power of beauty. In Kutaisi, light skin is highly prized, and no one thinks of me as plain. It makes me think how artificial the concept of beauty is and how much it owes to circumstance. The color of skin is inborn, and the society defining its esthetic value is likewise pre-determined by the place of birth. Then again, beauty can also be acquired or enhanced at any rate with a certain amount of effort. It is a combination of things: a gift of nature, a construct of society and an accomplishment. It involves the way you smile or turn your neck, the way you put up your hair or arrange the folds of your dress, the way you step out or proffer your hand to be kissed. It involves performance and costume play. So, in a way, it is up to me to be beautiful, in Kutaisi or in Vienna. But a person has only so much time and energy to go around, and on balance, I would rather write, see my thoughts turn into words and the words take form on a page, than stand in front of a mirror and practice beautiful gestures. In Kutaisi, no such effort is required. It is enough that I am light-skinned. In the eyes of the local men, I am naturally beautiful. So, I enjoy Totia's admiration and encourage it by accepting his flowers and answering his glances. I allow myself to fall into reveries. Totia has become the object of my secret fantasies and a partner in the erotic scenes I enact on my sofa bed under the cover of darkness. I greedily observe every detail about Totia, his glossy black hair, the muscles moving under the smooth brown skin of his arms, the angle of his hips as he walks. My nightly fantasies become more explicit until I can feel his skin against mine, except that his skin has turned to velvet, the sleek pelt of a panther, and his voice in my ear sounds like a purr. His rough tongue licks me until my body tingles, and my breath comes in gasps, and I reach the point where everything fades to black. Of all my fantasies this is the most sinful, an act of bestiality. I don't know why I turn Totia into a beast. Is it because everything about him is alien? I don't speak his language, I can't read his body or his eyes with any certainty. It is as if he belonged to another species. Is this how the people of Kutaisi see me in turn, the light-skinned woman who is not ashamed to show her face, whose words are as incomprehensible as the lowing of a cow? Do they have dreams about taming me, keeping me in a pen, or in a cage like a pet bird?

Then, on my last night in Kutaisi, Totia comes to me, and my dream turns flesh. He slips through the curtain at my door like a ghost. His bare feet make no noise on the carpet, although I can feel the air and the space shifting as if his body were giving off waves. He says only two words, *mon amour*, like a watchword to let me know who it is that has entered my room. I don't know what he would have done if I had screamed, but I accept the gift of his visit. I make room for him on my bed, and he lies down beside me. We lie quietly for a time, his chest pressed against my back. I can feel his lungs filling with air and emptying again. Then he sits up and takes off his clothes, while I pull off my nightgown. I am sorry that I can't see his mahogany skin and his red lips in the darkness of the shed, but when he lies down again, I pass my hands over his body and he over mine. We map out our territory in silence. We entangle our limbs and kiss with yielding mouths, our lips parted. He moans – a prayer, an incantation, a song? We have no words in common, but he attends to everything, and we find a common rhythm, our bodies rocking against the horsehair mattress until something within me quivers and scrapes to the surface, something supernatural, halfway between sacred and profane, between my old dream and this new reality. When our bodies separate again, I float into sweet blackness.

Totia leaves minutes or hours later, I have lost track of time. I hear the curtain move on the rod and see a sliver of night sky behind his head, but before he steps out into the yard, he speaks to me in his language – a declaration of love or a warning or an apology, I can't tell. Then he waits. I hear his impatient breathing. He is waiting for an answer, but I can't think of anything to say. In my arms, he did not turn into a panther. Skin to skin, he remained human, but our embrace was no meeting of souls. Our bodies communed in the way bodies do, and I have nothing to add to this organic process. It requires no words. In the end, because he is still waiting, I open my mouth and say *adieu*. I say it very softly, and it seems to satisfy him because a moment later, he slips out and pulls the curtain shut.

I wake up in the morning when the servant brings fresh water. I wake as from a deep and satisfying dream, although there are no images to go with my memory of the night, and a vague unease sets in almost immediately. The servant has pulled back the curtain and now points to my bed. I see that my nightgown and the sheet are stained with blood – my virginal blood, I think at first, but it is menstrual blood. My monthlies have always been irregular and hard to calculate. I am relieved when I see the blood. I am saved from agonizing over the consequences of what I have done. A niggling fear started up in my brain the moment I woke – what if Totia got me pregnant? An illegitimate child would mean shame, an illegitimate brown child would mean ostracism, but now I am free to push that thought away and tend to the immediate need of cleaning myself up. While the servant bundles up the bloody sheet and my nightgown for laundering, I rummage in my travel bag for one of Hartmann's Disposable Hygienic Towelettes, which I packed for just such an emergency. As I busy myself washing up, I listen to my conscience, waiting for a reproachful murmur, a warning to strike the fear of God into my heart, but it remains silent, and I wonder at my soul, at the hardened sinner I have become. A dull pain cramps my stomach, and that is all.

Bertie notes my discomfort. When I tell her it's that time of the month, she suggests putting off my departure by a few days, but I am reluctant to upset the arrangements she has made for me. In any case, I will be travelling only a short distance to Gordi, to stay with the princess for another week. I travelled outbound under the protection of a missionary and will embark on my return journey under the escort of a cousin of the princess, who is going to Istanbul. The plan is for me to board the Orient Express there. On the train, I will be safe in the company of businessmen and diplomats and their families travelling to the West.

My farewell to Bertie is melancholic and not only because it will be a long time until we meet again. Our friendship is fraying at the edges. Her amused comment when she first noticed Totia's devotion made me realize that we are no longer soulmates or perhaps never have been. Bertie is as obsessive as I, but her obsessions are on a grand scale. She wants to improve the lot of mankind. She lives on a higher plane than I and is carried aloft by her idealism. I am tied to earth by my animal instincts. I also think that life with Arthur has changed her. His idealism is infectious. Bertie is no longer interested in the mundane and cares only about ideas. I acknowledge the superiority of her motives and admire her principles, but her superiority has cast a shadow over our friendship. Friendship is perfect only among equals.

Totia is not among the people who bid me farewell in Kutaisi, and I don't expect to see or hear of him again. I think of him with gratitude as the dispenser of good things, a man who has essential knowledge, but he doesn't recede into the past and gently fade into a memory. He stays in my bloodstream. He lurks in the dark quarters of my mind, a jungle beast waiting to be summoned and pleasure me in my shameful dreams.

If I was a poet, I might be able to sublimate my instincts and turn my night with Totia into a paean of love, but since I am not, I try to bury it as well as I can under layers of civilized thought. I can't say that I am entirely successful. I gave into my shameful desires in the certainty that I would never see Totia again, and we would soon be a continent apart. But Totia has taken root in that secret place within me, the source of my daydreams. He has taught me to walk on the wild side – once in reality and often in my fantasy. My mind is flooded with jungle scenes in which he plays the leading role, the night beast. I fight against my sinfulness, I do. I try to deaden my body against this unholy desire and bury it deep down as in a crypt, never to be resurrected. It refuses to be kept trussed up in its grave. It comes to life. It wants to be fed. All it takes is a glimpse of a tall, slender figure and a certain squaring of the shoulders, and the memory takes hold. I am back in Kutaisi, and my thoughts start running in predictable cycles – the dark shed at the end of the garden, the stifling heat, a cool hand on my cheek, sliding down to my breast and my thigh, the climactic end and my unrepentant mind.

For a time Totia's panther eyes and sleek skin bury the images of Georg's death and keep my nights free of terror. I am beginning to think, I dare to hope that one obsession has driven out the other or will balance it at any rate, that my night with Totia, sinful as it was, freed me of my nightmares. There is a young doctor in Vienna, Dr Freud, who describes the symptoms of trauma and claims that it can be cured through hypnosis. I believe that's what Totia did for me. The ecstasy I felt in his arms was like a hypnotic spell. I relinquished all control over my mind and let go of my traumatic memories in the frenzy of the moment. The experience has eased my nights, but it also burdens my days with scruples. I am ashamed of my fall from grace. What bothers me most is the beastly nature of my relationship with Totia. A spiritual connection was impossible because we lacked a common language, but I never even cherished romantic thoughts about him. Surely there was a need for words like "love" or "promise" or "forever" to accompany such embraces, whereas we took our pleasure wordlessly, heaving and panting, satisfying our bodily desires like animals. And to add to the gravity of my sin, I am letting my fantasies run wild and do nothing to stop them, or perhaps I should say, *can* do nothing to stop them. On the contrary, I have come to depend on my sexual fantasies as an alternative to real life, as compensation for any unpleasantness or dissatisfaction. They are not terrifying like my nightmares but just as intrusive, and I realize: I have fallen into another rut too deep to escape.

The only way to fight those salacious dreams, I decide, is to revert to the earlier scenes, the imagined confrontations with Nobel, which have a certain legitimacy at least, which I can defend in my own mind because they are linked to a higher cause, my quest to avenge Georg. I introduce a few new elements into those daydreams: Let's say *I* answered the advertisement Nobel placed in the Viennese paper. Let's say he hired *me* rather than Bertie and I stayed on and accompanied him on his business trips. The imaginary scene takes off. I become Nobel's conscience. We have long and heated arguments about the inventor's responsibility for the use people make of his inventions. Nobel concedes... No, that is too implausible! Nobel isn't the kind of man who would concede anything. He would fire me. Immediately another, equally implausible scenario presents itself to my mind. Let's say I met Nobel on the Orient Express on my way back from the Caucasus. We share a compartment and talk about war and peace. I challenge him: You are nothing but an arms dealer, a merchant of death! He becomes increasingly uncomfortable and agitated. Finally, he excuses himself to go to the dining car. Shortly afterwards, the train stops with a jolt. Everyone runs out into the corridor to see what is going on. The conductor appears and says a fire has broken out in the dining car. As he talks, the corridor begins to fill with smoke. We all surge forward, making our escape. There is a tremendous explosion in the back of the train. The windows of the dining car blow out, and Nobel's mangled body lands in the ditch beside the tracks. The next moment, he is swallowed up by an orange ball of fire.

My fantasy about Nobel's death on the Orient Express is satisfying but has unfortunate consequences. The Heleneborg nightmares, in abeyance since my return from Kutaisi, come back with a vengeance. I suspect the imagined train explosion triggered them, and once again, I dream of Georg's bloodied body and wake up with screams lodged in my throat and sometimes escaping into the night air as shouts and moans.

I try a remedial process, thinking up a scenario in which Georg comes to life. I attempt to conjure up a happier scene from *before* he went to Heleneborg, but I discover to my dismay that I cannot find my way as far back as that. I cannot get beyond the photo displayed on my writing desk, in which Georg looks at me straight. All my attempts to remember him in profile fail. The side of his face remains a blur. I have begun to forget Georg's body, the arms that embraced me, the lips that kissed my mouth. Only the nightmares remain vividly present, with every detail of his torn legs and bloodied fingers in sharp focus. I suffer those renewed visions meekly. I deserve to be haunted by nightmares for allowing Georg to fade from my memory and betraying him in my lewd daydreams and in the shameful reality of my last night at Kutaisi. I deserve punishment for neglecting the principal task of my life – revenge on Nobel – and writing a travelogue instead.

Sophie

Nikki is pacing the room.

"Did you tell Czerny to get Gretel ready? It's unlike her to keep me waiting."

"It will only be a moment – *ein Momenterl.*"

"I wish you wouldn't use those diminutives, Sophie. *Momenterl. Passagerl. Kleiderl.* You aren't a child."

She curls her lip. "Everyone uses diminutives," she says, "except, of course, the people in the exclusive circles you are frequenting."

"And which you would like to frequent as well. Believe me, Sophie, they would take you up more readily if you behaved like a lady."

She starts up, words of protest on her lips. *Don't lecture me. I know what you think – I'm not good enough for you.* But she shuts her mouth and turns away from him to hide her annoyance. What did I expect, she thinks. It's a marriage of convenience, but does he have to be like that – so critical? He liked me well enough when we first met, in those heady days before I got pregnant. She misses the nights of music and dancing into the small hours, the snatched kisses, the touch of his hand on her bare shoulder, the baccarat tables at the casino, the popping champagne corks – the promise of unlimited fun. But when he resigned from his post in the army, it was as if he relinquished the spirit of exuberance together with his uniform. There was no more dancing and drinking, no more silly jokes and wild laughter, no more lovemaking. Once they were married, Nikki became calm and serious, well, not right away, but gradually so that she barely noticed it at first. He slowed down. He distanced himself from her and became aloof. Then, one day, he rented a place of his own in Hietzing, to be closer to his office, he said, but she knew what it meant. Separation. Officially, they were still a married couple. As for the rest – she sighed. And all that bickering about money.

"I realize that my little contribution to our household is just a trickle lost in the sea of your expenses," he said to her. "But you knew it would be like that when you married me. You knew I couldn't keep you in the style Alfred did."

It's over between them, but divorce is out of the question. Neither she nor Nikki can afford another scandal.

"I told Nanny to take her time because I need to talk to you," she says.

"About what?"

"I had a message from the lawyer. Alfred wants his letters back – the letters he wrote to me years ago."

"You still have them?"

"Of course I do. They are invaluable to me – the only memento I have of our time together. I won't send them back unless he pays me for them, and I meant to ask you what I should charge for them."

"I see. It wasn't nostalgia that made you keep those letters."

"It was, but now—"

"If you want my advice, Sophie, don't ask for money. Send those letters back and be grateful that Alfred keeps paying your allowance."

"I don't know why I should be grateful to him. It's only right for him to support me after what I had to put up with. I wrote back and told him: Those letters are mine. And I mean it. I won't part with them unless he buys them off me."

"You said that?"

"Not in so many words. I didn't say anything about buying and selling. I thought I'd talk to you first."

"For heaven's sake, Sophie, don't do anything rash or he'll cut off your allowance. In fact, I'm surprised he hasn't done so already, considering the impertinent letters you keep writing to him."

"I use plain words because Alfred treated me badly."

"Perhaps so, but you didn't treat him well either."

"You are like all men, Nikki. A woman is just a plaything to you. She must be amusing, or you can't love her." *Nothing is as repugnant to me as your endless crying and eternal reproaches,* Alfred had said to her. *Instead of bringing cheer into a man's life, you give it a bitter taste.*

"Alfred treated me like a toy poodle," she says. "I have every right to complain. You know yourself how difficult he could be. You know what I had to put up with: his morose talk and his insults. I stuck it out with him when no one else would. Was that not being good to him?"

Nikki shrugs. "Let's drop the pretenses, shall we? We know why you stuck it out with him, Sophie. And Alfred knew it too, I'm afraid. But let me ask you a question: Why should he pay you for the letters? What's in them? Are they indiscreet? Frankly, I can't see Nobel writing you torrid love letters. Or was he fool enough to do that?"

She twists under his probing eyes. Her mouth dips into a pout. "Well, I don't know about torrid, but—"

"But what?"

"Maybe not torrid, but soppy. Embarrassing at any rate. At least *he* thought they were embarrassing. At one point, he asked me to burn his letters, you know, but I couldn't get myself to do it."

Nikki raises his eyebrows and says nothing.

"I am attached to those letters," she says defiantly. "You don't believe me, Nikki?"

"Oh, I do believe you. They are valuable, no doubt, and embarrassing if you say so."

"Let me show you," she says. She goes to her bureau, unlocks a drawer and takes out a packet, tied with a red ribbon.

"Nice touch," he says when he sees the ribbon.

"Don't be sarcastic, Nikki."

"I try to stick to irony, but sometimes you are too much, Sophie."

"Sarcastic, ironic, what's the difference?" she says. "You are clever with words, that's what I mean."

She puts the letters on the coffee table, unties the ribbon and sorts through them.

"Here is one he wrote a few weeks after we met," she says, and reads it out to Nikki:

I wish I could be like my thoughts and fly to you. I wish with all my heart that I could see you again. I feel so lonely without you, Sophie dear, and I keep brooding in a terrible way because your last letter gave me the impression that you no longer care for me.

She looks up. "And he signed it: *Your Grouchy-Bear, who is always fondly thinking of you.*"

She sorts through a few more letters and reads out another passage: *I have never felt so lonely and abandoned. I press a fond kiss on your sweet mouth and think of you with love. Your old melancholic, Alfred.*

She looks at Nikki expectantly, but he shakes his head.

"That's just romantic twaddle," he says. "If you want my advice, return the letters and ask Alfred for a favor in turn – to convert your allowance into something permanent, an annuity."

"How does an annuity work? Is it like a bequest?"

Before Nikki can answer her, Nanny comes into the drawing room with Gretel.

"Here we are," she says, giving Gretel's coat a final brush. "Don't we look nice?"

"Beautiful," Nikki says. He opens his arms wide, and Gretel runs to him and gives him a big hug.

"How is my little princess?" he says.

"Did you bring Bella?"

"She is waiting for you downstairs, sweetheart. Let's go."

Gretel rushes to the door, pulling Czerny with her. "Did you hear what Papa said, Nanny?" she cries. "Bella is waiting for me."

"*Ein Momenterl,*" Sophie says to the child. Nikki frowns, but it's a perfectly good word, even if he doesn't like it. "*Ein Momenterl!* You've forgotten something, darling. You haven't kissed your mama goodbye."

Gretel gives her a dutiful kiss. She is in a hurry to see Bella.

The dog means more to her than her mother, Sophie thinks when they are gone. She can't help feeling deserted. Words start up in her head, conversations echoing in her mind in reverse order, last conversation first, *Let's drop the pretenses, shall we?* Nikki said. *We know why you stuck it out with him, Sophie. And Alfred knew it too, I'm afraid.* Alfred always questioned her motives, even when she was only being nice to him. *Don't think you can pull the wool over my eyes,*" he said. "*I know how it is when young ladies need money from old gentlemen. They feel obliged to make them wordy compliments.* He was always suspicious. She remembers the fuss he made about his nephew taking her out for a carriage drive. Emanuel had come from St Petersburg. It was his first visit to Paris. He fell in love with the city and, yes, with her. He was very handsome, almost too handsome for a man – with soft features and a ready smile. So what if she enjoyed a little flirting. Doesn't every woman? And he was such a lovable young man and extravagantly generous! Too bad he stayed only for a few weeks. Alfred couldn't wait to get rid of him and send him back to St Petersburg or the Caucasus or wherever those all-important oilfields are located.

She sits down and looks at Alfred's letters, fanned out on the coffee table, the red ribbon crinkling beside them. Those letters *are* valuable, she thinks. They are evidence. Alfred always made a great deal of his generosity, but it was a generosity laced with bitterness. If he wants the letters back, he has to give me something in return. He is an old man and in very poor health. If he dies, I am left with nothing. I need to find out more about annuities, she thinks.

She shuffles the letters. She wants to reread them, but something is holding her back; the fear of being hurt anew. She sits down on the sofa, undecided, but then she thinks: I need the reminder, even if it hurts. I mustn't feel guilty about taking his money. He owes me, he does. The bits she read out to Nikki were just *romantic twaddle*, as he said. She held back the worst She was embarrassed to let him know just how much she put up with.

She unfolds the letter she has put at the bottom of the pile, the ugliest of them all.

Perhaps you think my benevolence and forbearance are based on stupidity, but you are very wrong on that point. I am helping you out of goodwill. That's quite incomprehensible to you, of course, because you are a true daughter of Israel. Jews never do anything out of benevolence. They act only from selfishness or a desire to show off. So how could you understand a trait in another person which you completely lack yourself? Jews are the most selfish and inconsiderate people. For them, it is "me and my family" – all other people exist only to be fleeced. And you want a big cage for a little bird.

What a thing to say, just because she wanted to live in a nice place. Doesn't everyone? What does that have to do with being Jewish? And no one ever heard her brag about anything or *show off*. Why did he say such nasty things to her? She can't help it if her father is a Jew. And how is her family different from other folks? Everyone favors their own flesh and blood. Why shouldn't she give money to her brother or make presents to her sisters? She wanted to share her good fortune with them. *Jews never do anything out of benevolence.* That's a plain lie, but Alfred got mad if she told him so.

She reaches for the next letter, the one in which he broke up with her.

I will say only that our relationship isn't working out. For years, I've been searching for someone whom I could love, with whom I could spend my life, but that someone isn't you. Your outlook on life, your mindset has little or nothing in common with mine. You say that you are fond of me, but it isn't love. The time will come, and perhaps soon, when you will really fall in love with someone, and then you would feel tied down if we were married.

He wasn't entirely wrong about that. She did fall in love with Nikki, and now that she was married to him, she felt tied down and shackled to him. Their marriage hadn't worked out, but it wasn't her fault, even if Nikki blamed her. She was too selfish, he said. He sounded exactly like Alfred.

What worries me is your future, Sophie. Your selfish attitude will stand in the way of your happiness. These are words of truth that in all probability, you will not be able to understand, since it is foreign to your nature to make the slightest sacrifice for anyone else. I know you don't care for the opinion of others, which is a blessing and will save you from getting hurt in life. But no one can afford to disregard public opinion completely. You behave like a fool. Your education has been terribly neglected, and you have neither the ability nor the desire to catch up on what you have missed. That is the main reason why I am breaking up with you. I don't ask for an all-round education, I'm not even in favor of an all-round education for women, but I don't want to be embarrassed by every word a lady says in her own mother tongue. Your behavior in public is such that people would certainly question my judgment. You are making me a laughing stock. How many times did I tell you that you must work harder to improve yourself? But you are like a child and don't think of the future at all—

That's one lesson she has learned. She is thinking of her future. That's why she won't be giving away those letters. She carefully ties them up and returns the packet to her writing desk.

Ida

Carl's office is cluttered with books and manuscripts, some of them in piles that have the dusty look of neglect about them. Perhaps all editorial offices are like that, but I suspect it is a manifestation of Carl's personality. Clutter fits him. It goes with his mussed hair, untidy cravat, and missing button on his frock coat.

The manuscript of my travelogue is sitting on the desk in front of him. I have come back from the Caucasus with a clutch of essays and put the final touches to them with guilty joy. I should have spent my time writing about Nobel instead of my journey, but I relished using language that was not freighted with the purpose of revenge or, like my genealogies, bound by the conventions of a narrow genre. I filled my account with vibrant colors and exotic details. I relived my journey and enjoyed the sense of wonder a second time, but without the inconveniences or fear of things going wrong. That is the beauty of retrospection. You know nothing *did* go wrong, and anything that was not quite right can be corrected in your account, planed down or built up with words or cut out altogether. I wish I could amend my memories as well and transform the events of my last night in Kutaisi into a love unconsumed. A vague sense of remorse has taken hold of me, a whisper of conscience. I want to undo my sin and turn it into an innocent memory of Totia's admiration, to recall the desire in his eyes with a frisson of excitement instead of guilt, but my memory – unlike my travelogue – cannot be edited and remains stubbornly unalterable.

Three months ago, I brought the manuscript to Carl, in the hope that he would publish it. So far he hasn't said yea or nay. I suspect he is stringing me along to make me come back to his office. Perhaps he likes to see me beg. Perhaps he just likes to see me. I have my doubts about Mrs Olmuth's assertion that Carl is an entrenched bachelor. Sometimes, he has the look of a suitor.

"Well, Ida," he says and turns his loose-lidded, mournful eyes on me, the eyes of a loyal hound. There is something endearing about Carl, an embracing humanity. His moist, brown eyes make me think: this man is in love with me. But perhaps I am wrong, and this is a gentle look he has developed in the course of listening to all the authors who want to be published and don't have a chance.

Carl squares the pile of papers on his desk and moves them to the edge, like a man who wants to get an unpleasant job out of his way. He is finally going to reject my manuscript, I think. Politely, of course, saying something vague like: it's not the right time, it's not the right fit for his list. Or he'll go on dragging his feet and tell me: next year, perhaps.

But he just looks at me kindly and says, "Well, Ida, I reread your manuscript the other day. It was like having a conversation with you. I could hear your voice in every sentence. I could picture your face, the way you raise your eyebrows, the way you flap your hands when you are excited. There is something refreshingly personal about your essays, but that's not enough to sell a book, I'm afraid. It's a little thin."

Thin in more than one sense. It's a slim volume, even after I have added two essays on my earlier travels in France and England to the pieces about Mingrelia.

"I'll tell you what people are looking for in a travelogue," Carl says. "They want adventure. They aren't interested in ordinary lives, in modest cottages or comfortable hotels or churches and museums. They can look that up in their Baedekers. They want something more exclusive, a look behind the scenes. Women readers look for encounters with the rich and famous. Men want danger, firestorms, floods, death and destruction, the wrath of God. There's nothing like that in your essays."

"Well, I'm sorry I missed the Turco-Russian war."

He laughs. "I'm glad you did, Ida."

Much has happened since my return to Vienna half a year ago when I gave a sunny account of my journey to Mrs Kinsky, endowing Bertie's house in Kutaisi with the charms of a cottage in the Cotswolds. At that time, I could assure her with perfect honesty that her daughter was happy and that she and Arthur were safe. Kutaisi was a sleepy town then and far removed from the events that had the attention of the world, but the idyll soon came to an end. Not long after my return to Vienna, war broke out between Russia and Turkey. Kutaisi, which was close to the front, became a staging ground for military operations. I read about the battles in the pages of the newspapers I excerpted for Mr Olmuth and, of course, in Bertie's letters to me. She had joined the war effort in Kutaisi, she wrote. She organized benefits, offered herself as a volunteer nurse and provided food and drink for the troops marching through the town. But soon the mood of her letters changed. The resolute spirit she had shown in the face of danger changed to indignation. She had come to realize that the rationale for going to war was specious and trumped up. It wasn't about patriotism or defending the fatherland, she wrote. It was a power struggle that benefited crowned heads and arms dealers. *We were all caught up in Red Cross fever and melting with emotion*, she wrote, *but we could have offered the soldiers something better than our support: not sending them out in the first place.* But venting her indignation in letters to friends was not enough. She wanted the world to know about the horrors of war. That is why she wrote a book about her experience in Kutaisi and called it *Lay Down Your Arms.* It was a call to end wars everywhere and forever. She sent me the manuscript and asked me to recommend it to Carl, but he declined to publish it.

"I'm glad you got out of Kutaisi before the storm broke," he says to me. "Personally speaking, that is. Speaking as a publisher, I do want danger and excitement."

"Then, speaking as a publisher, why didn't you accept Bertie's manuscript? It's all about war."

"It's not. It's all about peace."

"Bertie may be advocating peace," I say, "but the descriptive parts are full of blood and gore. Villages burned down, women raped by marauding troops, men crippled or dead, their corpses left to rot on the battlefield – what more do you want?"

"I grant you the narrative was dramatic," Carl says. "We all know that acts of savagery were committed on both sides and thousands died on the battlefield. Dramatic, yes, but not the popular kind."

"I see. People want to cheer for the victor. Nobody wants to hear about the victims – is that what you are saying? They don't want to hear that the war was fought on the backs of ordinary men, that they died to secure the roads and railway lines transporting oil from Baku to the Caspian Sea. Tycoons and arms dealers like the Nobels prospered, while the common man risked his life on the battlefield and came back to find his house and fields devastated and his family suffering famine and epidemics."

"Indeed. Readers don't want to hear about the aftermath of war, and I don't want to get involved in the politics of war. Speaking of the Nobels – if you are still planning to write a book about them, Ida, I can tell you right now: if you take that angle, you won't find a publisher for your book."

"Not profitable enough, you mean?"

"That's exactly what I mean. Publishers make their living selling books."

He gives me a somber look. Then kindness returns to his eyes.

"As for your travelogue—" He clears his throat. "You know I am always ready to do you a favor, Ida—"

"I'm not asking you for a favor. I realize that this is a business proposition. I want you to be honest with me. You have decided not to publish it, am I right?"

He hems and haws – I know why he hesitates. He wasn't keen on publishing a travelogue written by a woman. If I had written a romance or brought him another genealogy, it would have been a different thing. But travel writing was best left to men. That was the received opinion. I did not have the option of using a male pseudonym, as some women writers did, because I had written my travel essays so clearly from a female point of view, telling not only what I had seen but also how others had seen and treated me, a single woman traveling in the East, I thought that the novelty would be in my favor. Apparently, it was not, and there was nothing I could do about it.

"I didn't say that, Ida. I said your manuscript was a little thin. Perhaps you could add to it."

"I'm afraid I'm right out of battle descriptions, but if peaceful scenes will do, I could add another chapter. Mrs Olmuth is going to San Remo next month. She has asked me to come along. I could write about San Remo."

The resort is fashionable. The crème de la crème of European society is staying in the grand hotels lining the bay. "I could capture the local color, write about who is wintering in San Remo this year, who's the darling of society and who's being snubbed – that sort of thing."

"It's a possibility," Carl says. "You might run into some interesting people there."

He gets up, folds his arms across his chest, as if he had just come to a decision, and walks around the desk. Seeing all of him does not improve the picture. Maybe it's shallow of me to think only of externals, of Carl's lumbering gait, his sloping shoulders, his jowls. Why don't I think instead of his accomplishments? Carl has an acute mind and a sense of humor. He is well connected and can offer a woman security. He is cultured. He can keep up an intelligent conversation. He has many good qualities, but he does not move me or quicken my pulse.

He gives me a soulful look.

"The Zuckerkandls have sent me an invitation to a soirée. She's trying for a literary salon, you know. Would you like to come with me?"

"I suppose I should. She might be interested in a genealogical study."

"If you want to put it that way, Ida, but I meant, would you like to spend an evening with me?"

What a boor I am. I dip my eyelashes at him.

"It's always a pleasure to spend an evening with you, Carl."

He leans forward in a kind of kowtow and takes hold of my hand. "I am glad to hear you say so, Ida."

I make the mistake of squeezing his hand to make up for my gaffe, but he takes it as encouragement and moves closer.

"Ida," he says. His breast rises as he fetches a deep breath. My heart skips a beat when I realize what's coming. He is going to declare himself.

I extract my hand and put a finger on his lips before he can say more. "Don't," I say. "Don't say anything you might regret later."

"I've thought about it long and hard, Ida—"

"Then it's only fair that you will let me think long and hard as well."

I see his courage ebb. He releases me slowly, reluctantly, and paddles away from the awkward situation. "You really are a heartless woman, Ida," he says, trying to give his voice a light, upbeat tone.

"Heartless? In a woman my age, it's called prudence."

"Your *age*, Ida! Counting years is completely beside the point. You are an attractive woman, with interesting thoughts and a charming way of expressing them—"

I'm trying to think of a charming way to put an end to this painful scene.

"Carl," I say, "I'm sorry, but I can't—"

"I won't press you for an answer," he says, "but will you give me another opportunity?"

"I will." I blush as I am saying it. No doubt he takes that for a hopeful sign, although I only blush because I am ashamed of humoring him for the sake of getting my travelogue published. I would like to say that it is loyalty to Georg that keeps me from accepting Carl's proposal, but that version is wearing thin and becoming untenable. The passing years have turned Georg's death into something abstract, an immobile picture, unlike the crashing, exploding night terrors. The only moving memory I have of Georg is his kiss, which still has the power to loosen my desire, and his touch, which still burns in my entrails. The rest of our last encounter, that walk to the railway station and our farewell have become fossilized, even as the nightmares remain vivid and continue to torment me, even as my fantasy battles with Nobel go on. There used to be a direct link between my anguish over Georg's death and my desire for revenge, but now, I fear I am no longer passionate about *his* death. I suspect I want to avenge my own suffering.

But none of that has anything to do with Carl. My relationship with him is embarrassingly straightforward. I don't want to disgruntle him at this crucial point – that is the reason why I don't give him a clear-cut answer and allow him to continue in his erroneous belief that I will give him another chance. Carl is a decent man and deserves better than that, I know.

I am burning with shame as he helps me with my coat, accompanies me to the door and bends over my hand to kiss it. I say goodbye without looking Carl in the eye. I can't wait to get out of his office. This is a turning point, I think as I cross the street and make my way to the train station to go back to my house in St Veit. After this, I can no longer call myself a woman of integrity, who speaks the truth however hard it may be. No, I'm deceiving myself. This isn't a turning point. There has been a gradual falling off, a decline in my moral standards. It started with small insincerities, acting the proper young woman to keep my mother happy and to satisfy the ladies who commissioned family histories. My hypocrisy is nothing new. It has gone up another notch on the scale.

Am I too hard on Nobel? I feel a twinge of guilt at setting a moral standard for Nobel to which I cannot live up myself. But there is a difference. Nobel's lack of ethics killed innocent people, mine brings shame only on myself. Maybe there are women who are able to abstract love and make it something laid up in heaven, like a prayer, but I am made of clay, earthy. I have felt the ecstasy of physical love, and I want to feel it again. But Carl – I can't imagine embracing him. His look, his shape, his movements – there will be no ecstasy with Carl.

*

Hindsight is a fine thing. Of course Carl is sorry now, that he rejected Bertie's manuscript. A publisher in Dresden printed it, and the book turned into an overnight success. *Lay Down Your Arms*, Bertie's plea for peace, struck a chord with readers. Even Arthur's parents laid down their arms and asked the couple to come home.

Bertie returned in triumph and was swamped with dinner invitations. The few times I saw her in Vienna, she was surrounded by a crowd. Not a chance to talk in private. But today will be different.

"Finally!" she says, as she leads me into the drawing room of her new home and takes her seat beside me. "Finally we have a chance to catch up on everything."

"So tell me," I say. "Are you enjoying your new celebrity status?"

"I do enjoy it, but I'm afraid I have disappointed my mother. She had visions of me hosting a literary salon in Vienna. Instead, we moved here. A rural estate! It's all foolishness to her."

"She has a point, you know. Harmannsdorf is rather remote from the center of things."

"But I love the old place."

"I can see why. It has a romantic air." The estate has been in Arthur's family for centuries and shows its medieval origins. It has a keep, a moat and a drawbridge, but the façade of the house and the interior court have been given a baroque makeover and look rather grand.

"It is beautiful, but what's more important, it gives me the peace and quiet I need to concentrate on my work," she says. "And let me tell you, it *is* hard work to drum up support for the Society."

Bertie hasn't been resting on her laurels. She has founded a society, *The Friends of Peace.* Advancing the cause of pacifism has become her mission.

"Of course, that's another bone of contention," she says. "You should hear my mother. 'You are wasting time and money on a hopeless cause,' she tells me. 'World peace! Whoever heard of such nonsense?'"

"You must admit the idea has a Utopian flavor."

"I admit no such thing. Universal peace has become the rallying cry of the world. Arthur and I have been travelling to conferences in London, Geneva and Paris—" She stops and catches her breath. "But I'm getting carried away. You must tell me about yourself, Ida. Are you still working on your biography of Nobel?"

"I haven't made much progress."

"And I wasn't very helpful the last time you asked me for information. But now I do have news for you. In fact, that is one of the reasons I asked you to come."

And the other reason? To make up an even number at the dinner table? – the role I usually play at the Olmuths.

"You remember our little adventure, when we called on Emanuel Nobel?" Bertie says. "Apparently, he mentioned our visit to his uncle. A few weeks later, I received a very kind letter from Alfred Nobel, inquiring about my life in Kutaisi. I sent him a copy of my book, and now we exchange letters regularly—"

At this interesting point in our conversation, Arthur comes in with a guest in tow and introduces me to Mr Herzl, a reviewer for *Die Presse.* The other guests arrive shortly afterwards, putting an end to our private talk. I'm still a little skeptical about Bertie's reasons for inviting me, but the pre-dinner conversation is reassuring. We are seven. Bertie is not afraid of odd numbers. And I'm definitely not a spare wheel. I am among fellow spirits. My natural tendency to speak up, which I have often been obliged to suppress, stands me in good stead tonight. I can hold my own and enjoy sparring with the gentlemen. Morals, bigotry, corruption and, of course, world peace all come under review. I feel at home.

The head servant throws open the doors to the dining room, and we troop in. The French windows look out on a formal garden. It is bare at this time of the year. The gravel paths, lined with ornamental vases, present a gray and cheerless picture, especially in the waning light of the day, but the company is lively. Bertie has seated me between Mr Kapy and Mr Herzl, who is clearly the guest of honor. I wonder why he has come without his wife. Perhaps the rumor of their impending separation is true. He is a passionate man, but his passion is for ideas, not for people. Herzl dominated the conversation in the drawing room with his firm voice. His face, narrow and obscured by a black, curly beard, was lit with ardor. Sometimes, he raised up his lean hands as if to start a prayer. I cannot picture him as a family man. He lives for his ideals – like Bertie and Arthur, but those two are united in their desire to improve the world. Perhaps Herzl's wife does not share his ideals.

I feel sorry for Arthur, who is flanked by Mrs Kapy and Mr Leschetizky, professor at the Academy of Music. He has only one subject: the awfulness of modern composers. In the drawing room, he went on a rant against Strauss and his lascivious waltzes. I wonder why Bertie invited him. In the interest of her cause? The professor is well connected, I know. He gives singing lessons in the best houses but only as a personal favor. His disdain for those who must charge fees has earned him respect in those circles. I think he is a pompous ass. And who are the Kapys? I find them difficult to gauge. How do they fit into Bertie's circle? Mrs Kapy is dressed in the newest Parisian fashion. She is a flirt but so far has managed only to attract the professor's attention. Arthur is immune to her prattle. As is Nikolaus Kapy, I notice. There is no love lost between husband and wife. He is a tall, elegant man with a quick smile and cultured voice, the kind of man that makes my blood rise in a hot and unpredictable way. It's been happening more often lately. Sometimes, I feel out of control. The desire for a man's touch will be my downfall. It has already led to improper situations, unbecoming looks and secretive brushes when I am in a crowd. It takes no more than a man's rude stare for me to be lost in fantasies and yield to unbidden thoughts. Kapy has given me no rude looks. He is very proper. Nothing in his words or his bearing suggests a personal interest in me, although he readily engages in conversation. As he talks, I come to understand why Bertie has invited him. He is a pacifist and speaks eloquently about the horrors of war.

At dinner, Bertie tells us that she has written a number of essays on the subject of universal peace and would like to see them published in the dailies. Newspapers reach a larger audience than books, she says, but so far she hasn't had much luck.

"The *Presse* did accept one essay I submitted. It will appear tomorrow. I suspect they accepted it only because I quote a letter from Alfred Nobel, in which he pledges money to the cause. The name of a prominent man, that's the drawing card. They have declined everything else I sent them."

Nobel supporting the peace movement! That's certainly new material for my "biography." His correspondence with Bertie may turn out to be a goldmine of information.

She is looking at Herzl as if he could or should have done something to prevent the rejection of the other essays, but he shrugs.

"I get no preferential treatment at the *Presse* when it comes to publishing anything with a political slant," he says. "They want me to keep to my subject proper: literature and book reviews. When I was their correspondent in Paris, I had a broader reach. I commented at length on Dreyfus and anti-Semitism – in fact, I may have said too much. The chief editor moved me to safer ground."

Mrs Kapy leans forward as if to make sure of Herzl's attention. "I lived in Paris for many years," she says, "and I could tell you stories about anti-Semitism. There are people in Paris who want all Jews killed. Even Alfred said—" She looks at her husband, hesitates and veers off, "—well he didn't say *that*, but he thought that Jews had certain traits that made them unpopular. They look only after their own, he said, and fleece everyone else."

Alfred? Does she mean Nobel?

A frown has appeared on Kapy's face. "Whatever he *said*, Sophie, his actions speak for themselves. He has shown you nothing but kindness and consideration." His voice is soft, but I hear a warning. Even when he is frowning, or especially when he is frowning, he makes my heart beat faster. The dark undertone thrills me. It speaks of something forbidden, like my own secret longings.

"Oh, I won't deny that he was kind," Mrs Kapy says. "Still—" She leaves the sentence hanging. There is a knowing look on everyone's face.

Until this moment, I thought I belonged, that I was a member of the circle around the table, but all of a sudden I am locked out. They know something that I don't know. Did Alfred Nobel befriend Mrs Kapy? I will ask Bertie later when we are by ourselves. And what about that essay in which she quotes Nobel? How can the inventor of dynamite be a supporter of world peace? It doesn't make sense. I turn my attention back to the conversation around the table. Herzl has picked up on Mrs Kapy's comment about the traits that make Jews unpopular.

"I used to think like that," he says. "I naively believed that it was up to us to change. If Jews embraced the culture of the country and became fully integrated into society, there would be no more prejudice against them. But the indiscriminate hatred I encountered in Paris has cured me of the idea. The same venom is now bubbling up in Vienna. There is no way the hatemongers can be pacified. Anti-Semitism is entrenched in Europe. There is only one solution: Jews must have a homeland, a country they can call their own. We must end the diaspora."

"A country of their own. I heard that phrase a great deal when I was in Budapest," Kapy says. "It's the slogan of the nationalists. We must fight the prejudice, they say. German-speakers are privileged in the empire. Hungarians are treated as second-class citizens. And what can be done about that? The solution, they say, is to have a country of their own."

Arthur looks glum. "Nationalist feelings run high in Prague as well, and among Slavs everywhere: in Slovenia, Serbia, Bosnia. If those sentiments prevail, the empire will break up."

"If the Jews emigrate, it may have economic consequences for Austria, but it won't lead to a break-up," Herzl says. "In any case, the newspapers are unwilling to give a voice to Zionists – that is what we are calling our movement inviting Jews to establish a homeland of their own. The idea is too outlandish for the general public, I suppose." He looks around the table. "This is perhaps the right moment – and the right company– to make an announcement: I have decided to launch my own paper."

Arthur is the first to congratulate Herzl. "I wish you every success," he says. "When do you expect to launch your paper?"

"The first issue will appear in the fall if all goes well. It will be called *Die Welt* because I am addressing the world. We cannot restrict ourselves to this country, large as it is."

I feel at one with the company again. I belong after all. I, too, find Austria too confining. I have become critical of Viennese society and am ready to speak up. Sometimes I wonder: am I too critical? There are so many conventions I find offensive now. Before my visit to the Caucasus, I was part of the fabric. I thought of Vienna as the arbiter of European taste. After all, the city has a long tradition of cultural leadership. It is the city of Haydn and Mozart, of Schubert and Strauss. The world's literati meet at the Café Central. The Ringstrasse, that grand tree-lined boulevard, is an architectural showplace. I have become a less charitable observer. I am no longer part of the fabric. I feel cut off. The night with Totia has uprooted my values. There may be another explanation for my unease as well. I am restless after my exotic adventure, or merely disgruntled to find that, after my glamorous interlude in Kutaisi, I am plain Ida again. I look at Mrs Kapy, who is the kind of woman Viennese men like: blonde and blue-eyed, with delicate hands and feet, a woman with a silly laugh and an empty head.

I shake off my uncharitable thoughts and join the others in wishing Herzl success with his new paper.

"You are right," Bertie is saying to him. "We must open our minds to the world. Coming back from the Caucasus, I find much of what I read in the Viennese papers insipid, not to say childish. People here take such a narrow view of things. You know what happens when you revisit places where you lived as a child? You remember the rooms as spacious and the front lawn as a vast expanse, but to your adult eyes, those same rooms appear small and cramped, and the lawn a tiny square of green. Something like that happened to me when I returned to Vienna. It seemed diminished somehow. The experience of living in the Caucasus disoriented me at first, then reoriented me. I find myself surveying the world anew and probing its relative worth: Vienna on the one hand, Kutaisi on the other."

"That's it, exactly," I say. "You put your finger on the spot, Bertie. I set out with a sense of Western superiority, but are we superior to the people in the Caucasus? Can we really claim to be more civilized? It seems that our idea of justice is as crudely retributive as theirs. We are as bigoted and judgmental, our clothes as ridiculous and, if anything, less practical than theirs." I want to add, *and our religion is just as irrational and superstitious as theirs*, but the professor cuts in with an ironic query:

"And their treatment of women is as liberal as ours? I understand that men of the Islamic faith are permitted four wives." He winks at Mrs Kapy who obliges him with a smirk.

"Ah," Bertie says, "perhaps women need a homeland, too, a country where they are free to fulfil their potential. I have always believed that women must be more than decorative elements in their drawing rooms, you know."

Herzl looks from Bertie to me and back again. "I see two potential contributors to my paper," he says.

"It would be a challenge for me," I say. "So far I've written only for magazines."

"But that's an achievement in itself," Kapy says with sudden warmth. Perhaps he too had difficulty placing me until now. He shifts his arm. The cuff of his shirt touches my hand, and my heart begins to flutter. My cheeks feel hot. Mrs Kapy is watching me, or am I only imagining it? No, nothing her husband does or says escapes her notice. It's as if they were tethered to each other, although I am not sure which of them is holding the invisible leash. She sends me a look that is hard to interpret, annoyed or ironic? She shapes her mouth into a little moue for a moment then turns to Arthur asking him a question. About me, I think, because he looks in my direction, fleetingly, as if he needed inspiration to answer her.

"Will you attend the international peace conference in the Netherlands?" Herzl asks Bertie. He is willing to pay her travel expenses.

"If you have money to spare, don't spend it on me," she says. "Donate it to the *Friends of Peace*."

"I'm afraid I can't do that," Herzl says. "I couldn't justify the expense to my fellow investors. We have no budget for charitable donations, but we do have a budget for paying contributors and correspondents. I would, of course, expect you to write a report on the conference for the *Welt*."

"In that case, I gladly accept your offer," Bertie says.

The servants are waiting to remove the dessert plates. Bertie rises from the table and nods to the professor, who has sat through the last bit of our conversation under duress.

"Shall we return to the drawing room? Professor Leschetizky has promised to give us a little night music."

By the time the guests leave, it is late, but I'm not ready to go to bed yet. It's been some time since I've had Bertie to myself, and that short conversation we had before dinner left me with many questions. I can see she, too, is eager to talk a little longer. We linger. Arthur knows he is one too many.

"If you'll excuse me," he says and gets up. "I'll retire and leave you to dissect the dinner conversation." Before he goes, he takes Bertie's hand. "Let me congratulate you, my dear," he says. "You always find the right mix of people. I had my doubts, you know. Herzl and Mrs Kapy in one room! But it all went well."

"Thank you, Arthur," she says. "I do think it was a successful evening."

"I share Arthur's reservations about Mrs Kapy," I say to Bertie when we are alone. "She is a little fool."

"Oh, I wouldn't say that. She grew up in unfortunate circumstances. It's not her fault that she was deprived of an education. And I do like her husband. He has the mind of a philosopher. You liked him too, didn't you?"

For a moment I think Bertie is onto me. I scrutinize her face. No, she has no inkling of my secret longings. She is not accusing me of flirting with Nikolaus Kapy. It's a straightforward question.

"I liked him well enough," I say, "but I was puzzled by the conversation. What is his wife's connection with Nobel?"

"I was about to tell you when Herzl arrived," Bertie says. "Mrs Kapy's maiden name is Hess. She is the secretary Emanuel Nobel met at his uncle's house in Paris. I thought she might be able to help you with your biography."

That vapid creature was Nobel's secretary? I remember Emanuel's enigmatic smile and the knowing looks around the table tonight. "You mean to say Nobel was her employer? Or were they lovers?"

Bertie bristles. "What a question. And why would you ask me?"

"Because everything about Nobel interests me. And I can't very well ask Mrs Kapy, can I?"

"I do hope you will be discreet if you decide to approach her for information."

"Before I do that, you must tell me about your correspondence with Nobel. I would rather have his own words than Mrs Kapy's second-hand impressions."

But Bertie is pulling back. I have spoiled the evening with my unfortunate question about Mrs Kapy.

"It is getting awfully late, Ida," she says. "We have all of tomorrow to talk about Alfred Nobel."

Bertie

I slip into the bedroom and undress in the dark. Why didn't I tell Ida the whole story? Because I am afraid of her judgment. Those bright, challenging eyes demand the truth. There is something relentless about Ida.

As I get into bed, Arthur turns to me. He isn't asleep after all, and I nestle into his arms.

"So, you think it was a successful evening?" I whisper as if someone – Ida? – could overhear us.

"A success, in the circumstances," he says.

What circumstances? "Herzl's wife sending her regrets, you mean?"

"No, I expected that. They have agreed to separate. It would have been awkward for her to come along. I was thinking of the Kapys. She has a loose mouth and is prone to gaffes."

"I know, but I wanted her to meet Ida. I thought she might be able to help Ida with her biography of Nobel. I have done all I can do for her. Or want to do. She can be very insistent, very pressing, you know."

"I see. You are passing her on to Mrs Kapy. Did you tell Ida that she was Nobel's lover?"

"She asked me: were they lovers? I said I didn't know."

"But you do."

"It's just a rumor."

"We know at any rate that people called her 'Madame Nobel' before she married Kapy."

"Arthur," I say. "Tell me, did I do the right thing when I accepted Nobel's donation?"

"The ends justify the means," he says, but so quietly that it doesn't soothe my scruples. I lay my head on his shoulder and talk with my lips moving against his chest.

"I didn't look him up in Paris just to solicit a donation, you know."

"I know that, my dear," Arthur says, but nothing more.

I go on, my words muffled by his rising and falling chest, "I wanted to see him again. He is a good man at heart and generous."

"You don't need to convince me, love," Arthur says, stroking my hair. "I am sure you have thought it all through. Now let's get some sleep. It's been a long day."

But I can't sleep. I keep thinking about the Kapys. He did the honorable thing when he married her. But how could she forget herself so completely and yield to a man's embraces without the blessing of the church? And how could Nikolaus Kapy take advantage of her weakness? Or Nobel for that matter? Kapy paid for his misstep at any rate. His family renounced him. He felt obliged to resign his commission – or did so voluntarily for reasons of conscience, as he says, because he is a pacifist – but now, he is reduced to working for a wine merchant. It must be... My mind starts to drift, and when I open my eyes, it is morning. Arthur is no longer by my side. I did not even hear him get up.

Sleep has cleared the tangled thoughts in my mind, but the feeling of unease is creeping back as I wash up and dress. I step into the hall and see Arthur below, coming out of the tea room. He stops at the foot of the stairs and looks up at me.

"Good morning, love," he says. "I just had breakfast with Ida."

"Oh, good. I was hoping you'd keep her company. You are both early risers."

"She was ahead of me. When I came downstairs, she was reading the morning papers. My advice to you is: abandon all thoughts of peace and prepare for battle. She's read your essay in the *Presse*. You will have to come to Mr Nobel's defense."

It will be best to pre-empt Ida. I should have had it out with her yesterday. I meant to tell her about my visit with Nobel in Paris when Herzl arrived. Ida will raise questions, of course, and I have my answers ready, but I hate to be a strategist with friends. I do consider Ida a friend. Or is our friendship under review, I wonder as I enter the tearoom and see Ida's probing look.

As soon as the maid has served my breakfast and we have gotten through the pleasantries, I take a deep breath and say:

"I didn't get around to telling you yesterday: I saw Mr Nobel two months ago when Arthur and I attended a conference in Paris."

The surprise shows in her eyes, but I don't wait for her to ask why I didn't tell her earlier. I go on quickly and talk about our visit to Nobel's house in the Avenue Malakoff. A marvel of interior decorating, I tell her, but sadly empty of life. Nobel has become a loner.

"He looked haggard and complained of ill health. The burden of managing his business is taking its toll, he said. He rarely ventures out into society. He has no time to spare. But you know, what shocked me more than his wretched appearance, was the decline in his mental powers. I think he was aware of it himself. He seemed embarrassed and said something about losing his ability to converse intelligently because he focused too much on his factories and laboratories and neglected the arts. Oh dear, I said, and you wrote such beautiful poetry! 'That was a long time ago,' he said, and his eyes filmed over. I felt sorry for him and asked him to come with us to Juliette Adam. I thought it might cheer him up. She is famous for her soirées, you know. The most distinguished writers and artists meet in her drawing room."

Ida is on the alert. She leans forward as if she needed a better vantage point to take in my words.

"And he joined you?" she says.

"He came along." I give her an account of the evening at Madame Adam's house. She wore a red velvet gown with a long train and a spectacular diamond necklace, I say, but Ida isn't interested in fashions. She won't be diverted from the subject.

"What did you talk about?" she asks.

"Everyone was preoccupied with Bismarck and his military preparations. There was a great deal of speculation among the guests."

"And Nobel? What did he have to say to that?"

"He didn't say much, but it was clear that he enjoyed the discussion. On the drive home, he promised me to go out more, read more literature and get back to writing poetry."

"Did you talk to him about your Society?"

"Of course I did. We had a lively discussion about the possibilities of world peace. I asked him to become a member of the Society."

"And to make a contribution?"

She puts her napkin on the table with a sweeping gesture, as if to throw down the gauntlet, and I must take it up.

"Don't look at me like that, Ida," I say. "Why shouldn't I ask Nobel for a contribution? He can afford to support a good cause. He is a wealthy man."

"He is indeed. He is making money hand over fist. His intellectual powers may have declined, but his business sense is intact. Or, let's say, he still has what it takes to make money: a lack of scruples and a disregard for the welfare of others."

Arthur was right to warn me. This is a duel.

"Tell me, Ida, why would you want to write about a man you so obviously dislike? Why don't you choose a more congenial subject – someone you admire?"

"And why do *you* admire him, Bertie? Because he gives money to your Society? Wasn't it a bit ridiculous to ask the inventor of dynamite to contribute to a group promoting world peace? How can Nobel be interested in peace when his factories supply the warring parties with ammunition?"

"You mistake him, Ida. He meant his invention to be used for peaceful purposes, in mines and construction. They used dynamite when they built the St Gotthard's tunnel through the Alps, you know."

"And they used dynamite to assassinate Tsar Alexander," she says. "Let's face it, Bertie: Alfred Nobel's enterprises provide the world with arms – that is how he makes his money."

"You are being judgmental." No, that was too harsh. Am I putting our friendship on the line? But I must defend Nobel, I must defend myself. "He has always shown a generous spirit," I say. "He has done a great deal for the public good. When his father died, he used his portion of the inheritance to set up a fund for medical research in Sweden. He gives to many good causes, and he is generous to those in need, and he never asks to be given credit for his financial contributions. In fact, he often gives to charity in the name of his mother. He is modest to a fault, you know. When someone wrote a book about famous Swedes, he insisted on having his portrait removed from the chapter that described his achievements."

"If you ask me, it is fear rather than modesty that makes him shy away from publicity. He does not want his picture published because he has enemies and prefers to stay out of the public eye."

"Why would he have enemies?"

"Because he makes his money selling dynamite. And dynamite kills people," Ida says. Her voice is hoarse with zeal. "So what if he gives money to medical research. So what if he is charitable. What does that amount to when you balance it against the shipments of dynamite that leave his factories every day? And you seriously expect him to support your peace efforts?"

"I do. And I am not the only one who thinks well of him. The University of Uppsala has given him an honorary doctorate."

"The question is: Were they honoring the scientist or the millionaire – in the hope that he would give them an endowment?"

"He is a great inventor and has earned his kudos," I say, "but when I congratulated him on the honorary title, he wrote back making fun of it. He has a tendency to make light of all his achievements. He called the medals he received trinkets and pieces of dross. He is like that, you know, too modest. He doesn't believe in himself and is pessimistic about everything. It's a sign of depression if you ask me. That's why he is hiding away. He thinks no one can possibly want to associate with him or like him as a human being. People seek him out only because he is wealthy. 'Grateful stomachs and grateful hearts are twins,' he said to me."

"Thank you. Another quip to add to my collection of Nobel anecdotes," Ida says. "But I don't see why you call that a sign of depression. It merely sums up his experience. People exploit him." She gives me a sidelong glance as if to say, "After all, didn't *you* ask him for money?"

"I give up, Ida. You keep asking me for information about Mr Nobel, but you don't want to listen to what I have to say. For some reason, you have conceived a dislike for him. And you sound so bitter!"

Ida struggles to compose herself. "I am sorry," she says. "I should learn to be a better listener." Her words are conciliatory, but her eyes remain implacable. I don't want to go on, but before I can come up with something to end our talk, Ida jumps in with another question.

"So, Nobel made you a promise to take a greater interest in the arts and return to his literary pursuits. Has he made good on his promise?"

I hesitate. "He has started writing again," I say. It seems I cannot extricate myself from this awkward conversation, Ida's sharp questions, my lame answers. She is waiting for me to go on. "He is writing a play," I tell her, "a historical drama."

Ida's eyes turn a shade more benevolent. "What about?"

I waver. "I'm not sure." I am not sure whether I should tell her. He has chosen an unfortunate subject.

"He hasn't told you?"

I shake my head and detest myself for the unspoken lie.

She purses her lips. "Machiavelli would make a suitable subject."

"Ida, Nobel is not amoral. He has a conscience, believe me. He struggles, as we all do – you should read his letters to me."

The moment the words are out of my mouth, I want to take them back. I spoke on impulse, but it sounded like an offer, and Ida pounces on it.

"By all means," she says. "Let me read them."

I demur. "I couldn't do that without his permission. It would be a breach of privacy."

She glares at me across the breakfast table. "You weren't worried about Nobel's privacy when you quoted his letter in the essay you submitted to the *Presse.*"

"You don't think I went ahead without his permission, Ida? He has made it very clear to me that he does not want his letters circulated. In fact, he asked me – and all his friends, he said – to return his letters. He is in poor health and feeling close to death. He is afraid of being misunderstood or misrepresented after his death. He wants to burn his papers. I begged him not to destroy all testimony to his goodness and to trust me. I would never harm his reputation."

"Letters don't make a man's reputation. His life does," Ida says and gives me a stern look.

"In any case, he was adamant about the letters, and I will return them as requested."

"Then perhaps you should introduce me to him, and I will put my questions to him directly."

I know when I am defeated. "Very well," I say, even though I am afraid she will offend him if she writes with her usual candor. "I'll tell him that you are planning to write about his life and work and would like to enter into correspondence with him. I'll let you know as soon as he replies."

"Thank you," she says, momentarily appeased. "I'm going to San Remo next week, but I'll give you my forwarding address."

I am thunderstruck.

"San Remo!" I exclaim. I am sure she can hear the apprehension in my voice, but she goes on casually.

"Not on my own money, of course. Mrs Olmuth has asked me to come along as her companion. The doctor advised her to spend a few weeks in the south, and San Remo is all the rage this season. Everyone is wintering there, everyone who can afford it. I thought I might write a piece on San Remo for Carl. He thinks my collection of travel essays is a little thin."

It sounds plausible. Perhaps it *is* a coincidence that Ida is going to San Remo.

We part on civil terms, but I cannot rid myself of the suspicion that Ida is pursuing a secret agenda. Our friendship has developed a hairline fracture. Perhaps the fissure has been there for a while, and I've noticed it only now because the gap has widened, and we are pulling apart.

I knew Ida would touch the sore spot, Nobel's donation to the Society. I knew we'd have an argument. She is right about the evil consequences of Nobel's invention, I admit that much, and yet I feel obliged to defend him. Can an inventor foresee or control the use of his invention? And when he becomes aware of the consequences, can he stop the process? I don't think so. He can only regret the past and atone for it. That is the reason Nobel offered to support my cause and why I feel justified accepting his gift of money. It is a gesture of atonement.

I admire his spirit. Someone ought to commemorate his life, his struggle, his successes and, yes, his shortcomings as well. He isn't a god. He is human after all. But is Ida the right person for the task? I wish Nobel a kinder biographer.

There has been so much grief and suffering in his life. He grew up in poverty. He was forced to sell matches on street corners, he told me. His childhood was bleak. He counted it a special day if he escaped a beating by his teacher or by the bullies in the schoolyard, he said. That is why he feels such compassion for the poor and disadvantaged. *I don't ask where a man's father was born, or what god he worships,* he said to me. *Helpfulness recognizes no national borders and seeks no confessions.*

Later, when his father made a fortune in construction, he enjoyed all the trappings of wealth, but he felt lonely and misunderstood even by those nearest to him. His father sent him abroad only to make him forget his "silly" ideas of becoming a writer. How different Nobel's life could have been if his father had nurtured his literary interests. He has a gift for language, no doubt about it. He is a talented poet. Of course, that only deepens the conundrum – how can a man be a poet *and* an arms dealer?

The ends justify the means, Arthur said, but he loves me and is indulgent. Ida makes no concessions. She doesn't mince her words. *Isn't it absurd to ask an arms dealer to support peace?* she asked. There is no simple answer to her question.

I know that Nobel is open to the idea of world peace. I have it in writing, and I am reluctant to let go of the proof. But he has asked for his letters back, and I respect his wishes. I have gathered our correspondence. The letters are sitting on my desk ready to be mailed, but before I return them, I want to read his words once more to reassure myself of his goodwill. He does want peace, even if he won't endorse my ideas wholeheartedly and camouflages his good intentions with black humor. When I sent him a copy of *Lay Down Your Arms* and asked him to promote my book, he replied: *It's a little cruel of you to expect me to praise your manifesto of peace, isn't it? Where do you expect me to sell my new powder if universal peace breaks out? You want to do away with arms – very well, but be charitable and do away also with poverty, prejudice and the bigotry of religion. Down with old Jehovah and his son, whose reputation is overrated, and the Holy Spirit who is no holy spirit, and the whole shop of worm-eaten antiquities!*

I can't defend those words. They are blasphemy. They are hurtful. He went on to say that my efforts were nothing but *fairy-land dreaming*.

My god, I replied. *I know very well that neither societies nor conferences can abolish warfare, but they can change public opinion! Don't ridicule my efforts,* I wrote. *Don't call my plans for world peace empty dreams. Speak more gently and give me encouragement.*

Yes, let him burn those letters. I don't want his sarcastic words or my pleas to become public knowledge. They give the wrong impression of Nobel. His words may be harsh, but his feelings are tender. He is a melancholic rather than a cynic. Byron is his favorite poet – that says it all, doesn't it? And in spite of ridiculing my idealism, he is an idealist himself. He told me that he will set up a foundation to promote arts and sciences. There will be annual prizes to honor achievements in physics, chemistry, medicine, literature and economics. And why not a prize for promoting peace? I said. He was not entirely averse to the idea. *I may fund a peace prize every five years, up to six times,* he wrote. *If, in thirty years, there is no success in reforming the present system of settling disagreements by means of war, it can't be done. And I rather suspect that will be the outcome. I still think that your idea of complete and lasting disarmament is a dream. It isn't possible to force nations to submit to an international court, as you suggest. A better solution would be for all countries to agree and oblige themselves to act against the country that attacks first. Such an agreement would be worth a prize.*

That is one letter I hope he will not destroy. But the play he is writing! I wish he would burn the manuscript. *The Rape of Beatrice Cenci*. I couldn't tell Ida. She would have turned the title into a weapon, and I would have lost that duel of words. Why did Nobel take up the infamous story of a father raping his daughter? Shelley wrote on the same subject, I know, but he is a notorious radical, fond of shocking people with his disregard for convention and morality. I can see why he would choose to write on the subject of incest and rape. He is an advocate of free love and unfettered emotions. But Nobel? I cannot imagine why he would be drawn to those themes.

He says he has treated the subject with discretion. *I was careful not to give offense and have aimed only at the effet scénique,* he wrote, but I don't know what he means by "scenic effect".

He enclosed extracts from the play to convince me of its merit or to move me perhaps.

You who read in my heart the misery of my whole life, you know that ever since my childhood days, I have been the victim of abuse of every imaginable kind. Hunger, lashings, insults – nothing has been spared me.

No doubt those words recall his own poverty-stricken childhood, but I know what Ida would say: Maudlin self-pity!

There were other lines that made me hesitate and wonder why Nobel would quote them to me. They are hardly to his credit.

Stupid moralists preach about improving people...

Ida would pounce on that line and say it proves his amorality. She would point a finger at another passage as well:

If an intelligent girl must choose between a youth and a mature man, she will always prefer the older one. Her instinct tells her that the man's experience of a woman's nature is an invaluable treasure. Young women do not thrive in inexperienced hands. The love of a young man is clumsy.

Those words are spoken by the abominable Cenci, but a critic might say they express Nobel's own opinion. If they do, I cannot agree with him. Arthur was very young when we married, and I found happiness with him. But Nobel is entitled to his opinion. He has written a play, not a philosophical treatise requiring cogent proofs.

When my book came out, I asked him to recommend it to his friends. Now he has asked me to recommend his play in turn. He will send me a copy once it is finished, he wrote. Did I have any connections to stage managers in Vienna? Even if I had connections and could persuade them to take on the play, it would do no good. The censors would never approve a play about incest. Nothing escapes their sharp eyes. Every day, newspaper editors are told to delete passages. The whited out patches in the dailies attest to the censors' zeal for public morality.

"I can't do anything for Nobel in that matter," I said to Arthur.

"Quite right," he said. "And there is no need to truckle to him."

Am I truckling to him?

I gather up the letters and ready them for the mail. Out of sight, out of mind? I doubt it. The scruples will stay with me.

Sophie

The man at the reception desk is buttoning his jacket as if he had just come from an afternoon tryst. He adjusts the brim of his cap as she passes by.

"Good morning, Mrs Kapy," he says, leaning forward, closing his lips over her name as if he was suppressing laughter, or is she imagining that? "There is a letter here for you, Mrs Kapy."

She takes it from his hand. An invitation, she hopes. Life has been so boring lately. There is always a lull after the ball season. In the elevator, on the way up to her suite, she opens the envelope eagerly, but it's only a reply from Ida Lassick. She thanks Sophie for her inquiry. She will call on her this afternoon. It was Nikki's idea. "Ask Miss Lassick to help you with your memoirs," he said. "She is discreet. Countess Fronberg paid her to put together a family history. Miss Lassick got the money, and the countess got the credit for the book."

Sophie isn't sure she wants to do it that way, but it may be the only way to let people know her side of the story. Everyone thinks she was lucky to find a wealthy benefactor. No one considers the sacrifices she made to keep Alfred happy.

The elevator boy opens the clanking doors, and Sophie turns to the apartment at the end of the corridor. The air is pungent with the smell of gas jets lighting the corridor. There are no electric lights on the fourth floor. The management has kept the renovations to the first two floors, the *belles étages*. Those refurbished apartments are too expensive, Nikki says, but they *could* afford them if he didn't keep a separate establishment!

She stuffs Ida Lassick's letter back into the envelope and unlocks the door to her apartment.

Czerny is getting Gretel ready for her afternoon walk. She can hear her whining. "I don't like those stockings, Nanny. They are itchy." And Nanny's steady voice: "They are not. It's all in your head, child."

Sophie stands in the door: "Be a good girl, Gretel," she says. "The new stockings look very nice. You want to look nice, don't you?"

Gretel gives her a martyred look.

Sophie hugs her close. "Oh, you are such a mug," she says, "but Mommy loves you anyway."

She goes back into the drawing room and takes up the sheet of paper sitting on the side table. She has started to write her memoirs. Nikki is right, she thinks, I need help. She looks over what she has written so far. The lines slope toward the right, the letters are a jumble. She doesn't have a neat hand, but worse, she doesn't have the words. She got stuck after three paragraphs.

She thought it would be easy. Call up the memories – the flower shop, the first kiss, the villa in Ischl and the rest would follow, with her mind dictating the words. She never thought it would be such a chore to write it all down. I can't do it, she thinks, but I can't give up now. I have to put my life with Alfred on record before I return the letters to him. I need something to hold on to and keep the story straight. I owe it to Gretel. I'm doing it for her. Well, perhaps I'm doing it for myself as well, to see it spelled out in black and white: it wasn't my fault that I lived the way I did. Alfred must take some of the blame. Why do people condemn me? Why don't they condemn him? But that's how it is. They talk of fallen women, never of fallen men.

At first, she only wanted to copy Alfred's letters before sending them back, to string them up in chronological order and add a few words, giving her side of the story, but Nikki said she couldn't do that. The letters were Alfred's intellectual property. "What do you mean?" she said. "When he sent me flowers or hats or gloves, they were mine to keep. They became my property."

"That's different," Nikki said. "He paid for those things and made you a gift of them. The letters remain his, and he wants them back. You can't use his exact words. You have to paraphrase them if you want to include them in your memoir. You need to change the words," he said, but she can't think of new words to put in place of the old ones.

One more try before Ida Lassick comes! She picks up a pen and looks at the sheet of paper in front of her, searching for words. Nothing, nothing. Her mind is blank.

She goes back to the top of the page and looks over what she has written so far.

Life was hard for me after my mother died and my father remarried. My stepmother didn't want me hanging around the house. She had a temper and when I said anything she didn't like she slapped my face and called me a stupid idjit. Paying for my education was a waste of money she said and I was old enough to earn my keep, so I started working in a flower shop in Baden. One day this gentleman came in and made eyes at me. He looked so elgant and I was a teenager and knew nothing of the world, so I blushed and one thing led to another and he asked me out. Then he asked me to come to Paris, that's where he lived. He rented an apartment for me there. Later we went to Ischl, where he rented a villa for me. Of course I was dazled. I had never seen so much money before, so much, that one day he asked his housekeeper what she wanted for a birthday present and she said 'What you make in one day, sir' and he gave her forty thousand francs, at least that's what he told me but maybe he was joking and I was naive to believe him. We were very close. I called him my Grouchy-Bear and he called me his sweet child and his little froggie. So of course I expected him to marry me but he said: "I never pretended to be a seeker of hearts and have, therefore, no obligations." Oh, he could be cruel! And he left me alone so much. I said "Why are your letters always so short?" And he wrote back: Women, and you especially, are egoists who think only of themselves. I am a busy man and can't always entertain you, so don't get too fond of me. The time will come when your heart will be filled with love for another man, and then you will be glad to get away. *He was wrong!*

She wasn't glad to get away. She did fall in love with Nikki, but it didn't last.

Marriage to Nikki was supposed to be her ticket to society, but she still sensed a small reservation in people's voices and in their eyes. She was on sufferance. That's why it's important to write her memoirs and let them know how it really was, but she needs help putting it all down on paper.

Sophie tucks away the sheet of paper inside a fashion magazine. Her visitor will be here any minute now, and Nanny is still arguing with Gretel. Now it's about her new doll.

"Czerny!" she calls out. "It's time for you to go." They are supposed to wait for Nikki in the lobby. He will take them for a ride in the park.

Gretel stands in the door of her room with the doll under her arm, pink lace trailing.

Czerny comes bustling after her. "No, child, put her back on the chair."

Gretel pulls a face. "Mommy," she says, "can I take along the doll?"

"You heard what Nanny said." Sophie can't keep the impatience out of her voice.

114

Gretel moans but takes the doll back to her room.

"Ready?" she says to the child when she returns, but Czerny is still fussing over her, smoothing out the band holding back Gretel's silky hair.

"There," she says. "Now we are ready to go."

Her sweet little girl! She is as cute as a button in her white coat with the pink braiding and those delicately ribbed stockings and black lacquered shoes. Czerny, standing beside her, looks like a crow in her long black coat and a hat like a bird's nest.

Sophie gives the child a fond kiss.

"Have fun, sweetie," she says.

The doorbell rings.

"Will you get it on your way out?" she says to Czerny and retreats to the sofa.

She hears Nanny open the door and ask Miss Lassick in.

Through the half-open door, she watches Nanny take the woman's coat and carelessly hang it on a hook by the hall mirror. She wants to tell me that it isn't her job to look after coats, Sophie thinks.

"Let's go," Czerny says to Gretel and pulls her out into the corridor, leaving Miss Lassick standing in the ante-room.

"Come in," Sophie calls.

She makes a feint of getting up from the sofa as her visitor comes into the drawing room. It wouldn't do to show too much deference to Ida Lassick, she thinks. This isn't a social call. Not really. I want to hire her services.

She sinks back onto the blue and gold striped cushions and stretches out a limp hand.

"Have a seat," she says. How dowdy the woman looks in that brown suit! It doesn't go with her complexion. If my cheeks had that healthy glow, I'd wear powder blue, she thinks. It's her favorite color, but her own complexion is a little too pale to go with powder blue.

The maid has set out a silver tray with coffee things on the table. She can see the sheet of paper, the beginning of her memoirs, peeking out between the pages of the fashion magazine on the settee beside her.

"Was that your daughter?" Miss Lassick says and sits down in the chair facing her.

Sophie breathes a sigh. "My poor child. Children always pay for the sins of their fathers."

She can see the question in Miss Lassick's eyes: Is Gretel Alfred's child? They all want to know, but of course, no one has the nerve to ask her straight out.

"I didn't realize—" Miss Lassick says.

Sophie holds up her hand. "Don't," she says. "Don't make me say more than I should."

Miss Lassick makes another attempt to get an answer without asking a question. "I didn't know there was a child."

Sophie gives her only an enigmatic smile.

"Coffee?" she says and pours two cups. "I told Nanny to take the child for a walk. Domestics are so nosy, always hanging around and listening for a bit of gossip."

"I understand your concern," she says. "It's a sensitive matter. You are planning to write about your life with Mr Nobel?"

"So many people want to know about me and Alfred," Sophie says with a sigh, "so many, that I've started to write it all down."

She can see the questioning look in Miss Lassick's eyes. Who are the people wanting to know about her and Alfred? But she doesn't ask that question either. Instead, she says:

"It's helpful to have a written record."

"Exactly. For one thing, people can't misquote me. But I find I'm not very good at the task. So when I heard that writing was your profession, I thought you could help me and look over my manuscript."

"You mean edit what you have written?"

"Whatever you call it. Fix it up. Could you do that?"

"Before we go on, Mrs Kapy, I should tell you that I was on the point of writing to *you* when I received your note. I meant to ask you about your life with Mr Nobel. I am working on his biography, you see, and have been collecting material for some time now."

"Oh," Sophie says. "In that case, perhaps we can do the biography together. I'll give you the information, and you put it in words. No one knows Alfred better than I."

Miss Lassick lowers her eyes, but Sophie has already seen the familiar reservation. She doesn't take me seriously, she thinks.

"It isn't as simple as that," Miss Lassick says. "We may find that we are pulling in different directions. A memoir contains personal reminiscences. My biography is more concerned with Mr Nobel's business ventures."

116

"It was only an idea," Sophie says. "If you don't think it's feasible, you can just help me with my memoirs, the way you helped Countess Fronberg with her genealogy. At least, that's what everybody says, that you wrote it for her."

"Who said that?"

Sophie shrugs. "Oh, never mind." She pulls the sheet of paper out of the magazine. "I've made a beginning," she says and hands over the page. "Why don't you read it and tell me what you think and if you are interested in editing it."

"Read it now, you mean?"

"It won't take you long, will it?"

Miss Lassick takes the page and runs an eye over the lines. When she gets to the end, she looks up.

"And he really told you that he felt no obligation toward you and did not want your affection to deepen?" she asks.

There is eagerness in her eyes now. I've caught her interest, Sophie thinks. I can tell she is dying to read more.

"That's exactly what he said. It comes straight out of his letters," she says. "I kept them all, you know. They are very dear to me."

"I'm glad you've kept the letters, and perhaps you will allow me to read them one day."

"No, I couldn't do that. They were meant for my eyes only, you know. But I felt I had to quote those bits, or people will say I made it up."

"I think you are wise to quote his words literally."

"But as it turns out, I can't. Nikki says the letters are Alfred's intellectual property, and I must paraphrase them. Is that true?"

"He may be right. Perhaps you should keep to your own reminiscences."

"I can't tell you how much it costs me to recall my life with Alfred. It was not all happiness."

She expects Miss Lassick to ask a follow-up question about her unhappiness. She wants people to know that it wasn't easy to live with Alfred, but instead she asks:

"Do you intend to publish your memoirs?"

"I've had offers, or maybe I should say, I've been encouraged to go on writing."

"Offers from publishers, you mean?"

Sophie hesitates. She hasn't received any offers, she hasn't even told anyone that she is writing her memoirs. Nikki is the only one in the know, but Ida Lassick needs to be taught a lesson. She has been so quick to dismiss the idea of cooperation. She wants her to understand that her life counts.

"I don't know whether to call them publishers," she says. "Scandalmongers, more like it. If I publish my memoirs, I want them to be taken seriously. It's a true story. Alfred was the love of my life, and I don't want people to make fun of my naivety, or say I'm a gold-digger. Men tend to think that way at any rate. I don't expect sympathy from men. I thought you – being a woman – would understand better what I've been through."

"Life must have been difficult for you, Mrs Kapy, but if you really want my help, you will have to let me read more than a sample of your writing."

Life must have been difficult. Sophie listens to the echo of those words. Is there condescension in Miss Lassick's voice, or pity? Will she be sympathetic when she hears the rest of her story? She can't make up her mind whether to trust this woman with her memories. What if she takes the information and puts it into her biography?

"I would need some security before I part with all the information."

"What do you have in mind?" Miss Lassick says.

She is so plain-spoken. Her words match the style of her clothes. Nothing to soften her words or give them a pleasant ring.

"I've been offered two hundred florins for the completed manuscript," Sophie says.

"I'm sorry, Mrs Kapy, I can't pay you for information, if that is your meaning." She pauses. "On the contrary. I make my living as a writer and would have to charge a fee for editing your manuscript or assisting you in writing your memoirs."

"Oh, please. This is getting too complicated," Sophie says with a little shrug. "Let's forget about the manuscript and just talk. I wouldn't have mentioned money if I weren't so hard pressed. The rent here… no, I won't complain. I just want you to understand how innocent I was when I met Alfred. He offered to buy me a villa in Döbling, and I said no, it's too far away from the center of the city. 'But it's a desirable location,' he said. 'Some very good people live there.' Then it must be horribly expensive, I said to him, and I don't want you to go through all that expense for me. 'Have a look at it at least,' he said. So I did, but it was too grand for my taste and too out of the way. No, I said to Alfred, I need to breathe the city air."

She waits for a response, but Miss Lassick only gives her a polite please-go-on smile.

"Well, even if he had bought me a place right here in the city, I couldn't afford it now. It's so expensive to keep domestics. That's why I live here. It's an economic necessity. I kept Czerny on because Gretel needs a nanny. The hotel takes care of everything else. And the heating is included too. Sometimes, I'm embarrassed to receive people in my drawing room here. It's so cramped, but the hotel still has a certain prestige. And it's centrally located." She checks her flow of words. "But of course you aren't interested in all that. You want to know about me and Alfred."

"You were his companion for many years?"

"Half a lifetime! But don't ask me the year we met. I have no head for numbers and dates."

"When you were a teenager, you said in your memoir."

"My memoir – you know I am beginning to dislike that word. It makes me sound like an old woman on her deathbed. I won't call it a memoir. I'll call it—" She lifts up her arms and spreads her fingers as if to indicate a marquee. "I'll call it *The Sad Story of My Love*—"

There is a knock on the door. She frowns.

Are they back already? But Czerny has a key. It can't be her. She would let herself in.

"Would you mind checking who it is?" she says to Miss Lassick, pulling rank. There has been a subtle shift in their relationship. As it turns out, Miss Lassick wants information from her. She is a supplicant.

Miss Lassick understands it too. She gets up readily, goes out into the hall and opens the door.

It's Livy. Mrs Mark Twain. Yes, the Metropole finally has a genuine celebrity among its residents – the famous American author. The hotel is definitely on the upswing, and that's good, as long as their rates stay the same. Mark Twain's name is golden. When Sophie mentioned it at her last visit to the Thurns, the baroness, who always lapses into a bored drawl when she talks to her, perked up and grasped her arm. *Oh, you've met the Twains, Sophie? You must tell me all about them.*

She can see Livy through the open drawing room door, craning her head, looking past Miss Lassick.

"Is Mrs Kapy in?" she says with her American twang. Her hand goes up to her hair, a braid tightly coiled around the top of her head.

"Livy, is that you?" Sophie calls out. She gets up and stands at the door of the drawing room.

"Mrs Twain. Miss Lassick," she says, introducing the two women. Then she gives them a helpless look as if to say, "What am I going to do with the two of you in this cramped space?"

"I am interrupting," Livy says in her correct German. "I shall come back another time."

"No, *I* am interrupting." Miss Lassick says. "Thank you so much for your time, Mrs Kapy."

She reaches for her coat. Sophie doesn't hold her back.

"Don't mention it, my dear," she says.

Miss Lassick's hand is on the doorknob. She turns. "May I call again another time?"

"Oh, of course. Call again," Sophie says lightly, carelessly, knowing she has won that round.

She takes possession of Livy's arm. "Do come in," she says. She loves talking to Livy. She is so understanding.

*

The afternoon creeps like the sun's shadow. Sophie looks at the half-empty coffee cups and the crumpled napkins. Livy didn't stay long. She was in a hurry. Miss Lassick barely touched the sweets and took only a few sips of coffee, as if she didn't want to be sidetracked.

She never took her eyes off me the whole time she was here, Sophie thinks. She isn't keen on helping me with my memoir, but she wants to know everything about Alfred. She reminds me of a hunting dog – the same alertness as if she was picking up a scent, the same concentration listening to the sound of my voice, as if I was her quarry. Perhaps that's what writers are like, on the lookout for other people's secrets, for material to put into their books. I didn't feel at ease with her at all. It was a relief when Livy called and put an end to Miss Lassick's visit. It would have been so nice to have a leisurely talk with Livy about everything – the memoir, Alfred demanding his letters back, Nikki keeping his distance, the constant want of money. But Livy never stays long. She is always in a hurry. In and out. That's how it is if you have a famous husband and a thousand social obligations, Sophie thinks. Samuel Clemens – Mark Twain as he styles himself – is in demand. And Livy looks after her man. She fusses about him and coddles him.

There was a time when Sophie fussed over her man. The memories rise up and escape with a deep breath. She can't help sighing. Alfred used to sign his letters *Your Grouchy-Bear* and expected her to take care of him. Mark Twain is a bear of a man, too, but more loveable, a fuzzy kind of bear, gruff-looking but harmless.

Livy is a lucky woman, Sophie thinks. Well, maybe not. Her daughter is ill. If Gretel ever – no, I don't even want to think about that. My sweet little girl. She's healthy, thank God. But Livy, poor Livy, she wants to spend as much time as she can with her daughter. She doesn't want to leave Jean by herself for any length of time. Of course. I understand. But it means we can never have a good long chat. And there is so much I want to talk about – to a friend. That's what I need: a woman friend.

She thinks of all that has been left unsaid between her and Miss Lassick. All those things she couldn't tell a stranger are crowding her head now. There is no one to share them with. There is Nikki, of course, but he is so distant. No, that's not the right word. He listens to her, but he doesn't really care. He doesn't care about anything. Life is a shrug for him now that he is no longer in the army.

She has always been unlucky in her choice of men. That's where the memoir comes in. She can write everything down, get it out of her head and onto paper, the good times she had with Alfred in Paris, the summers at the spas in Carlsbad and Trouville, the winters in Merano, the luxurious villas, the carriage rides, the shopping sprees – and the wretched time she had after Alfred lost interest in her. His accusations. She was frivolous, he said, and running around with a fast crowd. What was she supposed to do when he was away on business? Sit around and mope? Was it a sin if she went to a few dances or a private entertainment or placed a few bets at the tables in the casino? Was it surprising that she listened to the flatteries of gentlemen when Alfred left her soul parched and longing for gentle words? And there was Nikki, always ready to keep her company, never complaining of aches and pains or of the hour being late, never calling her frivolous or foolish. There was fire in his eyes then and on his lips, a teasing smile that stirred her soul, and sometimes a rush of laughter that gave her a thrill.

He has changed a great deal, she thinks. He used to be hungry for life, indefatigable when it came to having fun, almost desperate for it. Then he resigned his commission in the army and stopped being fun. When she asked Nikki what was wrong, he put on a quizzical smile. The look in his eyes became impenetrable. There was no more laughter, no more lively conversations. The words dried up. Silence descended on them. Is that what civilian life does to a man? Or is it the natural progression of an affair, passion congealing into habit or, worse, turning into distaste? She could see the same decline of affection in Alfred's letters. The first year, it was *my sweet Sophie, my little froggie, I am so lonely without you, I miss your charming prattle, I send you a thousand kisses.* Then it was: *Why don't you read some books and improve your mind? Why don't you learn French? Why don't you get a chaperone* – some doughty matron to stop the fun. And at the worst possible time, he told her it was over.

She hears the key turn in the lock and Czerny's voice in the hall:

"That coat will need brushing, Gretel. Dog hair all over it!"

Sophie calls to the child, opens her arms wide and plants a kiss on her rosebud mouth.

"You are back, sweetie! Did you have a nice ride in Papa's phaeton? Did he bring Bella along?"

"Yes, Mama. Bella was so happy to see me. She jumped up on me and wanted to give me a kiss, but Nanny—" She looks at Czerny accusingly.

"I put a stop to it and said to Mr Kapy: Don't let her kiss the dog. God knows where that animal has been rooting around. In the gutter, no doubt. But I get no help from Mr Kapy. He lets the child get away with anything. Well, the less said the better."

Sophie gives her daughter an indulgent smile. "You miss Bella, you poor thing, don't you? I miss her too, you know."

"Then why can't I bring her here?"

"The hotel would charge us extra, and Mommy can't afford it."

"Why would they charge us extra for Bella?"

"Because she is troublesome. She barks when other people are sleeping, and she doesn't know how to use the toilet. In any case, that's why I got you Wow-Wow. Don't you love your Wow-Wow anymore?"

"I do, but he isn't a real dog. He is just a toy," Gretel says.

She is too wise for her age. Sophie doesn't like to see so much knowledge in the child's eyes. She wants Gretel to be thoughtless and worry-free a little longer.

"So where did Papa take you today?" she says.

"We drove along the Ringstrasse."

"And was it fun?"

"It was all right, but Papa knows ever so many people, and we had to stop all the time and talk."

"What did you talk about?"

"Boring stuff. Plays people saw at the theatre. And a lot of names and places I don't know. And who will be invited to the dance at someone's house next Friday."

"Talk that was unsuitable for a little girl's ears, if you ask me, madam," Czerny says. "So we got out of the phaeton and walked ahead to the Volksgarten and met up with Mr Kapy there."

"Nanny says the Volksgarten used to be the emperor's private park, but he allows people to go for walks there now. That's nice of him, isn't it?" Gretel says. "I thought we might see the empress, but Nanny says she is spending the winter in Biarritz where it's warm. Can we go to Biarritz, Mama?"

"We might – well, maybe not to Biarritz, which is very expensive, but Merano, which is just as nice."

Those were the good days when Alfred was still in love with her. *Perhaps we could buy a little villa in Merano, Sophie. They say that the winters are very agreeable there. Or if Merano doesn't suit you, we could go to Switzerland, to Ragatz or Vevey.* He ended up buying a villa on the Italian Riviera, but that was after they parted ways.

"When will we go to Merano, Mama? Soon?"

"Next winter perhaps, my love – if everything goes according to your mommy's plans."

"And can Bella come, too?"

"I'll inquire about it." People in Italy were more understanding than people here, where everything had to be done according to the rules. It was really tiresome. "But you haven't finished telling me about what you did at the Volksgarten, sweetheart."

"Papa caught up with us and we went to a building in the middle of the park. It's made to look like a temple, Papa said, which is where people went to pray before they had churches, and Bella ran up and down the steps. We couldn't go inside the temple because the doors were chained up. I peeked through the gap between the doors, but it was all dark inside and smelled bad. Bella wanted to go in though, and I had to pull her back. Papa said she can smell other dogs because they did their business in there. And Nanny was annoyed with him for saying that."

"It wasn't polite," Czerny says with dignity. She frowns at the disarray on the coffee table. "Shall I ring for the maid to put the coffee things away, madam?"

"Yes, thank you, Czerny," Sophie says. She gets up and straightens her skirt. The sheet of paper, the beginnings of her memoir, is sitting on the side table, in plain sight. She wouldn't want Czerny or the maid to get her hands on it. She picks up the sheet and puts it back into her writing desk. Before locking it, she lightly touches the two bundles of letters there – Alfred's letters, tied with a red silk ribbon, and the copies of her replies, tied with a black velvet ribbon, almost as if she was grieving his death. Well, she is grieving the death of his love.

Ida

I'm fighting for my life among the ruins of a factory with blown-out windows and a caved-in roof. I struggle to get up, but my arms and legs are pinned down under a fallen beam. I am gasping for air. My chest contracts painfully, I push out a jagged cry and wake from my dream. Even after I've stopped flailing and lie on my bed, quietly looking up at the ceiling of the hotel room, I feel the devastation. The cry has shredded my throat. My breath comes in ragged bursts. I sit up. It's early morning, too early for breakfast, but I dress and go downstairs. Perhaps I can walk off my nightmare.

The sun has barely risen over the terraced hills of San Remo. The doorman of the hotel flashes me a doubtful look. He opens his mouth and closes it again, remembering the first rule of hotel employees: mind your own business. I brush by him and stand on the pavement, turning into the wind, allowing the morning breeze to carry away my dream.

If it weren't for those dreams, my stay here would be a holiday. Mrs Olmuth treats me more like a niece than a paid companion, but neither her kindness nor the genteel atmosphere of the hotel can keep the terrors at bay. At night, I stay up late, reading. I am afraid of going to bed and closing my eyes. I lie on my back, floating between waking and sleeping until I am overcome by exhaustion. Sometimes I try the remedy of an erotic fantasy. I call up the brown limbs of Totia or the elegant hands and sensuous lips of Nikolaus Kapy, but as soon as I drift into sleep, the amorous tussle with my dream lovers turns into a life-and-death combat and lands me back on the battlefield of Heleneborg.

Perhaps walking is a better remedy. Slowly, my breathing returns to normal, and I begin to see the outside world – the promenade, the glittering expanse of the ocean and the palm trees, their topknots swaying in the wind. Reason is getting the upper hand, telling me to live in the present and savor the mild climate, talk to people, take notes, think of what I might put into an essay about San Remo. There are only three days left before our return home, and I haven't met any interesting characters yet, just the usual

– society matrons in search of a wealthy husband for their daughters, young men in search of a dowered bride.

It's an ungodly hour for a woman to be out for a stroll by herself. The promenade is deserted. The only other person in sight is a gentleman. The distance between us does not allow me to judge whether he is indeed a gentleman or a cad, airing his sodden head after a night of drinking. He does, at any rate, move in an erratic way that makes me think he is drunk. For a moment, I consider turning around, but it is safer to keep him in sight than to have him in my back. Besides, this could be the interesting character I've been waiting for, the highlight of my essay on San Remo. So I walk on. As I get closer, I realize that he is not drunk at all but in distress.

He is an older gentleman, respectable, judging by his well-cut clothes, his carefully knotted cravat and the silver-tipped walking stick. Yet there is something wild about him – his hollow eyes perhaps, or his grizzled beard and thick black brows which meet on the bridge of his nose. He has come to a halt and is standing slightly hunched over, his cheeks pale and glistening with sweat.

I step closer and ask if he is all right.

He raises his head with difficulty and answers me in a raspy voice, "As right as I can be at my age." His Italian is slightly accented. A Prussian, I think and switch to German.

"Perhaps you should rest for a bit."

He switches to German as well. He is as competent in that language as he seemed to be in Italian, but he speaks with the same slight accent. German isn't his mother tongue.

"I refuse to rest," he says. "It's one of my principles. I reckon I'll have time enough to rest when I'm in the grave." He attempts a weak smile.

"But one ought to be flexible in one's principles," I say in the same spirit, "and make exceptions when advisable."

"Ah, madam," he says, "I see you are a philosopher. I shall yield to your superior wisdom."

He allows me to lead him to a bench. We sit down and make desultory conversation. He is the melancholy type, or maybe that's just a reflection of his age and ill health.

"I am keeping you from your walk, madam," he says after a while. "You are very kind to entertain me, but I assure you I am feeling better. You need not stay with me. All I need is rest. I only wish I had brought a book. I have a great dislike for wasting my time doing nothing."

I always carry a book with me, and not only for the pleasure of reading. It's a useful expedient. When I run into a chatty old woman or an importunate gentleman, I bury my nose in the pages of a book and there's an end to the unwanted conversation.

I pull the book out of my purse and offer it to him. It's Bertie's manifesto of pacifism, *Lay Down Your Arms.*

"I don't know if this will suit your taste," I say, "but you are free to borrow the book and return it at your convenience." I give him the name of my hotel. "Just leave it at the reception desk for me: Ida Lassick."

"Ida Lassick?" he says, and gives me a curious look, almost as if he was familiar with my name or wanted to know more about me, but he asks no question. Instead, he opens the book to the title page. "Ah, yes," he says, "Bertha von Suttner's book."

Before long we are engaged in a spirited discussion about war and peace. He is well spoken and a man of original thought. "What is needed," he says, "are weapons so frightfully effective and devastating that they will keep countries from starting wars altogether."

I could say a great deal about devastating weapons and their manufacture, but I hold back. It touches on my personal loss, and I have no intention of telling my story to a stranger.

Our conversation seems to revive the old gentleman. The color comes back into his cheeks. I get up to go. It is safe to leave him now. If he needs support, there are other people around who can help him. The promenade is no longer deserted.

I return to the hotel. Two letters are waiting for me. They have been forwarded from Vienna. One is from Bertie, the other from Mrs Kapy. I sit down in the lobby, impatient to read Bertie's news. Perhaps she has persuaded Nobel to enter into correspondence with me.

Dear Ida, she says, *I wrote to Alfred Nobel, as promised. I told him of your intention to write about his life and asked if he would assist you. I added politely,* unless, of course, you are planning to write your own memoirs. *I am sorry to say he rejected the idea out of hand. Here is what he wrote – I am quoting his own words:* I do not wish anyone to write about my life. Nor do I myself have plans for a memoir. What would I be writing about? I am a businessman, living a mundane and commonplace life. Who would want to read about the ledgers I keep or the scientific tests I carry out? The only popular biographies are those of actors and murderers.

I am sorry I can't give you better news, Ida. In view of Mr Nobel's objections, would it not be better to give up your project?

Yours,

Bertie

The only popular biographies are those of actors and murderers. And isn't Nobel a murderer? He has taken Georg's life. And isn't he an actor, pretending to support peace when he makes his money selling ammunition?

I don't know what Bertie said about me to Nobel, but I suppose she didn't recommend me warmly. She has reservations about my undertaking. I have never told her about Georg, but she realizes that I am not favorably disposed toward Nobel, while she is fond of the man and determined to see everything he says or does in a positive light. We have reached an impasse.

If I had been more diplomatic, I might have persuaded her to share Nobel's letters with me, but it felt wrong to disguise my feelings. Bad enough that I am withholding the real purpose of writing the biography – oh, let's call it what it is, the exposé. I didn't want to deceive Bertie outright. I was openly critical of Nobel and lost my chance to read his letters. I wonder why Bertie was so reluctant to show them to me. Was it really from a desire to protect his privacy, or was there something in those letters she did not want me to know? I wonder if Nobel ever mentioned the accidents that occurred in his factories and abroad. Even if there was nothing new or interesting in his letters, I would have liked to read his own words, rather than the quips floating around under his name.

I realize, of course, that letters, even private letters, do not give an unvarnished picture of the writer. It is likely that Nobel presented to Bertie an idealized version of himself, of the man he aspired to become or she had asked him to be. Bertie was a persuasive advocate for the *Society for Peace*. She was quite capable of shaming a man and making him fall in line with her idealism. Even so, I wanted to read those letters and see how the words looked on the page. There is something in the loops and slants of a man's handwriting, I believe, that shows his true personality.

Bertie was uneasy about Nobel's donation to her Society, I could tell. She felt obliged to justify accepting his money. It was an attempt to make up for the havoc his invention wreaked, she said. But that's not good enough! I am not content with the subtle manner in which Nobel goes about atoning for his sins, pretending to act out of benevolence and accepting kudos for his "philanthropy". I want a public acknowledgement that he has done wrong, that he is making amends for it, paying a penance, as it were. I believe that is the meaning of my fantasies, my imaginary sparring with him. I want to bring him to his knees.

My weekend visit to Bertie's new home in Hartmannsdorf did not go well. We argued on the morning of my departure. Arthur, who might have served as peace-keeper, had already left the breakfast table, and we confronted each other without a moderator.

"True, a scientist cannot control the use of his inventions once they become public knowledge," I said to Bertie. "But Nobel should have stopped his tests when he recognized the potential for misuse. He knew the danger of developing dynamite and chose to ignore it."

"I doubt that he could predict the abuse of his invention."

"We have his own word for it," I said and quoted from my extensive collection of Nobel's sayings. "He knew his explosives were demonic devices, *but considered purely as solutions to technical problems*, he said, *they were very interesting*. There's an unscrupulous scientist for you!"

"I don't believe it," Bertie said. "Whoever attributed those words to Nobel was out to blacken his name."

We kept on arguing. We disagreed on everything. The discussion only proved to me what I already knew – that we are drifting apart. Bertie has changed from the carefree woman she was when I first met her. Her daring confidence has turned into something more calculating or, at any rate, more cautious. Age, I suppose, has worn off the edges of her old heedlessness. Am I heading in the same direction without being aware of it? When I think of my younger self, the girl in love with Georg, it does seem impossibly far away. I call up Georg's face, but the image in my mind is only a reproduction of the photograph on my writing desk. I no longer remember his features. Georg has turned into a sepia hero, a tall young man with an enigmatic smile, standing silhouetted against a canvas sky – the set used by the photographer. The picture is a romantic vision, I realize. The train station where we said goodbye has also been transformed into a stage set. The locomotive disappearing in a cloud of steam has become a metaphor and Georg's hand waving adieu, a poetic line. I can no longer hear the actual words he said to me at the station. I make up dialogue, thinking of him and me in the third person.

Perhaps the same thing is happening to Bertie, and she has begun to think of herself and Nobel in the third person and is making up dialogue. She insists that he favors her ideas, but the letter she so proudly quoted in the

Presse isn't exactly a ringing endorsement. He offers only qualified support, and I doubt that those carefully worded phrases reflect his true thinking.

If I had to quote Nobel, which of the quips in my collection would I use to show his true nature? That's the problem. I can't quote what he neglected to say. I can't quote his silence on the mangled limbs, the torn flesh, the bloody remains, the cruel deaths caused by the explosions in his factories. He says he has no intentions of writing his memoirs, and I know why. He does not want to incriminate himself.

But there are witnesses to his life. I open the second letter forwarded to me, Mrs Kapy's note.

Dear Miss Lassick, she writes, *we didn't have enough time to talk about everything I wanted to say to you. Or maybe I didn't say it right. I still think we could work together on a book and I hope you will pay me another visit soon.*

Sincerely,

Sophia Kapy von Kapivar

Mrs Kapy may have answers to my questions. She will be more forthcoming than Bertie, I think. There was a lot of information on that first page of her memoirs, even if the style was primitive and the spelling bad. I knew at once that I had stumbled on a treasure house if she would let me in and show me around. I only wish I could get my hands on Nobel's letters as well. My mouth went dry when Sophie showed the packet to me. That's how badly I wanted to read those letters. The ribbon she tied around them isn't the color of red-hot love. It's the color of irritation. Her memoir will be a revenge piece. Should I tell her that I too have an axe to grind? Would that make her more cooperative? No, better not give anything away. Sophie doesn't strike me as a woman I can trust. She is good at camouflaging. Take her drawing room. It's an impressive room at first sight. The heavy drapes match the cream and dusty rose wallpaper. Nests of little tables and chairs are distributed around the room. The walls are decorated with a group of watercolors with naval themes: harbors and sailboats and caravans on blustery waves. All very handsome, but like Sophie, the room has hidden defects. The carpets are slightly worn, although pieces of furniture, strategically placed, conceal the worn patches. The china shepherdesses on the shelves are imitations of Sèvre porcelain, but that becomes apparent only on close inspection. The windows are large and give the room an atmosphere of air and light, but they overlook the quay with its embankment of rough stones. The preferred view would be the glassed-in courtyard or the street facing the center of the city and the Gothic spire of St Stephen's. On the quayside, there is nothing to see but a row of cabs waiting for customers. One can hear the clatter of the street traffic and the shouts of workmen loading the barges moored at the pier.

I suspect Sophie also knows how to camouflage the imperfections of her soul, how to hide them behind a façade. She knows how to dress to her advantage. Her blonde hair is arranged in perfect ringlets around her forehead, her chignon stuck with tortoiseshell combs. Judging by the length of her affair with Nobel, she must be in her thirties, but she has the porcelain skin of a young girl, delicate white hands and the languid movements of an Odalisque.

Mrs Kapy may not be an inane little woman – my first impression when I met her at Bertie's. That may be the pose she strikes when in company. Some men consider simpering fools charming. She lacks education, but she is intelligent or shrewd at any rate. She knows the value of things – of information, for example. I disparaged the idea of collaborating with her. I said we'd be pulling in opposite directions. Perhaps we have more in common than I thought at first. A memoir is personal but isn't my quest personal as well? And doesn't the title she suggested, *The Sad Story of My Love*, fit my case as well? There was a time when I thought I should follow in Bertie's footsteps and give my writing a larger purpose, turn it into a study of business practices and their effect on society, make it a protest against unconscionable profiteering. But I don't have Bertie's idealism. I can't see past my personal goal: vengeance. I want to pull Nobel down from the pedestal and shatter his heroic image. This is a man who put profit above human lives, a man who thought he could pay off his victims and atone for his sins with a show of philanthropy. I suspect Mrs Kapy was one of his victims, a woman used and discarded. The beginning of her memoir hints at something like that. She has suffered at Nobel's hands and wants to tell the world about it. The memoir may be her form of reprisal.

I will call on Mrs Kapy as soon as I return to Vienna.

*

It is our last day in San Remo. I am helping the maid pack up Mrs Olmuth's things when the bellboy brings a book and a bouquet of flowers. They are for me.

"Flowers!" Mrs Olmuth says. "Someone is sad to see you go, Ida. You must let me in on your secret. Who is your beau?"

"I'm afraid I must disappoint you," I say. "There is no romance. I lent the book to an elderly gentleman with whom I struck up a conversation."

I open the envelope that came with the flowers. It contains only a printed card of thanks.

I tell Mrs Olmuth of the encounter on the promenade and show her the card.

"Ah," she says. "He didn't sign his name. A secret admirer."

I would have expected a more personal note of thanks. Why did the old gentleman choose to remain anonymous?

A week later, back home in Vienna, I have my answer. I am in Mr Olmuth's library, looking through the stack of daily papers, and there is his face staring out at me: the man I met on the promenade in San Remo. His picture is on the front page of the *Presse*, under a headline announcing the death of the famous inventor and millionaire, Alfred Nobel – the killer I have been hunting for all these years. I run cold at the thought of our amiable chat, at the thought that I missed my chance to confront him.

I stare at the picture in the paper. I remember the man's cultured voice, his polite speech. That is the image Nobel presented to the world, a pleasant old gentleman. How carefully he concealed his true nature! I, along with everyone else, was taken in by his act.

Olmuth looks up from his book and says, "Are you all right, Miss Lassick? You look pale."

"I do feel rather peculiar," I say. "Do you mind if I step out onto the terrace for a breath of air?"

"Not at all," he says, "but you'd better ask Millie to get your coat, or you'll catch your death in that cold."

I nod and slip out into the hallway. I don't have the patience to wait for Millie to bring my coat. I am afraid I'll scream. I put my hands over my mouth to stifle the anguished cry that rises to my lips and rush to the back of the house. But what is the use of crying out now? If I had known, I could have screamed into Nobel's face, let fly the abuse stored up in my breast! I would have taken great satisfaction in raising his heart rate sufficiently to bring on the fatal stroke that killed him and to witness his death.

I pull my shawl over my head before I push open the door and step out onto the terrace. I pace up and down, taking deep gulping breaths, oblivious to the mist that saturates the air with moisture and glistens on the iron railing. I am hot with rage. I planned my revenge so carefully. I rehearsed my encounter with Nobel so often. I played the scene in my head, against a blurred background that could stand in for any place, urban or rural, seashore or mountainside – whatever the scenario might be when I met him. I faced off with him, fists clenched and feet planted in a fighting stance, but the old man in San Remo had nothing in common with the man I confronted in my imaginary encounters. My dream protagonist was robust, with a hard face and eyes of steely blue. I screamed accusations at him, spitting them out, every word hitting its mark. As my words pelted him, as he felt their impact, his face slowly changed. His eyes went soft, his face crumpled, his mouth twitched. He lifted his arms in defense as if I was pounding him with fists rather than words. He gripped his chest and dropped to his knees as if I had knifed him. I stood over him and felt the anguish pouring from my mind into his. Relief ran through my body like a spasm. But the imaginary scene never went further than that. I reached the climax and felt drained of all feeling, exhausted. A few days later, the anguish would rise again and pool in my mind. When it reached the tidal mark, the scene started over, a never-ending cycle of suffering and revenge. But Nobel is dead now. I've missed my cue. I'll never get to play the scene I rehearsed so often. It will remain a fantasy forever.

I stop pacing and lower my head in defeat, staring at the tiles, getting lost in their chessboard pattern. Too late to make him pay for his crimes! The fire in me collapses into a pile of ashes. I am suddenly limp and dull with regret, but coming out of my daze, I realize that my desire for revenge is not entirely frustrated. It's not too late to get even with Nobel. The pen is my weapon, and I mean to shame Nobel, to reveal him to the world as the criminal he was. I will go on writing my exposé. After all, a man's reputation survives him and can be ruined even after his death.

Now that I have made the decision to go on, my breathing slows and my surroundings come into focus again. I notice that my hands are stiff with cold and my toes frozen. How long have I been out here on the terrace? I pull myself together and return to the library, taking care to compose my face before I enter and to brush off the droplets of moisture that have gathered on my shawl.

"Feeling better?" Olmuth says.

"Much better, thank you."

He is looking at me with polite interest, waiting for an explanation of my odd behavior. The reading lamp gives a sheen to the top of his head, pink under his thinning hair.

"It must be the weather," I say. "The difference in temperature between San Remo and Vienna, I mean."

"That can be hard on the physique, I suppose, although it hasn't affected my wife in any adverse way. The doctor was quite right advising a sojourn in San Remo. Thank God, she is over her nasty cough." He runs his hands through his sparse hair and resumes reading his book.

I sit down at my desk and make an effort to work on the articles Olmuth wants me to translate, but my thoughts return to Nobel, and I scour the obituaries in the papers. None of them say anything about Nobel's victims. *Die Presse* reports only his achievements.

Alfred Nobel was born in 1833 in Stockholm, Sweden. His father moved his family to St Petersburg and became a supplier of military equipment to the Russian government. Nobel studied chemistry, conducted tests and perfected the commercial use of nitroglycerine. Since that chemical is extremely volatile in its liquid state, he invented a process of mixing it with diatomite, a clay-like mineral. The resulting substance, dynamite, proved useful in mining, and his business expanded to England and Spain. He found financial backers in France, where he lived, and established dynamite factories in Sweden, Germany, Austria, Italy and even America. Later, he formed a joint stock company with his brothers to drill for oil in the Caucasus. Nobel amassed a huge fortune and could have rested on his laurels, but he continued to direct the operations of his far-flung commercial empire in person. He repeatedly visited our city, where he was on intimate terms with Consul Philipp, director of the Viennese branch office. Alfred Nobel was the prototype of an inventor. He made a name for himself through his iron self-discipline, his energy and his restless striving. His friends praise him as a philanthropist who gave a great deal of money to charities. Nor was he a stranger to culture. In his youth, he had aspirations of becoming a writer. In later life, he was a patron of the arts and a promoter of young talent.

Nothing but praise and admiration for the man whose deadly invention supplied the means for mass murder on the battlefield. There are a lot of yes-men out there, obsequious to money and power. Nobel *gave a great deal of money to charities*! *He was a patron of the arts*! Well, he had to spend his loot on something, and those toadies of his won't tell the world that he sent blood money to grieving parents whose son he had killed. No, they carefully filter the information and give out only the nice bits that feed people's admiration.

The obituary goes on to say that he has endowed a foundation, which will award annual prizes for achievements in the arts and sciences. And for the promotion of peace! *His foundation will arouse the admiration of the entire civilized world, Die Presse* declares. *This is one of the most magnificent legacies to humanity.*

Bertie will be elated. She has always been eager to see the best in Nobel. He will be her shining white knight now. I wonder if she will take credit for inspiring him to endow a peace prize.

My first instinct is to call on Bertie and tell her of my chance meeting with Nobel. On second thought, I decide to keep the encounter to myself. It is an evasive move because speaking with Nobel in person has affected my image of him. When I asked Bertie to show me their correspondence, I hoped that his handwriting, the duct of the letters might tell me something about the man. Now, I have looked into the man's eyes and heard his voice. Did that tell me anything about him? I can't decipher the message of his eyes and mouth, but I'm afraid my encounter with him will flatten my anger. The memory of the frail old gentleman and his courteous talk has put a crust of pity on the deep layer of anger in my breast. That is why I am afraid of talking to Bertie. She admires Nobel, and I don't want to listen to her praise and run the risk of diluting my wrath. I want to hold onto my desire for revenge and keep my anger pure.

I stare at the lines in the *Presse* until they become elastic and swell up to engulf me and swirl around in my mind, a jumble of words. My thoughts are far away. I am thinking of Georg, his face obscured by debris and time, of the nightmares which haunt me still. Yes, my desire for revenge is intact. I deeply regret the lost opportunity to grill Nobel about the accident in Heleneborg. I resent the obituaries praising Nobel's generosity. The fire has not gone out of me.

Sophie

In the entrance hall of the apartment, she hangs up her suit jacket and takes a critical look at her reflection in the mirror. The jacket fits nicely, and the skirt of the dress is gathered and layered just so – Lise Bauer is a superb dressmaker. Sophie's hand goes up to the velvet band at her throat and the black brooch she has pinned to it. She straightens the sash of her gray dress – a half-mourning dress in memory of Alfred. Well, why not? They were lovers for fourteen years.

Nikki appears at the door to the drawing room.

"Oh good," she says to him. "You are here."

"At your service," he says and kisses her lightly on the cheek.

I wish he was at my service, she thinks and follows him into the drawing room.

He eyes her gray dress.

"For your benefactor?" he says with an ironic smile.

"Didn't you benefit as well?" she says and drops on the sofa with a sigh.

"You are right," he says. "And I am grateful for his help."

"And now you have to help me, Nikki."

"What can I do for you?"

"I can't possibly live on six thousand a year and bring up the child." She lifts her pretty face and gives him a pleading look, the kind that charms men.

"You mean you can't go on living the way you did when Alfred looked after you," he says. "You can't afford wintering in Merano and ordering your hats and shoes from Paris."

The magic is gone between them. He smiles down on her, but his smile means nothing. It's a habit. He is always civil, even when he disagrees with her.

"No, really, Nikki. Think of it. A miserly few thousand, out of all those millions Alfred made. I never thought he would be so stingy. I gave him the best years of my life. Fourteen years."

"Most people would consider an annuity of six thousand generous. Let me remind you that I live quite decently on a third of that."

"Are you saying I am a spendthrift? Well, perhaps I am, but I didn't stay with Alfred just because of his money. Deep down, I loved him, even if he was an old grouch."

When people ask for whom she is in mourning, she tells them for an uncle who passed away. She does feel lost without Alfred, truly she does. The arrangement with Nikki hasn't worked out. He is neglecting her. He no longer shares her bed. He no longer even kisses her or puts his arm around her waist. Life has become so dreary. It really is a life of half-mourning.

"Let it go, Sophie. Your feelings for Alfred are neither here nor there now. You asked me to help you, and I will if I can. What exactly do you want me to do?"

"You could negotiate with the executors on my behalf. They don't take a woman seriously, you know."

"What is there to negotiate? You have no legal claim on the estate. You want to challenge the amount of money Alfred left you? The executors will laugh you out of court."

"They won't laugh when they realize that I still have his letters."

It was lucky timing. She agreed to send Alfred the letters in exchange for converting her allowance to an annuity. He did. She intended to keep her side of the bargain, but she never got around to mailing the letters. When the lawyer notified her of Alfred's death, she held off sending them. Why surrender her treasure to that hateful man? He always treated her with contempt. She certainly felt no obligation to Nobel's lawyer.

"Here is what I want you to do for me, Nikki," she said. "Write to the executors on my behalf and ask them if they want to buy the letters."

He shakes his head and presses his lips together as if she was asking too much of him.

"Come on, Nikki," she says. "You have the words at your fingertips. It wouldn't take you long to write a letter and tell them: If they don't buy the letters, I'll publish them."

He sighs. "I'll leave the blackmailing to you, Sophie, but I'll do this much for you: I'll ask if they would be interested in acquiring the letters for the estate, since they are rather personal. That hint should be enough."

"If you think so. Just don't sell them too cheap."

He laughs, but it's only the sound of laughter. His face remains serious. "Sophie," he says, "a man has to admire your business sense if he can get past admiring your figure."

"I can never tell whether you are joking," she says. "You will write on my behalf? And soon?"

"They will want to know the specifics," he says. "How many letters are there altogether? How many years do they cover?"

"I haven't counted them, but there must be two hundred at least. Alfred wrote to me almost every day when he was travelling on business. Some of the letters go back to the time we first met. He didn't write much after we broke up, naturally, but he did send me the occasional note right up to last year. Let me see—" Sophie fetches the packet of letters from the bureau drawer and goes through the bundle, checking the date on the last one. "Nine months ago."

"It might be a good idea to include a few samples when I write to the executors. They won't buy the letters sight unseen, if they buy them at all, that is."

"I am not sending them the originals."

"I agree – not the originals. Why don't you transcribe two or three of the letters? Or perhaps I should do it, considering your poor handwriting."

Sophie pouts. "You do it then, Nikki, but you'll have to transcribe them right here. The originals aren't going anywhere."

"You don't trust your own husband?"

"You aren't much of a husband, Nikki. You only come to see me when it suits you."

"And whose fault is that? You can't say I haven't tried living with you, Sophie, but you've made it impossible."

"You are beginning to sound like Alfred. I don't know what men expect from a woman. Alfred said he couldn't live with me because I was 'uncultured', whatever he meant by that. That I didn't share his taste in music? That I liked waltzes better than symphonies? That I'd rather go to the comic opera than watch a bleak tragedy?"

Nikki doesn't answer. He is on Alfred's side, she thinks. The two men understood each other. Depressed and unhappy, both of them. At least Nikki had a reason. He was depressed because he hated the army, and his father was a tyrant. So, of course, when Alfred helped him to get away from both, he felt grateful. That's why he doesn't want to say anything against Alfred now.

"Well?" she says. "Why couldn't you live with me? What did you expect?"

"I thought I was very reasonable in my expectations," he says.

"I'm not going to argue whose fault it is that we can't get along, Nikki. You always get the better of me because you have a way with words. Every argument we have ends in you being in the right and me being in the wrong. You should have become a lawyer."

"I wish I was a lawyer and could charge the kind of fees they do, but as you so wisely say, my dear, let's not argue. Let me have a look at those letters, and I'll choose three samples that will make a good case."

"No, I'll make that decision if you don't mind. There's one letter that says it all, really. Well, two letters that are truly hateful, and if the executors have any consideration for Alfred's reputation, they wouldn't want them to become public."

"Fine. If you insist on making the selection yourself, go ahead. Let me have the two letters, and I'll transcribe them right now."

"Right now?"

"What are we waiting for? Or do you need time to sort them out?"

"No, no, I can put my finger on them immediately. I turned down the corners on all the letters I found hurtful. There are plenty of them. Just don't rush me. I don't like being rushed."

"All right, let's see what you can come up with."

"There are a couple of letters in which he calls me a selfish and greedy Jew, and that's after I converted to Protestantism. I'm sure the executors wouldn't want that to get out."

"Do you read the newspapers, Sophie? No, you don't, or you would know: that sort of thing doesn't get much attention. Last week, an old man was roughed up for no reason other than that he was a Jew, and the week before that, a boy stabbed his classmate and called him a dirty Jew. Were people shocked or outraged when those incidents were reported? No, they weren't. There were no protests of any kind. I'm sorry, Sophie, but I doubt the executors would sympathize with you over those slurs in Alfred's letters. On the contrary, I suspect a lot of people would secretly, or even openly, agree with him. You'll have to come up with something better, my child."

She keeps her head down, slowly sorting through the letters.

He comes around to the sofa, sits down beside her and lifts her chin. "Sophie," he says, "are you crying, sweetheart? It's nasty, I know, but that's how it is."

"I'm not crying," she says, "why would I be crying?" But her eyes have filmed over, and the whole room is a blur.

"The old man was just blowing off steam," he says and puts his arm around her shoulder. She leans into him.

"It's disgusting," she says.

"It is, but it's not something you can change. There are plenty of other things you could change to improve your life—"

She pulls away. "Don't lecture me, Nikki. I'm not a child."

She goes through the packet and hands him another letter. "What do you think of this one? I can't tell you how upset I was when I received it."

"Let's see," he says, looking over the lines written in Alfred's firm, slightly sloping hand. It's the letter in which he tells her that it's over, that he is ashamed of being seen in her company.

Nikki reads the letter, looks up and shakes his head. "I don't see how that is going to help your case, Sophie. It's a long harangue. Alfred was a tedious old man, but these *are* words of truth, a little harsh, perhaps—"

"Harsh?" she interrupts him. "They are insulting, don't you see?"

He reaches for her hands and holds both of her wrists as if to steady her and make her confront the truth. Alfred's truth, that is.

"Insulting? He was right, you know. You *should* make an effort to educate yourself. He says that the two of you are incompatible. That was a fact. He gave you warning that he wouldn't marry you. That was a decent thing to do. I don't see what's offensive about it."

"The tone," she says. "He always talked down to me, as if I was just a silly little goose. I'm not stupid, you know."

"Yes, but being smart isn't the same thing as being educated. Alfred is talking about sophistication and polished manners."

"And I have no polish, is that what you are saying, Nikki?"

He holds up his hands. "I'm not saying anything. I'm talking about Nobel's letter, but really, Sophie, what he says there won't help you a bit if you want to convince the trustees to buy the lot. They don't care about your hurt feelings, and they won't pay you for them. In fact, there are things in those letters that don't reflect well on you."

"They show what I had to put up with."

"That's not the point, Sophie. The only point of interest to the trustees is the illicit nature of your affair, the fact that you were Alfred's mistress. Even that may not sway them. Affairs like that hardly raise eyebrows nowadays."

She pulls out another letter. "I can prove that we were intimate if that's needed. He always asked about my monthlies because there was no sense in us getting together at that time. Here, for example."

This isn't the right time of the month to meet.

"Too vague, I would say. You have to read a lot into those words. Nothing more explicit?"

"Wait. Here. It showed that we shared rooms at any rate." She points to the line: *I have often warned you not to use my toothbrush.*

"God, didn't it turn your stomach to use the old man's toothbrush?"

"I've suffered worse." She compresses her lips and hands him another letter. "How about this one? He addressed it to 'Madame Nobel'. That should persuade them."

It's a short letter:

My dear, good, sweet little Sophie,

There is so much to do here that I can write only a few lines to you today and send you heartfelt greetings. In spite of the lack of time, I went shopping for your things. Isn't the old fellow nice? Virat's is the most shameless place I have ever seen. Imagine, for your little capot hat, which is a mere nothing, I paid 145 francs. Ten steps further down the street, one could buy an equally pretty (if not prettier) hat for 30 francs!

Take good care of yourself, my sweet child, and beware of colds, especially at this time of the month. On the train journey, when my melancholy thoughts left me some time, I started reading a novel. The story became more beautiful and more moving with every page. We'll enjoy reading it together.

With heartfelt greetings and fond wishes,

Your Alfred

Nikki checks the address on the envelope: "Madame Nobel, Villa Koppel, Ischl, Salzkammergut, Austria."

"That's good," he says. "Paints a cozy picture of you and Alfred huddling in front of the fireplace, reading to each other. And he even went hat-shopping for you! How very nice of him. Anything else like that?"

"There is a letter in which he says he'll take me to Stockholm and introduce me to his mother." She sorts through the packet again and reads:

It would be much more pleasant if we made the journey together. But you could not possibly stand the strain. In a few days, perhaps even tomorrow or the day after tomorrow, you will not be able to travel at all—

She looks up. "He is talking about my monthlies."

Nor would the stay in Stockholm be agreeable for you, for I couldn't spend much time with you. We will, therefore, have to defer our joint visit until the next year.

"And – did he introduce you to his mother?"

"No, Alfred never took me to Stockholm. He kept putting it off."

"It would have added a nice touch to the whole thing: you in the bosom of the Nobel family. But those letters will do very well as samples to send to the trustees. I'm almost sure they'll make us an offer after reading them."

"What do you mean – making *us* an offer? They are my letters, don't forget."

"You no longer want me to represent you, Sophie?" He smiles as if he considered the whole thing a huge joke, but Sophie doesn't feel like laughing.

"No, no. I do want you to represent me, Nikki. It's just that you need to understand—"

"Maybe we should put it all in writing," he says. He is no longer smiling. "I find the whole matter distasteful, you know. I will write to the trustees if you insist, but I don't want you to say afterwards that you never authorized me to write, that it was all a misunderstanding."

She sighs. It really is over between us, she thinks, listening for a pulse of regret in her heart, and finding none. Have they become tired of each other simultaneously, or was there never any love between them, and there is nothing to regret?

"Don't say things like that, Nikki. I ask you a small favor, and you make a fuss about it."

"I'm not making a fuss, Sophie. I don't particularly like getting involved in this transaction, but I am your man of business, so to speak. Sad to say, that's what our relationship has come down to: business. We may no longer be in love, but we have common interests, you and I, and there is no reason to be unpleasant or make life difficult for each other. We can still be friends."

That's what Alfred said. *We are not suited to each other as lovers. Let's just be friends.* But she wants a lover.

I have no luck with men, she thinks. Alfred turned cranky on me. He was good to everyone else, to all those people who wrote him begging letters and turned up on his doorstep and told him sob stories. But when I asked him for money, he balked. I guess he was exhausted. He spent all his goodwill on them and didn't have any left for me. In the end, he just wanted to shake me off, but at least he made good on his promise of an annuity. Nikki – well, that is over, too. He is a good father to Gretel. I have to give him that. But he is no husband to me. Still, it is worth something to have a man around. There are so many things a woman can't do by herself, so many doors closed to a woman on her own. It's tiresome always to depend on a man's goodwill.

He has pulled out a chair and is sitting at her desk, copying out the letters. At least he is good-looking, she thinks, a great deal better looking than Alfred and more civil too. He cuts a fine figure. His gray frock coat is nicely tailored. It brings out his broad shoulders and lean body. And he comes from a good family and is popular with society women, the ones in charge of sending out invitations to desirable balls and dinners. So, at least we get invitations, and life isn't entirely dreary. Nikki can't help it that he isn't wealthy, that he can't afford to live in style or keep me in style. We had fun for a time, and now it's over. Alfred arranged their marriage and took care of everything. It was probably the best he could do at the time. His final gift to her: a husband and a well-received name, Kapy von Kapivar. Nikki didn't come cheap. Alfred had to buy him a civilian position after he resigned his army commission. She still doesn't understand why Nikki did that. An officer enjoys prestige. In his present position, whatever fancy title it carried, he was just a man of business. If he was working for a bank, at least, or an insurance company, but Schlumberger! A wine merchant counted for nothing in society, even if he put *Purveyor to His Imperial Majesty* on his label. But there was Nikki's ancient name and his connections, and so, she really shouldn't complain. He moved among a nice set of people. She thinks of the life she used to live when she was Alfred's mistress, at spas in France and Germany and in the gentle climate of the Italian and French Rivieras. She thinks of the company she used to keep – the amusing talk, the lovemaking, the giddy ease, the whoops of laughter. Had it been worth exchanging all that for respectability and the deadly boredom of genteel drawing rooms?

*

Another visit from Miss Lassick. Her third. It's a curious relationship.

"Oh, please, call me Sophie," she said to Miss Lassick the last time they got together. "You know so much about me now, I feel we are quite old friends."

"And you must call me Ida," Miss Lassick said. It's a dance they are doing, stepping carefully, trying to make it look like friendship to camouflage the real purpose of their get-togethers. They want something from each other. Sophie wants help with her writing. Ida wants information.

There can be no friendship between us, Sophie thinks. Ida is one of those women who have never trespassed, who are lily-white and breathing virtue with every word they say. Ida believes she is better than me, but she suspends judgment for the time being and chooses her words carefully because she needs me. Sophie is amazed at the passion of writers, the sacrifices they make for their craft. To have the will to sit at a desk for hours, pen in hand, to coax words from their mind or, like Ida, from that leather-bound notebook in which she writes down the information and to arrange all those facts in a row so that they will make sense.

I could never do it, Sophie thinks. She was ready to give up after writing two pages. She had been sitting at her desk, looking at the sheet in front of her, a yawn creeping through her throat. Her fingers wanted to let go of the pen, her back and legs cramped up. She couldn't go on.

But she must go on. There is something cathartic about putting her life on paper and letting the world know what really happened between her and Alfred. There is a reward waiting for her at the end of the story – if only she can make it to the end – something more than a sigh of relief. Putting her life on paper is a cleansing of the soul, a delivery from all evil. That's what Sophie wants. To be redeemed. To be lily-white again. She doesn't want to obliterate the past and forget it completely. She can't even imagine that kind of amnesia. She only wants to put a solid layer on top of the past, a shiny new foundation for the rest of her life, so she can say: What happened wasn't my fault. But to reach that final point, she needs Ida's help. Luckily, she and Ida want the same thing, to put Alfred's life on paper. The reason for Ida's interest isn't clear to Sophie. Was there a secret connection between them, something Ida is keeping to herself? Then again, all the papers published obituaries and made a big fuss about Alfred's life. I suppose being a millionaire is enough to get people interested.

They have slipped into a routine. To begin with, coffee, petit fours and polite conversation for a quarter of an hour. Then Ida takes out her black notebook and begins asking questions. Sophie doles out the answers in small portions. This time it's about Alfred's poor health.

"What was he suffering from?" Ida asks.

"Oh, a lot of things," Sophie says. "Every day he came up with a litany of complaints. My head aches, my knees hurt, I can't sleep, my gums are sore. I had to listen to his complaints all day long, and I never said a cross word, never got impatient, just held his hand and told him how sorry I was for him."

The packet of Alfred's letters is sitting on the coffee table between them. She goes through them and reads a few words from each to show Ida what an inveterate complainer he was.

I have a continual headache and nosebleed so that the least effort is strenuous for me. In spite of cold compresses, I can hardly scribble a few words...

I'm in poor health, but that subject is of little interest to you. No one gives a hoot whether the old man does or doesn't have rheumatism, whether he lives or dies...

I drink iodized radish and grape juice. I don't feel it's of great use, but it helps somewhat. In any case, it's better than hanging about those stupid spas, where one kills time in the most idiotic way. Poor health is a thousand times preferable to intellectual death...

I can't write much because I've been sick now for five days, suffering from a serious bronchial catarrh. Today, I am a little better, probably because the doctor treated me with poultices and quinine and with a spray of carbolic acid...

During the night, I suddenly felt so ill that I did not have enough strength to ring the bell or unlock the door. I had to spend several hours all by myself, without knowing whether they were my last. Heart spasm, the doctor said.

She pauses. Is she giving away too much information for free? She watches Ida hunched over her notebook, jotting it all down. Her pencil is moving rapidly across the page to keep pace with Sophie's reading.

"We really need to come to some sort of arrangement, Ida," she says, putting the letters back in order and squaring the packet. "About working together on the book, I mean."

Ida looks up. "What sort of arrangement do you have in mind?"

"That publisher friend of yours, the one who printed your genealogies, would he be interested in a memoir?"

"I wish you wouldn't call them 'my' genealogies," Ida says. "It isn't my name that's on the cover of those books. I merely helped the authors to put them together and was paid for my services. Is that the kind of arrangement you have in mind?"

"Not really. I thought we could go on dividing the work between us, as we do now. I supply the information. You write it down, and when it's done, we put both of our names on the cover. We could draw up an agreement to that effect."

"I see," Ida says. Her eyes are trained on a spot above Sophie's head as if she was contemplating the painting hanging there, a lake and misty mountain scene.

She doesn't want to share with me, Sophie thinks and waits silently. She has put her offer on the table. It's Ida's turn to say yea or nay. Her eyes are on the packet of letters now. It's a covetous look. She won't say nay.

"Writing a book is a complex process," Ida says. "You can't draw up a set of rules to follow. You couldn't enforce such an agreement if you wanted to. Working together on a book requires trust." Her eyes are on the painting again, her brow furrowed as if a great effort was required to trust Sophie. "Or a consensus at any rate – what to include or exclude, how to arrange the chapters, the thrust of it all."

"Oh, I'll let you decide on that, as long as I don't come across as the black sheep, the guilty party as if I had done something wrong and Alfred had done everything right, when it's the other way round. I was young and innocent, while he knew exactly what he was doing."

"There will be no difficulty about that," Ida says. "I'll leave it up to you to describe your personal relationship. My concern is with Nobel's business practices, the lives lost in the accidents at his factories. I want to write about his production of dynamite and the dire consequences of his invention."

"You can write all you want about Alfred's business," Sophie says. "I won't interfere. In fact, I don't know anything about it. But will your publisher friend buy the book from us?"

"Carl Volker, you mean. He doesn't buy manuscripts unless he is sure of making a profit on them. More likely, he will ask to see the complete manuscript first and offer us nothing except royalties on sales."

Someone is at the door. A short rap, and Nikki steps into the room. I wish he'd let me know ahead of time when he comes, Sophie thinks. He will get in my way and disturb the balance of our talk. Then again, he doesn't visit unless he has something to tell me. He must have heard from the executors of Alfred's will.

Nikki stops at the door. "I beg your pardon," he says, quick to read her mood. "You are busy. Perhaps I should come back later."

"No, don't go," she says. "We are just finishing up." She is impatient to hear his news.

"Then I'll come in," he says, greeting Ida and politely kissing her hand. Ida's eyes come alive.

Sophie has seen that glint in her eyes before. When she looked at the packet of Alfred's letters. And when she sat next to Nikki at the dinner the Suttners gave. It's a hungry look. She is eating him up with her eyes. And Nikki gives her an appreciative look in turn. What does he see in her? Well, Ida isn't unattractive, just badly dressed. Sophie hasn't seen that appreciative look in Nikki's eyes in a while. He can be charming if he wants to, but he doesn't waste his charm on her. She only gets kind smiles, the ones reserved for pets and children.

A thought strikes her. What if Ida is as vulnerable as she was once? What if she could be ruined as easily? Would Ida fall for Nikki if he tried his luck with her? That would wipe out the superior look and the disapproving ring in her voice whenever the talk turns to Alfred and her life with him. Ida has no right to judge me, Sophie thinks. Someone should teach her a lesson in love and make her suffer. All it takes is falling in love with the wrong man, a man like Alfred – or Nikki because those two were alike when it came to taking their pleasure. They knew how to make an impression on a woman, Alfred with his wealth and power and Nikki with his golden words. Just listen to him flattering Ida, she thinks. He is full of compliments to make her feel important. Ida's cheeks glow. She thanks him. There is a new softness in her voice as she takes her leave from them. She is hungry for compliments. Perhaps she is hungry for love too.

Sophie accompanies her to the door. "Let's talk about our arrangement tomorrow," she says.

"We'll see," Ida says. "I'll think about it."

When she rejoins Nikki in the drawing room, he tells her the news. The executors of Alfred's will are interested in buying the letters.

"Those samples must have impressed them," Nikki says. "They have made you an offer." He holds out the sheet of paper for her to read and points to the figure. "They are willing to pay you twelve thousand."

"That's not enough," she says. "I expected at least fifteen thousand."

"Perhaps you expected too much."

Alfred always said that she wanted too much. *Tell me, how did you spend, no, excuse me, I meant to say "waste" all that money? You just don't understand the value of money until you are penniless, and yet you can be quite small-minded and fight over every penny.*

"Can't you negotiate with them, Nikki?"

"I can, but you would be taking a risk. It's a formal offer, drawn up by a lawyer. It's good for three days. And there are conditions attached, which you must accept as part of the deal."

Do you think they will give things away to you as a gift? Not even Rothschild can buy whatever he sees. Don't let yourself be persuaded by the Jews there that I am so rich – you could be in for a great disappointment. It is a strange business, my dear little froggie. Nothing is good enough for you. I don't know what dough you are made of. Can't you learn simplicity from me?

"Tell them I'll accept the offer if they make it – let's say, thirteen thousand, five hundred."

"It's not that simple, Sophie. If you sign the offer back, it's a brand-new deal. The old offer no longer stands. They'll have to initial the papers and accept the changes you made. And they may choose not to accept them and leave you hanging."

"Or they might come back and agree to pay more," she says brightly, although she can hear the brittleness in her voice. She isn't sure it can be done.

"I wouldn't take the risk if I were you. Twelve thousand isn't bad if you want my opinion. Not bad at all. This business of threatening them with publishing the letters – they might call your bluff. You won't get that kind of money from a publisher, not even close. I'm surprised they offer you as much as they do. I mean, the letters wouldn't do much harm to Nobel's reputation. They are embarrassing, but people already know that you were his mistress. You've never made a secret of it. The scandal, if you want to call it that, would soon blow over. I myself don't see why the trustees should care about the publication of those letters."

"But they do care, Nikki or they wouldn't offer me money for them And there are the postscripts in which Alfred asked me to burn them. Those people in Stockholm are supposed to execute his wishes."

His voice is polite but firm. "They will – to the tune of twelve thousand florins. I think that's a good price for his reputation. There are people out there whose accusations are more ruinous to his name. Do you know that

Strindberg called him 'the deliverer of ammunition to assassins'? – And don't give me that wide-eyed look, Sophie. You aren't sixteen anymore."

If you weren't the little, weak, senseless, undecided creature you are, I would have left you long ago. But as it is, your weakness has served you as a good weapon.

"Well, who is this Strindberg that his opinion counts for so much?"

"A successful playwright and a countryman of Nobel. But never mind Strindberg. Let's deal with what's on the table. Why don't you read through the offer before we go on discussing it?"

She takes the sheets from him reluctantly and leafs through them. Words, words. The lines blur. *It's useless to try communicating anything to you,* Alfred used to say. *I might as well save my breath. You don't understand me. You understand only what suits you.*

She reads out a line in the contract. "Not to make public or cite the letters on pain of forfeiting all remuneration – what does that mean?"

"I already told you. You can't quote Nobel's words. They are his property, and once you are paid off, they are the property of the trustees."

With a dumb show of fatigue, she puts the sheets of paper back on the table. "You know I don't understand lawyer's talk. That's why I asked you to deal with them on my behalf."

"Then you should listen to my advice and accept the offer, including the conditions. First, they want us to verify that the transcripts of the sample letters we sent them are correct. Someone needs to verify them and sign off on the copies. I was thinking of Miss Lassick."

"Oh, so she has made an impression on you, Nikki? I didn't think she was your type."

His brow creases – with amusement, or with annoyance, she can't tell which.

"My type? I don't know what you mean by 'my type'. She made an intelligent impression. And she has good manners."

"A good figure, you mean."

He puts his hand lightly on her arm. "My dear child, love can make a man blind, but a man in an arranged marriage isn't blind. He retains his esthetic judgment. Yes, I've noticed that she has a good figure and a pleasant face, that she doesn't simper or fish for compliments or look at a man sideways, gauging his status."

"In a word, you fell for her."

"Sophie, dear, I'm not a puppy who wags his tail for anyone who pays attention to him. I'm too old for that. I don't 'fall' for women, and if you want my advice, don't use that vulgar cant when you are in society."

"Don't worry. I won't use vulgar cant, and in any case, I rarely go into society. I wish you'd take me to the theatre occasionally. Or a dance."

She'd love to wear one of her off-the-shoulder dresses. The peach-colored one with the white sash, for example. What's the use of having shapely shoulders and nice round arms if you can't show them off? But Nikki doesn't answer. He gives her a thoughtful, determined look and presses his lips together, too polite to say what Alfred used to say. *I am forced by necessity to avoid meeting the people I come across. That is the result of keeping company with you. You deprive me of all intellectual nourishment, and I've lost all my brain power. And the way you behave—*

"You don't take me anywhere, Nikki, because you are bored with me, or ashamed of me, is that it?" she says. *I can't stand being alone with you,* Alfred said. *Either I have to have true company, that is, someone who offers me intellectual food, or I must occupy my intellect with work. I always miss that when I am with you.*

"You can be very, well let's say, free-spirited," Nikki says.

Silly, he means. But was that so bad? *Be a reasonable little woman, or if you can't be that, be at least consistent and wear short dresses so that your attire is in tune with your childishness.* Was she getting too old to be silly? She shudders at the thought.

"But to return to the offer we have here," Nikki says and hitches his chair closer to the table. "Ask Miss Lassick to confirm the accuracy of the transcripts. She has the right credentials. The other day, I paid a visit to Countess Fronberg – a business call, let me hasten to add, before you say the countess is 'my type'. She complained about the last shipment of wine, and Schlumberger sent me to pacify her. We can't have her complain. We need her endorsement. That's why I called on her. There was a book propped up on a side table in her drawing room, opened to a fold-out showing the Fronberg family tree, with ancestors going back almost to Noah's ark. It was a family history, compiled by the countess herself, supposedly, but when I asked a few questions, she confessed that it had been written with help from Miss Lassick. She 'edited' the text and arranged to have it published, the countess told me. Of course, Miss Lassick wrote the whole thing and was paid for it. As was the publisher for producing a limited edition. You may have to offer Miss Lassick a fee as well if you want her to certify the copies of Nobel's letters. It's a business transaction, so to speak."

"But then I'd have to let her read the letters."

He brushes his hand against the packet of letters sitting on the table. "Haven't you already told her a great deal about yourself and Alfred? That's the impression I got when you first mentioned her visits to me. She came at the right moment, I suppose, when you were upset and needed to talk."

"We talked, I quoted a few passages from Alfred's letters to her. That's all."

"And you showed her your memoirs?"

She twists uncomfortably under his steady gaze. "Only the first page. I thought she could help me with my writing, or we could work on it together."

"In any case, she knows about Nobel's letters. The alternative would be to have the transcripts notarized, but that would involve yet another party in a matter that needs to be kept private. And there are other conditions attached to the offer. One is to verify the accuracy of the transcripts, as I said. The other is an assurance that the letters have not been read by anyone except you and me and the person who certifies the transcripts. Can you give them that assurance?"

"I showed some of them to my father, and when Marie was with me, she saw one or two of them. Well, maybe more. She was the kind of maid who always snooped around, you know."

"Your father will keep his mouth shut, and we'll have to take our chances with your ex-maid. Have you stayed in touch with Marie?"

"Oh God, no. That little slut. I think she's an actress now. She slept with the director of a Vaudeville company, at least, that's what someone told me. I was on the point of firing her when she quit."

"Well then, we'll ask Miss Lassick to confirm the accuracy of the transcription and offer her a fee."

"I can't say I like the idea."

"What don't you like about it?"

Sophie busies herself with the legal papers on the table, shuffling them, squaring them. She doesn't like the idea because she isn't comfortable with Ida, who is one of the guardians, one of the women who think they are better than her, who pretend that they have never sinned, who hold onto their goods and give nothing away to a man until he signs the marriage certificate, who stay on the inside of the fence and keep to their set. Then again, there was something vulnerable in Ida's eyes when she took in Nikki's compliments. But it would be useless to say any of that in answer to Nikki's question, why don't I like the idea?

"Ida is nosy. She keeps asking me questions."

"You invited her. If you don't like her questions, you don't have to answer them. You can send her away."

"But I do want her to help me with my memoirs. You know I can't write them by myself."

"And you are going to pay for her services?"

"No, I thought we could write the book together, like friends, you know, and put both of our names on the cover."

"I can't imagine that she would go for such an arrangement. It isn't reasonable. She would do all the work."

Be reasonable, my child, Alfred said. *No, what am I saying? You can't be reasonable. And really, it's your silliness I find so attractive.* She looks into Nikki's impenetrable eyes. He no longer finds her attractive.

"Maybe you should ask me to help you with your writing," he says.

Is he serious? Is he teasing her? She can't decide.

"You would be of no help, Nikki. Certain things need a woman's touch."

"You mean it would be too embarrassing to let me in on the games you played with Nobel?"

She tries to smile, but it's hard to do because what Nikki says is true, although she never thought of them as games. It was a fair exchange. She gave Alfred what he wanted, and he rewarded her for it.

"I don't know what you are getting at, Nikki. I am trying to come to an understanding with Ida about working together. Until we have a definite agreement, I don't want to give away any more information. Not about Alfred's letters and not about my letters to him. No one can keep me from quoting *my* letters, right? They aren't part of the deal."

"I suppose you can quote your own letters, but judging by what I've seen, they are all requests for money and complaints about your health. With spelling mistakes."

Watch your language, Alfred used to say. *Don't mangle your words.*

"Don't preach at me, Nikki. Sometimes I'm so tired of listening to you. I want to go away, far away from here and start over again somewhere else. Did I tell you that Papa proposed for the whole family to go back to Odessa? He has a hankering to see the old place again, he says, to get back to his roots. We could all live there for a year on what I'm spending in a month here, he says."

Nikki draws an audible breath, a sigh of frustration or impatience.

"As your wedded husband, I think I should have a say in you and Gretel moving to Odessa. But you can't be serious, Sophie. At least I can't imagine that you would want to bury yourself in a provincial town in Russia."

"That's what I more or less said to Papa. How would I get on in Odessa? I said to him. I don't speak Russian. 'You could speak Yiddish to begin with,' he said. But I'd never learn Russian, not in a million years. I'm no good at languages. Alfred hired a tutor to teach me French, and I could never manage it, what with the words written one way and spoken another. And Russian is worse. Even the letters of the alphabet are different from ours. I could never learn that crazy language."

Who wrote that French telegram for you, Sophie? Someone helped you, I can tell. The style was rather good, although there were mistakes. "Monsieur" is spelled with an "n", for your information.

"I see I am in no imminent danger of losing you or Gretel to Odessa, so let's go on with the offer we have in hand. We'll ask Miss Lassick to read the letters—"

"I wonder if I should keep some of them back, for Gretel, I mean. As a warning."

"No, you can't keep any of them back. I gave the trustees a count – your count. Two hundred and sixteen letters. And the contract specifies that any other letters you may 'find' in your possession later will have to be surrendered to them and will be considered part of this transaction."

He scrapes back his chair. "Next time you see Miss Lassick, ask her to check the transcripts for you. I'll draw up something for her to sign." He picks up his hat and coat from the chair where he has laid them down, but she holds him back.

"The contract doesn't say anything that would prevent me from transcribing the letters for my own use, does it?"

"There's nothing about that in the contract. It would be too difficult to police, I suppose. They are interested only in keeping the letters out of the public eye."

"Then I'll transcribe a few of them."

"If it's really for Gretel's sake, you'd better make them legible copies, not your usual scrawl. And don't forget we have a deadline by which those letters must be delivered to Stockholm. You are very bad at keeping deadlines."

"And you are very bad about niggling me." As bad as Alfred, she thinks. He used to go on and on about her faults until she was sick and tired of listening to him. *You are a pampered little princess. Nothing is good enough for you. Nothing satisfies your little mind, such a very little mind.* "I'm tired of listening to your criticism, Nikki."

"You are right, sweetheart. I've been unkind, and I apologize. No sense in quarrelling. We are married for better or worse, so let's make it pleasant."

"I'm trying, Nikki."

"I know you are," he says soothingly and gives her a peck on the cheek before making his getaway.

He is treating me like a child, she thinks, the way Alfred did – no, Nikki is kinder. Alfred was blunt. A little brutal, I said to him. What do you mean, brutal? he said. *Your views have always been screwed up, and they don't seem to improve. And what else can be expected from a little, dependent, barely educated creature without any talent but with big ambitions, or rather pretensions? Believe me, Sophie, little birds, however fat, belong into little cages and will feel most comfortable there.* He knew how to make me feel guilty, she thinks. Everything was my fault. I made him sick. I made him stupid. I tired him out. I didn't appreciate what he was doing for me. I was going to desert him in his old age.

Well, it's all the same to me whether I live or die, he said. *If my old ragged heart still bleeds, it is only over the way you treat me, Sophie – a man who has always been generous to you and acted nobly.* He was afraid I would leave him, but in the end, it was he who deserted me. And now he is gone forever. Death is a kind of desertion too, she thinks.

Ida

On the way to the Metropole, I slow down and linger to look at the displays in the shop windows. I'm too early for my meeting with Sophie.

I don't know whether we can come to an agreement about working together. She is a crucial witness to Nobel's life, and I depend on her for information. She says she won't interfere with my writing, but I haven't told her much about my purpose because I am no longer clear about it myself. I said I wanted to write about Nobel's business practices, about an inventor's responsibility for the use of his inventions. I gave her my rationale, which is far removed from my visceral desire for revenge, the compulsion burning like lava and eating my innards. But Nobel is dead and revenge is no longer possible in the way I imagined it at first, running him to ground. I've turned from a hunter into a gatherer of information. Perhaps I'm following in Bertie's footsteps. She has transcended personal motives. In her book, she does not mourn the death of one man or even the collective deaths of men killed in the war she witnessed in Kutaisi. She wants an end to warfare itself. She mourns the death of humane and civil thought, of brotherly love. I have tried to go beyond the idea of avenging Georg's death and plead instead for an end to profiteering. At least, that's what my mind is urging me to do, but the voice of passion inside me still cries for revenge, for an end to my nightmares, to my own suffering. Revenge is not the only cure for my night terrors, I know. The ecstasy of lovemaking has the same purging power, but it isn't a cure I can take when I need it. Conjuring up Totia in a fantasy is not the same as being in a man's arms, and there is no miracle man in my life. Writing is the only remedy for my nightmares now, the only healing power on which I can draw readily. It, too, comes from within, a compelling desire. It flows out through the hand that holds the pen, issues into words that can be arranged in patterns that parallel life. No wonder the Bible gives to the word the mystic power of becoming flesh. Words can reshape the narrative of life and re-form it into something better. And words are always at my command. I can transfer my suffering to the page, pour my passion into words and end up with something tangible, a book, an object held in my hands. It makes sense to go on with my plan to write an exposé of Nobel, not only to avenge Georg's death and my own suffering or to raise a universal question, but to put together a story that gives me satisfaction, word for word, sentence for sentence until I get that quiet feeling of resting after a hard day's work. Can I trust Sophie not to interfere with that?

I pass the carriages lined up in front of the hotel and enter the lobby. The clock in the foyer shows a quarter to three. My appointment with Sophie is at three. I decide to go into the reading room and pass the time looking at today's newspapers. I am going through the stack laid out on a table when I see someone at the other end of the room trying to catch my attention: Mrs Twain.

She waves at me. To be exact, she waves a letter at me.

"Miss Lassick," she calls out.

An old gentleman by the window glances up from his book and gives her a disapproving look.

"Oh, excuse me," she mouths in his direction.

"I had better keep my voice down," she says in a half-whisper as she comes over to my corner and takes a seat beside me. "I wonder if you could help me, Miss Lassick. The concierge just gave me this letter. It is very formal – an invitation to the Concordia Club, or rather, that is my question. Is it an invitation or just an inquiry? I cannot make it out. My German is not good enough."

"But your German is excellent."

"It is good for most purposes. But sometimes I get lost in the thicket of polite phrases."

She hands me the letter. It's an invitation for Mark Twain to give a talk at the Concordia Club followed by a reception. The invitation is for him and three guests.

"Is the Concordia a respectable establishment?" she asks me.

"Most respectable. An exclusive press club. Three hundred members, or so. They rarely honor a foreigner with an invitation. I remember only one other occasion, five or six years ago, when they invited Henrik Ibsen."

"Then he will accept, of course. What is it like there? Sophie told me you are a writer. Are you a member of the Concordia by any chance?"

I laugh at the idea. "I've never set foot in there. No women allowed on the premises, you know. It's a male bastion."

"No women allowed? How quaint!"

The old gentleman claps his book shut and gets up. As he walks by us, he hisses: "This is a *reading* room, ladies."

"Perhaps we should go into the lobby," Mrs Twain says.

But we are the only people in the room now, so there is no need to move.

"I assumed the invitation was meant for the whole family, including myself and our two daughters," she says, "but if women are not allowed in the club—"

"I'm sure the invitation includes your family. This will be a special occasion, a gala, when members are permitted to bring guests, including ladies."

"I see. Well, if Sam accepts the invitation, we won't bring the girls. Jean is in poor health and Clara would probably be bored to tears. I wonder: would you be free to join us, Miss Lassick? I admit I have an ulterior motive for asking you. I'd be so happy to have an English-speaker by my side to interpret what I cannot understand. And then you are a writer yourself, and the evening might be of interest to you."

"Of the greatest interest. I'm very grateful for your invitation. It will be a pleasure to accompany you and your husband."

I'm elated at the prospect of an evening with the Twains. Herzl as good as invited me to write for his new paper. This might turn out to be the right material for an article.

"Maybe Sophie would like to come along as well," Mrs Twain says. "She goes out so rarely, on account of being in mourning. I feel sorry for her. She is lonely, I think."

Yes, and in need to talk to someone who is not intimately connected with her life. She wants a wailing wall.

"Of course, I do not know what the rules of mourning are here," Mrs Twain says. "Perhaps it is not considered right for her to attend an evening entertainment."

"I would think attending a lecture and reception at a closed function is respectable enough. It's not like going to a cabaret, although I understand your husband can be very entertaining."

"A humorist with an earnest touch."

"Then Mrs Kapy will be safe. After all, she is only in half-mourning, and I'm not sure for whom."

"For Alfred Nobel?" Mrs Twain says, suppressing a smile. "That is what I have been told, although I understand their relationship was difficult, or perhaps it is only her relationship with the executors that is difficult."

Perhaps so. Sophie likes to play coy and keep her visitors guessing. We are on a first-name basis now, but I've come no closer to understanding her relationship with Nobel. She is in two minds herself, I think, wavering between two versions. She was his constant companion and his neglected child. She was the good woman who looked after her man and the spoiled little girl demanding attention.

"But you were on your way to see Mrs Kapy," Livy says, "and I'm keeping you."

"Not at all. I'm a little early and came in here to take a peek at the papers."

"There is a nasty cartoon in that one," Mrs Twain says. She opens up the *Wiener Diarium* and points to a cartoon of Mark Twain surrounded by long-nosed Jewish merchants showing him bolts of cloth. The caption reads: *Looking for material, Mr Twain? Watch out they don't sell you crap!*

"Now tell me, Miss Lassick, what is that supposed to mean?" She looks distressed.

"An example of anti-Semitism, which is ubiquitous, I'm afraid. Sophie has had her share of it."

"That is what she told me. Mr Nobel used to bait her. Jews looked only after themselves, he said. They fleeced everyone else. And she had to listen to such things. Hard to believe that he could be so mean, don't you think? After all, he was her lover."

"And hard to believe that she stayed with him for so many years and put up with such hateful talk."

"And now the papers are going after my husband because they think he is Jewish – on account of his first name, I am told. Mark Twain is a pen name, you know. His birth name is Samuel Clemens."

"It may be his name that prompted the joke, but more likely, the cartoon is a reaction to his essay on the Jews of Vienna. It was too complimentary for some people's tastes," I say.

"Oh, you've seen the essay?"

Of course I've read it. It's the talk of the town. Twain is a celebrity, and Vienna is celebrity-crazed. They read everything he writes.

"I don't understand," Mrs Twain says. "What did he say that would offend people? It's all very positive and reflects well on Austria. He praises the emperor for striking down the laws discriminating against Jews."

"That's exactly what riles certain people. And, of course, the colorful expressions he used gave offense. If I remember correctly, he said the difference between the brain of the average Christian and that of the average Jew was the difference between a tadpole's and an Archbishop's. That's a bit strong, don't you think?"

"He meant it as a joke."

"That kind of joke doesn't go over well in Vienna. It would have been better to leave the archbishop out of it."

"You are right," she says. "What can I say? Sam always comes on strong. Too strong, I think. But he doesn't listen to me. He is a very stubborn man when it comes to his writing."

I discreetly check my watch. Not discreetly enough. Mrs Twain catches me out.

"I will let you go," she says. "I hope we have a chance to talk again soon."

We head back to the lobby. A gentleman is waiting at the elevator. He turns. It's Nikolaus Kapy. He gives us an urbane smile and bows. My heart begins to beat faster. I lower my eyes. Too late. Kapy has entered the orbit of my fantasies.

"Spring has finally arrived," Mrs Twain says to him. They start a desultory talk about the weather.

Kapy has the bearing of an imperial officer – straight-backed, clean-shaven, used to giving commands and in command of himself. And yet there is a soft edge to his words, a rounding of consonants that allows for a breath of doubt or hope, an expectation of more to come. He is the kind of man that leaves an imprint on my brain, the beginnings of a storyline, a fantasy. His eyes, amber in the glow of the wall sconces, darken as he turns to me. For a moment, I am the focal point of his inquiring gaze. A terrible appeal is coming from him. It makes me lose my balance. I feel myself blush, ashamed at the pleasure I take in his attention.

A fantastic scenario develops in my head: I see myself getting into the elevator with Kapy. Halfway between two stories, the cabin comes to a shuddering halt. The lights go out. I feel hot and short of breath. I stretch out my hand. My fingertips touch—

The doors of the elevator open. The lift-boy steps out and allows Gretel and her nanny to pass. My fantasy dissolves.

"Papa!" the girl shouts and jumps into Kapy's arms. He lifts her up and kisses the top of her head, disarranging her white bow.

"How is my little one?"

"Did you bring Bella?"

"She's waiting for you in the phaeton."

Gretel's nanny is standing by, her face inscrutable, but her stiff bearing gives away her disapproval of their whirlwind embrace which has knocked the child's bow sideways. She straightens it out.

Gretel makes us a curtsy. "We are taking Bella for a walk in the Prater," she tells Mrs Twain. "And then we'll watch the puppet show. Kasperle and the Crocodile."

"A real crocodile?" Mrs Twain asks, screwing up her face in mock fear.

Gretel gives a delighted laugh. "No, there are no real crocodiles in the Prater! It's a puppet made of wood, and it moves on strings. It's painted green and has a huge mouth with many, many teeth and eats everything in its way. Except Kasperle. He is too clever for the crocodile."

The fair-haired, amber-eyed Mr Kapy beams down on Gretel. "Well, then, sweetheart, I suggest we go, or we'll miss the performance."

Mrs Twain and I get into the elevator. I'm flooded with guilt. Why do I indulge in fantasies about Kapy? He is Sophie's husband. He is off limits. I'm afraid he will make his debut in my dreams tonight and become a regular.

"We'll stay in touch about the evening at the Concordia Club," Mrs Twain says, waving adieu to me as she gets off on the second floor.

I only nod. I cannot speak. I need all my energy to bar Kapy from entering my brain. I have never allowed myself to fantasize about a man I know by name and might meet again in the flesh. My dream lovers have always been anonymous or at least safely out of reach, like Totia. The elevator stops on the fourth floor.

Sophie is waiting for me. She takes her seat on the sofa, no, she arranges her body on the sofa, the folds of her skirt draped just so, as if she were posing for a painter. She is an actress, and what she has told me so far is a script for a play. She says only what furthers the plot. I suspect it will be the same with the story she wants me to put into our book. It won't be the whole story, his and hers. It will be Sophie's story, the bits and pieces that justify the grudge she bears Nobel. She has a grudge, of that I am sure, even if I don't know the details of her life with him. She has told me enough. She is wearing mourning dress, and she may be distressed over Alfred Nobel's death – naturally, after spending almost half her life with him – but the unhappiness in her eyes goes beyond mourning him. There is a permanent source of dissatisfaction in her life. Perhaps it's her marriage. *No one wants a woman who has been the mistress of another man for fourteen years*, she told me. She had to take what she could get. But Kapy is no second-rate man. Perhaps the discontent I see in her eyes has nothing to do with him and everything with Alfred Nobel. It is like my desire for revenge, deep-seated, visceral. It suits my purpose, but Sophie will not give away her resentment for free. She will make me work for it because in spite of her soft looks, she is a woman who drives a hard bargain.

That is the nature of our relationship, more than an acquaintance, less than friendship, an understanding perhaps. There is no more talk of a written agreement between us. Sophie has come to understand that our relationship can't be reduced to legal phrases. It's a give and take relationship, and I fear she will get the better of me.

*

I meet Mark Twain on the evening of the press gala in his honor. Livy has arranged for me to join them on the carriage ride to the Concordia Club. We meet in the lobby of the hotel.

I expect Twain to be stand-offish, as celebrities usually are when they are introduced to insignificant people like me and there is nothing in it for them. But he is cordial. He takes my hand and shakes it as if we were about to conclude a business deal. He doesn't kiss my hand. No Viennese *Küss die Hand* for him. He is a big shambling bear of a man with a flowing head of white hair and an untidy beard, looking disheveled even in his elegant evening clothes.

Mrs Twain had asked me to proofread the speech her husband will give at the club.

"I would feel better if you looked it over, Miss Lassick," she said. "Sam is too proud to ask for help, but I'll tell him to give you a copy. I'll say you asked for a sneak preview because you intend to give him a write-up."

"I'll read through his speech if you think it's helpful," I said. "As for the write-up, I'd be happy to oblige. I'm not a regular contributor to any paper or magazine, but Mr Herzl, the editor of *Die Welt,* has invited me to submit an essay."

"Oh, well," she says, "I'm not worried about publicity. Sam gets enough attention as it is. I'm worried only about bad publicity – like that cartoon I showed you the other day. That is why I would like you to read over his speech. I don't want him to offend anyone at the Concordia Club or make a fool of himself."

But Twain declined my help. I suppose he didn't want to give anything away and certainly doesn't need any publicity from me.

"Isn't Sophie coming along?" I ask as we get into the carriage.

"I invited her," Mrs Twain says, "but Gretel has a cough, and she wanted to stay with the child."

"Wanted to stay with the child?" her husband says. "My foot! Is that what she said? I'll tell you why she stayed home. She isn't interested in literary events."

"Or else she is scared of you," Mrs Twain says.

"Who, me?" He gives me a mock-pleading look. "Tell me, Miss Lassick, do you find me scary?"

"Humor can be intimidating," I say.

"Listen to her," he says. "She's a smart one."

I can't help smiling. He plays the endearing fool well.

"So we won't have Sophie's company," his wife says. "But Mr Kapy said he would come. He will meet us at the club."

In the carriage, on the way to the Concordia, I listen carefully to what Twain has to say and keep score in my head of what might go into an essay – the things Herzl would want for his readers, a personal profile, a few jokes.

"You are a friend of Mrs Kapy?" Twain asks me.

"We've met a few times. I was interested in what she has to say about Alfred Nobel. I am collecting material for a biography and was hoping to get a measure of the man."

"Nobel! There's a queer fish for you. At least that's the impression I got when I met him in New York years ago. His work is well documented, but the man? Good luck figuring him out."

My ears prick up.

"You've met Alfred Nobel?"

"I got interested in his patents – but I didn't think they had commercial value or potential. Besides, the ethics involved were a little too murky for my taste."

"You guessed wrong about the commercial value," his wife puts in, "but you were right about the ethical aspect. Who wants to invest in massacres?"

"And the man himself didn't inspire confidence," Twain says. "A morose character if I ever saw one. And plagued by rheumatism, I found out when we were in Aix-les-Bains, three years ago. He was the star guest of the season. Don't go to Aix-les-Bains, by the way. Dreadful place. Produces more noise by the square yard than any other place I've been to. The hackney drivers are the worst. Enjoy cracking their whips like pistol shots. And if those guys don't drive you crazy, the church bells will. There must be six thousand of them at least, all chiming five minutes apart—"

"Now, dear," his wife says and puts a calming hand on his arm.

"All right, I won't go on," he says, "but it was like that, believe me, Miss Lassick. As for Nobel, maybe rheumatism explains why he was so bleak, but I myself suffer from the gout, which is just as bad, let me tell you, and I haven't turned into a misanthrope, have I, Livy?" He gives her a droll look, and she squeezes his hand.

"Well," she says.

"What is that 'well' supposed to mean? I'm always in a good mood, gout or not. In any case, I don't know what drew Mrs Kapy to a man like Nobel. Or rather, I can imagine what drew her, but what kept her at his side for eighteen years—"

"Fourteen," Mrs Twain says mildly.

"Eighteen, she told me, if I remember correctly. But fourteen or eighteen. I admire her stamina. And would it have harmed him to acknowledge the child?" He turns to me again. "In any case, I doubt you'll get anything out of Mrs Kapy for your biography. She won't give anything away. She is planning to write her own story, I understand."

"She *says* she'll write her memoirs, but I doubt she will manage it," his wife says. "She doesn't have it in her, I don't think so."

"Right you are. When I think about that note she sent you – spelling mistakes even an English speaker can spot. 'Aspropos'."

"That was just an oversight."

"And 'desbarat' for 'desperate' – also an oversight?"

"Don't be so hard on her, Sam. It's not her fault that she didn't get an education. I blame her parents. Or rather, I blame fate – her mother died when Sophie was a child, you know."

"Then she was spared seeing her daughter's disgrace."

"Yes, she was spared seeing her daughter suffer," his wife says and gives her husband a melancholy look.

They both fall silent after that as if the air had suddenly dried up all words. Twain looks out the window at the passing traffic. After a while, he starts talking again, about his difficulties with the German language. He can't keep the genders straight.

"I haven't noticed you making any mistakes," I say.

"But it's hard. Take *das Mädchen,* for example. It doesn't make sense for 'girl' to be neuter, does it? And those long sentences with the verbs at the very end. By the time you get there, you've forgotten the beginning of the sentence." He goes on in that jocular vein, one quip after another. "So far I've driven three teachers to despair. I had to quit taking lessons. They were suicidal. I didn't want to be responsible for their death."

We arrive at the club to great fanfare. They have put up red-white-blue bunting, in honor of the American visitors, and a banner with the American motto "*E pluribus unum*". The potted palms and elaborate flower arrangements make the speaker's platform look like a winter garden.

Mr Gross, the president of the club, is waiting at the door to welcome us.

Twain cocks an eye at the decorations. "What – all this for me?"

Our host isn't sure whether to take his question seriously. Twain has a reputation for being a joker. It's hard to tell what he is up to. He has a way of gesturing in a theatrical manner. His unruly hair gives him a frantic, not to say clownish air.

Our host decides on a serious answer.

"Indeed, Mr Twain," he says. "We decorated the hall in your honor, and Mr Lehner was kind enough to supervise the décor himself."

"You will excuse the ignorance of a foreigner," Twain says. "But who is Mr Lehner?"

"The Emperor's Decorations Inspector."

"I take it the title is descriptive of Mr Lehner's responsibilities, which seem to me rather large, not to say insurmountable, unless I misunderstand the term 'decorations'. It does mean ornamentation, does it not?"

"That is the meaning," Gross says. He is ill at ease. This is no laughing matter. "Mr Lehner has the veto power on all stage design and all décor put up on public occasions."

Twain does not let him off the hook. "You don't say! Every bauble, spangle, and trinket?"

The Austrian censorship laws are severe. Our host squirms under the glitter of Twain's eyes. It looks as if he is going to launch a devastating joke at the expense of the censors, but Mrs Twain defuses the situation. She has spotted a famous opera singer and asks to be introduced.

Looking around the room, I see quite a number of celebrities from the stage and the music scene and, of course, the crème of the literati. The foreign press corps is represented as well, headed by the man from the

London Times, and there are several members of the diplomatic corps. And Mr Kapy. He has spotted us and is making his way through the crowd. He seems to know everyone. He stops to shake hands. Men clap him on the back and lean toward him in familiar talk. Ladies smile and nod. An elderly lady taps his arm with her fan. He helps her to a seat. At last, he arrives at our circle. He shakes hands with Twain and bends down to kiss my hand. Fantastic thoughts come into my head unbidden as I look down on his shock of hair. The scenario: I run my hand through his hair. He straightens up and gives me a melting look. Kapy seems to fall in with the imaginary scene in my head. He gives me a look of interest, though not exactly melting. I tamp down my lascivious thoughts and turn to Livy, who has returned from her chat with the celebrated soprano.

Mr Gross takes charge of his famous guest and leads him to the speaker's platform, while an usher shows the three of us to our seats in the first row. Mrs Twain is seated between me and Kapy. I am glad of the physical barrier. I don't trust my leaps of fantasy, but Kapy leans forward and says:

"Countess Fronberg keeps your book prominently displayed in her drawing room. I leafed through it. Impressive."

"I don't think my authorship is supposed to be public knowledge."

"But the countess confessed it to me, and she thinks very highly of your style of writing."

The audience falls silent, and Kapy leans back into his seat.

I don't know why I'm so inordinately pleased with his praise, or rather with his mention of Countess Fronberg's praise. Am I pleased because she gave me credit for the book, or because the praise came from Kapy's lips? I rather like his lips.

Gross introduces Twain. "We are honored to have with us one of the greatest sons of America: Mark Twain." The announcement is greeted with enthusiastic applause. Twain pulls out his spectacles and a sheaf of papers, apologizes for reading his speech, then continues to speak freely. Nice touch that, but I don't think he appreciates the intellectual level of his audience. He gives them a bantering, stand-up comic routine. He jokes that he has been told he speaks German "like an angel", but he is in no position to judge because he has never met an angel and is in no hurry to do so.

I must say, he is brave to address his hearers in German. His accent is very good, but the subject of his speech is miscalculated. His topic is "The Horrors of the German Language", which he illustrates with lame jokes, the same jokes he tried on me in the carriage. About the suicidal teachers. About the long sentences.

My mind wanders, looping into a fantasy. I imagine changing places with Livy and sitting beside Kapy. I can't take my eyes off the snug fabric of his trousers, his ankle boots made of matte kidskin. His leg touches mine. His hand creeps up to the armrest that separates our seats. His fingers touch mine. No, I shouldn't have thoughts like that! I snap out of my fantasy and look around. The eyes of the audience are riveted on the speaker.

Twain's voice fades back in. German is the most perplexing language, he says. The average sentence is a sublime and impressive curiosity to him, each one containing all ten parts of speech, not in the order listed in grammar books, but mixed and strewn with compound words put together on the spot – you can't find them in any dictionary. And the verbs are placed as far apart from the noun as possible. By the time you reach the end of the sentence, you have forgotten the beginning, confused as you are by the closing flurry of auxiliary verbs that don't seem to add any sense, at least not to his mind.

"I've come to realize," he says, "that it is a firm rule for typesetters never to have the subject and the verb on the same page." He brings up the neuter girl next – amusing to him perhaps, but hardly to a Frenchman or a Spaniard or indeed to German speakers, all familiar with the idea that grammatical gender does not reflect natural gender.

He repeats everything he has said to me in the carriage. It was a rehearsal, I realize. I got my sneak preview after all. I wonder whether he has any genuine conversation left in him, or is he on stage all the time and is everything he says fodder for speeches and articles? I like him well enough, but the thought of the rehearsed jokes diminishes him in my eyes.

Twain comes to the end of his speech. It couldn't have been longer than ten minutes. Or has my secret fantasy made time go faster? My fantasies, I notice, have a way of blocking reality and trumping it. Why would the scenarios in my head be more real than what's happening around me? Because other people are producing the external events, whereas my fantasies are my own brainwork, and that's more engaging.

I don't know whether Twain has been successful in engaging his audience. I think people expected something more profound. A comparison between American and European politics or customs. Not a comic routine. Ridiculing the German language isn't funny to a Viennese audience. There was a touch of boorishness about Twain. I expected him to be more sophisticated than that. After all, he took the trouble of learning German and spoke it very well indeed. The laughs he gets are thin, but people are generous with their applause in the end.

After the speech, we are treated to champagne. Waiters take around trays of *Gabelbissen*, fancy open-faced sandwiches. Mr Gross toasts the Twain party before announcing the program for the rest of the evening.

The entertainment begins: poetry readings, skits, and a piano rendition of Strauss waltzes. We reach the grand finale. A military band strikes up everyone's favorite, the Radetzky March. The conductor, in full blue dress uniform, waves his ebony baton. The audience is gripped with devotion to the imperial dream. Old men listen with pensive smiles, thinking of victorious battles, and young women tap their toes and part their lips breathing patriotic love for the smart men in uniform. The Kaiser himself looks out benevolently from the official portrait hung in every public place: the supreme commander in his snow-white uniform with the red sash. The last thunder of kettledrums fades. The audience applauds with fervor. It is the conclusion of the official program. The ladies are expected to depart now, leaving the men to serious drinking and cigar smoking and for all I know, a different kind of entertainment.

A little circle has formed around us. Mrs Gross offers Olivia Twain a ride in her carriage and asks where she is staying.

"The Hotel Metropole," she says, "but I have come with Miss Lassick, and we have a hackney waiting for us."

"The Metropole?" a bull-necked young man says. He is dressed in the Ulan uniform with a short, double-breasted jacket and a red sash. His boots are waxed to a smooth polish, a sheen that is matched by his close-cropped black hair. Mrs Gross has introduced him as her nephew, Franz, on leave from his regiment in Krakau. "Isn't Mrs Nobel staying at the Metropole?" he says. "Have you met her?" he asks Mrs Twain.

She gives the young man a confused look. Mrs Gross draws in her breath and looks at Kapy, who is standing next to her.

"She is Mrs Kapy now," he says to the man in uniform. His face is expressionless and his voice even. "You are speaking of my wife."

The young man pales. His body stiffens into subordination. "I beg your pardon, sir. My mistake. I meant no offense."

A fine smile appears on Kapy's lips. "If I hadn't resigned my commission, I might be obliged to call you out, but as a private citizen, I accept your apology. No offense intended and none taken."

Franz bows and clicks his heels together smartly.

Twain, who has overheard the exchange, frees himself from the cocoon of his admirers and says to Kapy, "What's going on? Have you just deprived me of witnessing one of your interesting native customs?"

"Oh, Sam," his wife says and pulls him away.

Franz has already made his getaway, and Kapy smiles and says nothing.

"I mean a challenge is a challenge," Twain says stubbornly.

I come to Kapy's aid. "I thought you had exhausted that subject, Mr Twain. I seem to remember a scene in your *Life on the Mississippi*—"

"Oh, you've read that?" Twain says and laughs. "You mean the shoot-out between Mabry and O'Connor? But that's a Wild West story—"

His admirers have closed in on him again and don't even let him finish the sentence. There is a storm of questions. Mabry and O'Connor? Who are Mabry and O'Connor?

"Let me see you out, ladies," Kapy says to Olivia Twain and me. "I don't think we'll be able to extract Mr Twain any time soon."

Mrs Gross gives him a grateful smile. We say our adieus and follow Kapy. He hands us into the coach. I feel his palm resting on the small of my back and lean into it to feel his touch a moment longer.

"Keep an eye on Sam for me, Mr Kapy, will you?" Mrs Twain says. "Don't let him get carried away."

"It's more likely that the adoring crowd will get carried away by him."

"Don't let him overindulge, I mean," she says, and he nods earnestly.

"Don't worry," he says, but his last look is for me. I feel the full power of his long and exacting look.

Mrs Twain and I drive back to the hotel. She has invited me to stay with her for the night.

"Oh, we won't let you go home after the performance," she said when we made arrangements to go to the club. "Stay with us. Clara will let you have her room. The girls can double up."

She is like that. Olivia Twain doesn't stand on rank or ceremony. She is good-natured and friendly with everyone. I gratefully accepted the invitation as well as her offer to call her by her first name and use the informal "thou".

Back in her drawing room at the hotel, we have a glass of sweet liqueur – "to climb down from all the excitement," as Livy puts it.

"Were those two men really talking about a duel?" she asks me.

"Well, yes, although the general sentiment runs against duels, and they are about to be outlawed. But old ways die hard, especially in the military and in the fraternities."

The talk turns to Sophie, whose honor was impugned by the young man's remark.

"Do you see a lot of her?" I ask Livy.

"Well, we are two women left to ourselves and looking for company. Sophie is really too young for me, or seems so much younger, at any rate. Her talk is all about fashions. My daughters would be better company for her, but Clara spends most of her time with her young man. She is up to her ears in love with Ossip Garbilowitch – a Russian concert pianist, you know, and Jean has taken a dislike to Sophie, I'm afraid. She thinks she is a 'fake'. But then, all of Vienna is 'fake' to her. She isn't used to ceremony and mannered talk, the hand-kissing and addressing everyone as 'gracious lady' – *Gnädige Frau*. 'I am no *Gnädiges Fräulein,*' she said to one young fellow who was merely being polite to her. 'In fact, I'll be very ungracious if you call me that again,' she said. 'Then what would you like me to call you?' he asked. 'Jean,' she said. 'That's my name.' He almost swallowed his tongue with embarrassment."

"She is still young."

"Seventeen. Too old to commit such a faux pas, and when I gave her a talking to afterwards, she was unrepentant. 'Oh but it's a stupid custom,' she said. She can't wait to get back to America. I think a little European polish will do her good."

"I can't imagine you giving anyone a 'talking to'. You are always so kind."

"It was only a mild rebuke. I don't have the heart to be stern with Jean." She sighs deeply. "She can be difficult and irritating, but it's her illness, you know."

"I'm sorry to hear that she is ill. It must worry you a great deal."

"I'm afraid so, and I don't like to talk about it much, but you are staying with us tonight, and I never know when the illness will strike next. So I'd better give you warning. Jean is suffering from epilepsy."

I remember the sudden silence in the carriage on the way to the club when we were talking about mothers and daughters, and I know now what

Livy meant when she said, "At least she didn't have to watch her daughter suffer." The same look is on her face now, and the same dense air spreads between us, an air of looming clouds and dark shadows. Then she breaks down and cries. "We have tried so many cures," she says, wiping away tears with the back of her hand.

I don't know what to say. I don't know how to comfort Livy. I put my arm around her wordlessly, but she goes on weeping. There has been so much grief in their lives, she says. They lost a son to diphtheria and a daughter to meningitis, and now there is Jean to worry about.

"But don't say anything about Jean or our private troubles if you write about Sam," she says.

"No, no, I won't," I promise her. "That would be cruel. But your older daughter, Clara. I hear she has a wonderful voice and is taking lessons from Professor Leschetizky."

Livy smiles at me through tears. "Oh, you may certainly mention Clara, but don't make too much of her voice. She has ambitions to become an opera singer, and that was one reason why we came here. She was keen on taking lessons from the professor, and Sam, who has always been too indulgent with her, engaged his services. But, of course, he can't work miracles, and he has already told us in so many words that her alto does not promise a great career."

After that, we pass on to lighter topics. I circle back to Sophie and the young man at the club calling her "Mrs Nobel".

Livy is very good-natured about it. "Oh, that. Well, everyone knows she was Nobel's lover. I guess it was only polite to call her Mrs Nobel in the circumstances. Perhaps he had intentions to marry her. She told me he left her an annuity. But now she is fighting with the executors over the money. Well, Sophie talks a great deal, and it doesn't always hang together. Or perhaps it does, and it's my poor German that's at fault. She is so voluble and talks so fast. Sometimes it goes right by me, and I don't want to be a bore and ask her to repeat what she said."

"If Nobel really intended to marry her, you'd think he would have done it when she was expecting."

"Instead, Sophie says, he arranged her marriage to Kapy. It's extraordinary, isn't it?"

Not extraordinary at all, I think. That is Nobel's mode of operation. He paid off his jilted lover, just as he paid off Georg's parents. Did Sophie accept the arrangement as meekly as they? Did she feel betrayed, or was she glad to put an end to her illicit affair and to the supercilious looks of servants, the knowing smiles, the silent snubs of society women which she certainly had to endure as Nobel's mistress?

"She could have done worse," I say.

"Yes, Mr Kapy strikes me as a nice man, cultured, intelligent – a brain wasted, Sam says. He is manager at a wine merchant's, you know. Schlumberger & Co. But what counts for me is the way he treats Gretel, so very kind and loving. You can always tell a man's character by the way he treats children. That is why I forgive Sam all his little – I don't know what to call them – all the odd things he says and does. I forgive him because he is a loving husband and father. Do you know that he kept a log book of all the cute and clever things our daughters said when they were little? I'll show it to you one day, Ida. Anyway, we were talking of Mr Kapy. He is a nice man. When he is around." She gives me a meaningful look. "Sophie says he has rented an apartment closer to his office."

In bed, I keep thinking of Kapy. I am ashamed of fantasizing about a married man – could it be excused as poetic imagination or was it sinful lust? There is a thin line between those two categories. It's difficult to sort out the difference. One is action, the other thought. That's the difference, I decide, but I suspect that kind of division will not stand up to doctrinal reasoning. I am a sinner.

I won't allow myself to slip into another fantasy. Not tonight. How can I sit in judgment of Nobel when I am a sinner myself? How can I be so eager to read his private letters when I would be mortified if anyone knew my own private thoughts, when I cannot get myself to confess my fantasies even to a priest? I know why penitents kneel in the dark confessional and whisper their sins to a priest through a grill. They relish the moment of absolution, when they can go forth relieved, with their souls intact once more. I, too, want my sins forgiven, and yet I cannot confess my salacious thoughts. I cannot tell the priest that I repent them or promise that I will not return to them. Those fantasies comfort me and satisfy my needs – my animal needs. I am weak. I am ashamed of my daydreams, but I cannot give them up. I am as powerless as I was in childhood when I went to confession and told the priests my sins but was unable to change my behavior. It would be the same if I told him about my fantasies. I can't stop them. I have sinned against God's commandment. Thou shalt not fornicate. Thou shalt not commit adultery. I am no better than Nobel, but here's the point: I have sinful thoughts. Nobel has sinned in deed. That's the mantra which finally soothes my conscience: Nobel's sin is greater than mine. I close my eyes. Tomorrow, I will go home and write my piece on Samuel Clemens aka Mark Twain, a task that requires no weighing of conscience. I know how I feel about him. I will gloss over his scraggly white mane, walrus moustache and fierce eyes under bushy eyebrows. I will forgive his tasteless jokes. Some time, in the early morning, I hear him come home drunk, bumping into furniture and swearing. I will overlook that too. For Livy's sake. Now that I know of Jean's illness and the death of their two children, I look at the Twains with different eyes. Their suffering has become visible to me. I can see it just below the surface of Mark Twain's zany humor. We each have our ways of dealing with loss.

Sophie

"Come in, Ida," Sophie says. "Make yourself comfortable."

She has come to like their talks. Ida writes down everything she tells her. One day, others will read about her life with Alfred and say: So that's how it was, now we understand. But what if Ida doesn't put it the right way? Sophie wants to make sure her words aren't twisted around and shaped into something she didn't mean. Those words belong to her, just as the words in Alfred's letters belong to him. That's why she wants her name on the book Ida is writing and the final say in how it's put together, because it is her life that will appear there on the printed pages. Ida needs me more than I need her, she thinks. I have all the information. She depends on me.

"The executors of Alfred's will have offered to buy his letters," she says as Ida takes her seat across from her. "Nikki says I can't talk about them in public once the sale is completed, or they'll sue me." She shakes her head. "But how can that be? I'm selling them the letters, not my life or my memories." She looks at Ida expectantly, making her the arbiter. Who owns the rights to Sophie's life?

"Then you shouldn't be talking to me about the letters?" Ida asks.

"I don't see how anyone can forbid me to say what's on my mind or in my heart," Sophie says. "We all need someone we can trust, someone to talk to, a sounding board."

Ida looks skeptical. "But surely—" she says, meaning surely there is someone closer to her heart?

"You mean why don't I talk to Nikki? I do. About everyday things, but when I talk to him about my feelings, he smiles in that absent-minded way which tells me he has stopped listening. Like Alfred. He used to ruck up his brows and say: 'What's this about your hurt feelings?' The way he said it – *feelings* – as if it was crazy to have emotions. 'Why are you tormenting yourself,' he said. 'You have no reason to be unhappy. You are living the good life – on my money, mind you.' He liked to point that out: I was living on his money. I can't help it if I'm unhappy, I said. 'I know,' he said, 'you don't have a mind capable of reasoning. So I have to forgive my little froggie if she succumbs to her feelings.' – You can write that down,

173

Ida, because those were his words. And those trustees can't oblige me to forget fourteen years of my life."

She watches as Ida obediently makes an entry in her notebook.

"But let's talk about something more cheerful," she says. "How was the evening at the Press Club? Nikki never tells me anything."

"Someone inquired after you," Ida says. "Franz Gross. He referred to you as Mrs Nobel."

"Oh? – Well, that's Alfred's fault. The confusion, I mean. He used to refer to me as his wife, to keep up appearances, you know. If we stayed at a hotel, the bell boy and the maid addressed me as 'Mrs Nobel'. It would have been awkward not to. Then other people began to call me 'Mrs Nobel', and Alfred criticized me for letting it happen. 'You have no right to use my name and give people a reason to gossip,' he said, 'you are ruining my reputation.' You can write that down as well, Ida."

She does.

"It's such a complicated story, now that I think how it all began and how everything between us changed over the years."

"What was it that changed?"

"Oh, I used to accompany Alfred to the train station whenever he left on a business trip, but then he told me to stay home. I attracted too much attention, the wrong kind of attention. And we used to write to each other every day when he was away, but I stopped because it was like writing reports for a taskmaster. He wanted to know how many pages I'd read in the book he'd sent me, how many hours I'd studied French, the company I was keeping, that sort of thing. It's all in the memoir I started to write, and now those people in Stockholm, the executors, say I can't talk about his letters." She throws up her hands. "It doesn't make sense!"

"Have you written any more since you showed me the first page?"

"A few more pages. Twelve altogether."

Ida lowers her eyes. To disguise her interest, Sophie thinks. She is keen on reading those pages, of course, but this time, I'll pin her down. I want a guarantee that I will have a share and a say in the book she is writing.

She gets up to fetch the pages from her writing desk. She presses the sheets against her chest to show Ida how precious they are, what a privilege it is to allow her to take a peek at them. I could get someone else to help me write my memoirs, she thinks, but Ida is the right person for the task. There is a glimmer of understanding in her eyes, more understanding than Sophie has seen in anyone else. It's astonishing, really. Ida is an old spinster. What does she know about life? And yet she seems to know.

"I'm almost ashamed to show you the pages," Sophie says, holding onto the sheets. "My handwriting is so bad."

"It's not that bad, judging by what I've seen."

"I tried to keep it legible, but after a few pages, I slipped back into my old scrawl. At least that's what Alfred called it, a scrawl. He said it was a disgrace, but then he criticized me all the time. According to him, I mangled the language. And I was too lazy to improve my style. All my troubles were caused by being lazy. I needed to set myself a goal and work at it, he said. Work beautifies everything. Such an odd way of putting it, but that's what he said. If I kept myself occupied, I wouldn't feel bored, he said, and run around shopping all the time. But not everyone can be a workhorse like Alfred. He kept buying me books and encouraging me to learn French. He even hired a tutor for me, but I have no talent for languages. Unlike you, Ida. You speak English and French, don't you?"

"I enjoy learning languages. It's a personal interest of mine."

"Oh, I am interested in languages too. I just don't have the brains to learn them. At least, that's what Alfred thought. A brain like a bird, he used to say. I really don't know why I stuck it out with him. Every conversation, every letter of his was full of complaints about me being stupid or ungrateful, about his health being bad, about the pressure of business. Paris was hell because people came from everywhere to see him, and he hated having visitors. They wasted his time, he said. Looking after his business didn't leave him enough time even to make an appointment with the dentist, although his gums were sore and bleeding. And then he had all those chemical experiments to supervise and accounts to keep. 'Be glad you are a little froggie,' he said to me. 'You have no worries.' But I did worry, about him and about myself too. I always came second or third. No, I came last on his long list of to-dos. I was just a bother to him, an interruption. That's how he made me feel. As if I was keeping him from more important things. You'll put all that into the book, Ida, will you?"

"I haven't started writing the book, Sophie. I'm just taking notes."

"I hope you will consult with me when you put it all together. I think of the book as ours, well, mine really, as far as my life is concerned. I know, of course, there are certain things you want to add. About Alfred's business, you said. But I want to make sure that the book tells the story of my life the way it happened."

"We both want the truth to come out," Ida says.

"Exactly, the truth, that's what I'm after."

"Of course, sometimes it can be difficult to establish the truth."

"Well, it's right here." Sophie touches her breast, "In my heart."

Ida gives her a probing look as if she needed to look into Sophie's heart. "I mean the truth is subjective," she says. "It is too bad that we can't quote Nobel's letters. But we have your memories."

"Oh, I remember everything Alfred said to me. That's the problem. I remember too well. Every hurtful word is etched on my brain. Every loving word, too. I can't tell you how much I miss Alfred. He could be a tyrant at times, but I suppose he knew what was best for me. It was so nice to have him take care of me and look after all those tiresome details and manage everything."

She suppresses a sigh. It's true. Nikki takes care of things only if she begs him, and then he does it reluctantly, as if it wasn't his business, as if she made unreasonable demands on him.

"And all Alfred asked for in return was love and gratitude," she says. "He said I was ungrateful, but it's not true. I always thanked him when we were together, and when we were apart, I ended every one of my letters to him with love and kisses and heartfelt thanks. But really, he loved his business more than me. He was never home. I was lonely. And do you know, all the time, *he* complained how lonely he was, that I was away too much. Well, what was I supposed to do, sit at home and wait for him? 'You are always away, having fun at some spa or other,' he said. When we were apart, he kept writing me letters saying how much he missed me, but when we were together, he was full of reproaches. I was keeping him from intellectual pursuits, from scientific experiments and I don't know what else. Sometimes, I had to stop my ears. He could be brutal."

"Brutal?"

"I don't mean in the physical sense. It's just that Alfred never had time for me, and yet he called *me* self-centered, can you imagine? Of course, he was always generous to me, but that's not the same thing as loving me. Money can't replace love."

"I know," Ida says rather forcefully and catches her breath, almost as if she had blurted out something she did not mean to reveal. There is pain in Ida's eyes, a shadow barely there, visible only to those who have known pain themselves.

"Perhaps you have experienced that kind of thing yourself, Ida. Have you?"

Ida hesitates.

"Have I touched a sore spot?" Sophie says. "You don't need to answer my question if you aren't comfortable with it." She gives Ida a roguish smile. "I know how it feels to be asked questions you don't really want to think about."

"You have been very patient answering my questions, Sophie. Why shouldn't you take a turn and ask about my life?" She hedges a bit longer. The shadow in her eyes deepens. Then she comes out with it. "You are right. Money can't replace love. I was thinking of my neighbors whose son died in an industrial accident." She keeps her voice steady, but the eyes give her away. She is no longer her steady self. She is weakening. And now her hand betrays her as well. She touches the black enamel locket at her neck. Sophie has noticed it before. It's a mourning locket, the type that contains a weave of hair, the memory of a loved one.

"I was engaged to him," she says.

So that's it. Ida was engaged. Or is that just a polite way of putting it. Perhaps she had a lover too.

"I'm sorry to hear of your loss," Sophie says.

"It happened a long time ago. The factory owner offered his parents money as if he could compensate them for the love of a son. And even that compensation came with a cold addendum from the company lawyer. The payment did not constitute an admission of fault, he told Georg's parents."

"That's lawyers for you," Sophie says. "They have no heart."

Ida puts her hands into her lap and clasps them together as if she was forcing herself not to finger the locket again. She is afraid of giving away too much, Sophie thinks.

"But to get back to Nobel," Ida says, looking at the manuscript of the memoir, the sheets Sophie has placed on the table between them. "I've read there were fatal accidents in his factories as well. Did he ever talk to you about them or about the loss of life they occasioned?"

"Not that I remember," Sophie says, but then she does remember. "No, wait. Alfred did mention an accident, in Hamburg it was, I think. Someone was suing him. The witnesses were lying through their teeth, Alfred said. He wasn't concerned about the money he might have to pay if the judgment went against him. It was a question of honor, he said. He was proud of the way he managed his business. He was always looking for

177

ways of improving things, always inspecting his factories and doing tests at his laboratories. He was doing too much if you ask me. The work took over and became more important than everything else, including me."

"It really is too bad we can't use his letters to you," Ida says. "But what about your letters to him? Have you kept copies of them, or are they included in your offer of sale to the trustees?"

"No, no," Sophie waves her hand in a vague swirl of sadness. "I am keeping those copies. I wouldn't sell Alfred's letters either, not for the measly sum the trustees have offered me, but what can I do? I need the money, and so I'm willing to sign the contract, against my better judgment and against what my heart tells me because those letters are part of my life. Which reminds me – I sent the trustees transcripts of a few letters, and now they want those transcripts verified before they send me the money. Could I ask you a favor, Ida? I need someone to compare the transcripts with the originals and sign a piece of paper to confirm that they are accurate copies. Would you do that for me? It's only three pages."

Ida can't disguise her eagerness. She is dying to read Alfred's letters!

"Of course I'll verify them for you," she says. "It won't take me long to read three pages."

"Thank you," Sophie says, keeping her voice breathy. "Oh, and another thing. I meant to ask you, Ida. This publisher friend of yours – Carl Volker – would he, by any chance, be interested in publishing the letters I wrote to Alfred?"

"I can talk to him," Ida says quickly, "but I would have to read your letters first so that I can get a sense of what's there. He won't be able to give me an answer unless I provide him with some information about them."

Sophie looks at the clock on the mantelpiece.

"We'll have to leave that for another time, I'm afraid. I have an appointment with the dressmaker in half an hour, and I still need you to verify those transcriptions. I've set them out on my writing desk."

It is time to ration her favors. Showing Ida three of Alfred's letters is enough for the time being.

Ida gets up obediently and follows Sophie to her writing desk, where she has set out the originals, the transcripts, and the verification document that Nikki had drawn up for her to sign. She watches Ida take a seat at the bureau and start comparing the two versions. My God, she is a fast reader, Sophie thinks. Her eyes fly over the pages. What a strange woman. She can't disguise her eagerness. Imagine getting so excited about someone else's life. What would she have made of the rest of Alfred's letters? Too bad they are off limits now. Sophie would have liked to show Ida what she was up against. She needs someone who can see her point of view. Nikki shakes his head and smiles when she complains. Like Alfred. Except that Nikki is more polite, or perhaps he just doesn't care.

I would have liked to show Ida the letter in which Alfred says I've made him stupid.

I feel so stupid and awkward now when I am obliged to talk to people. That's because I'm getting used to your childish ways.

Or the one in which he told her: *You took advantage of my generosity and undermined my spirit. I withdrew from all cultured relations and have lost my intellectual abilities, my self-respect and the respect of other people as well.*

And was that really my fault? Sophie thinks.

"Done," Ida says and signs Nikki's document "Let me just make a few notes about those letters."

"You do that," Sophie says. She is in a benevolent mood now that she has Ida's signature and that business is done without Ida asking for a fee. She takes up her engagement book and leafs through it. "Maybe you could come back tomorrow afternoon and look at my letters to Alfred."

179

Ida

Three letters in Nobel's handwriting. Now I have seen his hand, the hand of a law-and-order man, hard, disciplined, unwavering, so unlike the soft-spoken old man I met in San Remo. Now I have listened in on his conversation with Sophie, the words of a lover to his mistress before he turned into a disciplinarian and an ailing old crank. Sophie has been liberal supplying me with information, but she refers to the planned book as "ours" or even as her own. So be it. Let the book be hers. Let it appear under both of our names or her name alone, as long as it serves my purpose. But will Sophie be amenable to my plans and allow me to include what matters to me? If she doesn't, I may have to go back on my offer and write my own book. We will have to sort that out before long, but right now it's important to gather all the information I can, and here is my chance. Sophie is willing to let me read her letters to Nobel and has set out the packet on her desk. The letters are tied with a black velvet ribbon that looks funereal.

"I told Nikki that you are going to talk to your publisher friend about buying the letters," she says. "He isn't sure it's a good idea, but I have nothing to hide. Read the letters, I said to Nikki, and tell me why I shouldn't publish them. He went through a few and gave up. He said it took too long to decipher my handwriting. He couldn't be bothered to read the rest. He said the letters were boring. I wonder what you will think of them, Ida."

"I don't think I'll find them boring."

She pulls out a chair for me, and I sit down at the desk and undo the black ribbon.

Sophie isn't giving me much time to read the letters. She is keeping me on a short leash. She has been waving her engagement book at me. It's a day full of appointments, she says – the milliner, the hairdresser, the seamstress, a gown needs pinning up – but I think it's her way of keeping control of the situation. She knows how to manipulate people. Perhaps Nobel has taught her that skill. Last time, she rushed me through reading the transcripts she wanted me to verify. This time, she tells me I have less than an hour before she must be off, and, of course, she can't leave me alone with her letters. She has to keep an eye on them. She hovers, looking over my shoulder as I begin reading.

I can hear the clock on the mantelpiece ticking. The letters are in chronological order. First, I check the crucial year when Georg died. I go through the letters she wrote that year. I read rapidly, scanning for Heleneborg, explosion, accident. Nothing.

I go on to look at the rest. Sophie has retreated to the sofa. Out of the corner of my eye, I see her leafing through a book of fashion plates.

Most of her letters are from recent years, after her break-up with Nobel. I can tell already that they will be of little help in composing the kind of book I have in mind. Kapy is right. They are boring – short notes, mostly, compositions following the same pattern – complaints about her poor health, calculated to evoke pity, requests for money combined with polite inquiries after Nobel's health, aimed at keeping his goodwill and showing that she cared.

I make extracts.

I'm totally run down and have no energy left. I wonder if I will ever in my whole life regain my looks.

I am completely beside myself, so nervous and sick that I cannot stand it much longer, I am an unhappy creature who gets no advice or protection from anyone!

I beg you, dear Alfred, be kind enough to help me, I am in a terrible position. I have no money to pay the rent, and today, I had to pawn my last brooch, I have never been in such straits before.

The physicians are worried about my health. Your painful accusations have affected me so much that I now have an anemic brain and my limbs tremble.

I've sunk into a depression and feel lost. I never thought my life could be so wretched.

I am so nervous that I am dizzy. I need fresh air. I need to be outdoors as much as possible, but it is so windy out there. The weather is terrible.

I will end up a beggar. I beg you a thousand times, send me money. Every night I dream of them coming after me to seize my furniture, and one night, I even dreamed that they seized my child. I worry terribly.

I am puzzled about Sophie's health complaints. Was she lying, or was she really sick at the time? Was it a spiritual or a physical ailment? She looks the picture of health now – rosy cheeks and a well-rounded body, but then I remember Nobel's complaints and realize that Sophie merely echoes them. She pitted her anemia against his rheumatism, her anxiety against his migraines. It was a duet, call and response. If I could interlace their letters, they would make a play. Nobel was a playwright after all, and these letters were scenes from his life. He was on stage, playing the suffering king, or the benevolent protector of the weak, and Sophie took her cue from him and joined him in a lament or groveled and cowered and toadied to him. She went through her paces and gave him what he wanted.

I don't have time to read on or take more notes. Sophie is in a hurry to get rid of me.

"Nikki will be here any minute now," she said. "We are supposed to call on the Schönthals. I'd better get those letters wrapped up."

I square the letters, and she ties them up again and locks them away in her writing desk.

She wants me out of the way, I can tell, as if my presence somehow counted as evidence against her as if we were conspirators and she didn't want her husband to know. In a way, we are conspirators – two women with thoughts of revenge. Two women who want to get back at Alfred Nobel for what he has done to us.

"Sorry, Ida," she says. "I hate to be in a hurry. I like to take things at a slower pace, but every day is full of appointments."

"I'll read the rest another time," I say. "And we need to discuss how best to go on and get the story down on paper."

She walks me to the door.

"If you run into Nikki, don't tell him that I let you read my letters," she says.

I rather like the idea of running into Nikki.

"I probably shouldn't have shown the letters to you," she says. "For all I know, it violates some clause in the contract I signed with the trustees, and Nikki has a mind like a lawyer. Or maybe like a drill sergeant. He was in the military, you know."

"Why did he resign his commission?" I ask. As I say the words, I realize that I have no right to ask questions about him. Our business concerns Nobel, not Nikolaus Kapy.

Sophie doesn't answer me, just bundles me out the door. "Sorry to be so pressing, Ida, but time flies, and I have to get ready."

Nobel's letters are gone now, sold to the estate. The only sources remaining are Sophie's letters to him and the manuscript of her memoirs, which has grown to sixteen pages, still mostly quotations. She has finally entrusted them to me, "for editing" she says. We can't use the quotations, but they give me a sense of what was in the packet she sold, in the letters I'll never see. Sophie's memoirs are no substitute, but they say a lot about their relationship. They are an indictment of Nobel.

At home, I go over Sophie's memoirs. Nobel said terrible things to her. I would never have put up with such a man.

You complain that I don't use words of love in my letters. Yet for years, I have been pointing out that nobody can command anyone's emotions. It is part of my freedom-loving nature that I could not live day after day with someone like you: weak, jealous and childish. Solitude is preferable. You do not understand me, but I feel pity for you, all the more the better I get to know you. Your young, weak soul is thirsting for an affection I cannot give you.

He manipulated her, tried to make her feel stupid, told her that she was dragging him down to her level: *You understand only what suits you. You are incapable of seeing that I have, for years now, sacrificed, out of purely noble motives, my time, my duties, my intellectual life, my reputation, my whole interaction with the cultured world and finally, my business affairs to a child who is willful and without understanding, who is incapable of seeing the generosity of my actions.*

She was indiscreet, he said, and flaunted their relationship. He was worried about his reputation.

I don't want to become the target of gossip. A man can have many pieces of gold or obtain them, but he has only one reputation which he has a duty to keep as spotless as possible. And for years now, you have played a cheap comedy and kept all sorts of things secret from me. At my cost, you surround yourself with a crowd of admirers, have fun with them and make me a laughing stock.

If that was true, why did he not separate from her sooner? I can guess why. Because he wanted her adulation, her groveling thanks for his generosity. He wanted to lord it over her, make her feel inferior because she was uneducated. He wanted to make her feel guilty for depriving him of intellectual stimulation because he himself felt guilty for neglecting the arts. If I could use his words! But I must paraphrase them, and to paraphrase a man's words is to water them down.

Why did Sophie put up with him for fourteen years? She must have done it for the money. Perhaps not only for the money. What if she craved his attention and the closeness of another human body? What if she acted on her desires, as I did once, and did not know how to stop and keep those desires locked in her head? I don't know whether to pity her for putting up with abuse or despise her for being weak and letting it go on for so long. How could she stay with him and lead a life of lies and deceit? I understand temptation, but I have sinned in deed only once. The rest is fantasy. Could I lose my grip and act on my fantasies? No, I would never become a man's mistress! Such a life is beneath contempt.

*

When Carl took me to the soirée at the Zuckerkandls, I wasn't sure how I would get through the evening. It was our first get-together after that painful scene in his office when I rejected his proposal, or temporized at any rate. But the evening went well, and we are back on the old footing, or something even better, something more businesslike. He is staying away from the subject of marriage.

When I bring him my chapter on San Remo, he looks his good old self, sitting behind his desk, shuffling papers. "Good old" is the epithet that comes to mind whenever I see him. Carl has certainly recovered from my rejection and may even be secretly glad I didn't take him up on his offer. He is an old bachelor at heart. Mrs Olmuth had him pegged right when she warned me (quite unnecessarily) that I shouldn't get up my hopes.

"Here it is," I say and hand him the chapter on San Remo. "An essay about the rich and famous and about the question whether an inventor should be held responsible for the use of his inventions."

He looks doubtful. "Sounds heavy," he says. Then he makes the connection. "Ah," he says, "it's about Nobel! He died in San Remo, didn't he?"

I nod. "The elusive inventor of dynamite. I met him in San Remo shortly before he had his fatal stroke. We had an interesting conversation about war and peace."

"A personal conversation? That's a scoop, I'd say."

"Good enough to persuade you to publish the manuscript?"

"It will give your travelogue some heft at any rate. So you think Nobel should be held responsible for the use of dynamite?"

"I do."

"But a manufacturer can't control the use of the goods once they have left his factory. He can't tell his customers what to do with the product they bought."

184

"Nobel controlled the patents. He should have stopped manufacturing dynamite when he saw how it was used."

"Aren't you a bit hard on the fellow?"

"At the very least, he should have taken responsibility for the manufacturing process. I understand there were a number of deadly accidents at his factories and laboratories."

"From what I've read, justice was served. Nobel was sued and paid compensation."

"You really think a widow can be compensated for the death of her husband with a money order?"

I've never told Carl or any of my recent acquaintances about the circumstances of Georg's death and the nightmares I am suffering as a result. The Olmuths are friends of long standing and know about it. People in St Veit know that I lost my fiancé in an industrial accident. They made funereal faces at the time and offered me their condolences, but after eighteen years, I don't expect anyone to remember the accident or sympathize with me over Georg's death. No doubt, they think eighteen years is enough time to recover. Mind you, Freud recently declared that this kind of traumatic experience has long-lasting effects and could lead to permanent "hypnoid hysteria", uncontrollable emotions while in a state of sleep. Is that what my nightmares are – hypnoid hysteria?

"I suppose money can't compensate a widow for her loss," Carl says in answer to my indignant question, "but it was the best Nobel could do in the circumstances. Only God can resurrect the dead. And I hear he left millions to set up a foundation to support the arts and sciences. An admirable demonstration of public spirit, wouldn't you say?"

"Or an effort to atone for his sins."

"In any case, Nobel is an interesting subject. And topical. His name is in all the papers, so perhaps this is a good time to publish your travelogue and capitalize on the news value of your chapter on San Remo."

Those are beautiful words, like being handed a bouquet of roses. Carl is smiling broadly. Does he expect a reward, a greater reward than I am willing to give him?

"Thank you, Carl." I breathe the words and float them across the desk like a kiss, but I keep very still, waiting to see how he takes my response. Will he demand more than a thank-you? No, he seems to be content with gratitude. We argue a bit about the title. I want *European Resorts and Beyond*. Boring, Carl says. He wants *To the Caucasus and Back*.

"That's putting undue emphasis on the three chapters dealing with Mingrelia," I say.

"But it will attract more readers," he says. "Believe me, Ida. I know my business."

I won't quarrel about the title. I just want the book to come out. I can't wait to hold it in my hands. Those chapters are slices of my life, cast in solid type. Unlike my unsubstantial thoughts, unlike the fantasies in my head, unlike the memories of my journey to the Caucasus which are fading already, those slices of life will have permanence. And there is the chapter on Nobel, my first swipe at his reputation. I hold him responsible for his deadly invention.

"So what's your next project?" Carl says, still smiling, still full of benevolence after I have agreed to the title he wants, and he has as good as promised to send my travelogue to the typesetter.

"Keep working on a biography of Nobel," I say.

"Ah, that encounter in San Remo got you going."

"You might put it that way," I say. Carl doesn't realize how long I have been working on the book. Why am I so secretive? Because I am no longer sure of my motives? Of course, that is Carl's next question. What are my motives? Why do I want to write about Nobel's life?

"Still hung up on the question of the inventor's responsibilities?"

"I don't know why you'd call it 'hung up'," I say. "It's a perfectly legitimate cause."

"Legitimate – I suppose so, but academic, not to say Utopian."

We are definitely back to the status quo, chaffing each other and quibbling over words.

"It's a respectable cause at any rate – to shame a profiteering arms dealer. But more to the point, I've met a woman who was Nobel's lover for many years. Her name is Sophia Kapy. Now there is a story for you!" I don't say that the story I really want to tell is my own.

"Sophia Kapy?" He rubs his forehead, searching his mind. "Oh, yes. Now I remember – the notorious 'Mrs Nobel', made an honest woman by a Hungarian captain. Someone ought to write a play about her. A farce."

"Or else publish her memoirs. She wants to write about her years with Nobel, she told me, but she floundered after a few pages. She has asked me to help her."

"This 'Life of Nobel' is a commission then?"

"A collaboration."

"You want my advice, Ida? Don't collaborate. She will get in your way. That kind of arrangement works only if the partners are well-matched, which isn't the case here. You are an accomplished writer. Mrs Kapy is an amateur. Why collaborate when you can do it on your own?"

"That's just it. I can't do it on my own. Sophie has all the information, and she wasn't very forthcoming until I offered to collaborate. She lived with Nobel for fourteen years. Apparently, he didn't treat her very well. I believe she has an axe to grind, and her story will make for an interesting book."

I tell Carl about Sophie's correspondence with Nobel. "She sold Nobel's letters to the estate. They are gone, unfortunately, but she has kept copies of her own letters to him and is willing to sell them to a publisher. Are you interested?"

"Could be worth something," Carl says, "I'll take a look at them. Tell her to come to my office and bring the letters along. We'll talk. As for collaborating with her on a biography: remember, I warned you."

Carl is right, of course, but I need the information, and Sophie is the gatekeeper.

"We'll see how it goes. I'm still 'hung up' on my cause, as you put it. I won't allow her to turn the book into a scandal sheet."

"Although that would make for better sales," he says with a mocking smile.

"But it's not in Mrs Kapy's interest. She has an inclination to tell tales, but she wants the book to be a justification of her life, or rather a whitewash, and I'll go along with that as long as she has no objection to rounding it off and adding something about Nobel's business practices. And why should she object? It will reinforce her own complaints."

"Well, I'm curious to meet Mrs Kapy and hear what *she* has to say about your joint project."

I relay Carl's invitation to Sophie, but she plays coy. There is no sense in her going to his office, she says. She knows nothing about publishing. She'll send Nikki instead. He will make an appointment with Carl.

*

The two men have set up a meeting. Carl thinks I should attend. "This business concerns you as well," he says. Her letters would make a good appendix to the "Life of Nobel". He still considers my collaboration with Sophie a bad deal because I will have to do all the writing. I should at least attend his meeting with Kapy and guard my interests.

187

"You'd better watch out, Ida. Or let me watch out for you," he says.

I agree to sit in on the meeting – to guard my interests or to see Kapy again? The latter, I'm afraid. My fantasies about him have become almost as intrusive as my desire to expose Nobel, and while I believe that writing about him will liberate me, I can think of no way to be liberated from my desire for Kapy and put an end to my recurrent sinful thoughts. Well, I can think of one way: to act upon my thoughts. I don't mean in every detail and all the way, that would be despicable, but perhaps seeing Kapy and talking to him will take the edge off my desire.

So I have come to Carl's office and taken my seat across from his desk. He looks more together than I've seen him in some time. Tie straight, beard trimmed, hair carefully combed to hide the thinning part in front. His frock coat is buttoned up and brushed. He is dressed to meet the client, I realize. I haven't seen him in that role before.

"What did you tell Mrs Kapy about me, Ida?" he says. "That ladies aren't safe in my company? Why is she sending me her husband?"

"It's her mode of operation. He also negotiated the sale of Nobel's letters for her."

Perhaps I should have followed Sophie's example and let Carl negotiate on my behalf. I am no longer sure that seeing Kapy in the flesh is going to take the edge off my desire. I feel out of breath just thinking of my dream man. I am trying to make conversation with Carl, but my voice is clogged with half-remembered dreams of Kapy.

He arrives with his bowler hat side-raked. He takes it off and greets us. I keep my eyes down, looking modest, I hope. Before taking his seat, Kapy moves his chair over a bit, to give us room, perhaps, or to improve his sightlines, so that he can better divide his attention between Carl and me. He sits with his head erect and his back straight like the ex-soldier he is, with one leg slightly forward. His suit is immaculate, a smooth fit for his slim body. His hands rest on his thighs. They are pianist hands with long fingers. You'd expect them to dance, and yet they lie still, palms down flat, merely showing off their beauty. I am fascinated by their stillness, from which they are awoken occasionally to move upward, to emphasize something he is saying. They give his words an upward-drift. I long to hold those hands, take them between my own, stroke them. I steal a look at his face. A polite smile is playing on his lips. I feel the familiar warming of blood, which might bring on an unquiet dream. But I am determined not to give way to a flash fantasy until we are done with business. In spite of my resolve, a gossamer web of thoughts begins spreading between us, as if we had some secret understanding.

We talk about Sophie's plans to collaborate with me on a biography of Nobel, about the letters she is willing to sell to Carl. He has folded his hands over his avuncular paunch and put on an all-is-well expression. The posture is for Kapy's benefit. It is supposed to assure him that Volker Press is a solid business.

Kapy, meanwhile, doesn't look like a man needing reassurance. He is perfectly serene, looking at Carl as if he expected an instructive lecture on a subject of interest, though not of burning interest.

Carl has worked out two possible scenarios. He is willing to publish Sophie's memoirs – her life with Nobel – with the letters, or a selection of the letters, in an appendix. If it is to be a private edition, he will print a hundred copies and charge the cost to her. She can dispose of the copies as she sees fit. If I am willing to collaborate with her, it's up to me to charge her a fee for my services. He looks at me, expecting me to name my price. When I don't say anything, he goes on: "I suppose Miss Lassick will charge the usual. In any case, I know her work, and am confident that she will produce a good book, a substantial and well-written piece."

He pauses and gives me another look – expecting me to thank him for the compliment? But Kapy speaks up instead.

"My wife will need help, I know that," he says. "I'm sure she will benefit from Miss Lassick's skill and experience."

If the book is to be offered for sale to the public under my or Sophie's name – he leaves that decision to us, Carl says – he will pay us a certain sum for the manuscript, price to be determined on submission, and he will take the risk of selling the book. That's how he puts it. Of course, Carl never takes risks. He gauges the public appetite for a particular piece of writing, calculates its worth and offers money to the author accordingly. He has concluded that there is an appetite for a book about Nobel's private life if it involves a mistress, and he trusts in my ability to write that book. As for Sophie's letters to Nobel, Carl may be interested in buying the rights upfront, but that would be a separate transaction, he says.

"Did you bring the letters with you, Mr Kapy?" he asks.

"I'm afraid not. Sophie won't let them out of her sight. You'll have to call on her and look at them in situ." He takes out his pocketbook and hands Carl a card. "Her 'at home' day is Thursday," he says.

Carl takes the card and studies it. "I'll make an appointment with Mrs Kapy," he says. "I need to see how many letters there are and what's in them before I make an offer. Let's just say, if Mrs Kapy decides to go public with her memoir, I'd be more inclined to buy the letters. The book might whet the appetite of readers and lessen my risk as publisher – if I decide to buy them or take on the memoir, which is all hypothetical at the moment."

He has listed all the options and put them down on a sheet of paper, which he hands to Kapy.

"Talk it over and let me know," he says.

Kapy has listened with detachment to the inventory of options. His hands have remained still during Carl's enumeration of the available choices. But his eyes are roaming – in my direction – I can't help noticing. He is playing a game in which I am the loser. Our eyes meet and lock for a second. I half expect him to smirk. But he gives me a searching, thoughtful, even wary look. I can't read him, and I don't venture another look. I face forward and keep my eyes on Carl for the rest of the meeting.

But I can't deny that all the time, I was thinking of Nikolaus Kapy and thinking of him with longing. We leave Carl's office together.

"Which way are you going, Miss Lassick?" he asks as we step out into the street.

"To the train station," I say. "I live in St Veit."

"Then we are going the same way. I don't live far from you – in Hietzing."

He no longer shared Sophie's suite in the Metropole. I had begun to wonder about that even before Livy mentioned it. On the two occasions I met Kapy at the Metropole, he looked more like a visitor than a resident.

"I am a manager for Schlumberger & Co," he says. "Their winery is out that way."

The words are commonplace, but I listen for a hidden meaning. He lives close to me. He is close to me. I want to know more about his life. I want to get to the core, the layers under his skin, down to the heart. I want him. Desire has me by the throat.

"You prefer the civilian life to the military?" I say.

He gives me a surprised look. "You know about my career in the military?"

"I heard you say that you resigned your commission."

He looks blank.

"You were talking to Franz Gross at the Concordia."

"Ah," he says with what sounds like a breath of relief. Does he have something to hide? Is there something about his military career that he doesn't want to be known?

"Other people have asked me that question," he says. "Do I like being a manager rather than an officer? I tell them: Neither profession challenges the mind, but the production of wine suggests a more congenial context – dinners, dances, the communal spirit of sharing food and drink."

"Isn't the military meant to foster a spirit of camaraderie as well?"

I say it in a teasing voice, but he gives me a serious answer as if he was offering me his philosophy of life. Perhaps he is.

"Camaraderie, yes, but the context is adversarial. The idea is to sharpen the concept of them-versus-us. In the military, the purpose is to identify the enemy and kill him. But I don't believe in warfare as a way to settle conflicts."

"I know. You are in Bertie's camp. A pacifist."

"Let's just say I don't have it in me to defend the fatherland against her enemies," he says, smiling. There are many kinds of smiles. The straightforward kind, of happiness and affection. The amused kind. The ironic kind. Kapy's smile doesn't fit any of these categories. It's reserved, cagey, full of secret meaning.

"What enemies?" I say. "Prussia? I thought we were safe for the time being."

"I meant the enemy within."

For a moment, I think he means his inner life, but he is talking about domestic politics.

"There are too many parties in this country," he says, "each looking to increase their share of power. Too many hands upholding the roof. If one of them lets go, the monarchy will collapse. My cousin, who is a bit of a wag, likes to say: They each want their own little empire. The boozing Austrians, the bootlicker Czechs, the Polish smartasses, the Slovenian brushmakers—"

He stops because we've reached the train station. It's almost four o'clock, and the local train leaves every hour on the hour. Kapy takes my arm and steers me through the crowd of hawkers, luggage carriers and fellow travelers. I feel my hips brush against his.

"And the Hungarians?" I say. Kapy's family is Hungarian. Perhaps that's why his cousin hasn't included them in his abusive list.

"And the skirt-chasing Hungarians," he says and laughs as we get into a compartment occupied by an elderly couple. The man wrinkles his brow at the sight of the laughing Kapy. He gives him a questioning look that ends our conversation. It wouldn't do to speculate about the collapse of Austria in the company of strangers.

I take my seat beside the woman, who hugs her bag close to her chest as if she feared an attempt at robbery. Her husband eyes Kapy for a moment longer over the rim of his glasses before turning his attention back to the newspaper he is reading.

After a while, he lowers the paper and says to his wife, "They buried Strauss yesterday. Carried the coffin through the city. Thousands of mourners lining the streets."

She nods sadly. "Will there ever be another composer of waltzes like him?"

He purses his lips. "I hope not," he says sternly. How sure of himself he is, how unassailable in his disapproval!

"Oh," she says, "Oh, I didn't mean—"

The sentence hangs in the air, suspended on the ellipses of her meek uncertainty.

They get off at the next stop, leaving the newspaper behind.

Kapy picks it up. "Have you read Strauss' obituary in the *Presse?*"

"No, I haven't seen today's paper." I haven't had a chance to read them because I skipped my afternoon at the Olmuths' to attend the meeting at Carl's office.

"The waltz is a wicked dance," Kapy says with the same inscrutable smile that predicted the collapse of the empire. He unfolds the paper and reads a few lines to me:

"*It captures our senses in a sweet trance. Our limbs no longer belong to us. It is a storm let loose, an exorcism of wicked spirits from the body.*" He looks up, waiting for my reaction.

"And it certainly inspires metaphor," I say. "As for the waltz itself, I am no judge. I never go to dances."

"Then you must join us one evening and experience its bacchanalian effects."

"Better give me ample warning," I say, "because I'll have to practice."

It is Kapy's stop. He gathers his hat and coat. As the train pulls out of the station, he stands on the platform, raising his hand to me in farewell. I see his lips move but can't hear what he is saying. For a moment, two images merge: me waving goodbye to Georg, Kapy waving goodbye to me, his lips moving. Then the present erases the past.

At home, I think about the lines Kapy read to me: *The waltz puts us into a sweet trance. Our limbs no longer belong to us. It is an exorcism of wicked spirits*. I take a few dancing steps in my parlor. I imagine myself in Kapy's arms, twirling around the room, going into a sweet trance. Could a man like Kapy exorcise evil spirits and end my nightmares? I stop twirling. This is no fantasy. This is wishful thinking. I need to exorcise Kapy from my mind!

Sophie

"Oh, Livy! You are deserting me!" Sophie says. It's an unpleasant surprise. There are so few people she can talk to, so few who will listen. And now the Twains are moving to Kaltenleutgeben. They want to consult Dr Winternitz about their daughter, Livy says. He's experimenting with a new cure for epilepsy. Sophie is sorry to see her go and sorry also for the girl. I'm just glad Gretel is healthy, she thinks. I don't know what I'd do if she came down with some horrible sickness like Jean's. No, I don't even want to think about it.

Livy puts down her coffee cup. She gets up from the sofa and walks over to the window, looking down on the Donaukanal. Is she comparing views? The Twains' apartment overlooks the glass-domed atrium which is like a greenhouse, with palms and orchids and as quiet as a garden. Of course, they are paying for that view. But when Livy turns back, Sophie can tell that her thoughts are far away. Her eyes are blind to the outside world.

"We've rented a villa," she says, sitting down again beside Sophie and making an effort to be cheerful. "Recently built, eight rooms with all the amenities. There are balconies in front and back and a walled garden. It has large grounds, half an acre, and it's surrounded by hills and pine forests." She laughs. "Do I sound like a house agent?"

She does. It's because those are the house agent's words, she says.

"I've learned a lot of new vocabulary. Following him around was like getting a German lesson. He pointed to everything and named it. Sam thought the realtor was hilarious. The moment he left, he gave us a parody of the scene. 'On your right, you see a chair on which Lady Rich sat last week. On your left, a closet, which, only two weeks ago, held the elegant dresses of Lady Trendy. Straight ahead, the balcony. Breathe in, ladies and gentlemen, and fill your lungs with the scent of pines!' We were in stitches. Even Jean laughed out loud, and you know how she is, never letting on how she feels – happy or sad."

They are both laughing now, but Sophie can hear a note of desperation in Livy's voice. She doesn't know what to say, how to comfort her.

"I am sure you will enjoy yourselves," she says because she can't think of anything else to say. "Kaltenleutgeben is a popular town."

"So they told us when we tried to negotiate the rent. The owner wasn't prepared to reduce it, the agent said. It was a privilege to live there. He rattled off a list of famous neighbors we were bound to meet. Count Coudenhove, Countess Bardi, Princess Khevenhueller and the Queen of Romania, who writes novels under the name of Carmen Sylva, or so he said."

"I must look into that," Sophie says. The town was charming, but she had no idea the spa attracted such distinguished visitors. "Maybe I'll come and visit you." She wouldn't mind being introduced to a queen.

"By all means. Come and visit us, Sophie. It's less than an hour by train. We'll be back here for day trips if there's a concert or a play that interests us. I'll make sure to call on you when we are in town."

Sophie sighs. It had been nice to have Livy close by.

"I'll miss you," she says.

"We'll have a farewell dinner before we leave," Livy says. "Just a small affair. We need to keep things quiet. The doctor has cautioned us. Jean can't have any excitement. I hope you and Mr Kapy will be able to come, and I'll invite Clara's music professor and her young man, Ossip Garbilowitch."

"Oh," Sophie says. "Clara is engaged?"

"Not yet, but I fear Mr Garbilowitch is on the point of proposing to her. Not that I dislike him, but he is a Russian. I mean, where will they end up living? In Russia? He plans on making a career in the West, and the professor is helping him set up a tour in America, but what are the chances that he will succeed? I try not to think about it, Sophie. In any case, I need to think about the dinner party. I've sent an invitation to Bertha Suttner. You have met her, haven't you?"

"Oh, yes. She used to write begging letters to Alfred."

"Sam got letters from her too – well, perhaps I shouldn't call them begging letters. She tried to interest him in her cause and invited him to the meetings of her Society. Universal peace is a worthwhile cause. I told Sam she deserved his support. 'Then why don't you invite her to our farewell dinner,' he said, 'and I'll see what she has to say about her Society.' So I sent an invitation to the Suttners and another one to Ida Lassick."

"But how will Ida fit in? She is so—" Sophie was going to say so drab, so straight-laced, so ordinary. "I mean, she never goes out into society."

"She is a friend of Countess Suttner, Sam told me. He didn't realize there was a connection until he read Ida's travelogue – the book she published recently. Apparently, she visited the Suttners in Caucasia."

"There was some talk about Caucasia at a dinner Nikki and I attended," Sophie says, "but come to think of it, Ida never told me anything about her visit there, and I see quite a bit of her. Well, that just goes to show you. I talk too much. That's what Nikki says at any rate. I monopolize the conversation. But that's Ida's fault, you know. She is leading me on. She asks a million questions and tells me nothing about herself in turn."

"That may be in her nature. Some people are more reserved than others."

What else does Ida have up her sleeve? Sophie thinks. She was pretty smart about the contract with the publisher. I have to give her a cut if I sell the manuscript to Carl Volker. At least that's what Nikki says. Or was it Carl Volker who suggested paying her? Perhaps he is more than a friend to Ida.

"Countess Suttner accepted the invitation," Livy says, "but she will come on her own. Her husband has a previous engagement."

"That's awkward for you, isn't it? Four men and five women. You want to have an even number."

Livy shrugs. "That's just a silly convention. Odd numbers don't bother me. I wasn't sure the countess would accept. She is in demand on the social circle, I am told, but I suppose she accepted because she wants a chance to spread the word about her Society."

"She isn't going to spread the word very far at a dinner party," Sophie says.

"She only needs to get Sam's ear, and he is willing to listen. He may want to write or even just talk about her Society. The journalists report everything he says. It's like using a megaphone. If he mentions her cause, it will come to the attention of many people. I'm sure Mrs Suttner is aware of that."

*

The day of the farewell dinner arrives. Livy has given Mrs Suttner the seat of honor on her husband's right, Sophie notes. She is off to a good start if her purpose is to get Sam's ear, but Sophie gets a share of Mark Twain too. She is seated on his left.

Nikki is on Mrs Suttner's other side and will draw her off, she hopes, so she can have Mark Twain to herself. She likes Mark Twain. He is such an entertaining man. Nikki does make polite conversation with Mrs Suttner, but not enough to engage her. Instead, he keeps talking to Ida, paying more attention to her than he should. Sophie looks around the table. Has anyone else noticed how often Nikki's eyes are fixed on Ida?

The countess tries hard to steer the talk into the direction of the peace movement, but the music lovers at the other end of the table are in the majority and have taken over. When she finally maneuvers the talk back to her pet subject, Mr Twain has a few ideas of his own.

"If you want my opinion," he says, "world peace won't be achieved by signing papers or hearing cases in an international court. You'll never persuade countries to reduce their armament voluntarily. Fear of defeat is the only thing that will keep them from declaring war. I am very much in sympathy with your movement, my dear countess, but my head is not with my heart in this matter."

"That's exactly what Alfred used to say," Sophie chimes in. "Someone has to come up with a device that scares the dickens out of people, and that would be the end of war."

Maybe I shouldn't have used that word, she thinks. Mr Twain raises his eyebrows.

"The dickens?" he says and looks at Nikki as if he needed confirmation.

Nikki smiles. "Not in my hearing."

"I didn't mean to give offence," Sophie says. "But those were Alfred's exact words."

That clinches the argument. No one around the table has anything to say to that, or perhaps the next course, lamb cutlets à la menthe, occupies everyone's attention. In any case, the subject of war and peace dies. Too bad for the countess, who is desperate to keep it alive.

Livy, who is always an attentive hostess, would have supported Mrs Suttner out of courtesy, Sophie thinks, but she doesn't contribute much to the general dinner conversation. She is very quiet down there at the other end of the table, preoccupied with her daughter. Jean doesn't say anything all evening. She is one of those girls who feels awkward in company and fears the first look of judgment, afraid of speaking up and drawing attention to herself. Although tonight, it may just be lack of energy. She looks wan. Poor girl.

Ida doesn't have anything to say on the subject of war and peace either, although she is supposed to be Mrs Suttner's friend. She seems to be interested only in Nikki. There is something going on between those two, Sophie thinks, catching the brightness in Ida's eyes. There is something intimate in the way Nikki moves his hands and leans toward her when he speaks. You can't account for people's tastes. Her face is so ordinary, and she is a bit bulky in the shoulders. Is it jealousy that makes me look at her with such sharp eyes, Sophie thinks. No, not the ordinary kind of jealousy, at any rate. I'm envious of the moment – the moment of falling in love, the deep mutual interest, when everything you say has two layers, the ordinary meaning on top and below, the whisper of sympathy. I will never experience that again, she thinks with a pang. I am caught in a marriage which is no longer a marriage. Is it worth going without love for the sake of respectability, just so that people won't talk behind my back?

She strains to hear what Nikki is saying to Ida, but the general conversation closes in around her. All she hears are a few words. Something about Budapest and his oddball cousin, the one who comes out with the craziest things, the only one still on speaking terms with Nikki. And now, they are onto something more interesting: the theatre scene.

Nikki mentions that Sarah Bernhard's name has been put forward for the Cross of Honor. Either the award or the name of the actress catches the ear of the professor and makes him indignant.

"Soon every little actress will ask her admirers to submit her name to the committee, and the selection process will turn into a beauty competition."

"Then again," Countess Suttner says, "Why is it that so few women have been awarded the Cross? There are nurses who work at the front lines—"

Sophie doesn't hear the rest of the sentence, because Nikki says something about bicycle clubs and their political affiliation, and the professor is on fire.

"What business do those pedal-pushers have to interfere with politics?" he thunders, and they are onto the next topic. Sophie feels sorry for the countess. She can't get in another word about her favorite subject.

When the men go off to have their after-dinner cigars and cognac, Jean asks to be excused. Livy's eyes follow her with a worried expression. Sophie senses that she would like to go with Jean, but she can't leave her post as hostess.

"Jean dear," she says. "Why don't you ask Josephine to stay with you?"

Jean has her hand on the door handle. She turns. She reaches up to her forehead as if she had to prompt her mind, as if it was taking a special effort to answer. "Josephine is wanted in the kitchen," she says. "I'll be all right on my own, Mama."

The steep crease that has formed on Livy's forehead doesn't go away.

After Jean has left, Clara leans over and puts a hand on Livy's arm.

"Don't worry, Mama," she says. "I'll go and sit with Jean. I didn't want to offer earlier, because she would have refused me. But if I go now and stay with her, she won't object. She'll be too tired."

"Bless your heart, Clara," Livy says, relieved.

Later she tells the women: "The seizures aren't frequent, thank God, but they are quite unpredictable. The doctor tells us to avoid loud noises and strong colors, but I'm not sure that there is much scientific evidence to support his advice."

"I don't know whether this is a valid comparison," Mrs Suttner says, "but I have been told by returning soldiers that loud noises can set off nightmarish reactions in them, memories of battle scenes. The way they've described it to me, they freeze when they hear popping noises, their minds go blank – almost like a seizure."

The conversation turns to the cure the doctor in Kaltenleutgeben is offering.

"Alfred used to go from one spa to the next," Sophie says. "The doctors everywhere promised him the sky, but his rheumatism never got any better." Well, maybe that wasn't the right thing to say. "Of course, epilepsy is different," she adds.

Livy looks at her with tired eyes. When the men come back into the drawing room, Ossip, Clara's fiancé, sits down at the piano. Clara was supposed to sing, but she hasn't come back from her vigil and so he plays a sonata for them. Soon afterwards, the company breaks up.

Nikki will spend the night with me, Sophie thinks. For a moment, she considers the possibilities. What if she made love to him? But nothing comes of that idea. When they get back to their apartment, Gretel is still awake. Czerny is with her. The child has a stuffed nose, she says. That's because she refused to wear a hat when they went for a walk in the afternoon. Gretel clings to Nikki and starts crying.

"I tell you what, sweetheart," he says. "You can sleep with me and Mama tonight, in the big bed. Would you like that?"

"I would," she sniffles. She leans her head against his shoulder and closes her eyes.

Czerny shakes her head. "You'll end up with a head cold yourself, Mr Kapy," she says and retires to her room.

Bertie

Ida is staying overnight with the Twains. When I take my leave from them, she offers to come downstairs with me.

"I won't be long," she says to Mrs Twain. "But please don't wait up for me."

Before she can answer, Twain puts in: "Don't worry, Miss Lassick, we won't wait up for you. We'll treat you like family and ignore you completely."

I don't like his rude jokes.

"Oh, Sam!" his wife says. She is embarrassed and gently pats Ida's arm. "He doesn't mean it. Josephine has laid everything out for you. Just make yourself at home."

"The poor woman," I say to Ida when we are in the elevator. "She is drooping with exhaustion."

"She worries about Jean. That and moving to Kaltenleutgeben is sapping her energies."

The elevator boy ushers us into the lobby.

"I'm so glad you came downstairs with me," I say to Ida. "We've seen so little of each other lately. Let's sit down and talk a bit."

"I'm sorry Arthur couldn't join us tonight," Ida says as we take our seats in a quiet corner.

"To tell you the truth, he didn't want to come. He doesn't like Mark Twain's humor. Nor do I, but how could I pass up an opportunity to talk to him? I can't let my personal feelings get in the way of the greater good."

"You are hoping Twain will promote your cause?"

"It would be helpful if Twain wrote about the Society, even if Arthur doesn't think highly of his writing. The man turns everything into a joke, he says. Twain likes to play the stumbling foreigner tricked up by our customs, and then he goes and skews everything in a sly way. Writing is just a business for him, and he gives the people what they want – laughs, not earnest admonitions."

"Writing *is* Twain's business and his source of income. I don't see anything wrong with that, Bertie. I suppose he needs the money. His daughter's treatment is costly, I understand."

I nod in sympathy. "I only hope it will be effective. I feel for the parents. And that silly woman – Mrs Kapy! Prattling about spas as if the Twains were going to Kaltenleutgeben for a lark and their daughter needed no more than a bit of perking up. I thought it was only lack of education that made her talk such nonsense, but I come to think you were right in your assessment. She has no brains. I can see why Nobel got tired of her in the end."

"I doubt it had anything to do with her brain. I think he got tired of her body."

I bite my lips. No comment. I don't like to think of Nobel as Sophie's lover. It's another case where I can't allow my personal judgment to interfere with the interests of the Society.

"But it wasn't just Mrs Kapy's gaffe," I say. "The whole evening was frustrating for me. I was hoping to make a convert of Mr Twain, but I wasn't persuasive enough. I don't think he will write in support of my ideas, judging by what he said at table."

"Don't read too much into what he said. He likes to be contrary," Ida says. "If you like, I'll raise the subject with him over breakfast tomorrow."

"I'd appreciate that. In fact, I thought you'd speak up on my behalf at dinner tonight, but you were preoccupied." I search Ida's eyes. "With Mr Kapy, I mean. Is that wise?"

"I suppose it isn't," she says, locking eyes with me. "But you of all people ought to understand. Was it wise for you to fall in love with Arthur and elope to Mingrelia?"

"There is no point of comparison," I say. "Arthur wasn't married." I find Ida's comparison disturbing. Is she in love with Nikolaus Kapy? How can she think of my feelings for Arthur in the same vein as her shameful interest in Mr Kapy? I get up. I want to distance myself from her, literally. There is no excuse for adulterous thoughts.

"I hope you know what you are doing," I say. Of course, love is not a matter of knowing. The mind has nothing to do with it. Arthur entered my bloodstream. I could not help acting on my feelings. Some people may have thought they were improper. Arthur's mother did. But her objections were practical rather than moral. Ida's case is different. I hope she won't act on her preoccupation with Mr Kapy. It would be irresponsible.

Ida gets up as well. We look at each other silently. I can see our friendship dissolve.

"How is the Nobel biography coming along?" I say to overcome the silence.

"I am working on it. In fact, I have enlisted Mrs Kapy's help. She claims no one knew Nobel better than she."

"I wish you luck," I say. It sounds insincere. I am insincere. I wish Ida would let go of her unfortunate project. What can Mrs Kapy possibly add to a book on Nobel? Gossip, I fear.

We embrace before I go out to my waiting carriage. It feels like a final goodbye. There was a time when I thought Ida's project would bring us closer. I, too, wanted the world to know about Nobel, but it is clear by now that we take a very different view of him. I won't deny that his business put him in conflict with his conscience, and I suspect that Mrs Kapy was more than a protégé of his, that she was his lover, as everyone says. But he was a good man at heart, and I am convinced that his generous legacy was an attempt to atone for his sins and the evil results of his invention.

Arthur was surprised when he read that Nobel had instituted a prize for peace. I wasn't. It was his farewell gift to me. That's how I see it, although he left no message to acknowledge our friendship. The idea originated with me, I am sure of it. I had my reservations about accepting money from Nobel while he was alive, but I welcome his posthumous gift. It is no longer tied to the man, to a flawed human being. It is in the hands of a foundation whose credentials cannot be impugned, and it will, no doubt, be a great boost to the cause of universal peace. In a way, Nobel's death has been liberating for me. It allows me to take a more detached view of him and admit, yes, he had his shortcomings. He wasn't the hero I wanted him to be; he was human. I was biased in his favor, I admit. But Ida is biased as well, seeing only his negative traits. I thought Nobel's death would balance her judgment as it did mine, but now she has enlisted Mrs Kapy's help. I know where that will lead. The book will turn into a turgid exposé. It will be the end of our friendship.

Ida

When I get back to the Twains' apartment, only Josephine is awake. She makes me a curtsey, asking me if I need anything else before I go to bed. I tell her I can look after myself, and she says goodnight in a small, sleepy voice. The evening has gone by quickly. No polite conversations behind suppressed yawns. Nikki is an engaging talker, or perhaps it's a technique he has developed, forestalling my questions about his life by asking about mine first. I noticed the smoothness of his voice, gauged to reach only my ears, a melodious voice but with something else mixed in, a dissonance, a disturbance to break the calm. It's a voice to fall in love with, I think as I slip between the covers of the bed in Clara's room. Nikki's voice is in my ear, his lips are on my skin, but Bertie's warning is clouding my fantasy. I drift into sleep to the tune of her words, *I hope you know what you are doing, I wish you luck.* After a silent, dreamless night, in the sobering light of the morning, in that first instant of waking, I decide to heed Bertie's warning. I'll be wise and take Kapy off the mental stage. There will be no more fantasies with him in the lead. I will do battle with my new compulsion.

Twain appears at the breakfast table in a rumpled suit, his white hair flowing. He drank too much last night, but he seems to have recovered, judging by the hearty meal he is eating. There is a mound of stuff on his plate that I have never seen at a Viennese breakfast table: bacon, hash browns, fried tomatoes, toast, in addition to kaiser buns and a soft-boiled egg.

He is in a garrulous mood, speaking in his native tongue. For once, he does not put me through a German performance, punctuated with questions about grammatical and idiomatic intricacies. I always have the feeling that Twain uses me as a tutor. He gets a free German lesson out of me on every visit. But perhaps I'm unfair, and he speaks German for the benefit of the girls and has switched to English now because they aren't at the table. They are sleeping in. The three of us are breakfasting on our own.

"That bloody seating order – you'll pardon my language, ladies, but it really was a confounded business, Livy. Why did you seat me between those two, the countess and Mrs Kapy? On one side, a woman who tries to rope me into what I consider a lost cause, on the other, an insipid fool whispering sweet nothings into my ear."

"Sweet nothings?" Livy says, smiling.

"Okay, drop the adjective. Whispered nothings into my ear, is more like it."

"And peace is a lost cause in your opinion?" I put in. Here was my chance to speak up, as I promised Bertie.

"There is as much chance of two enemies settling a power struggle by signing a paper as there is of a wife bearing a child by signing the church register," he says. "There are instincts at work here, as I need not tell you, Miss Lassick. Enemies will fight, and – well you get the idea."

"But it is a worthwhile cause," Livy says, "and I think you should do your part and write something about the Society of Peace."

I second her and hope I've done my bit for Bertie now.

"Well, maybe I will write about it," Twain says. He decapitates the soft-boiled egg the maid has placed in front of him, takes a runny teaspoonful and wipes his beard with a napkin. "But seating me between those two women, really, Livy, that was too much. And I got no help from Kapy, who sat on the other side of the countess but was too busy paying court to our respected guest here," he says, waving his spoon in my direction. "I asked to be seated beside you, Miss Lassick, but Livy wouldn't let me."

"I am flattered that you wanted my company."

"Oh, you are flattered, are you? And I haven't even started flattering you. I wanted to talk to you about your book, *To the Caucasus and Back*. Volker sent me two advance copies, one for myself and one to hand on to someone else if I liked it."

"And did you like it?"

"You'll find out. I wrote Mr Volker a letter of thanks, two lines of which will appear somewhere in the guise of a review, I know. That's why publishers send copies to me. They expect me to comment, but I was glad to write on your behalf, Miss Lassick, since you made me out such a charming old bear in that essay you wrote for *Die Welt*. And don't go away without signing my copy." He turns to the maid and switches to German. "*Bringen Sie die zwei Bücher her*, Josephine."

Josephine fetches the books, my travelogue and one of Twain's own books, *A Tramp Abroad*. He wants to make me a present of the book. It's in the same vein as my travelogue, he says.

"I would have liked to give the second copy of your book to the American ambassador or to someone else who might trumpet your merits in august circles, but Kapy wiggled it out of me, you know. The moment he laid eyes on it, he took it up and asked where I had bought it, could he borrow it and so forth. And then Livy pipes up and says, 'Oh, take it, Mr Kapy, by all means, take it. Sam has two copies.' So she threw it away on that fellow—"

Livy protests. "But you like him, Sam. I thought you would want to make him a present of the book."

"Like him? I don't know about 'liking' Kapy. He is an entertaining man, I'll say that much for him. He has the gift of the gab."

"He is well-spoken. He is a civilized man, and you said yourself that he has an acute mind."

"Wasted on his present occupation – I know I said that. I suppose he had to resign his commission in the army when he married the current Mrs Kapy. Couldn't live down the scandal."

What scandal? Livy had been discreet when I asked her about the circumstances of Sophie's marriage. I want to know more, but I've missed the moment to ask my question. The conversation has moved on.

"You would look at Mr Kapy differently," Livy says, "if he had married someone of a more serious cast of mind, someone who could hold her own in company."

"Oh, so it's the wife's fault. He needs someone who will provide a more suitable background picture and set him off to advantage?"

"However you want to put it, Sam. But we do consider people in their familial context."

"Ah, that explains my success! And I stupidly thought it had something to do with my writing, but it turns out it's my good wife here who sets me off to advantage—" He stopped when he saw Livy's hurt expression. "No, that didn't come out right. I apologize. Sometimes I joke about things that aren't a joking matter."

"That's all right, Sam. I am used to your punning."

"Seriously, then," he said, winking at me. "I do like Mr Kapy, even though I feel he is tough competition. He jokes almost as well I do and is more civilized, if you listen to Livy. And his looks give him an advantage over me with the ladies. He beats me out every time, am I right, Miss Lassick? Whom would you have preferred as your table companion, young Kapy or Old Man Twain?"

I don't have to answer that difficult question because the maid announces Mr Kapy and his daughter. Livy has arranged for him to take me home in his phaeton.

"He lives out your way," she said, "and Gretel will be your chaperone."

None of us can get a smile out of the child. She looks solemn when she comes into the room with Kapy and makes us a curtsey. I, too, feel solemn saying farewell to the Twains. I have taken a great liking to Livy and even to Mark Twain who has a certain rough charm.

"We'll be in town at least once or twice every month," Livy says, "and we'll definitely look you up before we go home to Connecticut."

"Or rather, why don't you look us up in Connecticut?" Twain says. "You have a brother in New York, Livy tells me. She says he has invited you to live with him. So, how about it?"

"My brother only wants a governess for his children, someone to teach them pure Viennese," I say lightly, but the idea of visiting America is growing on me, and it's not just that I want to continue with my travel writing. The Twains got me interested in the American phenomenon – that's how I'm thinking of their easy-going manner and of Livy's tolerance for human foibles. Is it just their personality? I don't think so because Christine, my brother's American wife, has the same live-and-let-live attitude. I would like to explore that American phenomenon and study the effect of the Land of Opportunities on the mindset of its inhabitants. Does the wide expanse of the prairies open the mind? Does the vertical expanse of the buildings in New York allow the heart to soar? The World Building rises a hundred meters above the street, I've read. I'd like to see that. How does it feel to let your eye follow that upward sweep all the way to the sky?

I say goodbye to the Twains, my mind on the American phenomenon.

*

In the elevator, Gretel is very quiet and Kapy says, "She's under the weather." He gives her a friendly tweak. "Are we feeling under the weather, love?"

Gretel leans into him and buries her face in his cloak.

"Sophie didn't think it was a good idea to take her for an outing," he says.

Gretel looks up. "I'm not under the weather," she says. "I'm fine and I want to go to your house, Papa, and play with Bella."

"I know, sweetheart. You miss Bella," he says, stroking her head.

To me, he says, "I didn't have the heart to disappoint her. Let's just hope that whatever ails her will blow over."

As we cross the hotel lobby, I think: It isn't fair. Men look their best at forty, while women begin to fade at thirty.

He brings his phaeton around to the front of the hotel. It is a racy-looking gig, but the narrow roof does not offer much protection against wind and weather. It's the end of March. We've had a few spring days, but today is a throwback to winter: cold, gray, drizzly. Kapy lifts Gretel up into the carriage and lends me his arm as I mount the step and take my seat beside her.

"I hope the rain will hold off," he says and hands me a woolen blanket to keep myself and the child warm. I put my arm around Gretel's shoulder. She cozies up to me. It's the first time I feel a child's body – and a long time since I've felt any body resting against mine. She is soft and warm, like an extra layer of padded skin. I breathe a sigh of fuzzy happiness. Perhaps it was an audible breath because Kapy turns to me and gives me one of his searching looks that uncover secrets and play into my desires, I fear. His eyes wander to Gretel.

"Tired?" he says.

She doesn't answer. She burrows in under my arm and leans her head against my chest. The rhythmic turning of the wheels soon puts her to sleep.

"Now that we are alone, so to speak," he says, looking at the sleeping child, "let me ask you a question that's been on my mind since our talk at Carl Volker's office. Why would you want to work together with Sophie? You realize that you will do the lion share of the work?"

"Carl has asked me the same question, and I've given him an honest answer. I want to give Sophie an incentive to collaborate. I rely on her to tell me about Nobel."

"Surely there are better sources, or more objective sources, at any rate."

"I doubt it. I've scanned the papers for information on Nobel's companies. I don't know how objective journalists are, but they can only report what they are told, and Nobel played his cards close to his chest. I also talked to a number of people who knew Nobel personally, but I got only the most trivial information. He valued his privacy. Sophie may well be the only person who got close to him, the only one to see behind the façade. Of course, with his letters gone, I don't know to what extent she can reconstruct the story accurately."

"She remembers what she wants to remember. I'd say she has perfect recall and could quote you Nobel's letters word for word, like those freaks at country fairs who ream off names and dates without understanding the context. No, I shouldn't have used that comparison. Sophie doesn't lack intelligence, but she applies it only when she thinks it's worth her while."

"And the biography won't be worth her while?"

"She'll produce the information you need, but don't expect her to be impartial."

"Of course not. There is a personal angle to every narrative. The question is: what is Sophie's objective? What does she expect to gain from writing a memoir or collaborating with me on a biography of Nobel?"

"The usual objective, I would say. She wants to come out looking good. So take what she says with a grain of salt. Contrary to what she may tell you, Nobel did have redeeming qualities."

"Such as?"

He takes a moment to gather his thoughts.

"Compassion. He had a hard childhood. He understood suffering and was willing to help, but he didn't know how to give. He always wanted acknowledgment."

"I heard the opposite. That he often gave anonymously, or in the name of his mother."

"I don't mean official acknowledgment. On the contrary. He was a private man, as you said, a shy man even, and he hated public honors, but when he made someone a personal gift, he wanted to see wonder and admiration in their eyes. He wanted to see their backs bent in deference and humility. He wanted adoration. Sophie understood that. She was ready to light the incense and let the smoke blind him. But to get back to your project. So you will share the credit on the title page with Sophie?"

"This isn't about getting my name into print," I say. "It's about righting a wrong." I listen to myself and hear the echo of my words. Do I sound pompous? Can he tell that I'm keeping something back?

He eyes me with a steady gaze. "What wrong are you righting?"

Georg's death. I want revenge. I want an end to my nightmares. But I am not about to give that story away to him. Kapy is only a casual acquaintance even though he figures prominently in my fantasies, the ones I am desperately trying to suppress. In real life, I remind myself, we have met only a few times and never had a private conversation until last evening, unless you count the few words we exchanged on the train about waltzes that exorcise the devil.

He is waiting for my reply. What wrong am I righting?

"The way Nobel treated people," I say. "Like pawns on a chessboard, to be moved at his will and as it suited his purpose. Sophie certainly gives me the impression that Nobel did not treat her well."

"He treated her well in financial terms."

"But she complained that he was brutal. At first, I thought she was talking about violence, but she meant that he was brutally honest, or to be exact, cruelly honest."

I am steering Kapy away from my cause to Sophie's. She, too, wants to right a wrong.

"Nobel told her that she was an ignoramus and a bird brain," I say. "He did not strike her with his fists. He crushed her with words. She was an embarrassment to him, he said. And I am asking myself, if she was all that, why did he put up with her for all those years?"

"Why?" Kapy gives me an amused look. "Sophie has attractions, you know. She is a coquette, and she was young when she met Nobel. Youth is always charming to an older man. And Nobel was awkward with women, shy and courtly in an old-fashioned way. Sophie relieved him of the need to find the right words, to make the right moves. She took the lead. She is like that. She'll do the talking for you. She will tell you what you think before the thoughts are half formed in your mind. She will take you by the hand and make you realize that you wanted to do exactly that – take her hand. She suited Nobel, but from what she tells me, he couldn't make up his mind whether to play father to her or lover."

I remember the terms of endearment she quoted from his letters. *My little froggie, my sweet little child.* It was role-playing, and I'm not the only one who saw that. Kapy caught on to it as well.

"In the end, he settled on the role of benefactor. I think that's what kept the relationship going. He got his kicks out of lording it over Sophie. He paid for a villa in Ischl and an apartment in Paris. He gave her money, but he made her beg for it and thank him profusely, on her knees for all I know. Nobel liked to see her groveling and fawning. He enjoyed the feeling of superiority it gave him. Sophie, in turn, needed a father figure, someone to take care of her. That's how I see their relationship."

I agree. Nobel was good at manipulating Sophie. Perhaps she was a willing victim, but I don't think she got what she wanted – a caring father.

"He didn't show her any respect," I say. "I think that's what Sophie meant when she said he did not treat her well. He gave her money but ignored her emotional needs." Who knows what Sophie might have become if Nobel had not beaten her down, if she had met a man who was generous in spirit rather than with money. "She said she always came last on the long list of Nobel's priorities. His business and his scientific work came first."

"He was certainly more in love with science than with Sophie," Kapy says. "It all ties in with his shyness, his awkwardness in company. He knew how to handle equipment. He didn't know how to handle people."

I am amazed by Kapy's insight. "You seem to know Nobel well."

"I wouldn't go as far as that," he says. "Nobel visited Vienna frequently, and I saw quite a bit of him, but he was close-mouthed. He didn't open up to others. In fact, he struck me as slightly paranoid."

Why didn't I think of asking Kapy about Nobel? Here I was, trying to extract information from Sophie, who is often vague, who has her own agenda or lacks the perception to answer my questions, and in the meantime, I missed out on another, perhaps more reliable witness. Kapy surprises me with his perceptive comments on this elusive man. I never thought of him as a source of information about Nobel. I thought of him only as a dream man. But that wasn't Kapy. That was a creature of my imagination. I look at him more closely and take in the real man.

"Science definitely came first with him," he is saying.

"He spoke of his experiments to you?"

"In an apologetic manner. I read an article about a shipload of dynamite exploding in Panama and asked him about the dangers of producing and transporting his goods. And he said science itself was beautiful, even if the process involved risks. He was a hands-on chemist. I was amazed at the disregard he showed for the danger to himself – and to others. His experiments were deadly. His invention was deadly."

I feel a gust of shared feelings, a murmuring echo in my brain. Kapy – the real man – understands me. He has stopped talking, but I fill in the gaps. Words appear in the blurred space at the edge of my perception, the images of bloodied limbs and torn flesh, nightmare words that have never surfaced before in the light of day. I feel a surge of heat as if the sleeping child leaning against me had suddenly pressed closer.

"Nobel fed the war machine, and yet people think of him as a philanthropist." I can see my breath, a thin vapor in the cold air, like an image of my anger. I cannot suppress my bitterness.

"I suppose he tried to atone for his lethal business and his arms dealing with good deeds and by setting up a foundation to promote learning and peace," Kapy says.

"Yes, but how do you atone for lives lost? With money? With the profit made from a dirty business? Money can't replace lives. And Nobel atoned for his sins posthumously. He never apologized during his lifetime, as far as I know. He never stopped raking in the blood money. I specifically asked Sophie about those deadly accidents in his factories. He seems to have passed them over in silence."

My fervor catches Kapy by surprise. He gives me a questioning look. "I don't know what he said to Sophie, but when I brought up the subject, he said he had paid the price. His own brother died in an explosion at a factory in Heleneborg. He was only twenty years old, Nobel told me. But when I followed up and asked how the accident happened, he shut down. My feeling was that he couldn't bear talking about his brother's death."

Heleneborg. The word bursts into the air and fills the open space between us. It has been shut up in my mind for so long. It is a shock to hear it spoken out loud and coming from another person's mouth. Death at Heleneborg. But Kapy isn't talking of Georg. He is talking about the death of another man. Nobel's brother. I remember the letter Georg wrote me. The words are coming back to me in a rush. *I've made friends with the brother of the owner.* What was his friend's name? Emil. *Emil is my age, nineteen, and we get along very well.* The names begin to hammer in my head, a kind of echo to the clopping hooves of the horse. *Emil. Georg. Emil. Georg.*

Kapy has gone on talking. "I can't say what went on in Nobel's mind. I never got to know him that well. But I can tell you this much: he was a sad sack of a man. He suffered from depression."

I barely listen to Kapy. The horse's hooves keep up their knocking refrain: *Georg. Emil.*

"He may have been guilty of pride, ambition, cupidity – the usual array of sins men commit – but he paid for them. There was something unbearably bleak about him."

I try to shut out the names of Emil and Georg and remember instead the man I met in San Remo, his hollow eyes, the deep lines crossing his forehead and bracketing his mouth.

"In spite of his money and the deference people showed him, he always looked like a whipped dog. Of course, I knew him only as an old man. Perhaps he was different when he was younger. But judging by the letters he wrote to Sophie, he was just as crabbed and wretched then. Perhaps his poor health made him miserable. He complained a great deal about his aches and pains. Sophie picked up on that and started moaning and groaning as well. She didn't pick up on Nobel's learning or his manners – he was well educated, you know, and a proper gentleman. No, the only thing she learned from him was how to complain. She likes to pretend that she's sick, feeling dizzy or suffering from a headache. She likes to play the weak little woman. I suppose it worked with him. It doesn't work with me."

I should pay attention to Kapy's words. I am missing out on information, but my thoughts are stuck on Heleneborg. I barely listen to him. We have passed into the suburbs. I turn away and look steadily at the landscape, sodden fields stretching to the Danube and vineyards scoring the hills with trellised stocks, bare and black in the rain. My eyes follow the parallel lines of the stakes to their meeting point in infinity. I can hear the names in the soughing of the wind. *Georg. Emil.* Was Nobel's love for his brother more lasting than mine for Georg? Did his memories never fade?

Kapy notices my silence. "Have I said anything to offend you?" he says. "I would like to stay on your good side, Miss Lassick."

We have arrived at the turn-off to my house. I give him directions. The drizzle has turned into a steady rain, and the wind has picked up. The narrow roof of the phaeton is no protection against the slanting rain. It has soaked the back and shoulders of Kapy's spring coat and stained it dark brown. I have pulled the blanket all the way up over my shoulders and Gretel's blond head. When the phaeton stops in front of my house, she stirs and pushes off the blanket.

She looks flushed. I touch her forehead.

"I think she is running a fever," I say to Kapy.

He reaches over and puts the back of his hand against her cheek.

"I think I'll just let you off here and take her right back home."

The woolen blanket is glistening with raindrops. The roof of the phaeton is dripping.

"Is that advisable?" I say. "By the time you get back to the Metropole, you'll both be soaked to the skin. Why don't you bring her into the house and wait for the rain to ease?"

He carries Gretel up the path to the house. I go ahead and hold the door to the parlor for him.

"Put her down on the sofa," I say.

Gretel opens her eyes and mewls like a kitten.

"My poor little pet," he says.

I pull back the curtains to let the light in, but the day is so dull that the room remains in obscurity. I light a lamp.

Gretel is rubbing her eyes.

"Where is Bella?" she says. "Where are we?"

"In Miss Lassick's house," he says. "We'll wait here a bit until it stops raining so hard."

She sits up and looks around, at the china cabinet, the bookcases flanking the fireplace, the curios lined up on the mantelshelf, the grate where Olga, the charwoman, has laid a fire. It has burned down now, but the room is still warm, and I put on another log.

"I want my mama," Gretel says. She lies back again.

"Yes, love, I know." Kapy tucks one of the cushions under her head and sits down beside her on the edge of the sofa. "Just rest a bit until the rain lets up. You want Papa to tell you a story?"

She nods. Her throat works uncomfortably. Her lips are dry.

"I'll make you a cup of tea, Gretel," I say. Tea made of birch bark and sweetened with honey, I explain to Kapy. It depresses the fever.

I go into the kitchen and make tea and try to cool it down as best I can, pouring it back and forth between two mugs. When the tea has cooled, I bring it into the parlor. Gretel drinks gratefully then sinks back and closes her eyes again.

"Perhaps I should get Dr Stern. He lives just down the road," I say.

"Sophie may want to consult her own doctor. I'd rather let her make the decision." He hesitates. "I wonder – could I leave Gretel with you and fetch Sophie from the hotel? We'll come back in a closed carriage."

"You do that. I can look after Gretel," I say. I'm putting on a brave front. I'm not sure about my nanny skills. I know nothing about entertaining little girls. I have no stories or songs or toys or games to play, but my nanny skills are not called upon. Gretel sleeps while Kapy is gone. She wakes up once, shifts and sighs and closes her eyes again. My only duty is to change the damp cloth I've put on her forehead to keep it cool.

I look at her sweet face and think: I will never have a child of my own. I would have if I had married Georg. My mind wanders back to Heleneborg. I feel an urge to go into the study and look at the photo of Georg propped up on my desk, but I'm afraid to move and wake up Gretel. Instead, I search my mind for images of his face. I try to picture him walking by my side on the path to the railroad station, sitting beside me on a bench in the garden behind my house, turning his head to me, smiling at me or frowning or nodding his head. But I see only the one, sepia-colored photo, Georg against the photographer's drapery, looking out at me with a smile I cannot remember ever seeing on his face. I looked at him so carefully when he was alive and noted everything about him, the texture of his hair, the curve of his neck, the shape of his fingers. And yet he has turned into an object, into something less than an object, a flattened two-dimensional representation of what he was. The passing years have thinned out my memories. Soon, they will dissolve into nothing. Only the nightmares remain, repetitive and pointless. Did Nobel have nightmares about his brother? The refrain in my head starts up again: *Georg. Emil. Georg. Emil.* Did Nobel's head throb when he thought of Heleneborg? Did he keep a photo of his brother on his desk? I think of the old man in San Remo. Did he repent of his sins on his deathbed?

I hear the wheels of a carriage rolling up and coming to a stop in front of the house. Through the window, I see Kapy handing out Sophie and holding an umbrella for her as she hitches up her skirt and comes up the muddy path with mincing steps.

I greet Sophie at the door. For a moment, I stand in the rustling embrace of her dress, in a greeting that draws me in and makes me – a friend, a confidante? I pull back and move aside to let Sophie pass into the parlor. I can't help feeling envious. She looks beautiful. The movement of her hands is fluid as she shrugs off her wrapper. She no longer wears half-mourning. Her dark blue dress is cut in the latest fashion and is tied with a sash of light blue silk that matches her eyes. The bows on her suede shoes are charming, even though they are blotched now from the short trip over the gravel path. The water marks are the only visible flaw in Sophie's appearance. Otherwise, she is perfect. She has brought her own unique glow that leaves nothing in the shadows.

She looks past me at Gretel dozing on the sofa.

"How is she?"

"Better, I think. Less flushed."

She sits down on the sofa and strokes Gretel's cheeks.

The child opens her eyes and puts out her arms.

"Mama," she says and smiles.

"Mama will take you home," Sophie says. "Then you'll feel better."

It sounds as if she was blaming my house for making Gretel sick.

Sophie looks around my parlor, takes in the sloping floor and the dowdy curtains. Since she can't find anything to praise, she rests her eyes on the fire burning in the grate and says nothing. I have rekindled the fire and hung the blanket and my coat on a drying rack in front of the hearth. The air is steamy and smells of damp wool.

"My head hurts, Mama," Gretel says.

Sophie embraces her. Her eyes are moist with understanding.

"My poor little sweetie." She fusses over the child. I can't tell whether she is really worried or just acting the worried mother.

"I gave her a mug of birch tea," I say. "It's quite effective in lowering fever. Would you like to take some home with you? It might help to give her another mugful at night."

Sophie's mouth shapes into a moué. Have I challenged her motherhood?

"That's very kind of you, Ida," she says, "but I'd rather not rely on home remedies. We'll take her to my doctor. I trust him completely." She turns to Kapy, who has stayed in the background, waiting for a decision. "Let's go right away, Nikki," she says. "The sooner Doctor Bart gets a look at her the better."

I take the blanket off the drying rack and wrap it around Gretel. Kapy steps forward and lifts her up. Our hands meet as I tuck in the folds, an innocent touch but I feel the charge and dare not look into his eyes.

Sophie follows him. She stands in the open door and watches him carry the child to the waiting coach. The cab driver has jumped down from his seat and is holding the carriage door open for him.

"You live here on your own?" Sophie asks me.

"Yes, except for a charwoman who comes for a few hours in the morning and cleans and does the laundry and occasionally prepares dinner for me."

"Aren't you afraid to be on your own?"

"I have kind neighbors who keep an eye on me."

"Oh, neighbors," she says. "They *will* keep an eye on you, won't they?"

She is halfway down the path before she remembers and turns around to thank me for looking after Gretel.

Kapy helps her into the carriage then comes back and kisses my hand.

"You've been very kind," he says. "I hope I'll see you again soon."

Sophie observes us casually. Her look glides off me and takes in the house. Does she feel pity for me, a woman living in an unfashionable suburb, far from the inner city?

The rain has stopped now, but the air is hazy, sodden with moisture. There is a sharp smell in the air of wet leaves and decaying earth. When the carriage turns the corner, I take a few steps outside and look at the façade of my house. What do people see when they look at it from the street? A cottage, not much larger than Sophie's drawing room at the Metropole. There is a small parlor, a bedroom I shared with my mother while she was alive and another tiny room where my brother used to sleep, which is my study now. It is still furnished the way it was then, with a narrow cot and a plain table that serves as my desk. The kitchen has been added at the back of the house like a misshapen hump.

The wind beats down the smoke rising from the chimney. It rolls over the tiled roof and disperses into thin, gray air. The front yard is bare except for a few snowdrops and primroses. Tulips and narcissus are pushing up from the mounded flower beds. It's too early in the year for anything else.

I am glad of my shabby little house. Two years ago, my brother came from America for a visit. I was apprehensive. Surely, Fritz would raise the subject of his inheritance. We were co-owners of the house now. At the very least, he would want to charge me rent for his half. I just hoped he would not insist on selling the house. Neither of us had raised the question explicitly. We danced around it in our letters. I sheltered under the opacity of language, the trappings of the written word. But then he came to St Veit, and we were face to face. In addition to words, there were feelings that could not be entirely hidden. I was at his mercy. There would be the tone of his voice to contend with and his steady eye. It would be humiliating if I had to plead with him.

My brother is a man of means now. He acquired shares in a banking house in New York, married an heiress and fathered two children with her. The boy is six years old now and the girl four. His first move, when he visited me in St Veit, was to ask me once again to join him in New York. I would not have minded to pay him a short visit, but that didn't fit into his plans at the time. I suppose he had done the sums. To bring me to New

York permanently and take me into his household – there might be something in it for him. I could make myself useful as a companion to his children. To bring me over for a short visit – there was nothing to balance that expense. Would the fact that I was now the author of a travelogue restore the balance? I was planning to send him a copy of *To the Caucasus and Back* and tell him about Mark Twain's invitation to visit them in Connecticut. Would Fritz be more amenable to finance a trip to New York now, in the hope, perhaps, of seeing his name in the acknowledgments of my next book – *Travels in America*?

When my mother died, Fritz had offered me only one option: to join him permanently, and I demurred. The idea held no appeal for me. I could imagine the scenario: the spinster living in her brother's house. I would have to fit in and be on sufferance. Christine's laissez fair would not extend to a permanent house guest. I cherish my independence, and besides, I told my brother, I had my own life, translating for Mr Olmuth and writing family histories. I wanted to stay in St Veit. When he came to visit me two years ago, the talk soon turned to our joint ownership of the house. The fact that Fritz had no urgent need for funds would not keep him from calling in a debt, I thought. He had always been businesslike, and I feared he would finally demand a settlement.

Fritz isn't mean, but he knows the value of money. There was another person in the game as well. His wife, Christine, had come with him to Europe. We were civil to each other, although we did not have a great deal in common. She behaved well and showed no distaste for my modest lifestyle. She displayed the friendly nonchalance I have come to admire in Americans, but she did not stay longer in Vienna than courtesy required and travelled on to Italy with friends, leaving my brother behind to settle affairs. It all came out much better than I dared to hope.

"What would I do with half a house in St Veit?" Fritz said when we discussed our joint ownership. "If you can look after it and maintain it, it's yours and welcome to it."

I breathed a deep sigh of relief. His generosity came as a surprise to me, but perhaps it wasn't pure generosity. I suppose he had done the sums in that case too. So much in taxes. So much in repairs. So much in bother and lost time, which is money, according to the American creed. And so I am now the sole owner of the house, courtesy of my brother, and look after it in a fashion, or rather, Olga looks after it. She dusts, sweeps and scours and keeps the garden from going to seed. I keep to my writing. The location of the house isn't the best. It takes almost an hour to get from St Veit to the city on the local train, which stops at every church and hamlet, and another half hour to walk to the center where everything happens that a budding writer like myself might report or comment on. The center of the city, the *Innenstadt*, is where society goes to be seen, where the cafés are and the theatres, the concert halls and the opera. It's fodder for the articles and essays that top up my annuity and provide for those little extras that make life comfortable.

It occurs to me that I have one more chip to put on the bargaining table if the subject of travelling to New York comes up again. If Fritz agrees to have me over for a short-term visit and pay my travel expenses, I could reciprocate by writing a genealogy of Christine's family. That was one aspect of my life in which she took a lively interest: my genealogies. She is proud of her own family. The Joneses, she told me, are descended from the Pilgrims who came to America on the Mayflower. She was an only child, and it was a source of grief to her father that the family name would die out with him. Fritz obliged him by naming their firstborn Frederick *Jones* Lassick, but her father hoped his grandson would legally change his name to Frederick Lassick Jones on coming of age. My brother said nothing when Christine told me the story. Later, when we were alone, he spoke his mind. He thought Lassick was quite as good a name as Jones.

"My father-in-law fussed a great deal about the name business, but I kept my mouth shut. I don't want to quarrel with him. What's the use? He is old. He has one foot in the grave already. I'll bide my time."

That's Fritz for you, always counting – the years, in this case. I'm not sure we would get along in the long run, but I'm grateful he gave up his half of our inheritance. I may be unfair thinking he made the decision only after some calculation. I think he also felt pity for me. I am a spinster, and that makes me an unhappy case in his eyes. He brought out the old arguments: I must marry. Marriage would mean financial security. I wasn't trying hard enough to find a husband or not going about it in the right way. If I came to New York, he would take matters in hand and find me a suitable husband, he said, but there was uncertainty in his eyes. He wasn't sure he could bring it off.

I have no desire to enter the marriage market, but I think Fritz underestimates my potential. Carl, for one, was prepared to ask the question. It was me who held him back. When I think of his receding hairline, the lack of definition at the edges of his face, his little belly

218

bulging so that he has to unbutton his vest – no, I haven't reached the point where I have to make compromises on that scale. I am satisfied with my spinster life and my fantasies, in which the men are always ideally suited to my taste.

Besides, I saw the way Nikki looked at me when he took his leave and kissed my hand and said he hoped to see me again soon. Of course, he doesn't count in the marriage game. He is married, and I shouldn't think of him. I should certainly not think of him as Nikki. Yet, not five minutes after the carriage has rolled away and I have stepped back into the parlor, my resolve weakens, and a fantasy takes hold of me with Nikki in the romantic lead. Our hands meet. He draws me toward him. I close my eyes, but the bitter smell of dry wool stops me from playing out the scene. My coat is in danger of being scorched by the heat coming from the fireplace. I take the coat off the drying rack and brush it down vigorously until its nap is even and my fantasies subdued.

*

The next day, Sunday, is as dreary as Saturday was: leaden skies and drizzle. I've been to mass, the weekly ritual imposed on me by custom and society and my private rite of contemplating my relationship with God. Will I receive intimations of the divine if I pray harder? Is there hope of my soul entering into the ecstasies and transports of faith? Does God care about me, does he keep me in his omniscient sight, or am I too insignificant to warrant his attention, a tiny speck in the universe?

Every Sunday, I search the suffering faces of the martyrs flanking the altars. I look for meaning in their sinuous carved bodies, the pleated folds of their dress, in the Gothic pillars, the stained glass windows, the tinkling of the bells as the altar boys, in their lacy white tunics, kneel before the Eucharist. God does not answer my questions. I do not go to confession because I already know the priest's answer. I linger in church after mass and listen to the organist, who likes to stretch the closing hymn into a little concert. Sometimes, I think that's all the religious devotion I can muster – listening to the organist playing Haydn.

It's late in the afternoon now, and I'm sitting in the window seat, taking advantage of the last gleam of daylight to read over my notes for the Nobel biography and muse about my reasons for carrying on with it. The anger that drove me to write about Nobel is no longer red-hot. What Nikki has told me about Heleneborg has tamped down the flames. I know now that I am not the only one who suffered. Nobel lost a brother and may have been burdened with lifelong guilt because he involved Emil in the dangerous process of manufacturing dynamite. Is that punishment enough? Are we even on that score?

A strange feeling stirs in my heart, compassion, not for Nobel in particular, but for the price life exacts from each of us, pushing us into tight corners and turning us into cheats and equivocators as we try to make our way out of a bad situation. I hear Nobel speak in the voice of the old man I met in San Remo. I see him bent over, palpitating. Life defeated him.

A month ago, when I found out that Nobel was dead, I was furious that I had missed my chance to confront him. When Sophie agreed to speak with me, I was dizzy with excitement. I had a fresh source to draw on! And now, instead of being buoyed, I feel weighed down by my discoveries. I know too much and have lost my way. The more I hear about Nobel, the less certain I am of my ground. My image of him has become fractured like pieces of colored glass in a kaleidoscope. In Bertie's eyes, Nobel is a philanthropist and a genius. If I listen to Sophie, he comes across as mean and condescending. Nikki seems to think that he was a man subject to the usual faults and weaknesses, held fast by desire, ground down by brooding thoughts. I have nothing solid to go on. How do I know that these memories aren't inventions, illusions, constructs? I fear I can't get at the truth. I only know how Bertie sees Alfred Nobel, or Sophie, or Nikki. I find it hard to accept that kind of randomness.

Looking out the window, I see the row of poplars separating my lawn from the neighbor's and hear the piercing cry of a crow. It is like a clarion call and reverses the flow of my thought. There is no need to flounder, I tell myself. I have the hard evidence of his life lived – the chemical formula he developed, the quantity of dynamite he produced and sold, the deaths his invention caused, and I have the quotations from Nobel's letters in Sophie's memoir. This is how *he* presented himself to others. This was *his* idea of himself. Is that not truth enough?

But my mood remains dark. My eyes wander to the window again, across the lawn to the poplar trees and to the shed, visible between the rain-darkened trunks. The wooden boards are gray, as dull as cinders. The sight is dispiriting. I turn away and look at the familiar objects in my parlor instead, the books on the shelves, the lithograph of London Bridge on the wall, so familiar that I can make out every detail even in the gloomy light of the late afternoon.

Perhaps the diversity of witness accounts I've come across only means that Nobel was a complex man, too complex to be reduced to one character. That's a problem confronting every biographer. It has nothing to do with Nobel specifically. To tell a man's story, I must reduce him to the essentials, to the features that will carry my narrative. I would like to think that I am telling the truth, that I am presenting the man naked and without disguise. What if I am merely shrinking him down to a size that will fit the black and white pages of my book and am bleaching him of all color?

The past seems unreachable, but the book I want to write isn't only about the past. It's about my grief, which is still present. Georg's memory may have shrunk to the size of a photograph, Nobel, the man, may be unreachable, but his responsibility for Georg's death is as large and as clear as ever, and my nightmares are as terrifying as ever. Georg has become a relic, like the twist of hair in the locket I am wearing in his memory, but it is wrong to keep my memories locked up. I must air them, or they will serve no purpose and remain without effect. My case is not so different from that of the people who commission family histories. They commemorate the greatness of their ancestors and keep the record prominently displayed in their drawing rooms, where visitors will see it. I must commemorate Nobel's shame and put Georg's name next to his on the printed page for all to see: the murderer and his victim.

I *must* do this in memory of Georg, I say. I can't help noticing that the meaning of *must* has shifted. It used to be a compelling force, a command embedded in every fibre of my body, embraced with every thought and feeling, a persistent and irresistible force. It has become a cerebral thing and like all pure thought, subject to arguments and contradictions. It is no longer an imperative I cannot resist. I am helpless only against the nightmares, and when I wake up screaming, in those first moments of clouded consciousness, I am, once again, in the clutches of that primal force, the desire for revenge, but only in those first moments and then the desire abates, and I pity Nobel.

The evening descends, and the poplar trees at the end of the lawn are adrift on an ocean of darkness. I get up to light a lamp.

There is a knock on the door.

I answer it.

Nikki stands there with a picnic basket. My heart goes into an arrhythmic loop when I see him, a figure silhouetted against the night sky. I have a flash of memory, Totia with his hand on the curtain, his head shadowed by the moonlight

Nikki has taken me by surprise. I haven't heard the wheels of a carriage. I look past him. There is no carriage in the road.

He sees my questioning look. "I came on foot," he says. "I didn't want to alarm your neighbors. Or arouse their curiosity."

Have I encouraged this entirely inappropriate visit? Was our talk during the carriage ride too personal? When Nikki kissed my hand yesterday, did I leave it there for a heartbeat longer than necessary? I did look into his eyes when he said, "I hope I'll see you again soon," and felt a flicker of unease at the thought of Sophie watching us.

He has brought a picnic dinner and a bottle of champagne, to thank me for looking after Gretel, he says.

"I hope you will share the meal with me," he says. "It makes no sense for two people sitting at their separate tables in separate houses, eating their lonely meals in silence when they could have company and conversation."

"Being alone is not the same as loneliness," I say.

"I felt lonely at any rate, and hope you will not deny me the pleasure of your company, Miss Lassick."

Yesterday, I didn't have the strength to keep my resolve and dismiss Nikki from my fantasies, and now he is here in body, my daydreams replaced by reality. Of course, I yield to the plea in his eyes, or is it the pleading of my own heart? He unfolds the white cloth that covers the picnic basket and spreads it on the table like an obliging waiter. Then he arranges smoked meat and cheese on two plates. He takes a loaf of bread out of the basket and a jar of pickles. He has thought of everything, except the cutlery.

"I forgot the cutlery," he says, "but I did bring your book, *To the Caucasus and Back*. I got it off Mark Twain. He had two copies. Will you sign this one for me?"

He places the book on the table and opens it to the title page.

"How would you like me to sign your copy?" I ask.

"How about: To my devoted admirer."

"I didn't realize I had a devoted admirer," I say, escaping into the kitchen to bring cutlery. He follows me and stands at the door.

"There are only two explanations for that," he says. "Either I was too discreet in expressing my admiration, or I lack the necessary qualities to merit your attention."

He moves back to the table in the parlor and takes two champagne glasses from the basket. They are wrapped in linen napkins.

"There is a third explanation," I say. "I am bound to ignore a married admirer."

He folds the linen napkins into squares and sets them beside the plates.

"Even considering the status of my marriage?" His eyes are serious.

He is prompting me to ask a question in turn, but I won't oblige. He is trying to lead me to a place that is not safe for me, a dark forest where fantasies lie in wait. I put on my armor.

"I know nothing about your marriage," I say, "and I'm not interested in long tales of tragic love."

He pops the cork and pours champagne into the glasses.

"Come," he says, leading me to the table and pulling out a chair for me to sit down. "It isn't a long tale. In fact, it can be told in a few words: My marriage is in abeyance."

He stands behind my chair like a butler, but then he places his hands lightly on my shoulders and bends over me. I can feel his breath. Blood starts pulsing in my neck. He makes me tremble. For a moment, I think he will kiss the top of my head, but he only says, "It was an arranged marriage."

He sits down across from me and begins slicing the smoked meat. I watch him silently. I have no breath left to speak. I can't possibly eat. The skin around my mouth has softened. I can't move my jaw or swallow. My whole body is disordered.

I cannot fight him off. I carelessly allowed him to enter my head and play the lead in my fantasies, and now I'm afraid he will make me live my fantasies. I am thinking of that thin line between thought and action, the thin line that separates my misconduct from Nobel's sin.

I barely have the strength to hold out my plate for the slices of meat Nikki offers me.

"And how is it that *you* have avoided marriage so far?" he asks me. "It can't be for want of admirers. Has no one gone down on his knees and made you an offer?"

He says it lightly, with an amused smile, but I feel I have entered the dark forest of my dreams. How intimate our talk has become, how full of unspoken words, the makings of fantasy. I can't resist his line of questioning.

"No one has proposed to me because they are afraid of receiving an answer they don't like," I say, "but why are you asking me about that?" I make my voice hard, in an effort to break the spell. I push the book back across the table without signing it. "It's a rather personal question, isn't it? And we hardly know each other."

"*Ask and ye shall receive,*" he says. "What would you like to know about me?"

I need to get away from romantic talk about admirers and land on a safer topic. I take him up on his offer and ask: "You said the other day that you felt powerless to defend the empire against the enemy within. That's why you resigned your commission. I still don't know what you meant."

"I fudged. My motives weren't quite as noble as that. I didn't have a choice. I got involved in a scandal and felt obliged to resign my commission."

We are back on private territory. I meant to coax him into the open field of politics, but he has pulled me back into the thicket of his life. His words run dangerously close to my fantasy. He will cross over and make it real.

"You have heard about the scandal already," he says when I show no surprise. "Sophie told you?"

"Mark Twain mentioned it," I say. "But he didn't elaborate."

"The story has made the rounds, of course. I jilted my fiancée, who came from a distinguished family, and married a nobody, no, worse than a nobody – a notorious woman. I might have gotten away with it if I had allowed a decent interval to pass before making Sophie my wife. Going back on my promise to Elizabeth one month and marrying Sophie the next was outrageous. People called me a scoundrel and worse. I had to resign my commission."

Why does Nikki tell me about his broken promises and his disgrace? He is weaving me into the story of his life. I'm in it now. I can't cut the thread.

It's bad enough that I have fallen in love with Nikki before I knew anything about his life, and now I ask another question as if I intended to get even closer to him and stay in love.

"And why did you not delay the marriage?"

"Because Sophie put pressure on me. The child needed a name, Nobel's health was precarious. He was willing to make arrangements for her, and she was afraid he would die before they could be completed. By obliging her, I wronged Elizabeth, of course, and her family was not prepared to put up with it. They demanded redress and sued me for desertion. As you might have guessed by now: Nobel paid them off. And because I had to resign my post in the army, he arranged for a civilian position that paid a respectable salary."

He clips his sentences and keeps to the essentials as if he didn't want me to get sidetracked. But why would I want to know all that in the first place? To have a future, you must know the past, they say. But we have no future, Nikki and I. Yet I find myself asking questions and listening to the story of his life. Not just the externals, the banal and insignificant things which make up small talk. I have asked Nikki questions that take me inside his mind and show me around. His answers are testing me – do I like the furnishings of his mind? Will I condemn him for what he did? Will I agree with society and call him a scoundrel?

He should have withdrawn his promise to Elizabeth earlier, he says. They should have parted quietly, by mutual consent. It was a mistake to think that they could ever be happy together. Elizabeth knew it too after their long engagement, long because they were both afraid of taking the next step. When they first met, he thought she was the right woman for him. Like he himself, she came from a family of heroes. She was related to the Esterhazys and the Radetzkys. She was wealthy, placid, cultured. She was the ideal wife, he thought. But she was too placid, too cool.

The distance between them grew over the three years of their engagement. It was like sitting at opposite ends of a long table meant for two dozen guests, he says. There was no intimacy. There was a silence of the heart. Their marriage would have remained an empty shell.

He is telling me a great deal about himself, but he has me confused. Why did he feel obliged to give his name to the child? Sophie gave me the impression that Nobel was Gretel's father.

"Is Gretel your child?"

"Who knows?" he says. "Sophie is the only one who knows for sure, and she isn't telling. But whatever the answer to that question, I am Gretel's father now. I love her, and she loves me." He pauses as if he had second thoughts about that. "Well, in a pinch, she will take Bella over me," he says with a throwaway laugh.

"And Nobel took no responsibility for Gretel?"

"He took financial responsibility. He made sure, at any rate, that I would have the means to look after the child in case Sophie squandered all her money. He put us together like a business deal, signed and sealed. And that's all our marriage is, a business deal, except that I have taken to Gretel and love her – foolishly, because she keeps me tied to Sophie. But love is always unwise, isn't it?"

Everyone quotes that adage, and no one takes it into account.

We finish our meal and drink the bottle of champagne. The evening closes in on us. The space around us is peopled with the past. Nikki's words, as words always do, have seeped into the fabric of my mind, loosened it, and weakened me. I have no strength left, no will to resist. His mouth asks a silent question. We draw close without touching. Every gesture has a secret meaning, the way we lean forward, the way we breathe. When we get up from the table and he takes my hand, it is as if he showed me the key to decipher the coded language of our bodies. His hand is in mine, his skin against my skin, I can read the future clearly.

He takes me into his arms and kisses me. He says I am beautiful, and the words keep me in his arms. Now his lean body touches mine, his mouth presses against mine with a magnetic effect. I open my lips to him, and my fantasy becomes flesh. I take his hand and lead him to my bedroom. As I pass the armoire, the full-length mirror between the two doors, I am afraid of what I will see there, a woman who has no business to feel passion, but instead, I see Nikki's reflection, the shape of his shoulders, the blonde shock of his hair. He brushes against my arm. His touch removes all guilt.

We undress slowly as if we were going through a holy rite. Through the open door, by the light of the lamp casting a triangle on the floor, I see his bare feet. He lies down beside me, slides his body across mine and presses me against the pillows. His breath comes in stifled bursts as he strokes my breasts and my hips, attentive to the minutiae of my body, to intimacies in small places. I never thought there would be another man after Totia, another man to pleasure me like my dark-haired, dark-eyed lover in Kutaisi. I never thought I would feel such slim hips between my thighs again. A moan is swelling up in me. I hear night sounds, a dog barking, the wheels of a carriage driving by, then my ears go deaf to the outside world, and I hear only his cry and my cry.

When I open my eyes again, the light from the parlor spreading through the open door is vaporous. Then I realize it is a film on my own eyes, of tears or of heat. Nikki leans across and kisses me on my sweaty cheek, thanks me. His eyes carry the memory of desire fulfilled.

I fall asleep in his arms, sleep soundly until the first gray light filters through the curtains. I open my eyes and see that he is up, dressing quietly to avoid waking me. I watch him silently, secretly so as not to give away my wakefulness. He walks out of the room softly. Then I hear the front door close behind him and his steps recede. He said I am beautiful, and I wonder: can I be beautiful after all? I close my eyes again. This is the end of my fantasy – I have crossed over and can't go back. Nikki has become part of my life.

I sink back into sleep, and when I wake up again, it is morning. I smell the scent of the pine branches Olga has used to light the fire. She has let herself in and is in the kitchen, making her "camp coffee", as my mother used to call it, a brew of chicory and malt.

I allow myself to lie still a little longer and think of Nikki. No, I'm not thinking. I am listening to my body. Then my brain kicks in. The remnants of our dinner are still on the table in the parlor! Olga will ask me: Did you have a dinner guest last night? I feel the heat of shame rising in my cheeks. What will I say to her? A friend dropped in. What friend? A recent acquaintance. *She* lives nearby, I'll say to Olga. I get up, wash and dress hastily and with my hair still undone, join her in the kitchen. She has set out breakfast for the two of us – camp coffee and the braided egg loaf she bakes for me once a week. We sit down, but she asks no questions.

When the table is cleared and Olga starts on her housework, I follow her into the parlor and see why she has shown no curiosity. There is no trace of last night's meal. The picnic basket is gone. Nikki must have taken everything back with him. There is no need to make up an explanation.

I go on into my study. I spend most of my mornings here in this sparsely furnished room, writing under Georg's watchful eyes. Now I take his photo and bury it under a ledger filled with newspaper articles on Alfred Nobel. I have cut them out and arranged them on the pages with the name of the paper and the date of publication written below, as Mr Olmuth taught me when I started working for him. I also keep a file with quotations attributed to Nobel, and there is my black notebook in which I have written extracts from Bertie's and Sophie's letters. Sophie's manuscript, an untidy stack of papers, is sitting on the desk in front of me.

A few days ago, I started working on it, paraphrasing the quotations from Nobel's letters, but now I can't go on. Nikki and I are lovers. The rationale I had for carrying on has collapsed. The question of Nobel's responsibility, honoring the memory of the dead, righting a wrong – none of this makes sense anymore. I have put away Georg's photo to avoid his eyes, and I won't be able to look Sophie in the eye when I see her next. After my fall from grace, the book I meant to write is no longer the Garden of Eden, where justice prevails.

Sophie

"Mama," Gretel says. "Will that lady visit us again? The one Papa took me to when I was sick?"

"You mean Miss Lassick?"

An image pops up in Sophie's mind, of Ida standing at the door of her little house and Nikki kissing her hand. Observing them from the carriage, she thought: I know that devout bending of his back. And when he turned, she recognized the hungry look in his eyes and felt a pang of envy that it was not for her. But by the time Nikki took his seat in the carriage, she knew those feelings of envy weren't about their love. That phase was over. They were about a man's appreciative look and the desire in his eyes. There was nothing like a man's attention for bringing out the sweetness of life.

"Why does Miss Lassick have such a small drawing room?" Gretel asks.

"Because she lives on her own and doesn't need more space," Sophie says a little sharply and regrets the tone at once. It makes her sound old and disappointed.

"And what do you and Miss Lassick talk about when she visits you?" Gretel asks.

"My, we have a lot of questions today," Czerny says from across the room, where she sits knitting a charcoal shawl, which seems to take forever to complete, or maybe it's not the same shawl. Czerny always knits blackish things.

"I don't mind Gretel asking questions," Sophie says. "She's a clever child and wants to know everything. Right, sweetie? You are my clever little girl."

Czerny purses her lips, but Sophie ignores her.

"You want to know what Miss Lassick and I talk about?" she says to Gretel. "A book. We are writing a book together."

"Like my ABC book?"

"No, it's a story – the story of a famous man, who passed away a little while ago. Do you remember the reason why Mama wore gray dresses and black jewelry?"

"Because you were in mourning?" Gretel draws out the unfamiliar word as if to make it fit her mouth and her mind. "Were you in mourning for that famous man?"

"His name is Alfred Nobel. I'll tell you about him when you grow up."

"Miss Lassick was wearing black jewelry," the child says. "Was she in mourning for him, too?"

"No, she wears that locket in memory of a young man who died long ago in an accident."

Czerny puts her knitting away in the embroidered bag that is her constant companion.

"Come, Gretel," she says. "We'll go downstairs to the reading room. You can bring your ABC book along, and if it stops raining, we'll go for a little walk."

"No!" Gretel says. "I want to stay with Mama."

"You can stay if you promise to play quietly with your dolls," Sophie says.

"I promise, Mama. I'll be good."

Czerny sighs. "She'll be in your way, madam, but as you please. I'll go to the reading room by myself then. I suppose you don't need me here."

No, Sophie does not need anyone listening in on her conversations with Ida.

Czerny goes downstairs, and a few minutes later, Ida arrives.

"How are you?" she says, nodding to Sophie, but her eyes are on Gretel. "Are we feeling better today?"

I don't know what Nikki can possibly see in her, Sophie thinks. She always dresses so plainly and doesn't make any effort to bring out her good points. Such thick, glossy hair – it's a marvel – and she pulls it back and piles it on top of her head, so artlessly that you'd think she hates it. Her eyes are her best asset. They are enigmatic eyes, holding a promise or a secret. Some men find that attractive.

Gretel has settled on the floor and is serving "tea" to her dolls, two fine ladies in white lace with permanent smiles painted on their porcelain faces, a cheerfulness that will never be disturbed by life.

Gretel waves at Ida and keeps on playing with her dolls.

"Come, love," Sophie says. "Greet Miss Lassick properly."

Gretel puts down the tiny cup in her hand, gets up and curtsies to Ida. "I am having afternoon tea," she says primly. "Did you bring me anything?"

"Gretel!" Sophie says. "That's a very rude question."

"I didn't know I'd see you today," Ida says to the child. "Besides, I don't know what little girls like."

"Pretzels. I like pretzels best," Gretel says.

Sophie shakes her head, laughing.

"Then I'll bring you pretzels the next time I come," Ida says.

Gretel goes back to her dolls, and Ida is all business now.

"How is the memoir coming along, Sophie?"

"Not very well."

"Have you written anything more?"

She hasn't written a single line since the last time they talked, when she allowed Ida to take away the pages she had on hand. *You don't work, you don't write, you don't read. You don't even think*, Alfred said. She hasn't given any more thought to her memoirs. She has been thinking about the money the executors have sent and how pleasant it would be to spend it on going to Merano in the fall.

"I've read what you gave me," Ida says, "but it's almost entirely made up of quotations from Nobel's letters. I've started to paraphrase them since we can't quote them literally. When you go on writing, Sophie, I hope you'll keep that in mind. You can't use his exact words."

"I don't think I can go on writing now that I no longer have Alfred's letters," she says.

"You said you would have no difficulty recalling his words."

"Yes, but I feel lost without the letters. I feel as if I had lost Alfred a second time. Perhaps we could just talk, and you take notes."

"Mama," Gretel says. "We have drunk all the tea and eaten all the cake. What do we do next?"

"You put the tea things away and put your dolls to bed." Her eyes follow Gretel as she carries the dolls to her room, one by one. "That's a good girl," she says.

She turns back to Ida. "In any case," she says. "You'll want to read the rest of my letters to Alfred."

"Yes, I should finish reading your letters," she says as if it was a chore all of a sudden. A few days ago she was so keen on them.

Sophie gets up to fetch the letters. "I may not have them much longer," she says. "Mr Volker was here yesterday. He may buy them, you know."

Carl Volker reminds her of Alfred. *Are you eager to embrace your old uncle? Just one more little kiss.* That's what Alfred used to say, and Carl Volker has that same avuncular tone. She wonders whether he has the potential of becoming her protector, someone to take Alfred's place. Nikki is so stand-offish now. She misses Alfred's protective voice. *You are still a child and don't think of the future at all, and so it is good that an old, attentive uncle watches over you.* Volker has the same fatherly authority, but he doesn't look vulnerable to female charms, to her charms at any rate. She isn't even sure that he will go for the letters. He rifled through them and didn't say much. Perhaps she should send him a follow-up note.

She unties the ribbon and spreads the letters out on the desk. Ida pulls in her chair, looks through them, finds the place where she left off the last time and starts reading.

Sophie watches her for a while. Gretel is putting away the dollhouse, but she is dawdling. She's not very good at putting things away. And now there is Ida to distract her. She has stopped reading and is smiling at the child.

"Why are you smiling?" Gretel asks Ida, sidling up to the desk.

"Because I like you," Ida says.

"I like you too," Gretel says, "but not as much as Mama or Papa or Bella."

"And Nanny?" Sophie prompts her. "You like Nanny, don't you?"

Gretel wiggles her shoulder and whispers, "And Nanny." But she immediately glosses over that forced declaration of love by asking Ida another question.

"Why aren't you wearing your locket today? Mama said it's in memory of a friend who died in an accident. Have you remembered him enough?"

A faint blush appears on Ida's cheeks. "You could put it that way," she says.

Alfred used to say: *You will soon forget me, dear child. But do keep me in fond memory.* It is peculiar that Ida isn't wearing her keepsake, and the answer she gave Gretel is peculiar too.

"Come, love," Sophie says and pats the sofa. "Sit here with Mama. You mustn't talk to Miss Lassick. She is trying to read."

Gretel shakes off Sophie's hand.

"I won't talk anymore," she says. "But can I watch Miss Lassick read?"

"Just for a minute, love," Sophie says. "Then I'd like you to sit here with me, and we'll look at your alphabet book."

Gretel stands close to Ida's elbow, watching her silently for a while. Then she reaches up, touches her hair and tugs lightly at a strand.

"What are you doing?" Ida says, arresting her fingers.

Sophie gets up and firmly takes the child by the hand. "Stop that," she says.

"I was just trying to see whether your hair is real," Gretel says to Ida. "Nanny says you have such beautiful hair, it may be a hairpiece."

"It's real," Ida says, smiling again. But enough is enough, Sophie thinks. The child is making a nuisance of herself.

"I really think you'll be better off downstairs with Nanny, Gretel. You can look at magazines with her," she says. "I'll take you to the elevator. You can find your way to the reading room, can't you? Or do you want me to go downstairs with you?"

"I can find my way," Gretel says and gives her a defiant look. "I'm five years old, and I can find that stupid old reading room by myself."

"You are being naughty," Sophie says. "I'd better go with you."

I suppose it's all right to leave Ida alone with the letters for a few minutes, she thinks.

"*Ein Momenterl*," she says to her. "I'll be back in a short moment."

Ida gives her a stare as if she had said something astonishing. She seems distracted. Because Gretel pulled her hair?

When Sophie comes back, Ida is putting away her notebook and tying up the letters.

"Finished already?"

"Not quite," she says, "but I meant to ask you about Nobel's family."

"I don't know much about his family," she says. "I can tell you that he was very close to his mother. Too close, if you ask me. Every year, he went to Stockholm to celebrate her birthday. He always made time for her. When *I* wanted him to go on a trip, he said he was sick and tired of travel, but when it came to making that annual trip to Stockholm – not a word about business meetings or his rheumatism or his headaches and all the other things he kept complaining about to me."

And every Christmas he became maudlin, Sophie thinks. *I wish I could be there for the Christmas dinner. I want to hold out my plate for more dopp i gryta.* Some porridge his mother made, or was it bread pudding? A grown man crying for his mama!

"Did he have brothers or sisters?" Ida says.

She always takes a brisk tone with me, Sophie thinks. There's no sympathy in her voice. I guess she doesn't know what love is and how society makes you suffer when you love a man who isn't your husband.

You have no rights unless you are married. You have to sneak around and keep your eyes down and listen to them whispering behind their hands.

"He had two brothers," she says. "Ludvig was a hypochondriac. Alfred used to joke about him. 'He invents a new illness for himself every hour,' he said. 'In the morning, it's a heart murmur, at breakfast, gout, in the afternoon, tuberculosis, in the evening, blood poisoning, and at bedtime, cancer attacks his kidneys.' Alfred could be funny, you know. The dark kind of funny."

"And his other brother?" Ida asks.

"Robert. They are both dead now. A third brother, Emil, died young after some kind of chemical experiment went wrong. Alfred was broken up about his death and didn't want to talk about it. Talk to me, I said. It's better to get it off your chest, or you will have a stroke, like your father. You know, his father had a stroke shortly after Emil died, and he never recovered. But Alfred didn't want to talk about any of that."

"Did he feel guilty, you think?"

"Guilty? Why?"

"You say it was a chemical experiment. Perhaps his brother's death could have been avoided."

"How? I don't understand what you mean."

"Those experiments with nitroglycerine were dangerous."

"But that was Alfred's business."

"The business of death."

"Well, I don't know. That's a nasty way of putting it. Alfred used to complain about the way people talked of his business. He said he was only an inventor. He didn't mean his invention to be used for deadly purposes. It bothered him a great deal if that's what you mean by feeling guilty. I guess that's why he left money for a peace prize. If you ask me, he should have left it to his family. Maybe he thought they had enough money. They are wealthy in their own right, you know. But he could have left the money to me and Gretel."

"If he had regrets, why didn't he get out of the arms business?"

"That's what I said to him, especially when he complained so much about his health and said he couldn't take the pressure of business anymore. But he just put me off with jokes. 'Then you wouldn't have all those dresses in your wardrobe,' he said, 'or your fur coats. And there would be no nice presents on your birthday, no diamond earrings or strands of pearls. If I gave up my business,' he said, 'I'd be back in Russia, working the oilfields in the Caucasus, and you'd be back in Baden, selling flowers.' And in a way, he was right."

Ida says nothing. She just looks at me. No, the woman doesn't understand me at all, Sophie thinks. What's the use of talking to her!

"And the next generation of Nobels?" Ida says. "Have you ever met Emanuel Nobel?"

"Emanuel – I met him once, years ago when he visited Alfred in Paris. I suppose he's the head of the family now that everyone else is dead."

"Even though he is illegitimate?"

"Emanuel? He isn't illegitimate. What gives you that idea? Emanuel has always been the golden boy, the star of the family."

For a moment Sophie remembers Emanuel's handsome figure, his ardour, his whispered endearments, how exciting it was to feel wanted. It's all so long ago. Her life has become very dull.

"So, no more reading of letters today?" she says to Ida.

"I think I have enough information for the time being," Ida says and gets up. "It's time to take stock and put everything in order."

"Oh, well, let me know when you want to come back."

She looks deflated somehow or discouraged, Sophie thinks as she is saying goodbye to Ida at the door. Perhaps she won't come back. I hope she won't.

It's time to forget the past now that she has sold Alfred's letters. *No one will grieve over my death, least of all those whom I have helped.* Well, she doesn't mean to forget everything, just to move on, past Alfred who cannot help her anymore. Past Nikki, who never does anything for her without being prodded. Past the whole drab scene in Vienna, the quiet life of respectability that was forced on her by circumstances, the prosy people, the boring dinner conversations.

Her thoughts wander to Merano again. Italian men are more alive somehow, she thinks. She will go south in September and find a place which allows pets so that Gretel can have Bella with her. She will miss her papa, of course, but children forget quickly, especially if there are so many new things to see and do. Perhaps I should go earlier than September, she thinks. Next month even. But then I won't see the flowering of the chestnut trees in the Prater, the white candle-blossoms I love so much. But never mind the chestnut trees. There will be flowering fruit trees in Merano. There will be tulips, daffodils and forget-me-nots on the Tappeiner Path. And I'll make new acquaintances. It will be lovely to stroll along in a muslin dress on the arm of an attentive gentleman, or ride along the boulevard in a stream of carriages! She can hear the hollow hoof-beats of the horses, the jingling of the brass on the harnesses, the murmuring of turning wheels. She can see one of the gentlemen raise his hat to her and herself smiling and waving a gloved hand. She can feel the aura of gaiety and happiness. But how can she enjoy the attention of gentlemen when she is a married woman? There is the old expedient of pretending to be a widow. It's a nice way of putting it when you have been abandoned by your husband or have decided to go your separate ways. But perhaps it was better to make a clear cut and ask Nikki for a divorce. It didn't have the stigma it used to have even ten years ago when Strauss divorced his wife. And he had to leave the Catholic Church because they wouldn't allow his remarriage. He had to convert. The Protestants don't make so much fuss. Of course, a divorce costs money. The lawyers always exact their pound of flesh, and she would have to pay because Nikki didn't have the funds and would likely baulk at the expense. But all that was in the realm of possibilities now that the trustees had bought the letters and sent her the money.

Yes, it was sad not to have Alfred's letters anymore. But then, he never loved her as much as he loved his mother. *When life wanes and one is only a short step away from the grave, one does not form new bonds and moves even closer to the old ones. I wish I could stay with my mother.*

Would Gretel grow up to love her like that?

Ida

The flash is blinding. I am trying to find my way through the darkness. My fingertips touch dented walls, my feet stumble over the ground, ripped open by the explosion. The force of the blast is still rippling through my body. I am wading through blood. It eddies around my ankles, a river of severed arms and legs, torsos and heads tumbling in the current, hair flowing. I crawl up to the top of the bank and walk through a field strewn with bodies. I am looking for Georg and can't find him because my eyes are dim or because it is twilight or I don't remember what he looks like. But now I do see his body, I recognize the shape of his shoulders, I turn him over, and look into his lifeless eyes – it's Nikki! I scream. I want to run, but someone is pinning me down – the dead man's arm. He is strangling me, no, hugging me, calling to me.

"Wake up, love. Wake up. It's just a dream."

The image of the dead man dissolves. Nikki is holding me in his arms, soothing me. The drumbeat of my heart slows to a ticking. I feel his fingertips stroking my cheeks. I cling to my rescuer. When I dare to open my eyes, I see that he is safe, that I am safe in my bedroom. I am looking at Nikki's unmarked forehead, his serious eyes. He is unhurt. He is alive. My breath is coming back in a long moan.

"I dreamed you were dead," I say. "It's a nightmare I have. I can't shake it."

"Tell me about your nightmare," he says.

I turn to him. I can barely make out his face in the darkness, but his voice is full of tenderness.

"It's about a blast destroying houses and killing people. Even after I wake up, I feel as if I'd been through a catastrophe."

I don't want to explain it to him, but I can't hold back. The words are spilling out. I tell Nikki about the blast in Heleneborg that killed my fiancé. I don't say "Georg". It doesn't seem right to mention his name in the presence of my new lover. It would compound my infidelity.

"It's so many years ago," I say. "But the dream doesn't go away."

"You still miss him?" he asks. I can feel his breath on my cheek.

237

Do I? I barely remember Georg's face. It has crumbled into grayness. Only the dregs of terror remain. I fetch a deep breath. "I don't, and I feel guilty that I no longer miss him, that I am happy with you now."

"That's because your mind is out of tune with your heart. You think you owe a debt to someone, but you feel you have paid it already or didn't owe it in the first place." Nikki's breath comes like a sigh. He is right. I can feel the divide within me, but I'm not sure it is a divide between mind and heart. It's more like the present sending me in one direction and the past pulling me into another. But how does he know about these contradictions?

He turns on his back and floats his voice up to the ceiling. "That's how I felt when I was in the military. Gradually, the gap between who I was and who I wanted to be became so great that I felt lost, in a fog. Then I resigned my commission, and I could see clearly again. It was as if someone had released a cloud of vapor from my brain."

It's a relief to think of Nikki's past instead of my own. I let go of my dream, of my petrified memories. Why did he choose a career in the military, if it made him feel like that?

"Out of ignorance," he says. "I didn't know what I was getting into. I thought I owed it to my father. Serving in the army was a family tradition. My grandfather had a distinguished career. My father rose through the ranks and expected me to follow in his footsteps. I was sent to military school as a boy. Every talk I had with my father was about the military. He thought of civilians as an inferior species of man. He made me recite the army regulations. He quizzed me on the wartime strength of our regiments. He checked on my riding skills. I can still hear his voice. *Your horsemanship is a disgrace, Nikolaus. I shall have to speak to your instructor.*" Nikki's voice takes on a twang, a combination of dark vowels and soft consonants. Then he changes back to his own voice, the voice of the civilian he is now. "That's why I chose a career in the army."

It's hard to stand up to the expectations of your family – don't I know it? My brother expected me to get married while I still grieved Georg's death. Society expected me to become a wife and mother, not a writer of biographies and travelogues. But do you have to give in to other people's opinion.

"It seemed an unavoidable duty at the time," he says. "And I had no dislike for the military at first. I was eighteen. I saw it as a glamorous profession, as an adventure."

He remembers the day his regiment passed in review before the emperor, he says, the measured hoof-beats of the horses, his troop, eyes front, in full dress uniform, scoured and polished. He felt the gravity and importance of the occasion. The trumpets began to play the assembly march. The emperor spoke a few words of greeting. There was a roar of *Hurrah*.

"I remember the passionate devotion I felt to the fatherland and to the emperor. During the review, he stopped two or three times and asked questions. I envied the soldiers he singled out. If he deigns to address me, I thought, I'll die of happiness. But he passed me by."

The romance of patriotic love. The cult of heroism. It made young men dream of glory.

"I was eager for adventure," Nikki says. "I was impatient. I felt there wasn't enough action in my life. It was a decade of peace for Austria. We stood on the sidelines when Prussia attacked France. And when Russia declared war on Turkey, I was incensed that Austria did not join in the fray. I was raring to go. All of us were in a high pitch of expectation. And then finally, we got our marching orders – to occupy Bosnia and Herzegovina."

I see Nikki's face in the half-light of the moon, visible through a gap in the curtains. The memory of that day escapes from his eyes like a flash. I remember the call for mobilization myself. All the young men in St Veit were eager to join up. Some lied about their age and enlisted.

"We were all eager to go," Nikki says. "We felt invincible. I had no fear of being maimed or killed. After four years in the military, I still hadn't seen anyone die. We went out on maneuvers. We played at war. And then they sent us to attack Klobuk."

I had never heard of Klobuk.

"A fortress in Herzegovina," Nikki says. "Perched on top of a rocky outcrop, with one narrow track leading up from the river. It was a suicide mission, but we pressed on. We thought we could do it under cover of heavy artillery fire from our gunners. They would keep their artillery pieces trained on the ramparts while we forded the river and made our way up to the fortress."

But at night it started raining. A steady downpour. In the morning the river had turned into a torrent. By the time they crossed, Nikki says, the horses had to breast the water, and in spite of the artillery fire, the snipers on the ramparts managed to pick off a few of the men.

Nikki's voice is hollow now with the memory of death. He can't fight it off. I have learned to avoid the vision of death during my waking hours, at least. In the light of day, I know the things that lift the lever that opens the latch and allows terror to enter my soul. Asleep, I am helpless against dread.

"Don't—" I say to Nikki, meaning to caution him against those memories, but they have already taken hold of him. He can no longer stop the flow of words.

"The ground by the river was so soft that the artillery pieces sank into the mud. The gunners had a hard time keeping the cannons trained on the fortress and protecting us on our way up."

They left their horses behind, he says. Riders were an easy mark. They went on foot, keeping close to the rock walls.

"It's years ago, but I remember every detail of the climb, the grainy mud on the river bank, the stones crunching underfoot, my hand on the clammy rock wall."

The scraggy trees along the path offered them little cover, he says. The drifting fog camouflaged them, but there were stretches where they were in full view of the men defending the fortress.

"They opened fire on us, I saw the muzzles flash, saw the blue-gray smoke and heard the bullets whistle by, but it seemed as if I was invulnerable. A bullet hit the man beside me and pierced his leg. He fell to the ground screaming. A couple of us stopped and tried to drag him to the side, but the snipers had us in their sights, and we had to let him go."

His memories are like mine, a mass of dark ruminations blocking the escape route, an unnegotiable mountain he has to climb, step by step, reliving every moment of dread.

"We pressed our backs against the rock wall and watched as another volley hit the man on the ground, ripping into his stomach. I could see his steaming guts. His chest was a mess of blood, and still, he was looking at us and bellowing for help until death silenced him. Even then his mouth remained open, a frozen cry, an accusation because we didn't help him."

I know that face, the screaming mouth, death shutting out the light of life. I have heard the feral howl in my nightmare. I have seen the twitching hands, the ominous stillness of limbs in death. I can feel Nikki hold his breath. Such memories can make you forget to breathe.

Then he starts breathing again, ejects air forcefully, and I know that maneuver, too. A cry is stuck in his throat. He can't cough it up. I lean into

240

him, squeeze against him hard to make that cry come out so that it can dissolve in the air, but it is lodged deep down, out of reach.

"My coat was sopping wet from the river crossing, and I was shaking with cold, and yet I felt sweaty, burning up from the inside. We moved on through a hail of bullets," he says. "Scores of our men died, but we kept going. The snipers went on shooting at us until they had no ammunition left. It turned out there were only a dozen of them, but they defended that fortress to the last man."

For a long time afterwards, after Klobuk had been taken, after Herzegovina had been secured, and his platoon was back in Vienna, he was in mental turmoil, traumatized by the scenes of carnage. He kept seeing the faces of his dying comrades. One had a horsy face with a toothbrush moustache, he says, another had a habit of quirking his mouth. He couldn't forget them, even though they had not been close to him. "It must be worse for you," he says, "because you lost a man you loved."

"What was his name?" he asks softly.

Do I dare to say the name out loud? I make my mouth move and say, "Georg."

"Georg," he repeats as if he needed to memorize it. "I never had nightmares like you, Ida, but the memory, the terror was present in my mind for years, rising up anew every day and trailing like a streamer. It took only a swirling red skirt to call up the bloody limbs of dying men, or the sight of raw meat in a butcher's shop. Or the sound of pouring rain. There were so many triggers that brought the terror back to me. I could no longer listen to music. I heard the screams of my dying comrades in a violin's pitch, their pleas for help in the beating of drums. I saw terrified eyes fastened on me everywhere. The image of those dying men took years to fade."

The longer you keep it in, the deeper the impression left on your mind. The memory is stenciled into the coils of your brain. The sharp edges dig into your soft tissue. I know.

"You've kept it in too long," I say. I am amazed how well he has kept his memories locked up. The smiling face he shows to people and the calm voice he uses are no more than a truce with the terror in his heart.

"I couldn't talk to anyone," he says. "No one back home could understand me. They read about the war in the papers, but they continued to live a life of peace. They couldn't understand the ugliness of war. Not Elizabeth. Hero worship was in her blood. Not my father. He wanted to hear stories of bravery, not of dying comrades. Generations of soldiers looked down on us from the oil paintings on the walls of his library. They were mounted on dappled horses, raising their sabers in victory. Their chests were decorated with rows of medals. To my father, a man who feared death was beneath contempt."

He sits up, leaning back against the headboard. In the darkness, I see him lace his knuckles together and open his hands again. He wants to let go of that knot in his life.

"But your comrades would have understood," I say. "Didn't you talk among yourselves?"

"No. Talking of that wretched death march was taboo. It didn't fit the image of a victorious army. We were heroes, celebrated on our return. Every one of the survivors wanted to keep the sheen of glory untarnished by blood. But we weren't heroes in Herzegovina. We were the hated enemy there, the devil incarnate. Still are."

"And resigning your commission delivered you from the memory of death?"

"It saved me from despair. After Klobuk, I lost the will to live. The political situation was volatile, and I dreaded being sent into battle again. So I went out every night, drinking myself senseless, gambling and whoring my life away. I didn't care what I did or in whose company I was, as long as it made the time pass and kept me from thinking. Then Sophie got pregnant, and Nobel arranged for our marriage. Perhaps he understood what was ailing me and made me the gift of a new life. It was humiliating to accept his money, but I was like a drowning man. I didn't care if I was thrown a shiny new rope or a rotten plank. I grasped it. Anything to keep my head above water and allow me to breathe again."

Nikki's arm touches mine as if he wanted to check that I am still here, that I haven't deserted him. I squeeze his hand to let him know that I am listening.

"And your father?" I say, prompting him to go on.

"He couldn't live with my decision. He cut me off. He told me I had dishonored the family name. He wanted nothing more to do with me. No one in my family will talk to me now. Except my crazy cousin who is an outlaw himself." There was a sneer in his voice as if he despised himself. "If I hadn't accepted Nobel's help, I would have been left a beggar. Perhaps my father was counting on that and hoping I would reconsider. But I could never go back. Even getting out of the army didn't heal the wound. It only took the edge off the trauma. What remains is a sense of foreboding. We've won the battle, not the war. Those people in Herzegovina haven't forgiven us. Nor the people in the other territories we occupied, Bosnia and Serbia. There is unrest even in Hungary. When I visit Budapest, I hear complaints – German speakers are promoted over Hungarians. Why is German the official language? Isn't Hungary an equal partner in the monarchy? In Prague, it's the same story. There is discontent everywhere."

Nikki swings his legs over the side of the bed and picks up his clothes.

"We are sitting on a powder keg," he says as he steps into his trousers and buttons his shirt, getting ready to leave. "I give it another five years, and the dream of the multi-nation state will blow up. There will be war, and the monarchy will die a bloody death."

How did we get from nightmare dreams to a nightmare future? I can't help thinking that Nikki is right and that the emperor's policy over the last decade has been calamitously foolish. I, too, have a sense of impending collapse. I sit in Mr Olmuth's study and cut and paste newspaper articles. The headlines leave a trail of blood, like a wounded deer trying to escape the hounds, but the pack will hunt their quarry down and sink their teeth into its flank.

We are all saying *Lay Down Your Arms.* Bertie, Nikki, and I – we long for an end to violence because we have experienced the horror of violent death, but Nikki and I grieve for ourselves. Bertie hasn't lost a lover or seen a comrade die. She saw the horrors of war and grieved for others, took pity on humankind. She turned her grief into a cause, made it into something that went beyond personal suffering, into something more enduring than memories – a book, *Lay Down Your Arms,* a movement, the Society for Peace. I don't think my shoulders are broad enough to carry a cause. For me, it's about people: Georg, Nobel, Sophie, Nikki, me.

Nikki stands at the window. He parts the folds of the curtain and looks out into the gray dawn – it is almost daylight.

I get up and pull a shawl over my shoulder for warmth now that I no longer have Nikki's body to hold onto.

"I hate it when you leave," I say.

He comes back to my side of the bed and kisses me. "So do I, but it can't be helped."

He walks to the door and stops with his hand on the knob. "Then again, I didn't think there was a way out of my despair when I was in the army, and I got a reprieve. Maybe there is a way out of this dilemma as well."

"A divorce?" I say quickly, afraid I'll lose the courage to say it if I take the time to think and weigh the consequences of being the other woman, the co-respondent. But I'd rather be condemned openly than talked about behind my back. Scorn is easier to bear than scruples.

He shakes his head. "I doubt Sophie will give me a divorce. She married me for a purpose: to give the child a name and to become a respectable woman after being Alfred's mistress."

And now I am a marked woman like Sophie. I am Nikki's mistress.

"Besides," he says, "there is Gretel."

He stands in the door a moment longer as if to let the words thin out. He knows they are hard words, but he can't take them back. He doesn't want to desert Gretel. He is caught between two loves.

When the door has closed on him, I listen to Nikki's steps on the gravel path with longing in my heart. It is dawn, too early to begin the day. I go back to bed, but I crouch with my knees drawn up. I am afraid the nightmare will return, that Georg will rise from the dead and rebuke me for having betrayed him. I am afraid to close my eyes. I'm too tired to stay awake. I sleep finally, with no sense of time passing, and wake late in the morning with the sunshine turning the curtains to gauze.

*

Carl has invited me to see a play at the Burg. The theatre is a splendid structure, a pillared temple of the Muses with an auditorium shaped like a lyre. You could say it was built to show off the audience. The sightlines are terrible, even with the prohibition of hats which would have rendered the stage completely invisible to anyone in the mezzanine. But even if you can't see the actors, you can definitely see who's who in the theatre. Of course, I train my glasses on the imperial box – the ladies glitter with diamonds, and the gentlemen are in dress uniform, sporting rows of medals. I don't recognize anyone. They aren't members of the emperor's immediate family. No celebrity-watching tonight. Instead, I watch the antics of the students in the sky-high fourth tier and eye the fashionable gowns of the women taking their seats in our row.

Carl has been generous. He got us seats in the orchestra, right behind the section reserved for the nobility and the diplomatic corps, and so we do, in fact, both hear and see the play, Arthur Schnitzler's *Liebelei*. I would have preferred a light comedy, but Carl likes cutting-edge drama. This one is about an extramarital affair, a bitter-sweet dalliance with a fallen woman. Is there an ulterior motive behind Carl's choice? Is he onto me? I, too, am a fallen woman, one of those who take their female preparations – savin and pennyroyal – to stave off pregnancy. Soon I'll be wearing Dr Mensinga's diaphragm like a whore. I no longer think of Georg with love. I think of him only with the uneasy feeling that I've lost my moral bearings and with a dull fear of the nightmare returning. So far, I have been spared. Since I've told Nikki of my dreams, they have not recurred, or not in that bloody form. In the new version, I encounter a man walking through a ruined landscape, and although the light is hazy or dusky or gray in the dawn, he is eerily recognizable to me, and I feel a pang of remorse. He turns, and I see that it's Georg. Sometimes, it's Nikki. But more often, the man disappears in the haze, dissolves like a phantom, and I wake up with a gasp. The nightmare has been replaced by enigmatic dreams, full of guilt and longing. Am I longing for my former self?

Watching the play, I feel those dreamlike twinges again, mourning my innocent self. I suppose a play is like a dream, or like my dreams, in which I am the watcher. The characters on stage are unreal and unreachable, like the figures in my dreams, yet I recognize in them the archetype of people I have known and of the person I am now: an adulteress.

Afterwards, Carl and I sit in the Café Landtmann, next door to the theatre. If it weren't for the play, which is still holding me in its suffocating embrace, I'd enjoy the elegant setting, the dark paneled walls under crystal chandeliers, the plush upholstery in the booth where we are seated and the starched white tablecloths. It looks festive, I realize and come out of my stage-dream with a jerk. Carl looks festive too, in his cut-off and silk vest. Surely, I'm not in for another proposal so soon after my rejection of his last offer. Does he expect a reward for publishing my travelogue?

But Carl is talking about the lead actress, Adele Sandrock, who is all the rage these days. We are on safe ground. This isn't about him or me. It isn't leading up to another proposal. Sandrock wasn't that great, he is saying. She isn't the right type for the lead – a sweet girl from the suburbs. She was cast in the role only because she is Schnitzler's mistress.

"The role of the ingénue doesn't suit her," Carl says. "She's more the type of the femme fatale."

"I thought she gave a creditable performance."

"Maybe it just shows my bias. The innocent girl from the suburbs doesn't interest me – I prefer the cheater, the adventuress. More interesting."

"Really?" I say. "You'd go in for adultery? I didn't think you were the risk-taking kind, Carl."

He considers my question. "Not in real life," he says, "but in a play, adultery makes for grand scenes. The sweet young things are rather boring, don't you think? But I guess they create a light-hearted atmosphere."

"Until they get pregnant, like Faust's Margarete."

"And kill themselves. Well, I suppose that makes for dramatic scenes as well. But speaking of irregular love lives: I've finally met the charming Mrs Kapy."

"She charmed you, did she?"

He laughs. "Not really. Too insipid for my taste, but I can see what Nobel liked about her. She's got a certain pull. I understand he was a hard-nosed businessman who knew the value of things, but she managed him well. Even when he got tired of her, he didn't just drop her. He left her in style, gave her an annuity and bought her a first-rate husband."

"You think Nikolaus Kapy is first rate?"

"Well, he isn't old or ugly or fat or stupid. And he seems to have good taste – as his interest in you proves, my dear. I saw the way he looked at you that afternoon at my office. I'm not the only man who admires you, Ida."

Carl gives me a long look that makes me uneasy.

"Oh, yes, I'm a much-admired woman," I say with a laugh, keeping my voice light, hoping he will let go of the subject. He gives me another meaningful look and moves on.

"In any case," he says, "Mrs Kapy allowed me to take a closer look at those 'Dear Alfred' letters of hers. I don't think I want them."

"You read through the whole collection?"

"Just bits here and there. A dozen letters, maybe. Read one, read them all if you ask me. They follow the same pattern. Please send money. Thanks for sending money. How are you, dear Alfred. I'm in terrible shape, dear Alfred. That's about it. And her spelling is bad. So is her punctuation. Her non-existing punctuation."

He was right about that.

"Did you tell her you weren't interested?"

"Not in so many words," he says. "I didn't want to discourage her. If she decides to have those letters printed, I'll do it, of course, at the usual rate, and she can give them away or take the risk of selling them. If she can pull it off and wants more copies, I'll give her a discount. That's the sort of thing I told her, although I left the possibility of buying the letters open."

I need not have worried about Carl heading into another proposal. His mind is on business.

"What did she say to that?"

"She said she'd think about it. And how is that biography of Nobel coming along?"

"It's not. Or let's say, Sophie isn't going to write it, and I've lost steam."

"That's too bad, Ida. A book about Nobel has potential in my opinion. I'll take it off your hands whenever it's ready."

Of course he wants my next book, now that my travelogue has turned out to be a success.

"How very kind of you," I say.

"Don't go all sarcastic on me, Ida. I *am* being kind when I encourage you to work on your next book. Your travelogue is selling well. That's good, but you need to take advantage of your popularity. Follow up with another book while you have the attention of the public. Besides, the last time we talked, you were dead keen on writing that biography. So what do you mean – you've lost steam?"

"It was supposed to be an exposé, but I no longer feel about Nobel the way I did before."

I tell him the story of Heleneborg. For all these years, I've kept it to myself. I couldn't bear to say Georg's name out loud or mention Heleneborg to anyone, but now that I've told Nikki, it's out in the open. I no longer feel compelled to keep Georg's death to myself, to nurse my grief in silence. I can't even think why I wanted to keep it a secret. Perhaps I'm newly courageous because I've buried Georg's photo under a stack of papers. He no longer watches me from the sidelines of my desk. But I think it's because I've told Nikki and said Georg's name out loud in his hearing. Letting go of Georg's name has set me free.

I tell Carl my story. I wanted revenge for the death of my fiancé, but I discovered that Nobel, too, lost a man he loved. His brother died in the same accident that took Georg's life. I've come to realize that Nobel was an unhappy man. He was depressed and ailing. I feel sorry for him now, I say and keep on explaining my change of mind to Carl, without touching on the crucial point. I can't work together with Sophie. I can't face her because I am her husband's lover now.

Instead, I say, "I can no longer sit in judgment of Nobel. Whatever mistakes he made, he paid for them. You said it yourself when we talked about the accidents in his factories, and you were right. He couldn't work miracles. He couldn't bring the dead back to life, but he atoned for those deaths."

Carl nods. "So you've come around to my point of view, but I'm surprised you never told me about your fiancé. All the questions you raised about Nobel make a lot more sense to me now. But the fact that you have changed your perspective doesn't mean you have to give up on the book."

"I can't work together with Sophie."

"That doesn't surprise me. In fact, I told you it makes no sense to collaborate with her. You are better off without her. Go it alone. Just make it a well-rounded biography. Nobel is a worthwhile subject. If you really think you need those letters, I'll buy them off Mrs Kapy. Just change the emphasis of the book. A bit of an exposé – explosions, lawsuits, mistress – that's all good, but provide some balance. Make him more human. The man suffered. He was charitable to other sufferers. He was generous. That sort of thing."

"He was certainly generous to Sophie."

"She knew how to play him. Nobel must have been hooked on her." Carl shrugs and turns up the palms of his hands. "Oh well, the body is a tyrant."

Yes, the body is a tyrant. I know the power of carnal lust. The animal wants to be fed. Perhaps it was like that for Nobel. He couldn't stop his desire for Sophie. And I can't end my affair with Nikki.

"I'm not sure I can write the book you want," I say to Carl. "I'll have to think about it."

"You have to think about the book, or about publishing with me, Ida? You aren't holding out on me because of that proposal—" He laughs ruefully. "My *almost*-proposal."

"Don't be silly," I say.

"We are still friends?"

"We are still friends."

He pats my hand. "Thank you, Ida," he says humbly. He knows what he owes me. I am a bankable author now.

He pays up and walks me to the cab stand in front of the theatre. We say goodnight softly, glad we weathered the shoals and ended the evening on good terms. He hands me into the carriage, and I tell the driver to take me to the train station.

I enter the station, thinking of Carl's advice to get on with my book on Nobel. Just give it a different slant, he said. No, I can't write that biography now, even if I change the slant, even if there is a cause at stake larger than Georg's death. A man earns millions from an invention that kills people and will go on killing people. *Someone* ought to right that wrong and raise the question of Nobel's responsibility for the use of his invention, but I can't do it. This is a grand mission and needs an idealist like Bertie, who has the will and the dedication to carry her cause to victory. I no longer have the strength or the right to wave the banner of righteousness.

On the train, I share a compartment with a middle-aged couple. She is dozing. He stares out the window. There is nothing to see except a bright reflection of our compartment and the cloudy night sky beyond. I think he is afraid of meeting my eyes and being drawn into a conversation. How fragile we are, how uncertain of ourselves. This man is afraid of giving his thoughts away. Carl is embarrassed about his ill-timed proposal. I feel guilty about forgetting Georg. Nikki is ashamed because he accepted Nobel's money.

"You despise me now," he said to me after telling me about taking money from Nobel, while I was thinking, "He will respect me less now that I am his lover."

I tried to comfort him and myself, too. "We are both sinners," I said. "We are even on that score, you and I."

"What?" he said in mock surprise. "You have committed sins, too? Let me hear your confession."

"Nikki," I said, "confessions are best made to a priest. He can give us absolution. We can only forgive and forget."

He put his arms around me then and said, "Let's do that."

And so my untold sins are forgiven. I should forgive Nobel as well, or at least be a more lenient judge of his trespasses. Sins are the accidents of a historical moment after all. What we call sin today wasn't counted as sin in other times. In antiquity, the Amazons had lovers and were granted the blessing of myth. Elizabeth of England loved the Earl of Leicester and remained the Virgin Queen, and only a hundred years ago, Catherine of Russia had lovers and yet was hailed as Catherine the Great. Perhaps one has to wear a crown to be allowed the privilege of unmarried love or else there is a degree of passion, an elemental fire which surpasses moral considerations. Is my love for Nikki in that category – above human judgment?

I don't know, but it is, like all love, foolish. Carl called Nikki first rate. That was tongue-in-cheek. He isn't first rate, I know. I listened to his story about joining the army to oblige his father, about his fiancée who did not understand him, about accepting Nobel's money to save his soul. He is not strong in the face of adversity. He is no saint. If I weighed Nobel's sins on the same scale, would his sins be pardonable as well? That is the question I'd have to answer in a book about Nobel. If I write an exposé, I will have to add on an apologia for Nobel and for myself and for everyone else who isn't up to a saintly life.

The train pulls into St Veit. A few people get off with me at the station, none of them acquaintances with whom I would have to exchange greetings or strike up a conversation. That's good, but my affair with Nikki has made me cautious. I take my time and let the other passengers go ahead. I stand at the station exit and scan the plaza. The night sky is a starry haze, full of romantic promise. It is surprising how quickly I have become used to expecting love. Nikki is waiting for me at the corner, in the shadow of a chestnut tree. As I come closer, I see that he has a bottle tucked into the pocket of his coat, like a toper. He falls in step with me.

"How was the play?" he says, keeping a discreet distance, although the street is deserted now.

"All right," I say. "Not exactly cheering, but well acted."

"That's what I heard. I may go and see it next week. Sophie has been after me to take her to the theatre. She thinks I owe her escort services even though we are separated, or rather because she allows me to live a separate life. And there's a new development—"

Nikki stops talking. Half a block ahead, the door of a tavern has opened and a couple of men spill out, worse for drink, swearing and knocking into each other in a mock-fight. Nikki steps up his pace and moves deftly in front of me.

I hang back, staying in his shadow until the men move off.

At the corner, I catch up with him, and we turn into the narrow street leading to my house.

"What new development?" I ask.

"I'll tell you in a moment," he says, his hand on the fence. He unlatches the gate.

His reticence is making me uneasy. He has *something* to tell me. What is it? His words have a secret meaning. I am looking for hidden things in his voice.

We slip into the house, unseen by the neighbors, I hope. Nikki takes the bottle out of his coat pocket and sets it on the table. Sherry.

"This *something* you are going to tell me calls for a bottle of sherry?" I say as he uncorks it. "Is it that bad?"

"We might need fortification."

I bring two glasses from the kitchen, and we sit down, facing each other. I parse Nikki's face but get no reading.

"I'll come right to the point," he says, pouring us two glasses of sherry. "Schlumberger has asked me to set up a branch office in America. In Chicago."

I don't hear what he says next. I can muster only one thought: I'm losing him. Of course my happiness couldn't last.

When my ears unblock, Nikki is saying:

"We talked about it once or twice before. I said I couldn't leave Vienna. I had obligations here. But this time, I said I'd consider it. Schlumberger said to let him know by the end of the week. He can't put off the decision any longer. If I don't want to go, he'll appoint someone else."

"And your obligations in Vienna?"

"That's where the new developments come in," Nikki says. "The trustees have paid Sophie the money for Nobel's letters. It's burning a hole into her pocket. She's dying to spend it. She wants to give up her hotel suite and move to Merano. Rent a small villa there. The move will cost money, but she can live more cheaply in the south, she says. The climate is more pleasant and a villa would be nicer for Gretel than a hotel suite. I wish her well, but it means I'll lose Gretel." His voice thickens. He clears his throat. "I can't prevent Sophie from moving. I have no legal recourse. We are not living together. She might say that I deserted her, or that I'm not Gretel's father. And even if I could force her to stay, she might punish me by keeping Gretel away from me. So there is nothing I can do but accept the inevitable. She even promised the child that she could bring Bella along. Gretel loves that dog." He shakes his head. "I think I jinxed it the other day when I said to you: in a pinch, she'll prefer Bella to me. She will and forget me very soon."

He is smiling, but I can see the sadness at the core of his smile. His eyes are full of shadows.

"I'm seriously thinking about Schlumberger's offer," he says and reaches for my hand.

I pull back.

"And I?" The chill of desolation is in my voice.

He comes around to my side of the table, takes both of my hands and pulls me up into an embrace.

"You've already made your decision," I say. "You'll go." I can barely say the words. The thought of Nikki leaving me has taken my breath away.

"So far, I've decided only one thing: I won't go unless you come with me."

My breath returns. I feel as if I was rising from a deep well. *Unless* he said. But the condition is impossible to fulfil. How can I go to America with Nikki? What do I say to my neighbors? What do I tell my brother? How do I pay for the passage? Who will look after my house?

"We'll sail from Hamburg to New York," Nikki says. "From there, we'll take the train to Chicago." He says it so lightly, so naturally as if we were planning a holiday.

"And I will be Mrs Kapy – the way Sophie was 'Mrs Nobel'?"

I wrestle against Nikki's embrace, but he holds me fast.

"All right," he says as if he was giving in to an unreasonable child. "We book our passage separately – Miss Lassick, visiting her brother in New York, and Mr Kapy embarking on his new career in Chicago. We meet on board and fall in love."

"And the captain marries us." I laugh, although it sounds more like a sob.

Nikki is laughing, too. We have passed from vague possibilities into the realm of fantasy. The line between dream and reality is becoming blurred.

"Bigamy – well, perhaps not," he says, sobering up. "But there is a future for us now, Ida. To my surprise, Sophie mentioned divorce."

"And what did you say?" I'm shaky from moving so fast. Despair to hope in a few seconds.

"I didn't say much. I thought it was better not to appear too keen. Sophie is a sharp businesswoman. I expect this will take some negotiating. Meanwhile, Schlumberger is pressing me for a decision."

"But if I go with you, what do I tell my brother?" The moment I ask the question aloud, I realize what it means. I've made up my mind. I will go with Nikki. But that's crazy! I begin to laugh again.

We spin out a scenario. Nikki falls in so readily that I suspect he has been playing fantasy games before, just like me. Perhaps I have even figured in his fantastic scenes. I throw him a plotline: I write to my brother and tell him that I'm getting married. I couldn't inform him sooner. The arrangements had to be made in a hurry because my husband-to-be is being transferred to Chicago.

Nikki takes the lead now. "You could send him a wedding photo as evidence. We'll go and have our picture taken in front of a romantic set – a grotto with angels, say."

I can see it already. I make a frame with my hands. "I'm wearing a gown of China silk in virginal white and a delicate veil of tulle. There are fake pearls around my neck and a spray of flowers on my lap. You stand beside me, looking down on me lovingly."

"We have two copies made, one to send to your brother and the other for us to keep, to put on the mantelpiece in our new home in Chicago. And when the divorce comes through, we marry quietly and tell no one, and we'll always celebrate the date the photo was taken as our wedding day—"

We are both laughing frantically now, clinging to each other. Our laughter comes in great bursts, in cascades, in magnificent, sumptuous, mad, billowing waves of merriment.

"And we'll live happily ever after," I say through tears of laughter. "But seriously—"

There are questions in my head. How long would it take for a divorce to come through? Can all of this be done from America? How much does a divorce cost? Will I have to leave the church to marry a divorced man?

Then I hear the peal of the church bells. It's midnight, the witching hour, when anything can happen and everything is possible. Yes, why shouldn't Nikki and I live happily ever after?

About the Author

Erika Rummel has taught at the University of Toronto and Wilfrid Laurier University, Waterloo. She divides her time between Toronto and Los Angeles and has lived in villages in Argentina, Romania, and Bulgaria. She is the author of more than a dozen books of non-fiction, among them a translation of Alfred Nobel's correspondence with his Viennese lover, *A Nobel Affair*. She is also the author of five previous novels, *Playing Naomi, Head Games, The Inquisitor's Niece, The Painting on Auerperg's Wall*, and *The Effects of Isolation on the Brain*, an excerpt of which was awarded the Random House Creative Writing Award.

Made in the USA
Middletown, DE
21 September 2018